To Lou Collumb,
fellow Huu Driver
has, " been there, done that!"
Best Wishes,
  Ron Standerfer
  December 7, 2007

THE EAGLE'S LAST FLIGHT

THE EAGLE'S LAST FLIGHT

Ron Standerfer

iUniverse, Inc.
New York Lincoln Shanghai

THE EAGLE'S LAST FLIGHT

iUniverse books may be ordered through booksellers or by contacting:

iUniverse
2021 Pine Lake Road, Suite 100
Lincoln, NE 68512
www.iuniverse.com
1-800-Authors (1-800-288-4677)

ISBN-13: 978-0-595-36087-1 (pbk)
ISBN-13: 978-0-595-67328-5 (cloth)
ISBN-13: 978-0-595-80535-8 (ebk)
ISBN-10: 0-595-36087-4 (pbk)
ISBN-10: 0-595-67328-7 (cloth)
ISBN-10: 0-595-80535-3 (ebk)

Printed in the United States of America

To my loving wife, Marzenna, whose patient understanding helped me through the ordeal of writing this book.

PROLOGUE

▼

Republic of Vietnam
1969

Four F-100 Super Saber jet fighters, looking sleek and mean, circled the target like birds of prey impatient for the kill. Below them, the Mekong River lay steaming in the hot, humid air, surrounded by lush, green jungle, and red mud from the monsoon rains. Water-filled bomb craters gleamed dully in the late afternoon sun. Meanwhile, the forward air controller, or FAC, was scooting across the treetops in a small, propeller-driven aircraft, coordinating the final details of the strike.

The fighters had been airborne for over an hour, and Skip's flying suit was drenched in sweat. He was hot, uncomfortable, and impatient. Come on, come on, he thought, let's get on with it. Rain showers are moving in, and we won't be able to see the ground much longer.

"Icon Flight, Banjo Two-One is rolling in for the marking pass," the FAC said.

Skip saw an orange flash as the marking rocket left the FAC's aircraft, followed by a burst of white smoke on the ground that rose in a tall, straight column.

"Icon Lead, that's a good mark. Hit my smoke."

"Roger, Icon Lead's in. Got the smoke in sight," he responded.

"Cleared to drop, Lead."

Skip rolled the aircraft onto its back, and then pulled the nose through the horizon before rolling upright and into a steep dive. Things were happening fast, as the airspeed increased, and the altimeter unwound rapidly. When the target appeared in the windscreen, he began tracking it with his gun sight. Out of the corner of his eye, he could see bright muzzle flashes from a nearby tree line; then red tracers began streaming across the nose of his aircraft. Don't look at them, he thought. Keep your eyes on the target. Steady now. It'll be over in a second.

"Icon Lead, you're taking ground fire," the FAC said. "Over to the left."

"Roger. I see it. No sweat." His voice sounded cool and confident.

An instant later, two 750-pound bombs were sent hurtling toward the ground, as he pulled out, rolling sharply to the left, and then back to the right, trying to avoid the ground fire. In the rearview mirror, he could see the two bombs explode in a boiling column of mud and debris.

"Good bombs, Icon Lead. Put yours in the same place, Icon Two."

Suddenly, Skip's aircraft began to vibrate and shake, and a series of warning lights came on in the cockpit, one after another.

"Lead, you're trailing smoke," Icon Two called out.

"Not to worry. I've…uh…got a problem."

The aircraft was becoming harder to control as the vibrations increased. Now the flashing, red fire-warning light was on. Okay. Be cool. You gotta punch out. No big deal. Get more altitude…that's the first thing.

"Lead, you're on fire. The whole ass-end of the aircraft is on fire. Bail out!" Icon Two's voice was tense and demanding.

"Roger that. I have to climb first and head toward the water."

The cockpit was incredibly hot and filled with smoke. He could hardly keep the wings level. It's time to go, pal. You've done this before. Raise the ejection seat handles, and the canopy goes. Squeeze the trigger, and you go. It's a piece of cake. Holding the control stick steady with one hand, he reached down and raised the ejection seat handle, bracing for the explosion and rush of air as the canopy left the aircraft.

Nothing happened.

No problem. Eject through the canopy. It's been done. Carefully, he squeezed the exposed trigger in the handle, once again bracing himself for the shock. Again, nothing happened. Starting to panic, he squeezed it again…and again…and again.

"Lead, I repeat. You are on fire. Get out of the fucking bird, *now!*" Icon Two shouted.

"Roger. I…uh…can't. The ejection seat…it won't…oh shit!"

The control stick went slack. The flight controls were gone. Slowly, the aircraft rolled inverted like a wounded beast. Suspended upside down, looking at the jungle below, he knew it was over. "Bail out! Bail out!" Icon Two shouted one last time. Seconds later, the twilight sky was lit by a bright, orange explosion that disintegrated into flaming shards of silver aluminum drifting to the ground.

"Too late…" Icon Two said, in a flat voice, filled with resignation.

New York University Medical Center

December 27, 1999

Skip O'Neill awoke with a violent start, his bedclothes in tangled disarray from the thrashing they had received while he was dreaming. His heart was pounding, and his breath came in shallow, desperate gasps. He was confused and disoriented.

"Been out flying again, Colonel?" Nancy asked. Her hand was cool and reassuring on his forehead. She was a beautiful sight; her soft blue eyes wrinkled with concern, and her light brown hair cut short in that no-nonsense style all nurses seemed to wear. He wanted to reach up and touch her, just to make sure she was really there, but he was too weak.

"Flying? Yeah, I guess so."

"Well, we have to do something about that temperature. You're burning up."

"Burning up? That's what I was doing a few minutes ago."

"What?"

"Never mind…it was just a dream I get every once in awhile. The funny thing is it scares the hell out of me every time, even though what I dream never really happened."

She nodded sympathetically. "Well, now that you are back on the ground, I'm going to get ice packs to cool you down and get some fresh sheets for the bed. Meanwhile, try not to go flying again, at least not until I get the cockpit straightened out from the last mission, okay?"

Skip nodded miserably and watched her leave the room. He was awake now, and the view from his bed was cold and forbidding. There was a maze of wires, hoses, and tubes connected to his body and an oxygen mask over his nose. The smell of antiseptic was everywhere. His mouth was thick and dry, and he needed a drink of cold water. He tried to sit up but was too weak and nauseous to manage. Wearily, he threw his head back on the pillow and stared at the acoustical-tiled ceiling with its meaningless galaxy of small holes, his eyes vacant and unfocused. What's taking her so long?

The room was quiet, save for the sound of his breathing. "You're going to die," a small voice inside him said.

"Not yet," he replied to the voice. "Not until I say so." He shivered feverishly and waited for Nancy to return.

*   *   *   *

Skip was sixty-three years old when he was diagnosed with leukemia. The doctor said that it had been creeping through his body slowly, over a period of several years, maybe longer. Why had this happened to him? He often asked himself that question, but in his heart he knew the answer. He could not prove it, but he was certain that it all began in 1957, in the middle of the Nevada desert. There was no reason for him to be standing eight miles from ground zero watching an atomic test. He had volunteered to be an observer, because it seemed like the thing to do at the time. Besides, it got him out of northern Maine for a week, in the middle of winter. For a twenty-two-year old, fun-loving second lieutenant, that was reason enough.

He remembered the day he had arrived at Camp Desert Rock, a God-forsaken military base fifty miles from the nearest town. Its sole mission was testing the effects of nuclear explosions on military personnel and equipment. There was evidence of previous tests everywhere—charred and twisted hulks of tanks, trucks, and artillery pieces scattered about along the road leading into the camp. Living conditions were primitive. Visitors ate and slept in large tents with wooden floors, while sand and scorpions were propelled to and fro by the never-ceasing desert wind. When he arrived, he was given a dosimeter, a simple, crude device to measure radiation, to wear during the visit. Although it was obvious that radiation was an ever-present threat at the facility, neither Skip nor his fellow test participants gave much thought to the danger that surrounded them. They were, after all, participating in an official and tightly controlled test, and it seemed extremely unlikely that their government would put them in harm's way. By the time they realized their mistake, it was too late.

On the morning of the test, he was awakened before dawn by the arrival of paratroopers from the 82nd Airborne Division. The troopers spilled out of the trucks and began doing pushups in the chilly, predawn air, chanting, "Airborne...Airborne...Airborne." They would be positioned in trenches and bunkers, just three miles from ground zero. It was still dark when Skip and the other observers, mostly young Air Force, Navy, and Marine officers, arrived at the viewing platform. In the predawn light, they could barely make out the outline of the nuclear weapon suspended in a black canister from a seven hundred-foot tower, vaguely outlined by three, red navigation lights. It was an eerie sight; the red lights blinking hypnotically, creating a vision of something incredibly evil and destructive.

It seemed like they waited forever for the countdown to begin. In reality, it was only ten minutes. Meanwhile, they shivered and stomped their feet to keep warm. No one spoke. Each was wrapped in his own thoughts about what they were about to see. Finally the countdown began. They were instructed to cover their eyes with their hands. "Five...four...three...two...one." The flash from the detonation was so blinding that for a fraction of a second, he could see the bones of his hands as he covered his eyes. It was like looking at an X-ray. Then, he uncovered his eyes and looked with awe at the dark and dirty mushroom cloud, ascending skyward. He also could see a rolling wave of dust moving across the desert toward him. It was the shock wave from the blast. When it arrived, he felt it pass through his body with a resounding thud, knocking the breath out of him as it went. Then it was over. There was nothing left to do but stare at the lingering cloud and try to comprehend what he had just seen.

Skip never forgot his experience at Camp Desert Rock. Years later, he ran into a Marine at the officers club who had participated in one of the tests and the two of them compared notes about what they had experienced.

"It was the damnedest thing," the Marine said, "There we were, almost at ground zero. I mean we were sitting in trenches, three miles away. Three miles! Not on some piddley-assed platform eight miles away, like those Air Force and Navy pussies."

Skip let that comment pass, based on his longstanding belief that arguing with a Marine who has been drinking, was not a smart thing to do.

"And get this...right after the blast we were supposed to leap out of the trenches so we could be moved up to a point three hundred yards away."

"Three hundred yards?" Skip exclaimed. "Why so close, for God's sake?"

"Why? To set up a mock defensive perimeter against anyone who theoretically might have survived the attack."

"Yeah right…like anybody would."

"Exactly. When we moved into position, there was nothing to see, much less to defend against. I mean nothing, just a few piles of molten metal here and there. And, oh yeah, the charred flesh of sheep that were used in the test."

"Sheep?"

"Yeah, sheep. There I was with my men, tromping around in this fallout shit…you know…that white ash that crunches under your feet?"

"Fallout at three hundred yards, that stuff had to be big time radioactive."

"Right, but of course I wasn't afraid, because afterwards we were gonna get brushed off with brooms and hosed down. I mean, brooms, man. How dumb could we have been?"

"Anyway," he continued, "about the same time, this guy shows up over the top of the hill, all dressed out in some kind of shiny, silver, protective suit with a ventilator and face mask. When he sees us, he comes roaring over, like someone lit a rocket in his ass. What are you guys doing here? Where is your protective gear? He yelled. All the time he's talking, he's pointing this Geiger counter thing at us, which is going click, click, click.

I yelled back, we're just doing some reconnoitering, getting ready to kick some ass.

Well, you guys shouldn't be here, he replied. Are you crazy?

Well, yeah. I told him. We are crazy. I mean…we're Marines, which is basically the same thing…right?

It turns out this dude was some kind of technician from the Atomic Energy Commission. They were the guys who were supposed to be running the tests. And, get this…he didn't even know the military was operating that close to ground zero!"

"No way," Skip said.

"Yep, and when I got him settled down, I found out that he wasn't pissed at all. He was just scared…for us. That should have been my first clue."

"Don't take this the wrong way," Skip said, "but it sounds to me like the government was using you guys as guinea pigs."

"Guinea pigs?" The Marine snorted derisively. "We should have been so lucky. The laboratory animals they used in those tests were washed down with soap and water afterwards, and their health was carefully monitored. It's been fifteen years since that test and nobody has asked me shit about my health. It's like it never happened!"

"Or like you guys were expendable, so it didn't matter," Skip offered.

"We were *all* expendable. You, me, and the 250,000 or so troops who participated in all those years of testing. And that, my friend, is the way it is.

Twenty years later, Skip received a letter from the Center for Disease Control
in Atlanta. "Dear Colonel O'Neill," it said, "Our records show that in 1957 you
observed a highly classified nuclear test, code named, Smokey. It seems in that
particular test, an exceptionally large amount of radiation had been released into
the air, and in later years, a significant number of deaths from leukemia had
occurred among the participants." The letter went on to recommend that he
closely monitor his health in the future and gave him a questionnaire to fill out
and send in. He did so, and then forgot about the letter. And why shouldn't he?
His health was excellent, and there was nothing in his annual flying physicals to
suggest otherwise. By the time his illness was discovered, it was too late.

*   *   *   *

When Nancy returned, her arms were filled with fresh sheets and ice packs to
put under his arms.

"It's about time you got back," Skip said.

"Considering what they pay me around here, you're lucky I came back at all."

"Oh, you'll always come back. It's my intense good looks. You can't resist
me."

"And your modesty, don't forget that. Okay, let's get you untangled and back
in working order." Working quickly and efficiently, she arranged the new sheets
on the bed and tucked the ice packs securely under his arms.

He sank his head gratefully in the soft, clean pillow and watched through
blurred eyes as she adjusted the IV unit beside the bed. It was good to have company. He had been alone for much of his declining years. He wondered if she
would stay with him for awhile, but before he could ask, the morphine drip took
hold, and he drifted away.

He awoke at noon, feeling much better. Sharp, thin lines of bright blue sky
slashed between the blinds, flooding the room with light, and he could hear the
soft hum of cars passing by on FDR Drive. Looking toward the door, he saw his
doctor walk in, his lab coat buttoned neatly, a pair of horn-rimmed glasses
perched on the end of his nose.

When he had first met Dr. Benjamin Webster III, the chief oncologist at
NYU Medical Center, he decided he was a pompous, Ivy League jerk. Likewise,
Dr. Webster was put off by Skip's annoying habit of calling him "Doc," a title he

felt was disrespectful considering his position on the staff. But after several weeks, they had gotten to know each other, and now they were buddies. Skip trusted him completely and wouldn't have anyone else treat him. Typically, Dr. Webster's morning visits served as a backdrop for a nonstop barrage of sarcasm and gallows humor. Today was no exception.

"How are you feeling today, Colonel?"

"Okay, Doc. Hanging in there."

"I understand you were up flying last night. Did you shoot down any MIGs?"

Skip shook his head in mock exasperation. "What am I gonna do with you, Doc? If you're going be my wingman, you have to understand the mission. You and I are air-to-ground types—bombs, rockets, napalm—remember? Shooting down aircraft is for the fancy-pants World War II and Korean War aces. Air-to-mud, that's us."

"Yeah, sorry, I forgot…air-to-mud."

"I do have something significant to report, though."

"What's that?"

"I want to report that I felt damn lucky to be awake today."

"What do you mean?"

"What I mean is, that was some heavy-duty stuff you were pumping into my IV last night. Where did you get it anyway? From some dealer in the projects?"

"Aww, you figured that out and spoiled my surprise. As a matter of fact, I did get it from, umm…an outside source. I picked it up myself, just for you."

"Really?"

"Yep, I stopped by the finance office just before it closed, got a briefcase full of cash, and headed for the Bronx. Then, I pulled up to the first guy I saw and said, 'Hey man. I need two keys. Are you dealing?'"

"Wow, that was pretty dangerous, wasn't it?"

"Naww…lost two hubcaps on my Porsche while we were negotiating, though."

At this point, neither one could keep a straight face, and they started laughing. It felt good to laugh, but Skip's mood changed quickly, and his face clouded. "I know it doesn't look good, Doc. But it's not over. Not yet."

"I know." The doctor was all business now, leaning forward in his chair.

"In fact, it's not over until I say it's over."

"That's a good attitude to have."

"All this morphine, that's the problem. Every time I get strong enough to take another swing at the ball, to really fight this thing, I fall asleep, and you know what?"

"What?"

"I get pissed at you sometimes. I mean really pissed."

"At me? Why?"

"Well I keep thinking that it's a pretty crummy choice you offer me every day. What do you want to give up—incredible pain or a big chunk of what's left of your waking life? It's like choosing between a sharp stick in the eye and a kick in the nuts."

"Yeah, I guess it is. We're walking a pretty fine line here, between keeping you comfortable and getting some kind of treatment going. There are a lot of things in that IV besides morphine. It's tough. I know."

There was nothing left to say. The doctor had to continue his rounds. He rose and started for the door.

"Doc?"

"Yes?" he replied, turning around.

"You're still my wingman, aren't you? You're covering my six o'clock right?"

The doctor furrowed his brows for a moment, trying to remember the words Skip had taught him. He smiled, "I'm with you, O Fearless Leader. I'll follow you anywhere."

"That's my man," Skip said.

He fell asleep shortly after the doctor left and drifted in and out of consciousness for the rest of the day. When he awoke, it was after midnight, and the hospital was silent, save for the occasional sound of muffled footsteps, and someone coughing in another room. A small light on his bedside table was his only companion, its pale glow casting uneven shadows on the wall. Lying on his back, imprisoned by his surroundings, he thought about the voice that told him he was going to die. The voice was probably right, but was that such a bad thing? He had lived an incredibly full life after all, and everyone has to die sometime, Maybe so, but he decided to leave on his terms, and now wasn't the time.

The room had become noticeably cooler, downright cold in fact. As he shivered, and pulled the blanket tightly around him, his mind drifted back to the time and place where he took the first hesitant steps toward becoming the man he was destined to be, an Air Force colonel, a fighter pilot, and a decorated combat veteran. The picture of his life was sharp and clear, despite the passage of time and the debilitating effects of the morphine, and as he began to drift in and out of consciousness, he found himself living those days, as well as the months and years that followed.

The Journey Begins

Presque Isle Air Force Base, Maine
1956 to 1957

The radiators in the World War II-era building were cranked up full-bore, groaning and clanking, making the briefing room hot and stuffy. "The high today will be forty-nine degrees below zero," the weather briefer said. Second Lt. Skip O'Neill slumped in his chair in despair and disgust. He was going to freeze his ass off again today, as usual. As he stared gloomily out the window toward the Aroostook Mountains, a light snow began to fall. Might as well snow, he thought. It's been snowing ever since I got here. What's a few inches more? By now, the snow was several feet deep and getting deeper every day.

According to the orders in his pocket when he arrived at the base, wearing his shiny new gold bars and silver wings, he was assigned to the 76th Fighter Interceptor Squadron, 32nd Fighter Group at Presque Isle Air Force Base, Maine. His version of the story was that for some reason, he had been banished to a place so far north that he'd have been in Canada had he missed the exit to the city. His even shorter version was that he got screwed, or as his roommate in college used to say, diddled by the dangling digit of destiny.

At the age of twenty-one, Skip scarcely looked like a defender of America's freedom. Six feet, two inches tall, with a slender frame, he had chestnut-brown hair that characteristically hung down over one eye giving it a slightly disheveled look. He had warm, expressive brown eyes, and his face was smooth and boyish. He was the kind of young man high school girls would call cute. Older women wanted to pinch his cheek. The truth is, he shouldn't have been in the Air Force at all on this cold, miserable day. He should have still been at the University of Illinois, studying music. But he wanted to be a pilot, not a musician. That's why he quit school after two years, and enlisted in the Air Force's aviation cadet program. His parents were not very happy with his decision, but there was little they could do about it.

The real reason Skip was in Presque Isle was that for some reason the Air Force chose to train him as a radar operator, or RO, instead of as a pilot. But it was not in his nature to give up, and the minute he graduated from RO training, he applied for pilot training again. This time he was accepted but was told it would be at least three years before he got a class assignment. So there he was, cold and miserable, waiting for his life to change.

Presque Isle, Maine, had a population of less than ten thousand people and was mostly inhabited by potato farmers, military personnel, and moose hunters. When the first snow fell in late October, lawns, driveways, and sidewalks disappeared, not to be seen again until the spring thaw. Last, but certainly not least, there was nothing to do in town. You could walk from one end to the other in twenty minutes, passing one movie theater and a scant offering of bars and restaurants along the way. According to the people who lived in Presque Isle, there were only two single women in town, and neither of them liked Air Force guys. Skip always thought that was a gross exaggeration. If there were two single girls in town, he certainly hadn't seen them—unless you counted the waitress at the Aroostook diner, who had no teeth, and of course, Sister Mary Claire at Saint Boniface.

There were two fighter squadrons assigned to Presque Isle—the 76th and its sister squadron, the 75th. The mission of the two squadrons was air defense. In 1956, the Cold War was in full swing. The United States had hundreds of B-36 and B-47 bombers prepared to drop nuclear weapons on military and industrial targets in the Soviet Union. The Soviet Union with its fleet of "Bull" bombers was ready to do the same to the U.S. The Bull was a copy of the Boeing B-29 bomber, which ironically had been used to drop atomic bombs on Japan. It was a classic Cold War confrontation, with nuclear weapons on both sides.

Both squadrons were equipped with the F-89D Scorpion. The Scorpion did not look like a fighter aircraft. Heavy and ungainly, it weighed more than twenty-three tons when fully loaded with fuel and armament and required the best efforts of its two engines with afterburners to get off the ground. Although the aircraft was not sleek and aerodynamic, it was aptly named. Seen from a distance, it looked like a large, menacing scorpion. The rocket pods and fuel tanks, both mounted on the wingtips, resembled claws, while its long, upward-sweeping tail strongly suggested a stinger. It was not a supersonic aircraft, but it was faster than the bombers it was designed to attack. The aircraft was operated by a crew of two, a pilot and an RO.

Each pilot in the squadron was assigned his own RO, and the two flew together as often as possible. Skip was happy with his current pilot. Everyone agreed that Capt. Tom Denison was the best in the squadron. He was a combat veteran who had flown Black Widows in the Korean War. The Black Widow was a propeller-driven precursor to the F-89 that was flown almost exclusively at night on intercept missions. Although Tom's credentials were impeccable, he scarcely looked like the steely-eyed pilots you see in war movies. On the contrary, he was a tall thin man who walked with a slight stoop, and whose relatively plain face was featureless, except for bright blue eyes and a shock of unruly, blond hair. He was quiet, almost to the point of being shy, and spoke softly but firmly with a pronounced Midwestern accent. Tom had the best-looking wife in the squadron, or on the base, for that matter. The truth was everyone was in love with Penney, including Skip. Like Skip, Tom and Penney were from Illinois, and it was his ambition to marry a girl just like her.

The ROs could usually be put in one of two groups. The first included young lieutenants like Skip, who were just starting their careers. The second group included the older captains who had been enlisted men during World War II or flew as ROs in one of the earlier types of interceptors in the Korean War. There were few advancement opportunities for this group, and most of the men seemed to be holding on, waiting for their twenty-year retirement. Of the two, the second group was by far the most interesting.

Skip's favorite was Captain John "Cactus Jack" Kelly. He was the squadron RO, which meant he was in charge of all RO standardization and training. Cactus Jack had a style and panache that made him stand out from all the other officers in the squadron, and he worked hard to maintain that image. Each day, he arrived for work wearing black cowboy boots and a standard Air Force service hat, informally known as a "wheel hat." With the visor tilted back to the middle of his forehead and cocked to a jaunty angle, the sides pushed down in the classic fifty-mission crush, he looked like he had just removed his headphones and stepped out of the cockpit of a B-17 bomber. He wore the boots and hat whether he was dressed in a flying suit or a dress uniform. The majority of fighter crews would not be caught dead wearing a wheel hat with a flying suit, much less with a dress uniform. Their hat of preference was the standard blue flight cap, an elongated cloth hat that was worn perched just above the eyebrow.

Jack was also extremely fond of wearing his radar operator wings, which were not illegal, but rarely seen anymore. The wings were centered on a silver circle containing a radar logo. One had to look at his wings closely, because sometimes one might find that each wing had been cleverly depicted to show a woman's leg, thus creating the image of two legs spread obscenely around the circle in the center. "Night Intruder wings," he would say proudly. "Not many of these babies left anymore. I like to wear them every once in awhile just to keep everybody on their toes."

Suddenly, Skip's reveries about Cactus Jack were interrupted by the sound of chairs being pushed back, and everyone talking at once. The weather briefing was over. Caught by surprise, he looked up and saw Tom standing over him, with a look of amused tolerance.

"Ready to go, Tiger?" he asked.

"Yes sir," Skip said, scrambling to his feet. "Let's go get them!"

"Didn't wake you up, did I?"

"Me? Of course not."

"Good…let's pack up our gear and head over to the alert hangar."

"I'm with you, O Leader of Men!"

"Oh…and Skip."

"Yes sir?"

"Your briefing card."

"Pardon me?"

"Your briefing card and checklist…you left them on the chair."

"Oh right," Skip said, sheepishly. He scrambled back to retrieve them. By then, Tom was already out the door.

Checklists…briefing cards…who needs them? We're not going to fly anyway…just sit in the alert hangar all night doing nothing. Boring! Then he remembered something his instructor told him in training. Flying consists of hours and hours of boredom interrupted by a few moments of sheer terror.

*　　*　　*　　*

By 2 AM all activity had ceased in the alert hangar. Two crews were asleep in the bunkroom, flying suits on, boots carefully placed nearby. The rest lounged in easy chairs and sofas, some reading, others snoring softly as they dozed. It was the same downstairs. Ground crews slept, dozed, and read. Outside, falling snow silently blurred the taxi and runway lights. Occasionally, a teletype machine chattered details about weather conditions at nearby airfields. Otherwise, all was quiet.

The alert hangar consisted of a two-story building that housed the crews, flanked by four large, steel alert bays, two on each side. The four bays were interconnected, and inside each sat an aircraft fueled and armed with rockets. The bays were heated and enclosed. A massive steel door afforded access to the taxiway outside. Each aircraft was prepared for an immediate launch; power cart plugged in, parachute and shoulder harnesses ready to slip on, and cockpit switches positioned to save time when starting the engines. This was important, because two of the aircraft were required to be airborne within five minutes after being ordered to take off or "scramble." The purpose of a scramble was to intercept unknown aircraft penetrating the air defense system without prior clearance.

Scrambles were common at Presque Isle. The "unknown" was typically an airliner flying off course, or perhaps a large military transport lumbering its way down from Goose Bay or Greenland, unaware that its flight plan had not been passed to the air defense system, or that it had strayed from its planned course.

There was one sound in the crew lounge that was always present. A sound so subtle that it normally went unnoticed. It was a soft electrical hum from a squawk box that hung on the wall. It was connected to the command post and was used only to launch scrambles. When a scramble was about to be launched, there was a "click" as the transmit key was pressed, and then the humming stopped. The change was almost imperceptible, but it would send a jolt of adrenalin through anyone who was awake and had even been known to rouse a crewmember out of a dead sleep. At 2:30 AM there was a click, and the humming stopped.

"Alert…this is Smithfield. "

"Go ahead, Smitty," one of the pilots said.

"Scramble one, and put one on standby."

"Roger. Scramble one, and put one on standby."

The scramble order was followed by a long, jarring blast from a Klaxon horn located in the alert bays. The building came alive with sounds of urgent shouts and running feet. Before the pilots and ROs could start down the stairs, ground crews had already raced to the aircraft, starting electrical power carts and opening hangar doors. Meanwhile, the aircrews rushed down the steps, taking them two at a time, jostling each other as they raced to their aircraft. By the time they burst into the bays, power carts were running, and the bay doors were open, allowing flakes of wet snow to come swirling into the warm interior.

Tom was the first one up the ladder to the cockpit, and as he stepped over the canopy rail, he paused just long enough to activate the starter switch for the first engine. Then he settled into his seat, starting the second engine as he did so. By the time he had shrugged on his parachute and shoulder harness and put on his helmet, both engines were running, and Skip was all strapped in. They were on standby, ready to be used in the event that the first aircraft lost its radar or radio after takeoff. There was nothing they could do now but wait.

The number one aircraft, call sign Benny Alpha, pulled out of the adjacent bay and coasted down the short taxiway to the runway. Less than five minutes after the scramble order was received, it took off with afterburners roaring.

Three vertical lights were posted in each bay. Green for launch, yellow for standby, and red for abort. Fifteen minutes passed, and the yellow light was still on.

"Taking them awhile to make up their minds isn't it?" Tom commented.

"Yeah, I wish they'd pee or get off the pot. They're cutting into my beauty sleep," Skip replied.

Tom laughed. "Wouldn't want that now, would we?"

"Nope…and speaking of peeing, I have to…"

Skip never got a chance to finish. The light turned green.

"Uh-oh," Tom said, as he signaled for the crew chief to remove the chocks. "Looks like Benny Alpha needs help." Seconds later, they taxied out of the brightly lit hangar and into the night, where they were swallowed up by the snow and fog.

"Presque Isle tower, this is Benny Bravo on a hot scramble, approaching the active runway," Tom called.

"Benny Bravo cleared for takeoff. Wind is calm. Visibility is one mile in light snow showers and fog. Climb runway heading to two zero thousand feet."

"Roger. Cleared for takeoff. We're on the roll." As expected, just as the landing gear and flaps came up, they were sucked into a pitch-black mass of clouds and driving snow.

At ten thousand feet, they were passed over to the radar controller. "Benny Bravo, contact Eagle Beak on channel fifteen."

"Roger, switching to channel one five," Tom acknowledged.

"Eagle Beak, this is Benny Bravo climbing runway heading, passing ten for two zero thousand."

"Roger, Benny Bravo, radar contact. Continue climbing to…uhh…stand by one."

"He sounds a little nervous doesn't he?" Skip asked.

"Yeah, he's definitely tensed up about something. Might be a new controller, getting some kind of an evaluation."

"Bravo, continue your climb to two five thousand. Twenty-five thousand feet."

"Roger. What's my vector to the target?"

"The target…uhh…the unknown has been identified as friendly. It's not a factor."

"Eagle Beak, understand the scramble has been canceled? Do you want us to abort and return to home base?"

"Negative, Bravo. We have another problem. It's…uhh…Benny Alpha. He didn't check in after takeoff, and we don't have radar contact with him."

"No radar or radio contact?"

"That's affirmative, nothing."

"Okay, we'll start circling the field when we get to altitude, and then make some radio calls. Maybe it's a problem with your antennas."

"Roger, Bravo, sounds like a good plan. We'll keep the airspace open for you and stand by for further word."

It was a moonless night with several layers of clouds. Visibility was poor. "This is not good," Tom said. "Flying around without a radio in bad weather at night. I hope we can find him and get this sorted out."

"The problem is where to start?" Skip said. "Nobody has seen Benny Alpha or talked to him since he took off. He could be anywhere."

"Okay," Tom said, "I'm going to start making some radio calls. You keep your eyes peeled for his navigation lights or any sign that he is wandering around looking for help."

"Roger. You got it."

"Benny Alpha, this is Benny Bravo on channel fifteen," Tom called out. "Can you read me?"

There was no response.

"Benny Alpha, this is Benny Bravo. Can you read me?"

Still no response.

The calls continued for twenty minutes on several frequencies. Still no contact with Benny Alpha.

"I think he may have a complete electrical failure," Tom said finally. "If so, we'll have to find him somehow, join up, and then lead him down for an approach and landing on our wing."

"That's not going to be fun, especially in this weather."

"I know. But that's what we have to do. I'm going to start widening the search pattern and make some more radio calls. You crank the radar to max range and start looking for him farther out. Remember, he could be above or below us, so vary the antenna elevation."

They began tracing a grid pattern, starting over the runway at Presque Isle, expanding their search as they went. More radio calls on a variety of frequencies received no response. After two hours, they began to fear the worst. Soon, they would be low on fuel and would have to land. Because Benny Alpha took off before they did, he must be in the same condition, or worse.

"That's it," Tom said. "We're not getting anywhere."

"Maybe he landed at a different airport," Skip volunteered. "That would explain why there is no radio or radar contact."

"Yeah maybe. But why didn't they call the command post on the landline, so we would know what's going on? It doesn't make sense."

"I don't know. Maybe…" Skip didn't finish, and Tom said nothing. Neither wanted to suggest that Benny Alpha was indeed on the ground but not at an airport.

The weather at Presque Isle had deteriorated by the time they returned. They were lucky to land on their first approach. They had cut it so close that there wasn't enough fuel to try again. Taxiing up to the alert hangar they spotted an F-89 parked in the alert bay that Benny Alpha had vacated. For a moment their hopes rose, but upon closer inspection they could see that it was a different aircraft.

No one was sleeping in the crew lounge. Everyone was on edge, looking at the clock, and waiting for the phone to ring. They knew that Benny Alpha had to be on the ground somewhere. The F-89 didn't carry enough fuel to still be airborne. The day crews arrived at eight AM, but no one from the night shift left.

The jarring ring of the phone broke the silence at 9:45 AM. Everyone watched expectantly as Tom answered it.

"Alert. Captain Denison speaking."

"Yes right…so, what's the story?"

"Yes…Yes…Where? What time?"

"How about the crew? I see…Yes…I understand."

"Okay…Thank you."

Tom hung up and slowly turned to face the crews. The look on his face said it all. "The base helicopter spotted the bird fifteen minutes ago. It was on the side of a mountain about five miles off the end of the runway. The crash site is a mess. There's wreckage scattered over a two-mile radius causing a lot of small forest fires. Rescue and firefighter teams are on their way up." He paused for a second to compose himself and then continued.

"The chopper crew was able to get down low and get a good look at the site. There was no sign of life. And they didn't see any parachutes. We're pretty sure the crew went in with the bird." There was nothing more to say. Slowly, he walked across the room, picked up his parachute and helmet, and walked out the door. The rest of the night crew followed.

*   *   *   *

When Skip returned to his quarters, he took a long hot shower and lay down for some much-needed sleep. But sleep was impossible. Lying on his bed, his mind reeled with swirling sounds and images from the previous night as he tried to make sense of it all. Two of his squadron mates, Charlie and Ed, were gone, just like that. Where are they now? Shattered and crushed in a smoldering pile of twisted metal? At God's side in heaven, for eternity? Eternity…no beginning and no end. How can that be? Everything has a beginning and an end, doesn't it? If not, what happens before the beginning and after the end? As he pondered the possibilities of eternity, his mind began to spin crazily, and he felt dizzy, sick, and scared. For the first time in his young life he was forced to face his own mortality, and he was frightened.

He fell into a ragged and shallow sleep. While he slept, he dreamed that he was in a pitch-dark room, dashing to and fro, looking for someone. Or maybe someone was looking for him. He wasn't sure. In his frenzy, he smashed into walls, furniture, and all sorts of hard objects. On and on it went. The phone by his bed woke him up at noon. Groggy and disoriented, he picked it up.

"Hullo."

"Skip, it's Tom. Wake up. We gotta get moving."

"Get moving? Why? Where?"

"We've got to get over to Patty and Charlie's house. My wife is already there."

"Why do I need to go? What can I do? I wouldn't even know what to say."

"That's not the point. It's what we do when somebody buys the farm. We have to try and help."

"I don't know, Tom. I…uh…"

"I'll be over there to pick you up in thirty minutes," Tom said.

Tom arrived exactly thirty minutes later. "Well, it's official," he said. "The rescue team found both bodies in the cockpit. Or parts of them at least." Skip didn't ask for details. He didn't want to know.

When they arrived, Patty's driveway was overflowing with cars as visitors came and went. Skip walked up the steps filled with doubt and uncertainty. He didn't want to be there. Inside the modest frame, two-bedroom house, the shades were drawn, and the rooms were dimly lit. Dozens of people stood around uncomfortably, murmuring in hushed tones. In the kitchen, a small group of wives was busy making coffee, sandwiches, and other food for the visitors. Another woman sat by the phone, taking calls from sympathizers, carefully logging their names and numbers.

Patty sat on the sofa in the living room, flanked by her two best girlfriends, her eyes red and swollen from crying. Skip delayed talking to her as long as he could. She probably doesn't want to talk to me anyway, he rationalized. Finally, he walked over to the sofa, dreading what was to come next.

To his surprise, she seemed very pleased to see him.

"Skip! Nice to see you. How are you?" she said.

"Fine, Patty. I'm doing well. How are you?"

"Oh, I'm okay I guess. Charlie's been in an accident, you know."

"Yeah, I heard."

"Yep. Up in the mountains. He's there right now. He'll be home directly I suspect. Did you want to see him?"

"Yes…well…I…umm."

"Oh my God! Dinner! He's going to want his dinner when he gets home. He likes to eat first thing. I better get it started." She rose from the sofa, and then collapsed moaning and sobbing hysterically as she clung to her friends.

Not knowing what else to say or do, Skip mumbled a few words of sympathy and shuffled away. Out of the corner of his eye he saw the flight surgeon lean over Patty and talk to her in a consoling whisper. "No!" she cried out suddenly. "No pills. I don't want to be knocked out. I'm going to stay right here in case Charlie needs me."

For the next fifteen minutes, Skip wandered around the room, pausing to make listless conversation with those who remained. He felt trapped and wanted to leave, but he had to wait for Tom. Tom's wife, Penney, came out of the kitchen. She looked tired, yet her face was composed and had a look of resolve. She had done this many times before. "You guys must be pretty tired after being up all night," she said, taking Tom and Skip both by the arm. "Why don't you go home and get some rest? As soon as we clear this place out, we'll try to get Patty to sleep."

"Okay honey," Tom said, kissing her on the cheek. "I'll see you in a little while."

Skip felt like running out the door, but he forced himself to leave slowly. Once outside, he took a long deep breath of the cold frosty air. The weather had cleared since last night, and the sun was shining brightly "That was tough," he said, "tougher than I expected."

"I know," Tom replied. "It always is."

"It was my first time."

"I thought so."

"Does it get any easier?"

"No. The problem is you never know when it will happen again. Or who it will happen to."

Two days later, a memorial ceremony was held for the fallen crew. After the service, the squadron gathered at the officers' club for an informal wake. The party involved serious drinking and lasted well into the night. It ended with much laughing and shouting, as everyone told amusing or touching stories about their lost friends. It was a form of grieving and saying goodbye that everyone understood.

Tom was right. You never knew when an accident might happen, or who might be killed. Just three months after Charlie and Ed died, another crew was lost. And two months after that, still another. Six people died in just five months. All were in Skip's squadron.

The loss of lives and harsh living conditions in Presque Isle should have disillusioned Skip about Air Force life, but it didn't. He was impressed with the unwavering professionalism and courage of those around him, and with how they took care of each other. He decided to make the Air Force a career. It was the beginning of a new life for him—a life with a purpose.

Mayport Naval Air Station

They were beginning their descent. The engines on the old C-47 transport, a.k.a "Gooney Bird," were snuffling and popping as the pilot throttled back the engines. In the back, Skip and Cactus Jack sat hunched on bench seats attached to the wall, peering out the window at lush green vegetation, blue water, and a warm hazy sun. Soon they would be landing at Jacksonville Naval Air Station in Florida.

"I can't believe it," Skip said. "We were up to our ass in snow up in Presque Isle, and suddenly, boom. Here we are on a two-week assignment to Florida. It's unreal."

"Yep, and you can thank yours truly, old Cactus Jack, for getting us here."

"I know. How did you pull it off anyway?"

"Well, there I was, standing in front of the scheduling counter, when the ops officer comes up to me and says, 'Jack, I've got a very important assignment, and you are the only one who can handle it. There's gonna be a big two-week naval exercise off the coast of Florida, a big battle group with two aircraft carriers and a pisspot full of other ships. The Navy wants one Air Force guy on each carrier to check out the communication system with the air defense radar sites on shore. Pick another officer to go with you. I trust your judgment.' 'Leave it to me,' I said. 'I have just the guy, my main man, Lieutenant O'Neill.'"

"Wow, that's great," Skip said. "I really appreciate it."

"Okay, here's the plan. As soon as this bucket of bolts hits the ground, we grab our bags and head for Jacksonville Beach. We get a couple of motel rooms, take a quick shower, and head out. First we have a few drinks, just to warm up the old engine so to speak, then have a good dinner, and afterwards we get down to some serious drinking."

"I don't know," Skip said doubtfully. "The orders say we're supposed to report to the carriers this afternoon by five o'clock and…"

"Skip, Skip, Skip," Jack interrupted, "use your old noodle. There's gonna be how many men on board each carrier, two thousand maybe? Do you honestly think the Navy is gonna jump through its wazoo all evening looking for one Air Force type that didn't show up? Besides, the ships don't sail until four the next afternoon. It's gonna be fine, relax."

"Well, I guess it would be all right."

*   *   *   *

Skip stepped off the aircraft at Mayport Naval Air Station and was immediately enveloped by sun-kissed warmth and a light, salt-scented breeze from the nearby Atlantic Ocean. Looking around the base, he could see that the drab military buildings were surrounded by thick rows of flowered bushes, and the streets were lined with palm trees—not the squat kind found in the lobbies of second-rate hotels, but tall, graceful trees that reached toward the sky like monuments. It was Skip's first visit to Florida, and the contrast between his current surroundings and the snow-covered wasteland he had just left was overwhelming. It was heady stuff for a small-town boy from Southern Illinois who had traveled very little before joining the Air Force.

Jacksonville Beach was rocking and rolling. It always was when the fleet was in town, and even more so when they were sailing the next day. Sailors in their dress-white uniforms were everywhere, laughing, drinking, and looking for women. Cactus Jack's idea of a few drinks to warm up the old engine turned out to be four vodka martinis knocked back in less than an hour, after which they decided to find a place to eat. Pressing through the mobs of sailors on the crowded sidewalks, they spotted a quiet side street with a restaurant, flashing a blue neon sign that read, "The Blue Lagoon," and under that in red flashing letters, "Steaks, Seafood and Polynesian."

"Let's go," Jack said. "I've found the place. A good steak and more drinks are just what we need right now."

"Two for dinner, sir?" the petite Polynesian hostess asked.

"We're going to the bar first," Jack replied, eyeing her curvy, sarong-wrapped body appreciatively. "We'll be back though."

"Not bad," he whispered to Skip as they walked away. "We'll have to check her out later, for sure."

Skip nodded but said nothing. He wasn't sure he needed more to drink.

It was dark in the restaurant after being in the bright sunlight out on the street, but by the time they got closer to the bar, their eyes had adjusted, and they noticed two women perched on bar stools, an empty seat on either side of them. The first woman was short, squat, and had a missing front tooth. She was obviously very drunk and laughing uproariously at something the other had said. She wore a faded yellow, shapeless sundress. The second woman was speaking in a quiet manner, trying to maintain dignity for them both. She was dressed in a stylish, cream-colored skirt and blazer with a navy blue silk blouse.

Jack took in the scene quickly and maneuvered expertly to arrive at the stool next to the woman in the suit. "Follow me lad, and watch how I handle this," he said. "You'll learn something." Let Skip handle the dumpy one, he thought, it'll be good experience for the kid.

But the "dumpy one" grabbed Jack by the sleeve and pulled him onto the bar stool beside her. "Well shit, honey," she said loudly, "Don't be shy. Sit down and have a drink. We'll get piddley-assed drunk together."

Skip slid quickly onto the stool next to the other woman before her friend changed her mind. "Hi. My name is Skip."

"Pleased to meet you, Skip. I'm Dottie," she said, looking at him with frank and appraising eyes. She looked to be in her late thirties, a brunette with a lush curvy body and a sultry Southern drawl. She had been drinking awhile, he guessed, but he didn't think she was drunk. Not yet anyway.

"I watched you gentlemen come in," she said. "You're not in the Navy are you?"

"Well no. We're in the Air Force actually."

"The Air Force? My goodness. We don't see many Air Force men around here, that's for sure. You're officers aren't you?"

"Yes, how did you know?"

"I could just tell," she said, squeezing his hand gently. "You have this look about you that says you are...well...classier than the others. "

Suddenly, their conversation was interrupted by the sound of loud cackling laughter. Looking over his shoulder, Skip saw Cactus Jack's new friend leaning over, telling him a story with her hand placed firmly on his thigh.

"That's my friend, Lila," Dottie said. You have to excuse her. She's just the sweetest thing in the world, and I love her to pieces. She's so much fun to go out with, but she's taken to drinking a lot lately, and she likes to carry on with the sailors out at the base. I do believe they have taught her some of their ways."

"No problem," Skip said, "My friend…umm…Cactus Jack is a bit of a character too. I'm sure they will get along just fine."

Suddenly Lila announced in a loud voice, "Come on everybody, let's sit down and eat. I am so hungry I could eat a whole steer, asshole and all!" Her voice carried throughout the restaurant. Cactus Jack was so drunk by then that he barely looked up. Skip burst out laughing. He couldn't help himself.

Meanwhile, Dottie arched her eyebrows and said, "Well, that's Lila. What more can I tell you?"

The restaurant was cozy. Tiki torches lined the walls, along with ceremonial masks and straw mats of all kinds. At the far end of the dimly lit room, an organ player sat, playing mellow, romantic songs. Skip and Dottie sat side by side at one end of a semicircular booth with their legs pressed together gently, while Cactus Jack and Lila sat at the other end. The fresh flowery scent of the perfume in Dottie's hair made it very difficult for Skip to concentrate, as she spoke in his ear with her slow, seductive Southern drawl. Now and then, she would squeeze his thigh, as if to emphasize a point. Skip was becoming aroused. After awhile, he slid his hand under her skirt and began to softly massage her thigh. She did not resist, even when his exploring hand advanced well above the top of her stocking. The skin there was hot and silky smooth.

The teriyaki-marinated steak they had ordered was excellent, and a dessert of vanilla sherbet decorated with pineapple slices provided a perfect ending to the meal. By the time they finished dinner, it was nearly midnight. They had all been drinking since late afternoon. It was time to leave. Skip's head began to clear as he walked arm-in-arm with Dottie across the cool, deserted parking lot. Lila and Jack were close behind. He was pretty sure it wouldn't end here. He hoped it wouldn't anyway. When they arrived at Dottie's car she said, "Lila honey, I do believe we should escort these gentlemen back to their motel and make sure they get tucked safely into bed. Don't you?" Lila agreed.

There was no one in front of the motel they arrived. As the girls scrambled out of the car, Cactus Jack pulled Skip roughly to one side and began to talk in urgent, whispering tones, his face just inches from Skip's. His eyes were glazed from the night of drinking, and his breath smelled indescribably bad.

"Okay, Skip, I'm gonna do this. Just so you can get laid."

"Gee Jack, you don't…"

"This means you are gonna owe me, Skip. I mean really owe me," he said, repeatedly punching Skip's chest with his finger for emphasis.

"I understand, and believe me…"

"And Skip?"

"Yes sir?"

"If you ever tell anyone in the squadron about this, I'll kill you! Understand?"

"Oh, yes sir. And I want you to know…" he started to say. But Cactus Jack and Lila were already weaving their way toward Jack's room, arm in arm."

As soon as Skip pushed his room door closed, he and Dottie began making love. There was a flurry of zippers, buttons, snaps, and clasps, all coming undone. Kissing and holding each other tightly, they continued to undress each other, leaving a trail of clothes behind them, as they edged toward the bed, still locked in each other's arms. Once their clothes were discarded, they fell together upon the double bed. Dottie proved to be a woman of unbridled passion. Sometimes aggressive, demanding, and verbal, other times compliant, giving, and shy, she was filled with steamy contradictions. It was all Skip could do to keep up with her, but he did.

They made love until they both were spent and totally exhausted. When it was over, Dottie curled up in Skip's arms, laying her head on his chest as she listened to his rapidly beating heart.

"Oh wow," she said. "That was marvelous. You are a wonderful lover."

"Yeah, well, you are pretty wonderful yourself, you know, and a really special woman."

"Sugar, could I ask you one teeny question?"

"Sure. What?"

"Well, I was just wondering if you are…uhh…married. I mean, it's all right if you are."

"Me? Married? No. Absolutely not. Why do you ask?"

"Well, you seem so experienced. I mean, you seem to know just what to do to please a woman. And that takes practice I should think."

Before Skip could answer, he was interrupted by the sound of furniture crashing against the wall, followed by the furious squeaking of bedsprings and a high-pitched cackling laugh. "I do believe Miss Lila is in love," Dottie said giggling.

Their room was a disaster the following morning. Clothes, sheets, and pillows were strewn everywhere. The smells of cigarettes, booze, perfume, and sex filled the air. Skip told Dottie he would return in about two weeks and asked if he could call her when he did. He sensed she was waiting for him to ask her that.

Besides, he wanted to see her again. "Why, that would be very nice, sugar," she said. "I'll surely wait for your call."

*   *   *   *

The Essex and the Saratoga had been at sea for almost a week. Carrier qualification training for the aircrews was coming along nicely, and the two ships had performed smoothly in a series of exercises, working with cruisers, destroyers, submarines, and a variety of support ships. If all went well, they would return to port in a few days. Then, things began to fall apart.

The weather reconnaissance aircraft launched at 5 AM and lost its engine just after it was catapulted off the deck. It glided in the pitch dark and struck the water, skimming through the swells until it came to a stop. The pilot unstrapped and stepped out of the cockpit onto the wing. Within minutes a destroyer picked him up and transferred him back to the carrier. He was dazed, disorientated, and soaking wet. Meanwhile, rumors were circulating that the Saratoga had lost three aircraft over the past two days. It was a bad sign. But it was only the beginning.

The next afternoon Skip was standing in the superstructure watching aircraft land. It was a routine recovery of thirty aircraft. The last aircraft to land was a single-seat, prop-driven Douglas Sky Raider. All looked normal until it touched down. Suddenly, one of the main landing gear collapsed, causing the aircraft to veer sharply to the right. To make matters worse, the tail hook failed to engage any of the arresting cables. With no way to steer or even stop the aircraft, it continued straight down the deck, its collapsed wing dragging across the metal deck with a screeching howl, creating a dramatic shower of sparks. Finally, it smashed into a group of recovered aircraft with a sickening metallic crunch, scattering planes like bowling pins.

For a fraction of a second, there was silence. Then the fire started. People were running everywhere, running for their lives. The PA system broke through the confusion, "General quarters...general quarters. All hands man your battle stations. Fire on the flight deck." The call was repeated. Then came the steady, persistent clanging of an alarm that could be heard throughout the ship, as crews scrambled to their battle stations. Skip had nowhere to go, so he stayed where he was, watching the spectacle with slack-jawed amazement. The fire spread rapidly along the fuel-soaked deck, burning with intense heat and emitting an acrid smell that burned Skip's throat and watered his eyes. Within seconds, the fuel tanks in the Sky Raider exploded. Soon, the entire recovery area was transformed into a boiling inferno of greasy black smoke and twisted white-hot metal. Firefighters tried their best to gain control of the desperate situation but were driven back, as fuel tanks in other aircraft began to explode one after another. It was a scene from hell.

After two hours, the blaze subsided, and order was restored. By then, the forward end of the flight deck had been reduced to a wasteland of scorched aircraft and smoldering piles of metallic debris. Everything was smothered in thick, white foam that was used to quell the fiery inferno. Ten aircraft were lost in the fire. The wreckage, mostly piles of molten magnesium, was swept overboard. There was nothing left worth salvaging. Four other aircraft required extensive repair. Miraculously, no one was killed or even seriously injured. The pilot of the runaway Sky Raider escaped with minor burns. One ground crew member was missing for two hours and feared lost but was later found confused and in shock several decks below.

The commander of the carrier division decided enough was enough. Counting the weather reconnaissance aircraft, he had lost eleven aircraft on the Essex and three more on the Saratoga. It was time to regroup. The exercise was canceled, and the ships were ordered back to port.

The arrival of the Essex at Mayport was a somber affair. The excitement and enthusiasm that prevailed when they had set sail was gone. Two tugs guided the ship toward the dock too fast, and she smashed into a small barge that was tied up alongside. The barge was there to provide a buffer between the ship's hull and the dock. It did its job. There was no damage to the ship, but the barge was destroyed. It was a fitting end to a disastrous exercise.

The Saratoga was already in port when Skip arrived, and Cactus Jack had left for Presque Isle. Skip called Dottie and arranged to meet her that evening. They enjoyed a long, intimate dinner. She seemed even more feminine than before, with a hint of loneliness in her eyes. After dinner, she drove him to her home, a small neat house in a quiet neighborhood in Neptune Beach. After making love, they lay in each other's arms for a long time, Skip gently stroking her hair and listening, as she told him about her life. She had been divorced for several years, had a son who was away in college, and yes, she got very lonely at times. She told him that she rarely went to bed with a man she had just met. In fact, she rarely went to bed with men, period. But sometimes, she explained, she just couldn't help herself, as she needed to try and fill the voids in her life.

Soon, there was nothing left to talk about. Both realized, although neither said so, that this night and the one they had ten days ago were all they had. It was all they would ever have. When Dottie dropped him off at his motel the next morning, he gave her one last kiss and promised to keep in touch. They both knew that wouldn't happen.

Presque Isle Air Force Base, Maine

July 1958

Time passed quickly after Skip returned to Presque Isle, and he soon forgot about Dottie and his adventure on the Essex. For the past two years, he had been taking correspondence courses and attending night school, hoping to be eligible for "Operation Bootstrap". This was a government program that permitted military officers to take six months off to finish their college degrees. Colleges participating in the program offered compressed schedules that allowed students to take twenty four semester hours in six months, and some offered credits for military experience. Between the courses he had taken so far and his military experience, Skip figured that he was almost within twenty four hours of getting a degree. Soon he would be taking the final exam for the last course he needed to qualify. If he passed, he would send in his application right away.

Skip did pass his final exam, and a few weeks later he was notified that his application for the Bootstrap program was approved. He would begin classes at the University of Omaha the second week of September. It was August 15, 1958. He would be leaving in two weeks.

The day he left was picture-perfect, the kind you only find in Northern Maine in late summer, just before the leaves begin to turn and the air gets chilly. As he drove away from the base, he thought he might actually miss Presque Isle. Then he remembered that it wouldn't be long before the snows arrived, and everyone would be freezing again. All of his belongings were crammed in the trunk of his turquoise and white 1955 Chevy Bellaire convertible. Rolling down Highway U.S. 1 toward Bangor, the top was down, the radio was going full blast, and he was singing at the top of his voice, as Jerry Lee Lewis banged away at "Great Balls of Fire." It's gonna be all right, he thought. I have a feeling something is waiting for me in Omaha. Something besides a college degree. "Goodness, gracious, great balls of fire!"

UNIVERSITY OF OMAHA

Omaha Nebraska
1958 to 1959

The coffee shop was filled with excited students, all talking at once. It was registration day, and most were discussing class schedules, courses, and professors. Skip sat alone in the corner drinking coffee, feeling very much out of place. Everyone looked so young! He had his schedule in hand and was pleased with the classes he had selected; six, three hour courses in psychology, history, journalism, and political science. It was a heavy schedule but the courses were all relatively easy. He couldn't wait to get started.

Sipping his coffee and gazing idly around the room, he caught a glimpse of a girl sitting at a nearby table surrounded by friends. It wasn't love at first sight exactly, for their eyes never met. Nevertheless, the sight of her sitting there chatting easily with her friends, blissfully unaware of his existence, was one he would remember for the rest of his life, like a photograph that would never bend, curl, or fade.

To say that she was "good-looking" or even "pretty" would vastly understate her natural beauty, at least he thought so. Her dark brown hair hung down to her shoulders in luxurious waves with neatly trimmed bangs that framed a face with clear smooth skin and high cheekbones. She was dressed simply, in a soft white sweater, plaid wool skirt, white socks, and loafers. The sweater was loose fitting but did little to conceal a firm set of breasts. But it was her deep and expressive blue eyes that he noticed first. They seemed to send a variety of signals at the same time—warmth, shyness, curiosity, and a sense of mystery that he couldn't quite fathom. As he watched her chatting easily with her companions, he tried to figure out if one of them might be her boyfriend. He didn't think so but wasn't certain. He guessed her age to be about twenty or twenty-one. When it was time to leave, he gathered his things and casually strolled past her, trying to make eye contact as he went, but she never looked up. Just as he left the coffee shop, he heard someone call her "Christy."

Skip had made a simple bargain with the Air Force. They gave him six months leave with pay, and he in turn, promised to study hard and make good grades. He intended to keep his end of the bargain, and no one, not even Miss Christy whatever-her-name-was, was going to break his focus. Still, he found himself thinking about her a lot during the two days remaining before classes began, wondering if he would see her again. He decided if it was meant to be, he would. Besides, it was a small campus, and he was bound to run into her sometime.

When he arrived for his first psychology class, the classroom was already half full. As he sat down and arranged his study materials, the door opened, and Christy walked in. He watched her nervously out of the corner of his eye, as she glanced around the room trying to decide where to sit. Over here, he thought, sit over here near me. He was trying to will her to his side through mental telepathy. It was a silly notion, but it worked. She walked across the room and took a seat just in front of him. Yes! He thought exultantly. There is a God after all. After class, he casually introduced himself. She said her name was Christy Weber. She was pleasant and friendly, but it was obvious it wasn't love at first sight for her, far from it. Well, he thought as he walked away, I have to start somewhere. You never know where it might lead.

During the next two weeks, he made a point of "accidentally" bumping into her as often as possible. It made him feel like a high school kid, but he didn't care. He was in love, or at least thought he was. Each time they met, he would put his best moves on her, as the big boys back in Presque Isle would say. It was slow going. Sometimes, when he said something forward or slightly outrageous, her twinkling eyes seemed to say, "Nice try, big boy. Keep that up, and you might get somewhere…maybe." Once in awhile, he caught her looking at him, when she thought he wasn't watching. This gave him hope. Luckily for him, fate stepped in and gave him a break. Their psychology class was split into four groups to work on an outside project. He made damn sure he was in the same group as Christy. Better still, his group decided to break the project into a series of tasks and have two people work on each task. Miraculously, Christy asked him to work with her.

"What made you choose me as a partner?" he asked, trying to sound casual.

"Because you are older and in the military," she responded. "And you are used to following orders."

"Following orders?" he asked incredulously. That wasn't the answer he was looking for.

"Well…umm…I don't mean orders, exactly. Instructions, that's what I mean."

"Ahhh, instructions. Now I see."

"Yes, instructions." She was starting to stammer and blush. "From the professor, of course, not me."

"Oh right. Now I have it," he said, standing at attention and saluting smartly. "I'm ready for further instructions."

"Stop it!" she said punching his arm.

They both started laughing. The ice was broken.

*   *   *   *

They worked together after school for three weeks, mostly in the library. It was hard at first, being so close to her, smelling the sweet scent of her perfume while constantly being under the scrutiny of those ever-changing blue eyes. But he managed, and soon they developed an easy familiarity that was rapidly turning into friendship. Each evening after finishing their work, they would have coffee and talk. That's when he really started getting to know her. Christy was twenty-one years old and an education major in her junior year. She wanted to be a kindergarten schoolteacher. "It's such an important job," she said. "They are just little people, you know. And the kindergarten teacher is their first exposure to being in a classroom and learning."

"Yes," Skip nodded. "I can see that." And he really could. She's gonna make a helluva teacher someday, he thought, and be great with kids.

Christy lived in a small suburb near Omaha. Her parents were German immigrants, and she had an older brother and two sisters. They were not poor by any means. Her father was a jet engine inspector at nearby Offutt Air Force Base. But sending her away to a large university was out of the question. So she lived at home, commuting to and from school in a small sports car she had bought with her own savings. It was her only luxury in life. A 1957 MG. Skip's heart sank when she told him she lived with her parents.

"It isn't a long commute, only about twenty miles," she told him. "But sometimes when I have to study late, I stay with two of my girlfriends who have a nice apartment near the campus." Now we are getting somewhere, he thought. There has to be a reason why she told me that. He hoped so, anyway.

One evening they worked on their psychology project until almost ten o'clock. "Hey," Skip said, rubbing his eyes wearily. "I'm exhausted. Did you eat dinner?"

"No," she replied. "Now that you mention it, I sort of forgot."

"Why don't we grab a bite? I know a place nearby that makes great hamburgers. I'll even treat."

"Sounds good to me. Especially the part about you buying."

It was a balmy, early fall evening. The moon was full, and the sky was filled with bright, twinkling stars. Driving down Dodge Avenue, with the top down and the radio playing "Volare" by Domenico Modugno, they began to sing along, laughing uproariously as they stumbled over strange Italian phrases like *"nel blu dipinto blu."* They arrived at the restaurant much sooner than they both would have liked. The restaurant was noisy but fun. Christy had a beer, and he drank two. It was obvious she wasn't much of a drinker, and that was fine with him. They sat side by side in a curved booth. Being that close to her and feeling her warmth was driving him crazy. He wanted to touch her hair and bury his face in her neck to smell her perfume. But he didn't.

It was midnight by the time he drove her to the student parking lot and walked her to her MG. It was white, with a black racing stripe down the hood. "Hey I love your car," he said. "I almost bought one once."

"Well, if you play your cards right, I might let you ride in it sometime," she replied, as she leaned down to open the door.

When she stood up and turned around, their faces were almost touching. They didn't plan that. It just happened. For a second, neither moved. Then they kissed. It was a warm, sweet, soft kiss that lasted a long time. It was the best kiss Skip had ever had.

"Wow," Christy said, catching her breath. "You Air Force guys really move fast don't you?" And with that, she slid into her car, giving him a brief glimpse of exposed leg under her skirt as she closed the door and started the engine. "Good night Skip. Thanks for a super evening."

As her car disappeared around the corner, Skip stood rooted to the spot where they had kissed, his lips faintly smeared with lipstick, and a dopey, lopsided grin on his face. Yep, this is love all right, he thought, no doubt about it. We've come a long way in six weeks. So far so good.

*   *   *   *

Three days passed before they saw each other again. Christy had been intimidated by their encounter in the parking lot. That wasn't supposed to happen. But it did, and she loved it. Could she be falling for this guy? No way. For one thing, even though Christy was twenty-one, her father still made and enforced the rules. The most important rule of all was no dating military men. "I'm around them all day," he always said, "and I can tell you they are only after one thing." But Skip was an officer, and that should count for something. Besides, he was awfully cute and definitely more worldly than she was, and that fascinated her. She decided to dangle him along for awhile. He would be leaving in a few months anyway. Meanwhile, why not have a little fun? Skip, on the other hand, had no idea he was being "dangled." In his mind, their kiss told him he had turned the corner, and things were going his way. He felt confident, on top of the world.

They turned in their project on a Friday morning. They were sure they had done a good job. Even the other members of their group said so, assuring them that it would get an A, "Hey, I've got a great idea," Skip said to Christy when class was over. "Why don't we go out for dinner tomorrow night to celebrate?"

"Another trip to the burger joint?" Christy asked smiling.

"The burger joint...are you kidding? After that brilliant piece of academic research we just completed, we should go first-class. How about the officers' club out at the base? They have fine dining and dancing. But maybe you have other plans. It will be Saturday night after all."

"Well, I am supposed to meet someone," Christy said. This was a lie of course, but she was not about to admit that she didn't have a date for Saturday night. "But maybe that person would understand if I canceled."

"Great!" Skip said. He wondered if "that person" was a boy or girl. "Let's make it six o'clock. Where should I pick you up?"

"Where should you pick me up? At my house, of course. You didn't think you were going to sweep me away to wine and dine me without meeting my parents, did you? Au contraire!"

"No problem. Your folks are gonna love me."

"Well, we'll see. It all depends on what kind of mood my dad's in. Come to think of it, he hasn't beaten up one of my dates for a long time, so you might be okay."

"It will be a piece of cake," Skip said. "Gotta run. I'm late for my next class."

"Six o'clock sharp, Skip, and if you're late, you're out of luck. I'll move on to plan B."

"Eighteen hundred hours it is," Skip said. "See you then."

Christy watched him hurry away and felt a sudden grip of panic. What in God's name was she doing? First, she went with him for a sandwich and ended up necking in the school parking lot. Now, it's a fancy date at the officers' club…and he's going to meet her parents. Things are happening way too fast. Still, she was looking forward to going to the club. She had been there only once, on the night of her senior prom. She remembered the soft, quiet ambiance of the dining room with its crystal chandeliers and starched white tablecloths. It was the way she imagined rich people lived. Yes, having dinner at the officers' club was going to be wonderful. But Skip meeting her father? That could be a problem.

Skip was totally unaware of the thoughts and turmoil surging through Christy's mind. All he knew was that this was going be their first honest-to-God date. His big chance to show her what a cool and sophisticated guy he was. Oh sure, he realized that her father was probably going to be a real pain-in-the-ass. But he's gonna love me once he gets to know me. What's not to love?

*   *   *   *

The Webers lived in a neat, two-story frame house in a quiet middle-class neighborhood. As Skip drove up, he noticed the lawn was manicured, and flowers of all varieties surrounded the house. It was obvious that an avid gardener had been at work, probably her mother. The sidewalk leading to the front steps was spotless and gleaming. The grass along its edge was carefully trenched. All is in order, he thought, smiling to himself. Not a blade of grass out of place. Ernst Weber opened the door on the first knock. He was a handsome man, with a full head of wavy brown hair and finely chiseled Nordic features. His piercing blue eyes stared directly into Skip's as they shook hands firmly. Skip figured he was in his mid-forties. He wasn't smiling as he let Skip in, but he didn't look unhappy either.

"Christine is upstairs getting ready. She'll be down in a few minutes," Ernst said, settling into a large easy chair. Skip took that as his cue to sit down, but before he had a chance, Greta Weber, Christy's mother hurried in.

"Hello, Lieutenant," she said, "I am so glad to meet you. Christine is excited about going to the officers' club. I'm sure you two will have a wonderful time." Ernst shot his wife a "calm down woman and be quiet" look, but said nothing. The sight of Christy's mom made him smile and lifted his spirits. She had the same sparkling blue eyes, high cheekbones, and lush figure as her daughter. This is what Christy will look like when we are her parents' age, he thought.

"So, Mr. Weber," he began, "Christy tells me you work at the base."

"Yep, out at Offutt."

"A jet engine inspector, right?"

"Yep."

"What kind of engines do you inspect?"

"KC-135 engines."

The conversation was going nowhere so far. He wondered what to say next. But it was Ernst's turn to ask the questions. He wanted to know where Skip was from, who his folks were and so on; all the things a daughter's father isn't afraid to ask. Skip explained that he was from Southern Illinois, not too far from St. Louis, Missouri, and that his father was a postal clerk.

"A postal clerk, eh?" he said. "That's a damn good job. Civil service. Lots of security. Tried to get that myself a few years back."

Hurray, Skip thought, we have something going here. Not much, but it's a start. He wondered what to say next. Things were getting awkward. Then, he looked up and saw Christy coming down the stairs. She was wearing a black cashmere dress, with black high-heel pumps. The dress was cut just low enough to reveal a glimpse of cleavage. She was wearing pearl stud earrings with a matching single-strand pearl necklace. A small black-leather purse with a silver chain completed the vision of loveliness. Standing up to greet her, Skip had a catch in his throat and could hardly speak. She was beautiful. "Hi Christy," he said, taking her hand, "You look really nice."

She looked approvingly at his charcoal-gray suit, pale blue shirt, and highly polished shoes. "Thank you kind sir. You don't look so bad yourself. I like your uniform." They both laughed.

Greta looked at the young couple appreciatively and brandished a camera. "Both of you go over to the fireplace and let me take your picture," she said. "You look adorable together." Ernst squirmed uneasily and glared at his wife. Meanwhile, Skip slipped his arm around Christy's waist while her mom snapped the picture. They fit together perfectly.

"You kids have a really nice time tonight," her mother said.

"We will, Mom."

"What time can we expect you home?" her father asked pointedly.

"Oh Dad, you know, by midnight I guess."

"Okay, I will be counting on that."

"How did it go with my father?" Christy asked as they walked to the car.

"Oh great. Absolutely fantastic."

"No. I mean, how did it really go?"

"Well, I have to admit, it's gonna take some time for him to warm up to me."

"Know what I think?" she said.

"What?"

"I think he likes you."

"Get out of here. No way."

"Trust me. I know what I'm talking about. He seemed different tonight. I can't put my finger on it, but he did."

"Well, I'm sure glad he likes me," Skip laughed, admiring her legs as she slid into the car.

*   *   *   *

It was dusk by the time they arrived at the officers' club. Inside, soft lights cast a glow of warmth and elegance. Walking arm in arm into the main bar to have a cocktail before dinner, they were surrounded by mirrored glass and fine wood paneling. The dark blue carpet was thick and plush. Historical paintings were hung on the walls. At the far wall, a small group of people stood chatting quietly at a long mahogany bar. There were tables grouped throughout the room where couples sat talking and drinking. It was still early, and the bar was not crowded.

"Well, here we are," Skip said, leading Christy to a quiet table in the corner. "What do you think?"

"Not bad," she said, settling into a plush leather armchair. "Not bad at all. You Air Force guys certainly know how to live."

"I guess so," he said laughing. "But this is better than most clubs because Strategic Air Command Headquarters is here. You've been here before, right?"

"Yes. A bunch of us came here for dinner before our senior prom. They wouldn't let us in the bar, though."

A waiter in a white starched jacket arrived to take their order. Skip ordered a Dry Sack sherry straight up. Christy thought a minute and ordered a Dewar's Scotch and water. "I'm impressed, a broad with good taste in liquor."

"Well, you know, I don't drink very often, but when I do—"

"You like to go first-class," he finished for her.

"Right…and I am not a broad, thank you very much!"

"That you are not," Skip laughed. "I was just kidding."

"Tell me about Presque Isle," she said.

"Presque Isle? Well, to begin with, our whole officers' club could fit in the dining room here. And at this time of night, there would be at least two dozen guys in sweaty flying suits hanging around the bar, drinking, smoking, rolling dice, and making a hell of a racket. Oh, and the jukebox would be going full blast."

"That doesn't sound very appealing," she said, wrinkling her nose. "What about women? Are they allowed to join these gatherings of hairy-chested aviators?"

"Well, gosh, sure. The wives usually join their husbands for dinner right after happy hour."

"Wives and girlfriends, of course," she said.

"Girlfriends?" he scoffed. "No such thing in Presque Isle." Then he told her the joke about there being only two single women in Presque Isle, and they didn't like Air Force guys.

Christy was pleased to hear there was no girlfriend in the picture. But she tried not to show it. "Well," she said, "that's the officers' club. What about the rest of the base?"

"Not much else to talk about. There's the flight line, hangars, office buildings…the usual things. We also have two-and three-bedroom homes on base for married couples and their families. The single officers live in the BOQ."

"BOQ?"

"Bachelor Officers Quarters. Pretty much a dump, really. World War II-vintage buildings, common latrine and shower, that kind of thing."

"But surely there are some good things to be said about Presque Isle."

"Oh sure. It has some of the most beautiful scenery I've ever seen, with majestic mountains and crystal-clear lakes all around. In the fall, the leaves turn to such intense shades of red, gold, and brown that it's almost blinding. Flying over that kind of landscape on a bright sunny day is like surfing above a magic carpet that goes on forever."

"Sounds magnificent."

"It is. And the forests, you can't imagine how vast they are. Once in awhile during moose-hunting season, a hunter will get lost and never be seen again."

"Never?"

"Never. Search teams from the base and nearby towns look for them. But after two or three weeks, they have to give up."

"That's awful. What do you think happens to them?"

"I don't know," Skip said with a shrug. "They probably wander around in circles until they starve or maybe become delirious and end up getting mauled to death by a cougar or bear." Christy squeezed his hand hard at the thought. That's when Skip realized that they had been holding hands for a long time. He liked that. It seemed so natural. By now, they were warm and cozy, lost in their own special world. He was happy and didn't want the night to end. "Well," he announced, reluctantly, "it's time to slop the hogs."

"Slop the hogs? Oh Lieutenant, you have the most colorful and poetic way of expressing yourself!"

"It's one of my many endearing charms," he said winking. They walked arm in arm to the dining room.

The dining room was much larger than the bar and even more elegant. Crystal chandeliers dropped gracefully from the high-vaulted ceiling. The highly glossed parquet floor was spotless. There was a raised platform in one corner where a three-piece orchestra was getting ready to play. The room was filled with people and subdued activity. "Beats the hell out of the burger joint," Skip said, as the hostess lead them to their table.

"You've got that right," Christy giggled.

They chatted about the menu, and he ordered for both of them: shrimp cock-tails, followed by Caesar salad, filet mignon with baked potato, and crème cara-mel for dessert. The meal was excellent, and they ate leisurely, chatting and enjoying each other's company. Before the dessert arrived, the orchestra began to play a slow, romantic song. He wasn't much of a dancer, but he couldn't let the moment pass. He took Christy's hand and led her to the floor for their first dance together. The song was "It's Not For Me To Say," one of his favorites. She slid easily into his arms and moved in rhythm with him as though they had been dancing together for years. From the corner of his eye, he could see other couples watching them as they danced. The wives were giving them that "what a beauti-ful young couple, they look so much in love" look. The husbands, on the other hand, focused on Christy's sexy derriere, which was perfectly framed in her black dress. Dirty old men, he thought, laughing to himself. Eat your hearts out! They stayed on the dance floor even when the band switched to a fast song. Christy was a good dancer, no doubt about it, and they danced well together. Finally they sat down, out of breath and laughing.

By the time they finished coffee and dessert, she began to glance nervously at her watch.

"You're not getting bored, are you?" Skip asked.

"Gosh no. It's just, my dad gets…you know."

"Yeah, I understand. We better get going."

It was 11:15 by the time they walked out of the club and strolled to the car with their arms wrapped around each other's waist. There was more than enough time to get her home before the curfew. At the car, he gathered her into his arms and kissed her, pressing her body gently against the door. She didn't resist, and the kiss went on for a long time. When they finally broke away, he held her by the shoulders and said with mock severity, "Okay, you won't be able to escape by bugging out in your MG, like you did the last time. Get into the car woman."

"You're such an animal," she giggled as she slid into the seat.

They pulled up in front of her house at 11:45. Fifteen minutes to spare. He killed the motor and turned off the lights but left the radio on. Johnny Mathis was crooning away. "Chances are cause I wear a silly grin, the moment you come into view, chances are you think that I am in love with you..." A Johnny Mathis night, Skip thought. First the orchestra played "It's Not For Me To Say" at the club, and now, "Chances Are." I wonder what my chances are.

As if to answer his question, a full moon broke out of the clouds and lit up the inside of the car. By then, Christy had slid across the seat, into his arms, her legs tucked beneath her in a half-sitting, half-reclining position. Then she was on his lap, as they began a series of long probing kisses. He was stroking her hair and shoulders.

"Just because my composure slowly slips the moment your lips meet mine..." Johnny continued singing.

Skip was excited. He thought he was going to explode. "Chances are you believe the stars that filled the skies are in my eyes..." Johnny was still with them. He wondered how far he could take this.

Suddenly, porch light came on. "Shit!" they both said, as they broke away and sat up straight. Christy's lipstick was badly smeared, leaving most of it on Skip's face. "Is he going to come outside?" Skip asked.

"No, it's just his way of saying that he knows we're out here, and he's keeping an eye on us. Whew, Skip, you really had me going."

"Tell me about it," Skip said. "You have no idea how much you got me going."

Quickly she applied fresh lipstick and adjusted her dress and stockings.

"I'll walk you to the door" he offered.

"Thanks, but it's better if I go in alone. At least my mom thinks so. She doesn't want the neighbors to see any goings-on."

"So, it's okay to kiss up a storm and Lord knows what else in the car, but no goodnight kiss at the front door. Is that it?"

"You got it."

"And your dad, what does he think?"

"Nothing is okay with him," she said making a face.

She gave him a final peck on the cheek and opened the car door. "By the way," she said as she slid out, "do you ever cook meals for yourself, other than TV dinners?"

"No, not very often. I'm pretty much an eat-out kind of guy."

"That's what I thought. I will be at your place around five tomorrow to cook Sunday dinner for us. You do have pots and pans and stuff like that in your kitchen, don't you?"

"I don't know," he said. "I'll have to check."

"Okay, gotta go. I had a great time. Good night baby."

For a full minute, he sat in the car trying to make sense of it all. Good night "baby?" I'll be at your place tomorrow to cook Sunday dinner? It was almost too good to be true. As he drove away, his face broke into a wide grin, and he began singing, "Well, chances are your chances are awfully good."

*   *   *   *

Skip was still smiling when he woke up the next day. But when he looked at his apartment, his smile quickly disappeared. The place was a mess. There were clothes strewn from one end of his bedroom to the other. The bathroom needed a major cleaning, and the living room carpet couldn't be seen under the assortment of newspapers, magazines, and schoolbooks. The kitchen sink was filled with unwashed glasses and coffee cups. He had work to do before Christy showed up to cook dinner, and there wasn't much time.

The apartment was located in the basement of a well-kept, two-story home on a quiet, tree-lined street. It consisted of a living room, small bedroom, a dining alcove, kitchen, and bathroom and was sparsely furnished with old but comfortable furniture. It was all he needed. The elderly landlady who lived upstairs was quite taken with him and was quick to tell her neighbors that her newest tenant was a military officer and a fine young man at that. Of course, when he moved in, she gave him a speech about loud music, noisy parties, and rowdy behavior, and ended by saying, "I don't want to catch you bringing girls home at all hours of the night." The twinkle in her eye was unmistakable when she said that, and he was pretty sure the operative phrase was, "I don't want to catch you."

It took Skip most of the morning to clean and straighten the place up. He didn't want Christy to think he was a slob, even though he supposed he was. I wonder if she really can cook, he thought. I guess I'm going to find out this afternoon. The thought of the two of them alone in his apartment excited him but made him feel a little nervous too.

By one o'clock the apartment was spotless. It was time to attend to the last-minute details. He needed to buy flowers and a bottle of wine. He bought a fall bouquet of red, yellow, and white carnations in a green-frosted vase. It will look great on the dining room table, he thought. Then he bought a bottle of Chianti. Skip didn't know much about wine but thought the straw basket around the bottom of the bottle gave it a romantic touch. He had another Chianti bottle at home that he sometimes used as a candleholder. He would light a candle tonight and put it on the table next to the flowers.

His last stop was the grocery store to find something for dessert. After wandering down the aisles aimlessly for a few minutes, he ended up at a standstill, torn by indecision between the bakery counter and the dairy case. Cakes, pies, ice cream—there were so many choices. Which one to choose?

"Looks like you could use some help," a voice behind him said. Turning around, he saw a smiling, middle-aged woman standing by her shopping cart, looking at him with amusement. She was the motherly, I'd-like-to-pinch-your-cheek type.

"I have a date coming over to fix dinner, and I need to find a nice dessert."

"Oh, I see," she said. "Somebody very special, I'll bet. And you want to be creative and impress her, right?"

"Yeah, I guess so."

"Of course you do. Women love men who are creative. So, here's what you do. Buy a container of chocolate pudding and one of vanilla. Swirl the two together in a tall dessert cup. You know the kind they serve sundaes in. Then, top it with whipped cream and a maraschino cherry. You can prepare it in advance and have it in the refrigerator all ready to go. Believe me, you'll look like a master chef. And if you don't have the dessert cups, they have them over on aisle six."

"Gee thanks, that's a great idea. I'll do it."

"You're welcome," she said as she started to walk away. Then she paused, turned around and gave him a broad wink. "Good luck."

"Thanks again," Skip said, blushing.

Having taken care of the house cleaning, shopping, and preparation of the dessert, Skip fell back into a living-room easy chair and looked at his watch. It was 4:30 PM. Christy would be arriving in half an hour. There was nothing left to do. He was nervous, so much so that her knock made him jump, even though he had been expecting it. He hurried to open the door. She stood there in a sweater and skirt looking every bit as delicious as she had the night before. She was holding two large grocery bags. She looked around the apartment appraisingly. "Nice," she said. "You have this place fixed up really cute. I love the flowers and red and white checkered tablecloth on the dining room table…a very nice touch. I don't know why, but I sort of pictured your place as being a little bit messy, you know, typical bachelor's pad."

"Messy?" he said, indignantly. "How could you think such a thing?"

"So," Skip said, "what's on the menu at Chez Christine this evening?"

"Pot roast with carrots, potatoes, and onions, and a tossed salad."

"Yum. Pot roast is my favorite"

"I know," she said, "I called your mother and asked."

"You what?" He was speechless.

"I called your mother to find out what you liked. Did I do something wrong?"

Christy tried her best to keep a straight face as she looked at him innocently, but it got too much. "Boy, are you easy!"

"Oh, right, you're joking. Very funny! I can see it now. This little girl from Omaha calls my mom and asks her what to fix her son for Sunday dinner."

"Little girl? Look at me," she said, twirling around, thrusting her breasts out in an exaggerated pose. "Do I look like a little girl to you?"

"Well no, not exactly. You're not Marilyn Monroe by any means, but…" She socked him on the arm before he could finish.

"Hey," he said, rubbing his arm, "take it easy. It was my turn to make a joke."

"Okay, I guess we're even." They both laughed.

When dinner was ready, Skip poured the wine and lit the candle while Christy served the salad. The roast was delicious. He ate the first serving, and she quickly brought him seconds. When the main course was finished, he got up and brought out dessert. Christy was impressed with the swirled pattern of the vanilla and chocolate pudding topped with whipped cream and the cherry. "Very creative," she said. Skip thought of the lady in the grocery store and silently thanked her once again. They decided to sit on the couch to enjoy it. By now, the wine was nearly gone, and they were both a little tipsy as they navigated their way across the room.

Looking back, it was hard to remember how it all started, or who started it. But suddenly, they were kissing in a way that made last night's activities in the car seem like a handshake. Christy struggled to catch her breath. Things were out of control now, but she was past caring. "Honey, the couch, it's so…I mean, don't you think…" He didn't wait for her to finish. After pulling her gently to her feet, they went arm in arm to the bedroom.

The bed was freshly made with clean linens and turned back. There was a small lamp on the night table casting intimate shadows on the walls. Christy sat on the edge of the bed and started to undress. "No," he said, "Let me. I like to unwrap my own presents. That's half of the fun." Pushing her gently onto her back, he began to take off her clothes, while kissing and caressing her all over. It was a ritual rich in sensations of touch, smell, and taste. As he slid her panties off, he found that she was incredibly wet and ready for him. Everything was happening naturally, as if preordained. Now it was his turn to undress. Holding her close to him with one arm, he shrugged off his trousers using his free hand, and then within seconds, the rest of his clothes were laying in a tangled heap on the bedroom floor. She was eagerly waiting for him to take her, and he did. She was not a virgin, nor had he expected her to be. Still, he could sense in her an untapped reservoir of sexual power. She knew a lot, but she didn't know everything. The possibility of teaching her more thrilled him.

When it was over, they lay in each other's arms and talked. She told him about her high school sweetheart. They were going to be married when she graduated from high school, but he was killed in a car accident in his senior year. The pain had been unbearable. She confessed that she still wasn't sure if she was over it or ever would be. Skip didn't say so, but he was happy there was no rival in the picture. Christy was relieved to have the whole thing off her chest and out in the open.

Finally the wine, passion, and lovemaking took its toll, and they began to drift off. Before they did, Skip leaned over and whispered, "I love you, Christy Weber. Do you know that? I really love you."

"I know that, sweetie. I love you too."

At 4 AM, he stirred slightly and felt her warm body curled up spoon-style behind him, with her arm thrown over his back. She was breathing with a contented purr. He smiled and fell back asleep.

He woke up the next morning confused and disoriented. The room was bathed in soft warm sunlight that was streaming in through the small bedroom window. Did last night really happen? Or was it only a dream? The bed was still warm, and he could smell her perfume. Rolling lazily over on his side, he looked at the alarm clock and then bolted upright. Eight o'clock! He was late for class. "Relax honey," Christy said, walking toward him from the doorway. "No classes until ten o'clock today. Remember? Even I know that, and it's not my schedule." She was wearing his white terry cloth robe, loosely tied around her waist, and was holding a fresh cup of coffee. The apartment was a disaster. The dining room table was filled with dishes crusted with unfinished food, empty glasses, and crumpled napkins. They hadn't snuffed out the candle when they went to bed, and it had burned to nothing, leaving the bottle covered with melted wax. Sitting untouched in the midst of it all were the two desserts Skip had so carefully made. The puddings and whipped cream had all run together in a sodden mess.

"Looks like there was a fire, and everyone left in a hurry," Christy commented.

"Yes," he nodded solemnly, stifling a grin "You might call it a fire. By the way, how did you get away with staying out all night?"

"Oh, I told my folks it would be a late night for studying, and that I would stay over at my girlfriends' place."

"Well, I have my reputation to think about," Skip said, "and having your little black and white bomb parked in front of my place all night doesn't do it any good."

"Your reputation? Ha! I should think it would help it. You should pay me to park it there from time to time."

"Now, Miss Christine, you know what they say about women who do things for money."

"Phooey," she replied, sticking her tongue out at him.

When it was time to leave and they were walking to the door, coats on, and books in hand, he said, "You're pretty good at remembering my class schedule, but do you remember what we said to each other before we went to sleep?"

"Yup," she replied, kissing him on the end of his nose. "You're in big trouble now, Skip. Let's get this show on the road, or you're gonna be late for class."

*   *   *   *

Looking back on the night they spent together, Christy realized that she had crossed the line when she told Skip she loved him. The idea that their relationship had changed from a casual college campus flirtation to a serious affair frightened her. Did she really love this man or had she simply given in to a moment of tenderness? Her heart told her she was in love with him, and that her response to his declaration had been honest. But did she love him enough to take their relationship to the next level, a step that would ultimately lead to marriage? She was not sure. What would happen next spring when he returned to Presque Isle to await his assignment to pilot training? She also wondered what it would be like to live the nomadic life of an Air Force wife. It sounded exciting enough, but was it really? She didn't know. She needed more time and more answers before she made up her mind. Hopefully, there would be plenty of both in the months ahead. Meanwhile, if Skip thought nights of wild and joyous sex would be a regular occurrence, he was sadly mistaken. She did visit regularly, mostly to study, but only occasionally did she spend the night. It drove him crazy, but she made it clear that's the way it had to be.

*   *   *   *

By December, Skip began to feel the pressure of time. The fall semester was almost over and after the first of the year, he would take two more courses in an abbreviated session that would be over in March. Then he would graduate. As for pilot training, he had no idea when he would start but surely not before late summer or fall. In the meantime, he would have to return to Presque Isle without her. He couldn't bear to think about it. Christy was also torn. She wanted to finish college, but spending a year or maybe longer without him would be lonely and painful. She was sure of it. It was a touchy subject for both of them, and they never talked about it.

Skip planned to spend a week with his parents during the Christmas break. They hadn't seen much of him since he joined the Air Force and were looking forward to his visit. Since he wouldn't be in Omaha during the holidays, the Webers invited him to their home for dinner, the week before Christmas. Although Christy didn't say so, the message was clear. It was time for him to be introduced to the Weber clan. She was the youngest in the family. All of her siblings were married and had children. Bob, her brother, was the oldest. He was a tall, muscular man like his father. He was a mechanic at the local Ford dealer and his gruff, tell-it-like-it-is manner intimidated Skip at first. But sometime before dinner, Bob motioned him to the garage, away from the watchful eyes of Greta Weber, and produced a six-pack of beer. After knocking back a couple of cans each, while talking about cars, he decided they were going to get along just fine.

The oldest sister, Ingrid, looked a lot like her mother and had the same bubbly personality. The other sister didn't look like either of her parents. Christy always referred to her as "my obnoxious sister, Karen." Skip didn't see what was obnoxious about her. In fact, he thought she was pretty sexy. But of course, he never mentioned that to Christy.

By dinnertime, the dining room was transformed into a joyous collage of sights, sounds, and smells. The menu was a mixture of Midwestern American and German dishes, including ham, potato salad, sauerkraut, and numerous other vegetable dishes. The platters of steaming hot food with mouth-watering aromas filled the table to overflowing. There was barely enough room for all of the family to sit, even with two extra leaves in the table and a separate table in the next room for the children. It was hard to get a word in edgewise with all the talking and laughing going on. This was okay with Skip, because he knew he was under scrutiny and wanted to keep as low a profile as possible.

When dinner was over, the ladies went to the kitchen to wash the dishes, while their husbands went out in the backyard to smoke. Bob and his wife had to leave early, which left Skip pretty much alone except for the grandchildren who were eager to get to know him and bombarded him with questions. Thankfully, after a few minutes of trying to keep up with the kids, Skip was summoned to the study by Christy's dad. "Come in, Skip," he said. "I want to show you something."

Skip walked into the small room. A bottle filled with clear liquid sat on the table with two glasses beside it. Each glass had a small plum in the bottom.

"Schnapps," Ernst explained proudly. "I brought it over from Germany. You can't find this kind in America. I don't drink it much, only on special occasions. It's served chilled, poured over a small plum." As he was speaking, he filled the two glasses and handed one to Skip.

Skip had to admit it tasted good. It went down smoothly, leaving a warm, radiating glow all the way to his stomach. By the time he drained the glass, he was relaxed.

The room was quiet except for the gentle ticking of a small antique clock on the mantle. "So..." Ernst said, refilling their glasses, "what's going on with you and my daughter?"

The question caught Skip off guard, and for a moment, he was at a loss for words. "Well, I...err, like your daughter a lot, sir. She is a fine person."

"Like...what does that mean?"

"Well, it means..." Suddenly it became clear that this was no time to back down. He had to stand his ground. He wouldn't be able to bullshit him anyway, so what did he have to lose? "Well, actually," he began again, "I love Christy. I love her very much. Have for quite some time."

"Oh ho! Love, now that's a different word entirely."

"I know, and as a matter-of-fact, it goes even further. I intend to marry her one day."

Now it was Ernst's turn be caught off guard. He hadn't expected this. He was only having some fun with this young man. But now...marriage? This was a different story. "I do hope," he said, measuring his words carefully, "that one day doesn't mean anytime soon. Christy has another year of school, and then she will become the first college graduate in our family. We have high hopes for her."

"I understand that, and I have pilot training ahead of me. That will take over a year, after I finally get started."

"And what does Christy think about all this?"

"Well, actually, I haven't told her yet."

They were on their third glass of schnapps now and feeling the effects. "Tell me something," Ernst said, his blue eyes twinkling. "I know I am just an old-fashioned Kraut who doesn't know all the ways here in America, but back in Germany, the man would ask the woman to marry him. We called it proposing. You have heard of this custom…yes?"

Skip smiled. He knew his leg was being pulled.

"I think you should ask her. What have you got to lose? I doubt she will turn you down."

"You don't think so?"

"Of course not. Nobody else is banging the door down to marry her."

Skip was dumbfounded and didn't know what to say. Then Ernst burst into a hearty gale of laughter. It was the first time Skip had heard him laugh. Now he knew where Christy had learned to play the "J-o-k-e" game. He started to laugh too.

At that point, Christy opened the door and poked her head in. The sight of Skip and her father grinning at each other was not what she had expected. "What were you guys laughing about?"

"Oh nothing, just man's talk," her father said.

"Yeah," Skip said, his voice slightly slurred, "man's talk."

"Well, if you 'men' are finished talking, it's really nice out, and I thought we might take a walk, Skip, and burn off some of that food."

"Sounds good to me," Skip said, draining his glass.

"Don't forget what I told you," Ernst said, giving Skip a broad wink.

Christy left the room shaking her head. What's going on here? They are acting like children. It must be the booze, she thought.

It was a beautiful December evening. Strolling down the sidewalk, their breath frosted as they savored the crisp, clean air. Stark, leafless branches of trees lining the street were silhouetted against the bright orange of the dying sun. The neighborhood was still, save for the quiet rumble of an occasional passing car.

Christy waited for Skip to say something. Finally she could stand it no longer. "Okay, what was going on between you and my dad?" Her voice was filled with exasperation. She didn't like to be kept in the dark.

"Oh nothing much. He just wanted to know what the deal was between you and me."

"And what did you tell him?"

Skip shrugged, "I told him I was in love with you, and that I intended to marry you after your graduation."

"Damn it, Skip, stop teasing me. I want to know what's going on." She was getting angry now.

"I'm serious, honey. That's what we talked about."

"Oh my God. What did he say?"

"He asked if I had proposed yet. I said, no. Then he said, maybe I should."

"He said that?"

"Yep."

They stopped walking as Christy waited for him to continue.

Skip gave his head a shake as he tried to focus on the matter at hand through the haze of schnapps.

"I'm sorry, Christy," he said. "I guess I should have talked to you first. It just somehow came out when I was talking to your dad."

Christy said nothing. Her face was filled with conflicting emotions. Then, before she could stop him, he was on one knee staring up at her. "Christy Weber, you are the girl I want to spend the rest of my life with. I've known that for a long time. I love you dearly, and I am asking you to marry me. Will you?"

The sight of him down on one knee proposing made her want to laugh. It was so theatrical. But she knew he was sincere. This is happening so fast, she thought. I'm scared. What should I do? What should I say? I need time…more time. For a few agonizing seconds, her answer hung in balance. Then the words tumbled out. "Yes, Skip O'Neill," she said. "I love you and want to spend the rest of my life with you." He quickly got up, and they began hugging, kissing, crying, and laughing, all at the same time.

Suddenly, the spell was broken by the sound of applause coming from a young couple standing on the other side of the street, clapping and smiling. Christy looked embarrassed, yet pleased. Skip smiled back at them, shrugged his shoulders elaborately and said, "What can I say? I love her."

"We understand," the young woman said. The man gave Skip a vigorous thumbs-up.

They walked hand in hand for another hour, basking in the afterglow of their new commitment to each other. As they approached the house, Christy stopped, grasped his shoulders with both hands, looked him straight in the eye and said, "Okay Skip, you had a lot to drink today. Do you realize that you proposed marriage to me in front of God, my parents' neighbors, and the world?" She wanted to be reassured it was all for real.

"I'm absolutely sure about wanting to marry you. I want you to be my wife and have our children and live happily ever after," he replied, kissing her on the nose. "By the way, your dad said you would probably say yes."

"Oh? How did he arrive at that conclusion, may I ask?"

"He said he doubted if anyone else would want to marry you."

"I'll kill him. I'm gonna absolutely kill him."

"Before you do, are you going to tell him about our engagement?"

"I'll tell him tomorrow," she said, laughing. "And I hope he has a hangover when I do. It will serve him right."

"Well, good luck," Skip said, hugging her.

I wonder if I need to ask her dad for her hand, he thought. *Probably not. After all, it was his idea that I propose.*

Christy's folks took the news well, especially her father. The way he looked at it, the wedding would not take place until after Christy graduated, and that was over a year away. Things could change in the meantime. On the other hand, Skip's parents had no idea how serious things had become. Skip had mentioned dating Christy in a couple of letters, but that was all. When he called them to break the news, they were shocked. He decided they needed to meet her soon. After much discussion, Christy agreed to fly to his parents' house in Illinois the day after Christmas and drive back with Skip four days later. It seemed like a workable plan, and he was looking forward to spending time alone with her during the long drive home.

"They're going to love you," Skip told her. "No doubt about it."

"We'll see," Christy replied. She wasn't so sure.

*   *   *   *

Skip's parents came out on the porch as soon as he and Christy drove into the gravel driveway alongside the house. Skip's father was a good-looking man, just over six feet tall, with brown eyes and slightly graying brown hair parted neatly in the middle. Gene O'Neill had lived a hard life but carried his burdens with dignity. He was the second eldest in a family of seven. His mother had died of pneumonia when he was sixteen. Gene's father was not the nurturing type, so the motherless children grew up devoid of discipline and love. Consequently, he and his eldest sister were the only ones in the family who were not alcoholics or had not been married more than once. He was a kind and gentle person with a reputation for seeing the good in everyone. Skip was positive that his father would love Christy right away, and she would love him.

Skip's mother was a petite woman with coal-black hair set in tight waves and sharp brown eyes. Sarah O'Neill had been a "surprise baby," the youngest of ten children, born seven years after the last sibling. Her father died three years after she was born, which left everyone in the family contributing to her upbringing in a caring and doting fashion. Those who knew her well would say that even at the age of forty-four she could be a spoiled brat if the mood struck her. Skip was her only child, and she loved him dearly. So much so, that it was doubtful any woman would match her expectations for her son. If anyone in the family is going to have a problem with Christy, it's going to be my mom, Skip thought.

After introductions were made, everyone went inside. The two-bedroom, white frame house was Gene O'Neill's pride and joy. He bought it after World War II when he returned from the Navy. Every square inch of it, inside and out, had been painted at least once, and nothing lacked for repair. It was a small house, and when they gathered in the living room to visit, it was filled to over-flowing.

Christy had prepared well for this meeting. As Skip's "surprise fiancée," she would be under close scrutiny, and she knew it. She was wearing a soft gray sweater, a gray tweed skirt, bobby socks, and loafers. Her jewelry consisted of a delicate, gold chain necklace with a small pearl and matching pearl earrings. Her hair and makeup were perfect. This was no accident. She had insisted on freshening up before they left the airport. Sitting in an easy chair across from Skip's parents she looked like a Norman Rockwell painting of everybody's college sweetheart—shy, yet confident, without being pushy or aggressive.

There was an awkward silence. Skip's father was the first to speak. "So, Christy, how was your flight?"

"It was wonderful, Mr. O'Neill, and much faster than driving. I'm glad, because to tell you the truth, I was pretty anxious to see Skip and to meet you and his mom, of course," she amended quickly. "I really missed him," she continued, glancing at Skip shyly. "Seems like he grows on you."

"Yes," Gene chuckled, "Grows on you. "He has a way of doing that. But then, so does mold." Everybody laughed, except Skip's mom. She sat on the sofa with her lips pursed, and her arms crossed solidly across her chest.

"How did you and Skip meet, Christine?" Sarah asked.

"In school. We were in a class together. The professor teamed us up to work on an outside project."

"A psychology class," Skip added.

"In psychology class. Uh-huh," Sarah said doubtfully.

"Yes, and it took me awhile to warm up to him. I mean, I liked him okay, but I am a small-town girl, living with my parents, and Skip seemed so mature, so experienced, being in the Air Force and all. It was a little overwhelming."

"You live with your parents?" Sarah said, relaxing a little.

"Yes," Christy smiled, "and I can tell you that at times it's like living in a convent. My father is, shall we say, very aware of my comings and goings."

"Very aware," Skip interjected, rolling his eyes in mock exaggeration.

Gene nodded sympathetically.

"Anyway," Christy continued, "the project required a lot of work after school, and afterwards we spent time drinking coffee, talking, and getting to know each other. One evening we went out for hamburgers after a long session working on the project. And then, two weeks later when the project was finished, he invited me out for dinner at the officers' club to celebrate. That was our first real date. He came to my house to pick me up and got the third degree from my dad. But, it ended up being a very romantic evening, and afterwards I realized I was falling in love. One thing led to another and well…here we are."

"Yes, here we are," Sarah said. "I must admit it sounds romantic. It reminds me of our courtship. Gene was persistent too." She looked tenderly at Skip's father as she spoke. "But marriage? Gene and I dated for four years before we got married."

"Don't forget, that was in the Depression," Gene interjected. "I'm sure we would have gotten married sooner if I'd had a job."

Sarah gave her husband a sharp "whose side are you on anyway?" look.

"I understand what you are saying, Mrs. O'Neill. My parents are saying the same thing, and I totally agree. My dream is to become a kindergarten teacher, and I need eighteen months more of college before I can do that, and quite frankly I'm not about to marry your son until I finish school." Christy's words were firm, almost defiant, as she looked Sarah straight in the eye. "Of course," she added softly, "it's not going to be easy being without Skip when he goes back to Presque Isle. I still have this, umm…mold problem."

This time everyone laughed.

The conversation reverted to small talk for a few minutes, and then Sarah rose and motioned for Christy to follow her. "Let me show you where you will be sleeping tonight, dear," she said. "Then I have to get dinner started."

"May I help you?"

"Yes, if you like."

"It's not going to work, you know," Sarah said when they arrived in the kitchen. Her eyes were sharp and penetrating.

"What won't work?" Christy asked, returning her gaze.

"This whole idea of marrying my son."

"Why not?"

"He's not ready to get married yet. I know him."

"All I know is that we love each other very much. And he's the one who has been courting and pursuing me. He's the one who proposed. Not the other way around."

"I realize that," Sarah said. Her demeanor softened, although her eyes did not. "Look, Skip has a lot of growing up to do yet. He is full of ideas and promises, but he doesn't always deliver. Like the promise to go to college and get a degree. His dad worked hard to earn the tuition money, and what happened? He called us one night to say that he had dropped out and had joined the Air Force. Just like that. He can't be trusted."

"As I see it," Christy said, measuring her words carefully, "we have a year, maybe more, to change our minds. If we don't, I intend to be his wife and spend the rest of my life with him. It's that simple."

"You intend to keep your promise to wait until you graduate?"

"Indeed I do."

"Good," Sarah said, rising abruptly and patting her arm. "Then we have an understanding. Now, let's get dinner started."

That night, after Christy went to bed, Skip sat with his parents at the kitchen table, the traditional meeting place for family talks. They told him that they liked Christy a lot. They also pointed out that it would be a long time before the two of them would get married, and that was good. It would give them a chance to really get to know each other. It was a start.

The next day Skip took Christy for a tour of Belleville. It was not a large town, scarcely thirty thousand people, but it was steeped in history starting two hundred years ago, when the French trappers and explorers worked their way down the Mississippi River to Southern Illinois. Skip told her that thanks to the influx of German and Dutch immigrants in the early 1900s there were no fewer than five breweries in town, not to mention numerous bakeries. By the third day, the mission was accomplished. Both sets of parents were in agreement with the young couple's plans. After a breakfast of bacon, eggs, and pancakes, they all gathered in the driveway for fond goodbyes and hugs. Skip and Christy loaded up the car and left for Omaha.

They drove home relaxed and happy, planning and dreaming about their new life together. It was going to be perfect.

*   *   *   *

In early March, Skip got a telephone call that changed everything. "Skip," his operations officer said, "I have your pilot training assignment. You are to report to Moore Air Base in Mission, Texas, June fourth."

Skip was elated. This was much earlier than he had expected. "Great," he said. "I can't wait to get started. That's only ten weeks after I graduate from college, though. What will I do in Presque Isle in the meantime?"

"I thought about that. I have a friend who works in SAC headquarters at Offutt. Maybe I can arrange to have you assigned there temporarily for sixty days. You know, some kind of liaison job…shuffling papers."

"If you could arrange that, it would be perfect."

"I'll see what I can do."

The next day his ops officer called again. It was all arranged. He would stay in Omaha until it was time to go to pilot training. Although his future was now clear, he became uneasy and decided that he had been lying to himself, to Christy, and to their families. The truth was that being separated from her for over a year was not going to work. But there was another way…if he had the courage to choose it.

The next day, he asked Christy to come by his apartment after school. She was reluctant at first. "Oh honey," she said, "I've been there a lot recently, and my folks are getting suspicious, you know?"

"It's not about that," he replied, looking very serious. "I just need to talk to you."

"Well, okay. Is everything all right?"

"Yes, everything is all right."

"Are you sure?" She could sense that something was wrong. She wondered if he had changed his mind about the engagement.

"I'm sure honey. Just come by after school, okay?"

She looked frightened when she arrived at his door. So he got right to the point. "To begin with, I have a class assignment for pilot training. I report the first week in June."

"That's wonderful, and much earlier than you expected, isn't it?"

"Yes, and there's something else. I am being assigned to Offutt for sixty days after I graduate from college, so I won't have to go back to Presque Isle."

"Oh honey, that's perfect. It means we will be able to spend more time together. So why all the gloom and doom?"

He paused and took a deep breath. It was time to get down to business. "The problem is, I've thought long and hard about all this and have decided that I cannot and will not leave you for a whole year. I just won't do it."

"What are you saying?" she said, her voice filled with alarm.

"I'm saying that I want us to get married before I leave."

Christy was shocked. She couldn't believe what she was hearing. "Skip, you know we can't do that. We promised our parents I would finish college, and that's what I want to do too."

"I know, believe me I know, and I am one hundred percent behind you on that. I am going to do everything in my power to help you get that last year of college."

Christy was becoming angry and started to raise her voice. "Oh sure, you're one hundred percent behind me, and you are going to help me finish. Well, I'll tell you something, Skip. I don't need your help to finish college. I want to do it now, not when it fits your schedule."

"You don't understand," Skip said. He was beginning to falter. "If we were to separate now, it would be like…well, like leaving something precious and irreplaceable out in the open where anyone could come along and fool with it or even steal it. Don't you see?"

"That's ridiculous. I'm your fiancée for God's sake, not a tricycle left on the sidewalk for anybody to come along and pick up."

"That's not what I meant. It's just that I…"

The argument went back and forth for some time until finally he grasped her shoulders gently and said, "Look Christy, I'll make this real simple for you. Just look me in the eye, and tell me that you are okay with us being separated for a year, and I won't say any more about it. Agreed?"

"Damn, that's not fair. You know I can't do that either. You know I want to be with you. But my parents…they are going to be furious. I don't know if I can deal with that."

"You're not going to deal with them alone. We are going to talk to them together, you and me. We are a team, right?"

"Well," she said, "I hope you know what you're getting into."

"I do baby. Trust me, I do."

Christy was still angry when she left his apartment. How could he do this to her? In one irrational moment, he had swept away all the time she had counted on to prepare for their marriage. And what about the promise he made—that they wait until she finished college before they married? "My son is immature and doesn't always keep his promises." That's what his mother had said. Christy was beginning to think she was right, and that disturbed her. What did she really know about this man, other than she was in love with him? She decided she would go along with him this time, but the next time he changed his mind or broke a promise, she was going to stand her ground.

*   *   *   *

To say that her parents were furious was a gross understatement. Greta Weber was in total shock and could hardly speak. Both parents believed there had to be a reason for this hasty decision, and they were pretty sure they knew what it was. The thought of his pride and joy leaving college without graduating, with a bun in the oven, made her father insane. So much so, that he began to stutter and mix German and English words together. It took more than a half an hour for Christy to convince them she was not pregnant. She pointed out that if she were lying, the truth would be there for all to see in a few weeks. "Oh *ja*, sure," her father said sarcastically. "But I guess a modern young woman like you could find a way to make that problem go away, and we would never know about it."

Christy looked visibly stung but kept her temper in check. "Yes, I suppose I could, if I believed in such things, which I don't. I'm Catholic, remember? Besides, if I did that, why would I bother getting married? I mean, what would be the point?"

Neither parent answered.

"You know," she continued, "I remember the story of another couple about our age in Germany who promised their families they would wait before getting married. Then, the man got a chance for a better life in America, and they decided to marry right away so she could go with him. There was hell to pay for that I'm sure, but they did it." Christy paused and looked straight into her father's eyes. "I assume that young lady was pregnant also, right?"

"Of course not," Ernst snapped angrily. "How dare you suggest such a thing? Our situation was much different."

"How was it different, Father?"

"I loved your mother very much and didn't want to leave her behind."

"Exactly, that's just what Skip said to me last night."

Ernst started to reply but fell silent. It was clear that he had painted himself into a corner.

Once the pregnancy issue was put to rest, the discussion turned to other concerns—Christy's age, the need for her to finish college, the need for both to get to know each other better, and on and on. Speaking in calm, measured tones, Christy began to slowly but surely wear her parents down.

"Two months to plan a wedding," her mother wailed. "It's not near enough time."

"Church," her father interrupted, glaring at Skip. "I want my daughter married in church, not by some clerk."

Christy's voice was soft and reassuring now. "Of course we are going to be married in a church. It will be a proper wedding with bridesmaids and everything. We can have it at the base chapel."

"And we can have a fine reception at the officers' club," Skip volunteered. It was the first time he had spoken since the discussion began.

"But the wedding gown," her mother protested. "You can't get a wedding gown made in two months. It's impossible."

Christy looked at her mom softly. "The wedding gown shouldn't be a problem. I've always dreamed of wearing the gown you wore when you were married, Mom. You looked so beautiful in the wedding pictures. Could I please wear it?"

Her mother nodded, looking as if she was about to cry. "Yes dear, of course you can wear it. That would make me so happy."

When it was over, Skip realized that he had spoken just one time in the past hour. Meanwhile, Christy had patiently and with steely resolve bent the will of her parents into agreeing with what they were about to do. It was a side of her he had never seen before, and he was impressed, if not somewhat in awe. Clearly, his bride to be was no pushover, and that was a good thing—or was it? He wasn't sure.

"Well, you've really done it this time," she said, as they walked out to their cars. "You'll have to marry me for sure now."

"Hmm," Skip said, "maybe I should knock you up, just to be on the safe side."

"Not a chance. We have to have sex to do that, and we're not going to do that anymore until we get married."

"But…"

"Good night, Skip. See you at school tomorrow."

But it wasn't over yet, not for Skip anyway. He still had to call and break the news to his parents. He began by explaining the situation to his father, who listened patiently but with obvious annoyance. Like Ernst Weber, his main concern was the pregnancy issue. Skip did his best to allay that concern using the same arguments Christy had used with her parents. He could tell his father was not convinced. Then his mother got on the phone.

"Well, you've done it again. It's just like the college thing. You make promises but never keep them. You just can't be trusted."

"It's not the same thing as college, Mom. This is much more important. We're talking about the rest of my life here. I love Christy and don't want to be apart from her, certainly not for a year."

"And your poor fiancée," Sarah continued as if she had not heard him. "If you've done anything to that poor girl I swear I'll…"

"She is not pregnant, Mom," Skip replied wearily. "I just went through all that with Dad."

"I just don't see how the two of you could do this to me. Christy sat right at our kitchen table and promised she would wait until after graduation. I thought *she* at least would keep her word."

"Don't be so hard on her, Mom. This was my idea, not hers. She's having a tough enough time of it with her parents. They're not thrilled about it either."

"Well, I should hope not. But…"

"It's going to be a beautiful church wedding, with bridesmaids, flowers, and everything."

Sarah said nothing but began to sniffle.

"Mom, you're coming to the wedding aren't you? You have to."

"Well, probably, but it's up to your father."

He continued to reassure his mom for another ten minutes. Finally he said, "I've gotta go, Mom. This call is costing me a fortune." Then they said their goodbyes. Whew! Skip thought. I'm glad that's over!

He had one more telephone call to make. Tom Denison answered on the first ring. He and Penney were home for the evening, and he could hear their children shrieking and laughing in the background.

"Hey Tom, this is Skip."

"Well hello there, Tiger. It's been awhile since we talked. How's life treating you out in Omaha?"

"Great, I'm doing really well."

"Feel any smarter since you graduated from college?"

"Not much," Skip admitted, "and what I have learned, is fading fast, hanging around those bomber pukes at SAC headquarters."

"They'll do that to you," Tom chuckled. "So, what's up?" He was beginning to sense that this was more than a social call.

"I sort of need a favor."

"What kind of favor?"

"Well, the thing is…I, um…met this girl and uh…we're getting married in a month. I was wondering if you would be my best man."

"Getting married? Good God! How long have you known this girl? Where did you meet her?"

"Actually, I met her during the first week of school. She was in one of my classes. She's wonderful. You'll really like her."

"I'm sure I will. As for being your best man, I could probably arrange…" Penney snatched the phone away from him before he could finish. She had obviously caught the drift of the conversation.

"Okay, Skip," she said. "What kind of trouble have you gotten into this time?"

"Trouble? No trouble here, lady. I just happened to finally find my own Midwest girl. Her name is Christy. I love her, and we are going to get married."

"Oh my God. She isn't…ummm…"

"Knocked up? Christ, you sound just likes her parents. No Penney, she is not. Thank you *so* much for your confidence in our good judgment and our respect for each other."

"No need to get huffy. I just wanted to make sure. By the way, does she know what she is in for, marrying you, and becoming an Air Force wife? I mean, does she really know*?*"

"Of course she does."

"I seriously doubt that. That's why I am coming out to Omaha a day or two before the wedding. To check her out and tell her the way it really is."

"Oh Penney, you don't have to do that."

"Nonsense. It's for her own good and yours too. See you in Omaha, hon." She hung up.

"Can you believe that, Tom? Our boy has fallen in love and is going to marry a girl named Christy."

"Well, I think it's all your fault."

"My fault, why?"

"You always said that we had to get him married, and I always said we had to get him laid."

"And I said it was all the same thing. Remember?" Penney responded.

"Yeah, so?"

"So, Miss Christy comes along, and he gets laid and married. Like I said, it's all the same thing."

"Skip didn't say anything about getting laid," Tom said doubtfully. "His fiancée might be a virgin, you know."

"Trust me on this one, I know what I am talking about."

*   *   *   *

The base chapel and the officers' club came through with confirmed dates for the wedding and reception. Christy and her sister Ingrid handled the details. There was one glitch, though. Christy insisted on a formal military wedding, which meant passing through an arch of crossed sabers when leaving the church. Tom talked it over with the squadron commander at Presque Isle, and he agreed to let six men fly to Omaha on the weekend of the wedding to be the honor guard, providing they rode out on the base gooney bird.

Finding six guys to go to Omaha was not the problem. After all, "I'll do anything to get away from Presque Isle" was practically the squadron motto. But flying there in a beat-up old prop transport and wearing their dress uniforms for a wedding ceremony? That was asking a lot from a group of men whose credo was "speed is life," and who only wore dress uniforms when given a direct order to do so. But Tom laid it on thick about how cute the bridesmaids were and how susceptible they would be to the advances of handsome men in uniform. This was a bold statement considering he had no idea what they really looked like. In the end, six stalwart men agreed to do the gallant thing and make the trip, mostly because of the rehearsal dinner on Friday night which, Tom implied, could well turn in to the drunken orgy to end all drunken orgies.

*   *   *   *

Penney arrived two days before the wedding and stayed at the Webers' house. She wasted no time whisking Christy away for lunch at the officers' club so they could have a long talk and get to know each other. "Get to know each other" was code for "checking her out," and Christy understood that.

The dining room at the club was almost deserted. It was midweek and not a lot was going on. They chose a table in the corner where they could talk quietly and not be disturbed. Penney ordered a glass of white wine. Christy thought that was very sophisticated and ordered the same, although she rarely drank wine. The two women made small talk for a few minutes and then, under Penney's gentle prodding, Christy talked about herself, her family, and her dreams of being a schoolteacher. She also explained in detail how she and Skip met and fell in love. The latter amused Penney greatly. Some parts of the story sounded like the young, irresponsible Skip whom she knew so well. Other parts reflected a romantic and sensitive man that she had never seen.

Then it was Penney's turn. She talked about the struggles she had faced being married to an Air Force officer. Packing up and moving every two or three years, dragging the kids along to new schools, and sometimes living in real dumps off base. She talked about husbands being away on temporary tours of duty, or "TDYs" as they were called. TDYs could last weeks or even months, sometimes with so much secrecy that the wives didn't know where their husbands were, much less when they would return. She also described an Air Force wife's biggest nightmare, finding the squadron commander and chaplain on the doorstep; how they would stand awkwardly in the doorway, with sadness and compassion in their eyes, struggling to convey the message that her husband wasn't coming home. It happens a lot, she told Christy, and the wife suddenly finds herself both a mother *and* a father, with small children to raise alone.

"There will be times," Penney said, "when you will become so overwhelmed and stressed that you will want to beg him to get out of the Air Force and find another life, a safer, saner line of work." Christy nodded, trying to grasp what she was saying, but in reality, she could not. "But it is not the right thing to do," Penney continued. "Believe me. You see, men like my Tom and your Skip are in the Air Force because they want to be. It is not a job to them; it is a way of life. It's who they are. If you persuade them to change, they won't be happy, and they'll never forgive you. Better you should leave him than do that."

"I would never do that," Christy said firmly.

"Do what? Leave him or beg him to get out?"

"Either one."

"Well I hope not, because it's not going to be easy. And speaking of not being easy, Skip can be well, how should I put this…"

"A little childish sometimes," Christy finished for her.

"Yes. It's not his fault really. He was only twenty years old when he graduated from training and became an officer. He has always been the youngest guy in the squadron and wants so badly to fit in. The trouble is he doesn't always choose the best role models. There are some obnoxious characters in the squadron. World War II and Korean War veterans, mostly. A hard drinking, womanizing bunch with more guts than brains, as the saying goes."

"Like the guy called Cactus Jack?"

"Good example. Skip thinks the sun rises and sets on him. In reality, he is a disgusting, lecherous man with a drinking problem. At one time or another, every wife in the squadron has slapped him for trying to pinch her butt."

Christy giggled at that. She couldn't help it.

"So, when Skip starts doing his happy hour at the bar routine and begins to get out of hand, you…"

"Have to whack him alongside the head and straighten him out, right?"

"Right. You got it. But don't get me wrong. It's not just Skip. Most flyers, especially fighter pilots, tend to be immature, when they are not flying. I don't know why. Maybe it's their way of compensating for the dangers and stress in their lives. Anyway, just when you get fed up with their childishness, along comes a war or major crisis, and they become the calmest, most steadfast, decisive, and heroic bunch of guys you ever want to meet. Then you can't imagine being married to anybody else."

"I can't imagine being married to anybody else now."

"Well said," Penney said with a smile. "Welcome to the Air Force family, Christy!"

*   *   *   *

Two days before the wedding, Skip and his father sat down in Ernst Weber's study for an after-dinner drink of schnapps and plums. Skip's parents had arrived earlier in the afternoon and had been invited to dinner. It was a pleasant and relaxed evening. The two sets of parents were close in age and alike in many ways.

Ernst finished serving the drinks and settled into a deep, leather easy chair.

"This schnapps tastes really good," Gene said.

"Careful Dad," Skip warned. "You've gotta sip this stuff, not knock it back. It'll go right to your brain if you do. I learned that the hard way."

Ernst smiled but said nothing.

"I've never been much of a drinker," Gene admitted. "A highball on New Year's Eve, and that's about it."

"Neither am I," Ernst replied. "But I do like a cold beer once in awhile, especially when it is hot."

"Well," Gene laughed, "you can find plenty of beer in Belleville. It's a Dutch-German community. There are three breweries in town, and a tavern on almost every corner."

"Really?"

"Yes, and in the summer the old-timers sit in their front yards passing around a bucket of beer carried from the corner tavern."

"Hmm…I never saw such a thing in Germany. Must be a Dutch custom."

"Could be," Gene acknowledged. Skip listened to their exchange about drinking and smiled to himself. They wouldn't last two rounds at happy hour in Presque Isle, he thought. Two martinis would knock them right on their asses!

After a few quiet and awkward moments, Ernst cleared his throat and said, "Well, the past few months have been full of surprises, haven't they?"

"Yes," Gene sighed. "That's my son. Always full of surprises."

"Let me tell you something honestly, Gene," Ernst said, leaning forward in his chair. "When your son started dating my daughter, I was dead-set against it. Nothing personal, mind you, but your son is in the military and is older than my Christine. He has, how shall I put this…been around. But after I got to know him, I realized he was a fine young man, and I found myself hoping that the two of them might marry someday. In fact you could say that he proposed to her because of me."

"Really?"

"Well," Ernst said smiling, "let's just say drinking my schnapps gave him the courage to ask her."

"Oh, so that's the way it was," Gene said, laughing.

"Yes, that's the way it was. But when they decided to marry so soon, I was not happy. In fact I was ready to kill him. My daughter is special. She has, or should I say had, dreams. Dreams to be a schoolteacher and to be the first member of our family with a college degree. Will her dreams come true now? I wonder."

"Well, I can certainly understand how you feel. Skip is a fine boy, but frankly speaking, this isn't the first time he's pulled something like that."

"Really?"

"Yes. Six years ago I sent him off to be the first person in our family to get a college degree, and I worked damn hard to earn the tuition money. After two years he announced that he was leaving college to join the Air Force. I was sick about it. I'm just now getting over it."

"On the other hand, Skip will soon have that college degree, will he not?" Ernst offered.

"Yes, and that is a huge relief to his mother and me. I can also tell you that my wife and I are absolutely delighted with your daughter. She is beautiful, kind, and has a good head on her shoulders. We couldn't ask for a better daughter-in-law."

"Well then, the matter is settled," Ernst said, rising to refill the glasses. "Things didn't work out as we expected, but in the end it is the same, is it not? Two young people very much in love who will marry and begin a new generation. Let's have a toast to the Webers and the O'Neills. May our two families prosper!"

"To the Webers and the O'Neills," Gene echoed, after rising unsteadily to his feet.

"And to my beautiful bride-to-be," Skip added.

*   *   *   *

The afternoon before the wedding, Father Jack McMahon, Chaplain, United States Air Force, was explaining the duties of the wedding party. Suddenly, he was interrupted by a raucous commotion as both doors at the chapel entrance flung open. Looking up, he saw six men in rumpled flying suits weaving as they peered into the darkness of the church.

"We're here everybody. Did we miss anything? Let's get this show on the road." The speaker was none other than Cactus Jack.

"The honor guard is here," Tom Denison mumbled. "I'll take care of it."

"Where have you guys been? You're late." Tom whispered as he approached the back of the chapel.

"Headwinds," Cactus Jack replied. "The fucking gooney bird…"

"Shhh," Tom hissed. "You're in a church for God's sake."

"Oops, sorry," Cactus Jack replied, as Tom grasped him firmly by the elbow and pushed him outside.

"And by the way," Tom said, "you smell like a brewery. I could smell you all the way from the front of the church. What's the deal?"

"Ah yes, the results of a very fortuitous accident." It was a struggle for Cactus Jack to say "fortuitous," but he managed.

"Accident?"

"Yes, someone carelessly left two cases of beer in the back of the aircraft before we took off."

"Well, I don't have time to bullshit around. First, I am appointing you in charge of the honor guard. You're the senior ranking officer here."

"A wise choice sir, and I assure you that…"

"In that car over there," Tom continued, cutting him off, "are six ceremonial sabers, courtesy of the local ROTC detachment. We have to return them in good shape. The instructions for the ceremony are on this piece of paper. They are very simple. Even a monkey could follow them."

"A monkey? I 'resemble' that remark!"

"Whatever. Run through the routine a few times to make sure everyone understands it, and then wait for me. I'll be back as soon as the rehearsal is over."

"Your wish is my command, *mon Capitan*. Okay men. Listen up. Here's what we're gonna do."

"Sorry about that, Father," Tom said, resuming his seat.

"Fighter pilots I assume," the chaplain said with a faint smile.

"Yes, some of them anyway."

The chaplain resumed his explanation of the ceremony but was interrupted again, this time by the sound of stumbling feet and the clash of metal. Oh shit, Tom thought, as he scrambled to his feet and hurried toward the door.

The scene on the steps of the chapel was chaotic. Five men were fencing vigorously, advancing and descending the steps amid shouts of *en garde* and *touché*. Cactus Jack was in the middle of the melee waving his saber overhead shouting, "Advance! Advance men, victory is close at hand." Everyone fell into an embarrassed silence as Tom walked out the door.

"Sorry, Tom," Cactus Jack said. "We were just warming up a bit, getting into character so to speak."

"So I see," Tom said without emotion. "Okay, let's try this approach, in thirty minutes the bar will be open for happy hour. If you can run through your routine and get it down pat, you can be there when it starts. If not, I guess you'll have to wait until I get finished, and we can practice later in the day."

Cactus Jack brightened at the words happy hour. "Okay men," he said, "you heard Captain Denison. We have a critical mission to accomplish, and time's a-wasting!"

Tom sighed wearily and walked back inside.

*   *   *   *

The rehearsal dinner was a festive occasion, a gathering of the young, old, naïve, and worldly. Everyone was determined to get an early start on celebrating the upcoming union of Skip and Christy. The tables in the small, private dining room in the officers' club were covered with white linen and arranged in a U-shape so that everyone could mingle easily. Skip and Christy sat at the head table, flanked by Tom and Penney, Christy's older sister Ingrid, who was the matron of honor, and her husband. There was plenty to eat and drink, all served using fine crystal and good china with the Strategic Air Command emblem emblazoned on each piece. Neither Christy's nor Skip's parents had ever been to an officers' club. They were impressed.

Each guest celebrated the event in his or her own special way. Some sipped their drinks cautiously while eating heartily. Others drank copiously but scarcely touched their food. Father McMahon managed to do both. Cactus Jack was on his best behavior for a change. Charming, witty, and urbane, he was polite and complimentary to every female at the dinner, young or old. There were a few tense moments when he flirted outrageously with Skip's mother, but soon he redirected his attentions to Greta Weber, reducing her to fits of blushing and giggling. The two fathers took it well, looking at each other and rolling their eyes in amusement. It was hard to not like Cactus Jack.

Cactus Jack and the honor guard had finished their rehearsal early and were already drinking by the time the dinner started. This, plus the two cases of beer they had consumed on the gooney bird, gave them a decided head start over the other guests. They were determined to set just the right tone for the celebration, a tone that reflected the fighter pilot's view of life. After a round of pro-forma speeches and toasts by the wedding party, they began a long series of toasts of their own, drinking to everyone and everything imaginable. The guests tried their best to keep up, but eventually many of them became glassy-eyed and began to fall behind.

At last, Penney took control, standing up to announce that the rehearsal dinner was over. The guests rose from the table somewhat unsteadily and headed for the door.

After everyone had said their good-byes and left, Skip cornered Christy to kiss her good night. As he did, she whispered in his ear, "You better enjoy your last night alone, baby, cause you're going to find me in your bed every night for the rest of your life."

"I'm going to hold you to that."

"You can count on it," she replied, slipping out of his arms. "I love you…you know."

"I love you too, honey," Skip replied. "Good night."

"Good night," Christy said. Then she was gone.

For a moment Skip stood outside in the cool night air uncertain what to do next. Suddenly a hand gripped him firmly by the arm. It was Cactus Jack.

"Ready to party, lad?"

"I thought I'd go home. Tomorrow is a big day."

"Oh no, no, no…that's not the way it's done. There is a protocol to follow. This is your last night as a single man. You have to seize the moment."

"Gee, I don't know."

"Look, if you show up at the wedding tomorrow bright-eyed and bushy tailed and not hung over, do you know what the guys are gonna say?"

"What?"

"They're gonna say, 'Look at him. He didn't even take advantage of his last night of freedom to drink with his friends. He was probably afraid his bride would find out. The poor guy is pussy-whipped already, and he's not even married yet.' Is that what you want people to think?"

"No, but…"

"No buts about it," Cactus Jack continued, leading him back into the club. "Now, here's my plan. I made a little reconnaissance mission to the stag bar downstairs. There's a pretty good crowd there. It's not anything like Presque Isle, mind you, but hey, what can you expect from a bunch of bomber pukes? They seem like good guys, and your fearless honor guard is there waiting. So what we're gonna do is have a couple of celebratory drinks."

Cactus Jack was right. There was a sizable group at the bar, at least forty, and they were good guys. Everyone knew about the wedding and wanted to buy the bridegroom a drink. When Skip arrived, the honor guard was teaching the SAC guys some typical fighter pilot songs. They started with a few simple ones like, "Sing hallelujah, sing hallelujah…throw a nickel on the grass, save a fighter pilot's ass" and "Ringa dinga dinga, blow it out your ass." They sang hesitantly at first, but after several drinks, everyone started to loosen up.

For the finale, Cactus Jack led the crowd in an old fighter pilot favorite, "Sammy Small." When the "chorus" reached the final stanza, which went, "Oh my name is Sammy Small, and I've only got one ball, but it's better than none at all so fuck 'em all," everyone literally shouted out the words, "fuck 'em all!" They could be heard throughout the club. It was hilarious.

Five minutes later, the club officer walked into the bar. He was a short, middle-age major who looked like he'd rather be any place than where he was.

Before he could speak, one of the pilots yelled, "Let's all say hello to the club officer!"

"Hello, asshole!" the crowd responded.

"Let's all say hello to the asshole!" another pilot yelled.

"Hello club officer!" the crowd responded.

After the gales of laughter subsided, the club officer spoke in a soft but firm voice. "Gentlemen, there is a party of senior officers upstairs having a late dinner with their wives. They are complaining about the noise and the obscenities coming from down here. So, it's very simple. Either you hold the noise down, or you'll have to leave." He composed himself and walked away with as much dignity as he could muster. Just as he reached the door, the pilot who led the last cheer turned to the crowd and shouted, "Let's sing a hymn to the club officer."

"Hymn…Hymn…Fuck hymn," the crowd intoned sonorously.

The club officer left without looking back

By eleven o'clock, Skip was a happy man. Gone were the jitters and the nervousness in the pit of his stomach about the wedding. He was with friends having a great time, and life was good. At the far end of the bar a noisy discussion broke out between Cactus Jack and a young SAC captain.

"I'm telling you," Cactus Jack said, "it's not as easy as it looks." He was holding a small lime and a funnel.

"It looks pretty easy to me," the captain said.

"Well, let me just give you a demonstration, so you can see how hard it is. You place the funnel down the front of your trousers like this." he demonstrated, weaving somewhat. "Then balance the lime on your nose. When you think you have everything lined up just so, you drop the lime so it falls into the funnel. And remember, no hands."

"I can do it," the captain said.

"I doubt it. In fact, I have five dollars that says you can't do it in three tries."

"You're on," the captain said, reaching for his billfold. As he did, people all along the bar began placing bets, some for him, some against. A circle quickly formed around the captain as everyone watched intently. Putting the funnel in his pants, he placed the lime on his nose, arched his back, and began balancing it in preparation for the drop. As Cactus Jack predicted, it was not easy. On the first try he almost dropped it in, but the lime bounced off the rim of the funnel and fell to the floor. There was a chorus of frustrated groans.

"Not bad, lad," Cactus Jack commented. "Not bad at all. You aren't perchance a bombardier are you?"

"Yep, I'm a radar bombardier on a B-52. And I'm going to get it this time."

"Well," Cactus Jack said worriedly, "you just might."

On the second try the captain was a picture of intense concentration. Head and shoulders thrown back for balance, he stared fixedly at the ceiling as he maneuvered the lime over the funnel. Suddenly, with lightning fast speed, Cactus Jack produced an opened, ice-cold bottle of beer, up-ended it, and jammed it neck-down into the funnel.

"Yoww...shit!" the captain screamed, as the cold beer flooded his crotch. Hopping from one foot to the other across the floor, he struggled to retrieve the bottle. But it was too late. Beer was running out of both trouser legs. The crowd broke out in a deafening roar of laughter. It was the highlight of the evening. After the excitement died down, Skip turned to the bar and ordered another drink. This is fun, he thought. I can't believe that Cactus Jack got away with that old joke. Just thinking about it caused him to start laughing again. Suddenly, he realized that he was the only one laughing. In fact he was the only one making any noise at all. The bar was quiet. Turning around he saw the reason why.

Standing tall and erect in the doorway was a two-star general. He was wearing a dress blue uniform; blouse buttoned, tie adjusted perfectly, and shoes shined to a high gloss. On his blouse was a pair of command pilot wings along with no less than five rows of service ribbons, reflecting valor and combat flying in World War II. He was a relatively young man with short-cropped dark hair, showing only a few flecks of distinguished gray. The club officer was standing behind him, looking anxiously over his shoulder.

The general paused at the doorway for a moment, savoring the drama he had created among the embarrassed, half-drunk officers. Slowly his eyes moved across the room looking at each one of them, as if memorizing their nametags and faces. As his eyes swept past the young captain with the beer-soaked trousers, a faint smile crossed his face. He walked slowly into the bar, the heels of his shoes tapping a steady cadence on the hardwood floor.

"Good evening, gentlemen," the general said in a measured, authoritative voice. "I apologize for interrupting the festivities, but frankly I'm here out of curiosity. My wife said she heard hymns being sung and wondered if you were conducting some kind of religious ceremony, and when she mentioned a certain four-letter word used in one of the hymns, I decided to come down and find out what church you belong to."

Nobody moved as he spoke, save for a few young officers who shuffled nervously and tried to hide behind the others. "Anyway," the general continued, "I understand that I might find a Lieutenant O'Neill here."

"Oh shit," Skip thought. "I'm Lieutenant O'Neill," he said, struggling to stand at attention. In his present condition the best he could do was lean vertically against the bar.

"So, Lieutenant, you are the guest of honor here, are you not?"

"Yes sir."

"And hence, it can be said that you are the reason for all this loud and drunken behavior."

"I suppose so, sir," Skip replied. His knees were beginning to shake now.

"Well, let me tell you something, Lieutenant," the general continued, "You are at a Strategic Air Command Base, the site of SAC headquarters in fact, and in SAC we take great pride in our discipline and professionalism. Loud and disruptive behavior in the officers' club is a very serious matter."

"Yes sir."

"On the other hand, it can be fairly said that you were not the senior ranking officer here tonight," the general continued, glancing significantly at Cactus Jack.

"No sir."

"Hmm, what to do here? On one hand, such undisciplined behavior should not go unpunished, but it would be a shame to spoil the evening." The general paused here for effect. "I tell you what. I am willing to forget the whole thing, on one condition."

"One condition, sir?"

"Yes and that condition is that I be permitted to buy a round of drinks for you and everyone at the bar so we can toast to a long and healthy life for you and your bride."

There was a stunned silence as the reality of his words sunk in. Everyone realized they had been had. Then the collective tension in the room escaped like air from a punctured balloon, and a loud cheer broke out. Everyone bellied up to the bar to collect their free drinks. The party lasted until 1:30. The general himself authorized the bar to stay open after normal closing hours and stayed until the very end. He had a few more tricks up his sleeve. He had not, as it was supposed, been a bomber pilot in World II but instead, he had flown P-51 Mustangs escorting B-17s into Germany. In other words, he was a fighter pilot. Furthermore, he knew by heart every song that had been sung that night. He even taught the group some new ones.

*   *   *   *

"What time is it?" Skip asked.

"Ten after one," Tom replied. "Five minutes later than the last time you asked."

"The wedding was supposed to start at one. What the hell is going on?"

"I told you, the photographer is late."

"Oh yeah, I forgot."

The two of them were waiting in a small chapel adjacent to the main part of the church. Both were in Air Force formal attire. Skip was uneasy and on edge as he paced the floor.

"You should see the honor guard," Tom said, trying to divert Skip's thoughts. "You wouldn't recognize them."

"Really?" Skip replied absently.

"Yeah, they really look sharp. They're even wearing white gloves if you can believe that. And Cactus Jack…he looks like General Patton with all the service ribbons on his uniform. He's such a clown sometimes that people forget how much combat he's seen."

Skip continued to pace the floor, only half listening. Then he flung himself on the front pew with a heavy sigh. "This is unreal; I can't believe I'm actually going to get married."

"Having second thoughts?"

"Well yeah, I mean no…of course not. It's just that…what if it doesn't work?"

"Look, everybody has second thoughts just before their wedding. It's perfectly normal. No big deal. You're just nervous."

"Yeah, I guess I am."

"In fact, you know what this whole thing reminds me of?"

"What?"

"The time I lead my first sixteen-ship formation takeoff."

"Sixteen-ship formation takeoff?" Skip asked, looking puzzled. It was obvious he didn't see the connection.

"Right. As we were walking out to the aircraft, my squadron commander said, 'Tom, have you ever done this before?' 'Nope,' I replied. 'Well it's really not that hard. Just remember, after you start rolling down the runway, don't abort the takeoff and don't look back.' I think that's pretty good advice. Don't you?"

Skip paused for a moment to absorb his words. Then he broke into a wide smile and visibly relaxed. "You're right," he said, "that's very good advice."

Their conversation was interrupted by the swell of organ music followed by a soft knock on the door. "We're ready for you," a voice said. Skip sprang to his feet, stood perfectly erect, and checked his uniform one last time. Then he strode with confidence to the door. As he placed his hand on the knob, he turned to Tom, gave him a self-assured wink and said, "Don't abort and don't look back, right?"

"You got it. Go get 'em Tiger."

They both walked out the door.

The church was lavishly decorated. Lush, colorful baskets of yellow and pink spring flowers adorned the altar and filled the church with a variety of sweet scents. White ribbons and bows were strung along the pews on both sides of the center aisle. It was an unseasonably warm day, and the two massive doors at the back of the church were open to let in the soft wafting breeze. It was a perfect day for a wedding. The church was filled. Everyone was dressed in their finest. The women wore gloves and fashionable hats. He caught a glimpse of his parents watching him anxiously. He gave them a brief nod and a lopsided smile. He was really nervous now. I can't do this, he thought. Yes you can…and you will. Don't abort and don't look back.

At last the organist began the wedding march, and the parade of flower girls, bridesmaids, and their escorts began to slowly walk down the aisle. The guests turned their heads and crowded against each other to watch the procession pass. Meanwhile, Skip shifted impatiently waiting for his bride to make her entrance.

Then he saw her. She was glowing as she walked through the church doors, arm in arm with her father. It was a breathtaking sight. Her wedding gown was a soft and elegant creation of white silk and lace. The style was different in a way that gave her a look of European sophistication. Her hair was done up simply in the back and interlaced with a small garland of tiny flowers. She looked more beautiful and radiant than he had ever seen her.

Skip watched with fascination as she approached the altar. She took her place beside him and quickly whispered, "You look quite well, considering last night."

"You heard about that, huh?"

"Yep."

When he took her hand, it was shaking. He gave it a gentle reassuring squeeze.

Looking back, Skip could remember nothing about the actual ceremony. It was all a blur of words, music, prayers, and vows. When it was over, they were man and wife, gliding down the aisle through a sea of happy, well-wishing guests. Flashbulbs popped all around them. As they stepped into the bright sunlight, they were greeted by Cactus Jack's crisp clear command, "Honor guard. Atten-shun! Present sabers!" Six gleaming steel sabers swept upward in a graceful flashing arc and met overhead with a solid metallic clang. Skip and Christy descended the steps under the saber arch and rushed excitedly through a shower of white rice to the getaway car, a white 1955 Cadillac sedan owned by one of Skip's bootstrap buddies, who had volunteered to be their chauffeur for the day.

"Hey," Christy said, settling into the plush, red-leather seats, "this is nice. I could get used to this real quick."

"On a lieutenant's pay? Not a chance."

"Shucks."

For a moment, neither spoke as they held each other tightly, the tension draining out of their bodies. Christy's hands were still shaking,

"Well, Mrs. O'Neill," Skip said finally, "what do you think?"

"I think I'm glad it's over."

"Me too. Pretty scary wasn't it?"

"Uh-huh. I must love you a whole bunch to go through all that, don't you think?"

"Could be. It's official now, we're married," Skip said.

"That's a good thing. That's a very good thing."

The main dining room in the officers' club had been blocked off with screens to accommodate the wedding reception. Like the church, the room was lavishly decorated with baskets of spring flowers on tables set with white linen, gleaming silverware, and fine china. There was a choice of prime rib, chicken cordon bleu, or grilled swordfish. Small open bars were positioned strategically around the room ready to serve champagne, wine, beer, or mixed drinks to the guests. A five-piece orchestra was setting up for after-dinner dancing.

Skip and Christy had no time for a drink. There was a reception line to attend, plus more photos to pose for. The reception line seemed never-ending. Skip had never shaken hands with so many strangers in his life. It seemed that the Weber clan extended well into Wisconsin, Minnesota, and Iowa, as well as California. Greta Weber's oldest sister even made the trip from Germany. A tall, elegant, gray-haired woman, she looked Skip up and down appraisingly and pronounced in German to her sister that he looked like a "good catch."

The pre-dinner ceremony began with the traditional toast by the best man. Tom gave a touching speech about Skip's life in Presque Isle, the loneliness, and the need for him to have someone to share his life with. He described how he and Penney decided it was time for him to find his own Midwest girl, and how he gave Skip that advice one quiet morning when they were alone. "I have to admit," he said, wryly, "that Skip didn't always follow my instructions, much less advice. But this time he did a magnificent job, and he couldn't have made a better choice for a wife. To Skip and Christy O'Neill. Health, happiness, and a long life together!" Everyone rose to their feet, glasses in hand and cheered.

As the toasts and speeches went on, Cactus Jack's turn came, and he gave a toast that was so outrageously risqué that it was almost obscene. But to the relief of many, it ended on a wholesome note, and everyone clapped appreciatively.

The food was elegantly prepared and ceremoniously served, starting with the bride and groom. Although neither had eaten since breakfast, they could scarcely touch their food. They were just too excited.

When the meal was over, the happy couple was called to the floor for their first dance together as husband and wife. Picking the song for the first dance had been easy. They both agreed on "Chances Are" by Johnny Mathis. As he held her in his arms, her cheek pressed to his, Skip thought back to that night in front of her house when they listened to that song together on his car radio, and he realized he was in love. The very next night they consummated their love for the first time. It had all happened so fast. Yes indeed, he thought, chances were pretty good after that night. I am a lucky guy.

Looking over Christy's shoulder as they danced, he decided that the wedding reception was a subdued affair compared to last night's party. Thank God for that, he thought. But everyone seemed to be having good time, and the room was filled with happiness and love. He was pleased to see some significant mingling between his friends from Presque Isle and the bridesmaids, thus fulfilling the promise Tom had brashly made. Everything was working out perfectly. Later in the evening, he danced with Penney.

"She's a keeper," Penney said, as they were dancing. "You done good, so don't screw this up."

"I won't, Penney. I promise. I love her very much."

When it was approaching time to leave, Christy slipped away and changed into her traveling clothes. There was no time for a honeymoon, but they would have this whole glorious night all to themselves. The white Cadillac with Skip's friend at the wheel was waiting at the curb outside the club. "This is wonderful, sweetie," she said as they settled once again into the deep leather seats in the back. "I am so happy. What a beautiful wedding. When we get back to the apartment I'm gonna…"

"Apartment?" Skip said. "Did I say anything about taking you to our apartment? We are going directly from here to our honeymoon suite in the Hotel Creighton…without passing go, thank you very much."

"The honeymoon suite? Oh my God. You're really spoiling me, you know."

"Nothing is too good for my wife," he said proudly.

Their entrance into the lobby of the hotel was impressive, with Skip in his dress uniform, and Christy in a smart gray traveling suit. The hotel staff had been alerted to the arrival of the newlyweds and made much fuss and ado over "Lieutenant and Mrs. O'Neill." When they arrived at the honeymoon suite, Skip made his new bride wait in the hallway until the bellhop left with a generous tip in his pocket. With a flourish he carried her over the threshold.

The suite was spacious and richly appointed with thick, blue-velvet drapes and elegant antique furniture. The bed was wide, and its crisp white sheets were turned back just so with a Belgian chocolate truffle on each pillow. Everything was bathed in a soft warm glow from the two bedside lamps. A bottle of champagne sat chilled in a bucket of ice on one of the night tables.

They were both close to exhaustion but too excited to think about sleep. They had not made love in several weeks. It had been Christy's idea, a compromise for their decision to marry early. They fell into each other's arms and made love slowly, for a long time. When it was over, they both fell into a deep and peaceful sleep.

When Skip awoke the next morning, Christy was asleep beside him, purring softly, just like the first time she spent the night with him. Except this time, she wouldn't be leaving. Drawing her into his arms, he softly kissed her awake. They had a leisurely breakfast delivered by room service and then left for Skip's apartment, which was to be their new home. Christy had classes the next day, and final exams were only two weeks away. The honeymoon was over. It was time to start their married life.

✳   ✳   ✳   ✳

While Christy attended classes and studied for exams, Skip busied himself organizing and packing the things they would take to Texas. They decided to take the MG, thinking it would keep her from being stuck at home all day while he was at the base. But they were not about to drive all the way to Texas in two cars, so Christy's brother installed a trailer hitch on the back of the Chevy so the second car could be towed. Taking the MG was good for another reason too. It had a trunk plus space in both seats to store luggage. They needed all they space they could get. Both cars were going to be packed.

On the day of their departure, they went to the Webers' house for breakfast. The whole family had gathered to see them off. Everyone was happy for them, but no one wanted to see them go. Finally Skip and his brother-in-law hitched up the MG, and amidst many waves and wishes for good luck, they pulled out of the driveway and drove off.

The road heading south was unusually quiet that morning as it stretched out in front of them through the rolling plains as far as the eye could see. They likened it to how their life would be—clear, bright, full of adventure and promise. "Pilot training," Skip said, "is going to be a piece of cake. I've been in an interceptor squadron for four years now, flying in the old Scorpion. Compared to that, learning to fly a piddley-ass little prop plane like they do at the local airport should be no sweat. You'll see."

"Whatever you say, honey," she said snuggling up beside him.

✳   ✳   ✳   ✳

The IV relaxed its grip slightly, and Skip felt himself drifting slowly toward the surface, back to the conscious world. But he did not want to wake up, not yet anyway.

There was nothing waiting for him there, except a bleak hospital room filled with gnawing, persistent pain. He was much happier where he was, sharing the life of the man he once was and his beautiful wife as they started their new life together. They were so young and naïve! Clearly, they took everything in life at face value and were open to all the possibilities the world offered. Pilot training was only the first small step in their journey, but it was far from a "piece of cake." But they didn't realize that until much later.

PRIMARY PILOT TRAINING

Moore Air Base, Mission, Texas
July 1959

The blazing Texas sun beat down on the canopy of the small prop-driven trainer. Skip sat hunched forward, holding the stick and throttle in a death grip, trying to see through the rivulets of sweat that were running down over his eyes. They had only been airborne a few minutes, but already his flying suit was soaked with sweat. The Beechcraft T-34 was a small, low-wing, single-engine monoplane that carried a crew of two, sitting in tandem. The student sat in front, and the instructor in back. Both had access to a full set of flight controls. It was not a high-performance aircraft. In fact, many of the old-timers referred to it as a "ninety-knot bird" meaning that it took off at ninety knots, cruised at ninety knots, and landed at ninety knots. Most pilots found it fun and easy to fly, but not Skip. He had received over eight hours of instruction so far and still hadn't soloed. If he didn't solo soon, he would be eliminated from the program, and his career as a pilot would be over.

Although he didn't need another reminder that the pressure was on, he got one every morning when he lined up with his classmates for roll call. Those who had soloed were given green baseball caps to wear. Those who had not still wore their standard-issue flight caps. There were only three people wearing flight caps this morning. The problem was his landings. He could do a halfway decent job of flying the "traffic pattern," which meant circling the field and making the final approach, but just as the aircraft hovered a few feet above the touchdown point, something always went wrong. Sometimes he would wait too long to pull the power back and round out, and the aircraft would slam onto the runway with a spine-rattling thud. His instructor liked to say those weren't landings but merely "arrivals." Other times, he would round out too high and too fast, causing the aircraft to start flying again instead of landing.

His instructor was a sadistic son of a bitch. There were times when Skip was sorely tempted to reach across the briefing table and jam the unlit cigar stub he always clenched between his teeth right down his throat. Unlike most instructors, Gordon Ross did not scream or shout when he was instructing. He simply communicated his displeasure using a mixture of snarls, sarcasm, and nasty comments.

Skip's face was a picture of intense concentration as he approached the auxiliary field for the first practice landing. On initial approach now, he told himself, get ready. Here we go…over the end of the runway, rolling in to sixty degrees of bank for the pitch-out. Throttle back to idle…I need a nice smooth 180-degree level turn here. Easy does it. Be smooth.

"Watch your altitude," Ross said.

Damn…he's right. I just lost one hundred feet of altitude. That's okay…keep going. Rolling out on downwind. Pre-landing checks…turn to base leg…gear down and checked…flaps down.

"Goddammit Lieutenant, I want to land at this auxiliary field, not on some friggin' runway in east Jesus somewhere. Check the wind. The wind is blowing you away from the runway. Can't you see that?"

"Yes sir," Skip replied. He made the base leg a little flatter to compensate for the wind. Lined up with the runway now…hey, this looks okay!

When the aircraft was over the end of the runway, he eased back on the control stick and pulled the throttle to idle. It rose briefly as if to fly again and then dropped abruptly onto the runway. It wasn't a smooth landing, but they were on the ground. He paused for a second, waiting for his instructor to say something. "Okay," Ross said finally, "take it around." Skip pushed the throttle forward and took off for another try.

The second pattern and landing was about the same as the first, except he let the wind blow him too close to the runway and as a result almost overshot the turn to final approach. This earned him another sarcastic snarl from his instructor, but he managed to correct his error and make a halfway decent touchdown.

"Again," Ross ordered, as they coasted down the runway.

The pressure was building. I've got to get this one right, he thought. This might be my last chance. Ross is so damn quiet back there. What is he thinking? Is he giving up on me? He flew the next traffic pattern by the numbers; airspeeds, altitudes all on target. This is it, he thought as he glided down final approach, throttle at idle, and the engine popping and purring. This is going to be a perfect landing, and it would have been, except for one thing. He rounded out just a fraction of a second too late, and the aircraft slammed into the runway, bounced back into the air, and then dropped onto the concrete with a resounding thump. It was the worst landing so far. He slumped in the cockpit in stunned silence waiting for the volley of abuse that was sure to come. But his instructor said nothing. Uncertain what to do next, he advanced the throttle for another takeoff.

"No," Ross said, pulling it back to idle. "Turn off at the next taxiway." His voice was flat and without emotion.

The cockpit was quiet except for the soft rhythmic chugging of the engine as it coasted down the runway. Oh shit, he thought. It's all over. Damn, I just needed a little more time.

"Turn left here."

Skip did as he was told, oblivious to where they were headed. He felt like a man headed to his own execution.

"Pull over here," Ross said, "and set the parking brake."

Skip saw they were near the approach end of the runway, about fifty yards from the mobile control unit, a small, glass-enclosed cabin on wheels used to observe takeoffs and landings. As soon as they came to a stop, Ross leapt out of the back seat and stood on the wing, glaring down at him.

"Listen," he said leaning over, so Skip could hear him above the idling engine, "I'm tired of this crap. You're going to kill somebody one of these days. It's all right with me if you want to kill yourself, but I'm not going to let you kill me. I'm out of here. Now, get back up there and make two touch-and-goes, and a full-stop landing. And Lieutenant…"

"Yes sir?"

"Try not to bust your ass." Then he jumped off the wing and walked to mobile control.

For a minute Skip was too stunned to do anything. He was going to solo! He was both excited and afraid. Finally, he pulled himself together, taxied up to the runway, closed the canopy, and in the most professional voice he could muster, called for takeoff clearance.

"Mobile, T-Bird 42 is number one, ready for takeoff. Request permission to remain in the pattern for two touch-and-goes and a full stop."

"T-Bird 42, cleared for takeoff."

As he pulled onto the runway, he saw the glow of Ross's cigar through the tinted window of the mobile control unit.

He was lined up for takeoff. After checking the cockpit one last time, he pushed the throttle to full power, released the brakes, and started down the runway. The engine responded with a muffled roar. Seconds later he was airborne and alone. It was up to him to get the bird back on the ground. For a moment, he was seized with panic. But he shook it off. I can do this. Relaxing a little he pulled the aircraft up to downwind for the first landing.

The first landing was a little rough but okay. The second was better. His confidence began to rise. It was a lot easier when that asshole with the cigar was not in the backseat.

Ross had been very specific. "Two touch-and-goes, and a full stop." It was time for the full-stop landing. The feeling of being in the air alone, free to do what ever he chose, was intoxicating. He didn't want to land. He was having too much fun. His last traffic pattern was nearly perfect. Gliding across the end of the runway, engine throttled back and purring quietly, he knew it was going to be a good landing, and it was. As he pulled back on the stick and retarded the throttle, the aircraft hung in the air hesitantly and then softly kissed the concrete. It was over. His first solo flight.

When he left the runway and taxied toward the parking ramp, he wanted to leap out of the aircraft and do a dance on the wing. He was overcome with joy and excitement. Instead, he reached in his pocket, tore out his flight cap, and flung it onto the grass beside the taxiway. "There," he said, watching with satisfaction as it tumbled end over end in the prop-wash, "I won't need you for awhile." As expected, his classmates were waiting for him, armed with buckets of water. Dousing pilots who had just soloed was an old tradition in the Air Force. He climbed down the ladder, grinning from ear to ear. Then he dropped his parachute and helmet on the ramp and rushed headlong into a torrent of cascading water. When it was over, he was drenched.

His flight commander stood waiting in a small grassy area beside the parking ramp. He was holding the coveted baseball cap made of green twill with a small squadron emblem on the front. As his classmates gathered round, Skip saluted the flight commander, accepted the cap, and perched it on top of his water-soaked head. Everyone cheered, pounding him on his back, and shaking his hand. Ross shook his hand briefly but said nothing. His first solo! He finally made it. He couldn't wait to get home and tell Christy. She would be thrilled.

It took more than two hours to dry out and escape his classmates who insisted on buying him several beers at the club. At last he was on his way, driving Christy's MG with the top down and wearing his new green baseball cap. It was a fine afternoon, and he was in high spirits. They lived about ten miles from the base in a small rented house. Driving home in Christy's car was one of his favorite things to do. He liked to navigate the twists and turns of the back roads using the gear shift to decelerate while taking special care to run the RPM into the yellow zone to get max torque before shifting to a higher gear. During such times he imagined he was the famous British race car driver Stirling Moss, driving at Sebring or in one of the Grand Prix events in Europe. Today he drove with even more exuberance than usual.

Their house sat in the middle of an orange grove and was surrounded by trees, bushes, and multicolored flowers. It was a frame house with a red barn and storage shed in the back. It was a quiet place, although sometimes they were awakened just after dawn by the sound of a crop-dusting aircraft flying low over their roof. "Flyboys," Christy would always say, "you can't get away from them, no matter what." The Chevy was in the driveway when he pulled up, so he knew Christy was home. But she didn't come out on the porch to meet him. I wonder where she is, he thought. I want her to see the baseball cap right away. Leaping out of the car and bounding across the front porch, he flung open the front door and shouted, "Hello, I'm home. Your fearless aviator has returned." The house was quiet, but there were mouthwatering smells coming from the kitchen.

Suddenly she appeared in the doorway, a pitcher of martinis and two frosted glasses in her hand. "Welcome home, honey. I understand somebody in your class soloed today. That calls for a celebration, don't you think?"

"Damn! How did you find out? I wanted to surprise you."

"I have my ways. Actually, Marcia called me. Barney called her from the club to say he was over there helping you celebrate. Anyway, I needed the extra time to fix something special for dinner, which is almost ready. But first, tell me all about it. I want to know every little detail."

They sat for almost an hour, sipping the ice-cold martinis while he relived the experience of the day. He told her everything. About starting the day with the sinking feeling that he was only one of three students left who hadn't soloed. And about the frustration and pressure he felt flying round and round the traffic pattern trying to make a decent landing, until Ross abruptly left him to solo with the admonishment, "Try not to bust your ass." Finally, he described with passion the exhilaration he felt, in the air alone, free to do as he liked, confident that he would get the bird back on the ground just fine and then join his classmates wearing the green baseball hat he wanted so much.

By the time he finished, the sun was settling below the canopy of orange trees, leaving streaks of soft golden light. A gentle breeze blew through the open window, making a soft clacking sound as the blinds drifted to and fro. It's going to be okay, he thought. I'm going to graduate and get my wings someday. The worst has passed. I can feel it.

*   *   *   *

Ross leaned back in his chair and glared at Skip. "Lieutenant, I think it's time for you to consider the possibility that you may not graduate."

Skip stared impassively across the briefing table and said nothing. As usual, he was fighting the urge to jam the unlit cigar into his instructor's sneering face. This blunt act of defiance had become a fixation lately, and at times he had to struggle to keep his hands at his sides.

"The way I see it," Ross continued, "you barely learned to fly the T-34. But your performance in the T-28 is even worse and not improving. The way things are going, I'll have to recommend a progress check flight. And if you flunk that, we'll have to turn you over to the Air Force for an elimination check. It's all for the best. I mean, let's face it, you're just not the flying kind."

Once again, Skip remained silent, save for a muffled "Yes sir." In his opinion, the pointed reference to "turning him over to the Air Force" was symbolic of the problem. The instructors at Moore Air Base were civilians whose company had a contract with the Air Force to provide initial pilot training. Many had been teaching there since World War II. In general, they were tired, cranky, and old. Most were burned out from watching the same boneheaded mistakes day in and day out. There were a handful of Air Force pilots assigned to the base to make sure the program ran smoothly and to conduct elimination checks. The elimination check ride was usually the last stop on the way out of the program. During the flight, the Air Force instructor would evaluate the student's abilities and decide whether additional training was warranted, or whether he should be eliminated or "washed-out."

"Well," Ross sighed, standing up and gathering the briefing materials, "we can only hope for the best. Maybe you'll get lucky and…" His voiced trailed off as he turned and walked purposefully to get his parachute and helmet, with Skip at his heels.

A typical Rio Grande Valley morning greeted them as they stepped out of the small white building and onto the flight line. The morning fog had just burned off, and all that remained was a layer of fat clouds drifting over the airfield. Skip could see there was no chance of a weather cancellation. It was better that way. It would only delay the agony.

Comparing the T-34 to the T-28 was like comparing the family lawn mower to a large tractor. Both were single-engine, prop-driven trainers with a tandem cockpit, but that's where the similarities ended. The T-28 was massive when compared to the T-34. It was not possible to jump on the wing and scramble into the cockpit as in the T-34. Instead it was necessary to climb a set of steps built into the side of the fuselage to reach the cockpit. The T-34's engine hummed and purred when idling; the T-28's 800-horsepower radial engine throbbed with a throaty chugging sound that increased to a deafening roar when the throttle was advanced to the takeoff position.

Sitting in the cockpit with the battery switch turned on, Skip was ready to start the engine. "Prop clear!" he shouted to the mechanic.

"Prop clear!" the mechanic responded.

After pausing nervously to gather his thoughts, he depressed a small button with his left index finger. There was a whine as the starter engaged, and the prop began to turn. Holding the starter button down, he tapped a second button with his adjacent finger. This fed fuel to prime the engine. Depressing the primer button too long would flood the engine and cause it to stop. Releasing it too soon would cause it to backfire, and all hell would break loose from the instructor. The timing had to be perfect. After several turns of the prop, the engine coughed and sputtered, sending puffs of blue smoke drifting past the cockpit. He released both buttons and gingerly advanced the mixture control lever. The engine accelerated smoothly to idle. He breathed an audible sigh of relief.

As they taxied out to the runway, he occupied himself with going over what would be expected of him during the flight. After takeoff, there would be a forced-landing exercise where he would demonstrate his ability to make an emergency landing after an engine failure. Then they would proceed to an open area to practice aerobatics such as loops, rolls, and spins. It would be the same as yesterday. Except today he had to do better. His flying career depended on it. Meanwhile, the cockpit was quiet except for an occasional snarling complaint by Ross that he was taxiing too fast or too slow.

As soon as the aircraft was airborne and climbing, he applied himself to making a series of turns, first in one direction and then the other, all the while scanning the sky for other aircraft. This was called clearing the area, or in Ross's words, keeping your head out of your ass. The air was smooth, and the aircraft was climbing well. He was almost at the base of the clouds when suddenly the throttle was wrenched out of his hand and pulled back to idle. "Forced landing," Ross said.

Aha, you son of a bitch, Skip thought, I'm ready for you this time. Aligning the aircraft into the wind, he began to descend at optimum glide speed, all the while looking for a suitable place to land. There were plenty of choices. The land below was flat and filled with cultivated fields, all framed by section lines created by roads, fences, and trees. Looking to his left, he saw a field that would do just fine, long and wide, with a smooth, green surface. It was a pasture of some kind, and there were no trees, rocks, or large animals to get in the way. Keeping the field in sight, he began a lazy, spiraling descent, taking care to play his airspeed and altitude so as to arrive on the final approach in just the right position.

It was a good pattern, and as he lowered his landing gear and turned to final approach, he could see that he would easily make the field. The aircraft glided noiselessly toward touchdown. At one hundred feet above the ground, Ross pushed the throttle forward and told him to resume his climb. "That was okay," he said, "the pattern was a little wide, but it was okay." His voice was noncommittal.

Okay? Skip thought. You bet your ass it was okay. It was more than okay. It was a damn good pattern!

By the time they started practicing aerobatics, his self-confidence began to fade. This was his weak suit, and the reason he was in such a jam. He wasn't afraid or uncomfortable performing aerobatic maneuvers. In fact, he thoroughly enjoyed the rush of freedom he felt at being able to defy gravity and place the aircraft in any position he chose. But flying aerobatics required him to think in three dimensions. Sometimes, he would become confused and disoriented during a maneuver, with disastrous results.

They started with the aileron roll, the simplest maneuver of all. This was performed by pushing the stick to one side to make the aircraft roll around its axis, all the while applying rudder to keep the nose straight. But Skip forgot about the rudder, and the nose wobbled from side to side throughout the maneuver. Not a good beginning. After the rolls, they began a series of aerobatics that started with chandelles, lazy eights, and clover leafs, and progressed to more demanding maneuvers such as loops, Immelmans, and Cuban eights. By now, he was sweating profusely as he clenched the flight controls, performing each maneuver with dogged determination. The harder he tried, the worse things got.

"Climb back up to ten thousand feet and give me a spin to the left," Ross said.

Skip hated spins. Most pilots did. It was the only planned maneuver he knew of where the aircraft was truly out of control for a time. The sight of the nose crazily rotating around the horizon was disorienting enough, but the fact that the aircraft was rushing toward earth at the same time was downright scary. Each time he was in a spin, the thought crossed his mind, "What if I can't pull out?" When he leveled off at ten thousand, he took a deep breath, brought the throttle to idle and raised the nose above the horizon. As the aircraft began to shudder and stall, he brought the stick full aft and kicked in full left rudder. The aircraft bucked wildly and then snapped into a vicious flat spin. Take it easy, he thought, you know what to do. Throttle idle. Stick full back. Rudder against the spin. We're spinning left, so apply right rudder. The aircraft continued to spin, and Skip became uneasy. Then, mercifully, the rotation stopped. Quickly he neutralized the rudders, brought the stick forward and advanced the power. The aircraft was under control again.

"Took your sweet time recovering, didn't you?" Ross commented. "Give me another one, this time to the right."

He climbed back to altitude and repeated the procedure. This time something unexpected happened. The aircraft rolled over and went into a violent inverted spin. As it did, the sideway forces caused his helmet to rotate on his head, thus covering his eyes, as the spin wound tighter and tighter. Panic stricken and virtually blind, he knew he needed to act quickly. Instead, he froze.

"I've got it…I've got it!" Ross shouted, ripping the flight controls out of Skip's hands. After stopping the spin, he righted the aircraft and brought it under control. "Jesus Christ! You do have a death wish, don't you? Okay, you have the aircraft back. Get me on the ground."

The debriefing took more than two hours. Slumped in his chair, Skip listened as Ross went through five pages of notes he had written on his kneeboard. Each criticism, each error or failure pointed out, jabbed him like the stab of a needle, and he sank lower and lower in his chair.

Finally, it was over. Ross leaned back and gazed reflectively at the ceiling. "I hate to do this…" he began.

Here it comes, Skip thought. This son of a bitch is actually enjoying himself.

"But I really have no choice. I've done my best, but I can't do anything more. I'm going to ask my boss to give you a progress check ride. Maybe he can figure out what the hell to do with you."

"I'm not going to make it," he moaned, more to himself than to Ross.

Ross gazed at him with a steely-eyed stare that showed not a trace of pity. "No," he said calmly, "you probably aren't. Not with that attitude anyway." Then he rose and slowly walked away.

Ross's last words stung him like a brutal slap in the face, and he was overwhelmed by a white-hot wave of anger. He wanted to follow him, to grab him and fight back. It wasn't fair. He just needed more time. When his anger cooled, he felt his body fill with a core of cold, steely resolve. Fuck you, he thought. Fuck you, your shitty little cigar, and the horse you rode in on. You're not going to get rid of me that easily. In fact, you're not going to get rid of me at all. How does that grab your happy ass? I am going to make it, whether you like it or not. Just thinking those words made him feel stronger, more confident. He was not about to give up, not now. He had come this far, and he was going to finish it.

The next morning, he awoke with a fever and sharp pains in his right ear. He was too sick to get out of bed. As the morning wore on, the pain increased, and a pale yellow discharge appeared on his pillow. By afternoon, Christy decided to drive him to the base to see the flight surgeon.

"An ear infection," the flight surgeon said, removing the scope from his ear. "How long has this been going on?"

"Beats me. I just noticed it this morning."

"Well, it's serious. We have to get you on penicillin right away. It's going to take awhile for it to heal."

"What's awhile?" Skip asked.

"It will be a least at least ten days before you can return to flying status…maybe even two weeks."

"Two weeks? But…"

"I know, I know. You're gung ho to get back to class and worried you'll fall behind, right?"

"Right."

"Well, don't be. It's no big deal. It happens all the time. Take this DNIF slip over to the school secretary's office, and they'll know what to do." DNIF was an Air Force acronym for "duty not including flying".

The flight surgeon was right. It wasn't a big deal.

"Ear infection," the sergeant at the school secretary's office said. "Nasty break."

"What happens now?" Skip asked.

"Hmm," the sergeant said, taking out his training folder and looking at it. "You're in Class 60 Golf, graduating on or about May fifteenth. Is that right?"

"Right."

"Well," the sergeant said, pulling out his pen and ceremoniously making some notations, "as of now, you are officially in Class 60 Hotel, graduating on or about June fourth. Check back with me in a week, and I'll have the name of your new instructor, along with a time and place for your new class."

"Sounds simple enough," Skip commented. "I can do that."

"It usually is. Oh, and by the way Lieutenant, you ought to go home and get into bed. You look like shit."

"Thanks for your warm words of sympathy," Skip laughed, as he left the office.

"What's the word?" Christy asked.

"I've been reassigned to the next class. Meanwhile, it looks like I'll have to shack up with you for a couple of weeks. Is that okay?"

"I'll see if I can fit you into my schedule. And I'll expect my usual fee in advance."

"In your garter or tucked in your bra?"

"Wherever."

The penicillin and pain pills the flight surgeon gave him were powerful, and he spent the next two days drifting in and out of sleep. Christy kept the blinds drawn, and he soon lost track of day and night, sensing only the soft hum of insects and the soft breezes rustling through the orange trees. Sometimes he dreamed, and when he did, it wasn't pleasant. Once, he dreamed of doing aerobatic maneuvers, sweating and straining, but never getting them right. In one dream, his aircraft was inverted and spinning crazily to the ground. Try as he might, he couldn't make it stop. Meanwhile, Ross was screaming, "I told you. I told you. You're not the flying kind. You'll never make it."

On the morning of the fourth day he was awakened by gunfire. The shots came from all around the house and seemed much too close for comfort. "What the hell?" Skip shouted, rolling over to shield Christy with his body. But she was already on the floor beside the bed. Crawling to the bedside table he managed to pick up the phone and dial the sheriff's department.

"We're under attack here!" he shouted into the phone when the dispatcher answered. "There's shooting all around us."

"Take it easy, sir," the dispatcher drawled. "Where are y'all located?"

He told him.

"Oh there, I see. That ain't nothin' to worry about. It's dove-hunting season. Only happens a few days a year. And that grove where you live is a favorite spot. My advice is to just lay low until midmorning. That's when the hunters usually pack up and go home. Those peckerwoods usually can't hit nothin' anyway."

"What did he say?" Christy asked, after he hung up.

"He said it's just a bunch of dumb peckerwoods out dove hunting," he said, doing his best Texas drawl imitation. "And they usually can't hit nothin'."

On the Wednesday before he was to resume training, the flight surgeon cleared him to fly. The ear infection was healed. He had just four more days to prepare for the challenge ahead.

*   *   *   *

Skip's new instructor, Robert McPherson, was a Southern gentleman from the old school who took a calm, measured approach to everything he did. As a matter of principle, he went out of his way to be kind and considerate to everyone who passed his way, be it other instructors, students, or strangers. When it came to teaching, he strongly believed that words of praise and encouragement were far more effective than criticism and sarcasm. He was an ordinary looking man who wore his salt-and-pepper gray hair cut short, constantly had a pipe in his mouth, and spoke with a slow Southern drawl. Everyone called him "Mac," including his students.

"Hmm…" Mac said, as he slowly leafed through Skip's grade folder. "You've been having some trouble with aerobatics I see."

"Yes sir," Skip replied, shifting nervously in his chair.

"Well, it doesn't look like a big deal to me. I have a feeling you just haven't got the big picture yet. Sometimes the body can be pretty dense when it comes to learning. In the beginning, it relies on the brain to give very precise instructions, or it won't do much of anything. After awhile, it settles in and begins to learn on its own. So, you need to teach your brain and muscles to learn together. Understand?"

"Yes sir, I do."

"I see that Gordon Ross was your instructor."

"Yes sir."

"He can be a real pain in the ass sometimes, can't he?"

Skip smiled but said nothing.

"Well, anyway, here's what we're going to do today. When we get to the practice area, we'll go through all the aerobatic maneuvers, just like you've been doing. Except I'll demonstrate each one the first time around. When I do, I want you to put your hands and feet lightly on the controls so you can feel what I'm doing. At the same time, listen carefully as I describe what I'm thinking…and of course, look outside so you're seeing what I'm seeing. Feel, listen, and watch. Got that?"

"Yes sir,"

When the briefing was over, Mac gathered up his flying equipment and walked with Skip toward the door. "By the way," he said, almost as an afterthought, "have you decided what you want to fly after you graduate from pilot training?"

The question took him by surprise, and for a moment he couldn't think of an answer. His only thought for the past few weeks had been will I graduate, not what will I fly when I graduate. "I, umm, haven't given that much thought yet."

"Well," Mac said, "it's not too early to start. You'll probably want to fly interceptors after flying around in the back seat of the F-89."

"Interceptors, yeah, that would be good. Or fighters of some kind."

Skip was waiting for the other shoe to drop. Surely this guy would change his easygoing ways once they were in the cockpit. That's what instructors do, don't they? But the shoe never dropped, and by the time the flight was over Skip "had the picture." It all seems so easy now, he thought. Why was it so hard before? Three days later he completed aerobatics training and moved on to the next phase. There was no further mention of evaluation check rides or elimination from the program. He had finally turned the corner.

During the second week of December, he took his final check ride and passed with flying colors. He would definitely be graduating from primary pilot training. Later that day his class received their assignment for basic pilot training where they would begin flying jet aircraft. Classes would start the first week in January. Everyone in his class gathered at happy hour to celebrate their graduation. Skip was in the middle of it all, laughing and drinking with joyous abandon. On the way home he put the MG through a challenging course of twisting turns, down-shifting and up-shifting, taking hairpin curves with ease. He was lost in a dream world of Grand Prix racing. He took the checkered flag in his driveway as the car screeched to a halt, its small motor popping and throbbing as it was shut down.

Christy met him on the porch wearing blue jeans, a red-checkered shirt with a black string tie, and a pair of handmade cowboy boots she bought in Mexico. "Hold on there, partner," she said in her best Texas accent, "What's all this fuss about?"

"Oh, nothing much, ma'am. I just passed my check ride and got my assignment for basic."

"And where might this basic pilot training be, handsome stranger?"

"Laredo, Texas, little darlin'…just up the Rio Grande apiece."

"You don't say," Christy said, jumping into his arms. "Well, let's herd 'em up and head 'em out!"

Basic Pilot Training

Laredo Air Force Base, Texas
January 1960

Four gleaming, silver T-33 jet trainers approached Laredo Air Force Base in tight echelon formation. When they arrived, their leader rolled into a brisk sixty-degree bank to downwind. Three seconds later, aircraft number two followed suit, followed by the others. In less than five minutes, all four aircraft were on the ground, taxiing toward the parking ramp.

"Wow," Skip said, admiring the spectacle. He was standing by a small highway, just outside the base. The Chevy sat on the shoulder, filled with boxes and suitcases, with the MG hitched behind. They had just arrived in town.

"You like that, don't you, Skip?" Christy linked her arm into his.

"Yeah, I really do."

"Well, you'll be doing that before long."

"I hope so."

"You hope so? Of course you will. Training starts on Monday, right?"

"I just don't know if I'm good enough."

Christy's voice softened. "Still a little off balance from that bad start at primary, aren't you?"

"That could be it, I guess."

"Well, remember what you told me when we left Omaha. It's gonna be a piece of cake. And it will be, you'll see."

They arrived at the base on Friday afternoon and checked into the guest quarters. The next day they began looking for a place to live. There were plenty of apartments available in town, but Christy wanted a small house and they were not easy to find. After two days of fruitless searching, they answered an ad in the local paper for a two-bedroom, furnished house. The house sat on a dusty street, just five blocks from downtown Laredo. Its front porch sagged slightly, and the place was in need of paint and repairs, both inside and out. The lawn had long since given in to an onslaught of weeds and crabgrass. The backyard was barren except for a few bushes and wildflowers growing alongside a rickety wooden fence. The inside was clean, but the walls and floors showed weary scars from a constant procession of renters over the years. "This is it," Christy said, after the landlady gave them a tour of the house.

"I don't know." Skip said, eyeing the place doubtfully. "Are you sure you want to live here?"

"Absolutely," she replied. "It's going to be darling when I get it fixed up."

The next morning, a small moving van arrived with what little furniture they had accumulated so far. The movers were greeted by a volley of furious barks from a small white dog tied up on the neighbor's back porch. The house belonged to Maria, their landlady. "Blanco's a very good dog," she had explained, "but he gets excited when strangers come around. Both my husband and son work in the evenings, so Blanco keeps me company and makes me feel safe."

As the movers began unloading, Christy walked over to the fence, smiling warmly at the dog. "Blanco," she said, "why are you barking at these nice men? They're here to help us get settled in. We're going to be your new neighbors." The dog stopped barking and cocked his head inquisitively. "That's a good boy. When I get the kitchen set up, I'll cook my husband a big juicy steak and give you the bone. Would you like that?" Her words had a soothing effect on the dog, and by time Christy walked back into her new home, he was already snoozing in the warm afternoon sun.

By mid-afternoon the movers had gone, and Skip and Christy were hard at work, rearranging furniture and unpacking.

"Oh my God!" Christy screamed. "Skip, come here!"

He rushed into the kitchen tripping over boxes along the way. Christy was standing in the corner with a large broom raised over her head. Three feet in front of her was the largest, ugliest spider he had ever seen. It was black, hairy, and measured at least six inches across.

"Stay calm, it's a tarantula. I'll…" Before he could finish, Christy slammed the broom down with a resounding thwack. The spider tumbled backwards from the blow and tried to scurry away. Thwack…thwack…thwack. She hit the spider repeatedly. Finally it lay crushed and dead on the linoleum floor.

Skip looked down at the remains of the spider and then at Christy holding the broom in her hands, ready to strike again if necessary. "Thank God I was here to rescue you," he said.

Christy put the broom down looking slightly embarrassed. "A gal has to defend herself doesn't she?" she said finally.

Just when I think I really know my wife, she exposes another layer of her personality, and it's usually made of steel, he thought. He walked away shaking his head.

✳   ✳   ✳   ✳

The atmosphere at basic pilot training was much different than in primary. It was less intense and more relaxed. The instructors were all Air Force officers, mostly lieutenants and a few young captains, who had been flying fighters, bombers, tankers, and transports before becoming instructors. Each instructor was assigned three students. Every morning they gathered at their designated tables for a general briefing and to discuss the day's activities. The students usually flew once a day. When the day was over, they gathered once more to review what had been accomplished.

Skip's instructor was Lt. Craig "Robbie" Roberts. He was a tall, slender, soft-spoken man with blond hair and blue eyes. Each instructor was allowed to choose his own call sign. Robbie's was "Brahma." A graphic picture of a snorting, angry bull flexing a whip was painted on the visor cover of his helmet. At first, the sight of the snorting bull made Skip uncomfortable. Here we go again, he thought, another flaming asshole like Ross. One of the students asked Robbie why he chose that call sign. "It was actually my flight surgeon's idea," he said with an embarrassed laugh. "He suggested it, because I've got seven kids." Skip and the other students all laughed along with Robbie. He was a good-natured guy after all. Skip felt much more at ease.

Skip's tablemates came from other primary bases. Bob Lewis had been an RO like Skip. He was a stocky man with sharp aquiline features and a military-style crew cut. He had a dry sense of humor, and when he shared a joke, he liked to cover his lower face with the back of his hand and talk conspiratorially out of the side of his mouth. His wife, Jan, was the same age as Christy. The third student at the table was "Corky" Myers. He was three years younger than Skip and unmarried. He had entered pilot training immediately after college graduation. He was a slender, blond-haired Virginian who went about every task with the enthusiasm of a young puppy eager to please. So eager that Bob Lewis once commented, "I am always afraid that in his excitement he is going to pee on my foot." Skip, Bob and Corky got along well together. They vowed to stick together during pilot training and help each other graduate. One night at happy hour, they decided that they should have a call sign, just like the instructors did. After several rounds of drinks and much raucous debate, they decided to call themselves the "Blunderbirds," a play on the name of the Thunderbirds, the Air Force aerial demonstration team. It seemed appropriate.

Training began with a one-week course on the aircraft and its systems. The T-33, or "T-bird," as it was called, had been around since the late 1940s and was designed by lengthening the cockpit of the single-engine Lockheed P-80, the first jet fighter designed for combat in World War II. The systems were simple and easy to maintain. The flight controls were moved by cables and pulleys. There was a hydraulic system to raise and lower the landing gear. Fuel was carried in tip tanks, one on the end of each wing, as well as in fuel cells inside the wings. There was a system of generators and alternators to power the electrical system and instruments. The two pilots sat in tandem. It was considered a fast aircraft when first developed, with a max speed of 525 mph.

Skip flew his first flight in the T-33 as soon as ground school was over. He had ridden in the back seat of the T-Bird several times while he was at Presque Isle, but it hardly compared to sitting in the front seat, actually flying the plane himself. It was surprisingly easy to fly but difficult to taxi. Unlike the T-34 and T-28, it had no nose wheel steering. Steering the aircraft on the ground was a matter of tapping the brake on whichever side the pilot wanted to turn. This was especially tricky when leaving the parking spot. The key to this maneuver was the use of engine power to get the aircraft rolling. Too much power would scatter chocks and other equipment in the wake of the jet blast. If too little power was used, the nose wheel was apt to cock when a brake was tapped, causing the aircraft to skid to a stop. It was extremely difficult to get the aircraft moving again once this happened.

Robbie said there were only two kinds of T-Bird pilots: those who have cocked the nose wheel while taxiing and those who will. I sure hope it doesn't happen to me anytime soon, Skip thought. But of course it did happen—on his first flight, and second, and third. After the three failed attempts, Robbie took him to a vacant area on the ramp just to practice taxiing and turning. His classmates took great delight in his misery. "That's our boy Skip," they would say. "He's a hell of a pilot, once he manages to get the bird out of the parking ramp." It was embarrassing and frustrating. What if this happens when I am flying solo? he wondered.

*   *   *   *

The Blunderbirds were gathered around the table for the afternoon debriefing. It was Friday, and they were shuffling their feet under the table like children waiting for the recess bell. It was five o'clock, and happy hour was about to begin at the club. "This is probably against my better judgment," Robbie began, "but all three of you are going to solo on Monday. Skip, you'll go first on the early flight, then Bob, and then Corky. Any questions?"

"No, sir!" they chorused.

"Okay. Then get out of here. And try not to destroy yourselves at the club over the weekend. I need you bright and fresh on Monday morning."

"It's going to be great," Corky said elbowing his way up to the bar. "My very own jet to drill around in the sky. All by myself. It's about time."

"Yep." Skip raised his glass in a toast, "To the Blunderbirds."

"To the Blunderbirds," Bob said. "All for one and one for all. Speaking of which, Skip, I want you to know that if need be, Corky and I will be happy to help you taxi the bird out on Monday morning."

"Yeah," Corky smirked. "What are friends for?"

"Fuck you both," Skip replied, then drained his glass.

*   *   *   *

"It's going to be a piece of cake," Robbie shouted over the sound of the idling engine. He was standing on a ladder outside the cockpit, giving Skip some last-minute encouragement. "It's just another mission, except I won't be in the back seat." Skip nodded, glancing at the instruments nervously, making sure everything was ready. "Good luck," Robbie said finally, giving him a pat on the shoulder. Then he climbed down and took the ladder away.

Skip fastened his oxygen mask, snapped the sun visor down, and signaled the crew chief to remove the wheel chocks. When he was ready to go, he advanced the power, and the aircraft moved smoothly forward. But just as he retarded the power and started to turn, it began to slow down. In an instant, the nose wheel cocked, and he skidded to a stop. Oh shit! he thought. Desperately, he gave the engine a blast of power, hoping to get it moving again. It didn't work. Looking in his rearview mirror, he saw equipment flying in every direction, as people scrambled to escape the devastating effects of his jet blast. The ladder Robbie had been standing on just a minute ago was now spinning crazily toward the aircraft in the next parking spot.

He slumped in the cockpit feeling defeated and discouraged as two crew chiefs raced toward the aircraft. They had gone through this many times. One of them signaled for him to advance and retard the power while they pushed their shoulders against the side of the nose trying to muscle the aircraft and nose wheel back into the forward position. It was tough going for a minute or so, much like rocking a car back and forth when it's stuck in the sand, but finally the aircraft broke free and started moving toward the taxiway. The crew chiefs gave him cheery thumbs-up and trotted back to the parking area.

He reviewed the mission profile one last time as he taxied toward the runway, trying to shake off the embarrassment of what just happened. Taxi to the runway; take off; climb to fifteen thousand feet; proceed to the training area and then...and then what? He tried to remember. "Warm up by doing some steep turns," Robbie had said. "Then, acrobatic maneuvers. Keep it simple at first. When you feel more comfortable, do more complicated ones. When you have two hundred gallons of fuel left, return to the base." Take off, get the job done, and go home; just like the big boys do, he thought. This time won't be anything like my first solo in primary, with that cigar-chewing weasel, Ross. They didn't even have jets when he was in the Air Force, so what does he know? No sir, no more bullshit from Ross. You're in the big leagues now, my man!

As he approached the runway, he closed the canopy and locked it. The noise of the engine dropped to humming whisper. "Laredo tower, Brahma 51 is number one for takeoff...initial solo," he called.

"Brahma 51, taxi into position and hold."

"Brahma 51, Roger. Into position and hold."

Checking over his shoulder for approaching aircraft, he eased onto the runway and lined up on its centerline. It was an unusually bright day with a cloudless sky. Even with his tinted visor down, he had to squint to read the instruments through the glaring sunlight flashing off the silver nose of the aircraft.

"Brahma 51. Cleared for takeoff."

"Brahma 51, Roger. Cleared for takeoff."

Holding the brakes, he pushed the throttle to full power, and the engine responded with a muffled roar. There was a welcome rush of refrigerated air from the ventilation system. All the instruments were in the green. It's show time, he thought.

"Brahma 51 is rolling," he called out, as he released the brakes.

The aircraft hesitated briefly and then gained speed. Fifty knots, ninety knots, the nose began to lighten and rise. Yeah baby! You want to fly, and I want to fly. Let's do it. He was ecstatic. At 120 knots, he eased back on the stick, and the aircraft leaped into the air. He raised the landing gear and flaps. There was no turning back now. He was on his way.

The climb speed increased rapidly to 270 knots. Raising the nose to hold that speed, he turned out of the traffic pattern and headed for the practice area, which was thirty miles from the base. At fifteen thousand feet, the city of Laredo was nothing but a dusty postage stamp-size smudge. To the south, the Mexican city of Nuevo Laredo sat brooding in the heat, with sporadic spots of greenery dotting the unpaved streets. Between the two cities, ran the Rio Grande River, its muddy water reflecting dully in the morning sun. It all seemed so small and insignificant compared with where he was, and what he was doing.

Skip started the maneuvers cautiously, with a few steep turns, enjoying the sensation of being totally alone and unsupervised. Then he did a series of rolls, starting with some sharp, crisp aileron rolls, followed a series of slow, easy barrel rolls. On the last barrel roll, he paused while inverted, enjoying the view through the top of the canopy. Laredo, the base, and Nuevo Laredo were still there. Except this time, they were above him instead of down below. Viewing the world while hanging upside down was an exciting experience. He didn't want it to end.

The fuel gauge read, two hundred gallons. It was time to go home. He had been airborne over an hour. Where had the time gone? Rolling the aircraft inverted one last time, he pulled the throttle to idle, dropped the speed brakes, and buried the nose below the horizon. He descended at a rapid rate with the air rumbling around the open speed brakes. The base was dead ahead. He barely made it to traffic pattern altitude before turning on initial approach. Now he was lined up with the runway, his airspeed on target at 240 knots.

"Laredo tower. Brahma 51 is on initial approach for a full stop. Initial solo."

"Roger, Brahma 51. Check base with gear down and locked."

Crossing the end of the runway, he rolled smartly into a sixty-degree bank, pulled the throttle to idle, and dropped the speed brakes. He decided to make an honest-to-God fighter pilot's overhead pattern. The aircraft buffeted its way around the turn to downwind as the airspeed bled off rapidly. He paused just long enough on downwind to drop the gear and flaps and raise the speed brakes. Then he made a descending turn to base leg.

"Brahma 51 on base. Gear down and checked."

"Brahma 51 cleared to land."

The traffic pattern was almost too tight, and he barely had time to roll out on final before the aircraft streaked across the end of the runway. Pulling the stick and throttle back at just the right time, it touched down with a comfortable thump. Not bad, Skip thought, holding the nose off the runway as the aircraft slowed down. Not bad at all.

Skip was still on an adrenaline high when he walked into operations. He was greeted by a ring of students, some cheering, and others laughing. The cocked nose wheel, he thought. I forgot all about that. But I don't care. It's been an extraordinary day, and I feel great.

Robbie walked up to him, holding a gray silk flying scarf with red polka dots. It was the traditional reward for soloing. "Skip, under the circumstances, I should probably tear this scarf in half and give one part to you and the other to the crew chiefs who helped un-cock your nose wheel." This brought a gale of laughter from the students. "But," he continued seriously, "I was in mobile control when you landed and saw the traffic pattern you flew. It really looked sharp. Congratulations. Wear this with pride. You earned it."

Skip took the scarf, held it triumphantly over his head, and then draped it around his neck. He turned to Bob. "Okay, Ace, it's your turn now. Try to remember everything I taught you and…um, don't bust your ass." This brought another round of applause and cheers.

"All right," Bob laughed. "I'll do my best."

*   *   *   *

The afterglow from his first solo didn't last long. The next day, he returned from a routine mission with Robbie in the back seat. Everything was going fine until just before the landing. He knew he was too fast when he rounded out but pulled the power back anyway. Instead of touching down, the aircraft continued to fly. Too late, he increased the power. The aircraft dropped onto the runway with a jarring thud and bounced hard. Then it landed on the nose wheel and bounced hard again. "I've got it!" Robbie shouted, advancing the power to go-around.

Skip's next approach was okay, but by no means a smooth landing.

"What the hell was that all about?" Robbie asked.

"I don't know," Skip replied. He honestly didn't.

The next day was no better, or the day after that. It was as if he had forgotten how to land the aircraft. Robbie was perplexed and concerned. He had never seen a student lose a recently acquired skill so quickly. "I don't know what's going on here, Skip, so I am going to recommend that you fly with Captain Sparks. Maybe he can help you." Skip nodded glumly. Captain Sparks was their flight commander.

"We definitely have a problem," Sparks said after their flight. "The flight was okay, but your landings were borderline dangerous. It's probably only a temporary lapse, but there are rules. You've had four failing or marginal flights in a row. That kind of performance requires a progress check ride—there's no way around it."

Once again, Skip could do nothing but slump in his chair, listening with dogged acceptance as his dream of being a pilot began to dim. A progress check meant he was only two flights away from being eliminated from the program. It felt like he was back in primary pilot training all over again. Except this time there was no sarcasm and no suggestion that he "wasn't the flying kind." He was under intense pressure, and it came from within. "I'm going to make it," he vowed. "I swear to God I am."

*   *   *   *

The young check pilot strolled up to the briefing table looking like he didn't have a care in the world. The zippers on his flying suit were mostly unzipped, his flying scarf hung loosely around his neck, and his sleeves were rolled up to the elbows. He was wearing sunglasses. "Well," he said, plopping unceremoniously into a chair, "we're doing a progress check today, right?"

"Yes sir," Skip replied.

"Do you know what a progress check is for?"

"To decide if I should stay in the program."

"Nope. That's an elimination check. My job is to find out if you can keep up with the other students. As I see it, you were doing fine until you soloed. After that, you had a significant memory lapse, and you forgot how to land. Give me a good ride today and show me that you have regained your 'memory,' and then we'll both move on to bigger and better things, fair enough?"

"Fair enough." He was determined to do his best.

"Good," the check pilot said, standing up. "Let's go."

The check ride turned out to be marginal, at least in Skip's view. It could go either way. Now he was back at the briefing table, watching the check pilot write furiously in his grade folder. Finally, he looked up, closed the folder, and tossed it on the table. "Well, that's that. Geesh, look at the time. I'm supposed to meet my buddies at the club." He rose and turned to leave.

"Wait a minute. Did I umm…?"

"Pass? Sure. You'll be okay. Just don't get any more of those brain cramps when you're landing."

"That was a close call," Corky said. "I thought we were going to lose you." The Blunderbirds were at the club celebrating Skip's successful check ride.

"I didn't give a rat's ass about that. I was just afraid you wouldn't be around to buy us drinks," Bob said, rattling the dice cup under Skip's nose, pointedly.

"Your concern touches me," Skip grinned. "Put the friggin' cup away. I'll buy this round."

"Aw, I like it better when you lose and have to buy," Bob said. "You always get so pissed. It makes my day."

"By the way, who was your check pilot?" Corky asked.

"Captain Hopper," Skip said.

"Never heard of him."

"He's the guy at the end of the bar with all those people. The one with the sunglasses."

"Looks like he's celebrating something," Corky said. "Maybe he's happy you didn't kill him today."

"I heard someone say today was his last day," Bob said. "He got an assignment to fly fighters in Europe."

"Lucky guy!" Corky was impressed.

The check pilot looked up and noticed the three of them talking and looking his way. He raised his glass in a solemn toast in Skip's direction. He had a satisfied smile on his face. Skip raised his in return.

This guy had my whole flying career in the palm of his hand today, he thought, and he let me stay. I wonder if I really did okay, or if I got a free ride because it was his last day. Of course I did okay! He would have never passed me otherwise. He thought about walking over to talk to him but decided against it. Quit while you're ahead, he thought.

*   *   *   *

"Was that neat shit, or what?" Corky exclaimed. Skip and his friends had just returned from their first formation training flight and were having a "debriefing" at the club.

"Yeah," Bob responded. "The Blunderbirds strike again. I thought we did quite well, despite your rather ratty join-up after takeoff."

"Ratty join-up? Bullshit. I…"

"Yeah, I was going to mention that," Skip interrupted. "Thanks ever so much for not hitting me when you did that gross overshoot and had to pass under me."

"That's okay, Skip. Rave on. You can't piss me off, no matter what you say. After all, I hung in there during every one of the in-trail maneuvers, while you were bouncing around the sky like a friggin' yo-yo. I figure if I can follow you, I can follow anybody."

"He's got a point," Bob commented. "Meanwhile, we gotta start cleaning up our act. They'll be here any minute now."

"Who?" Corky asked.

"Our wives. We promised to take them out to dinner tonight. You can join us if you want. That is, unless you plan to go to Papagayo's on your endless quest to get laid." Papagayo's was a large nightclub and brothel in Nuevo Laredo just five miles from the base that was popular with the Air Force guys.

"Gee, I don't know. On Wednesday nights they usually have the girl and donkey show. I'd hate to miss that. It's one of my favorites."

"I'll bet," Skip said. "Is it true you were once offered the chance to play the donkey?"

"You should have done it," Bob said, before Corky could reply. "With your mentality you would have been perfect."

"Aww, fuck you guys. I…"

Corky was interrupted by the sight of three women waving from the doorway. Christy and Jan were wearing white summer dresses with matching sandals. They looked cool, confident, and beautiful. The third woman was a stranger. She wore a pale yellow dress with a matching lace shawl thrown casually around her shoulders. She was tall, with a curvy figure and shoulder-length, dark brown hair. Long silver earrings complimented her soft brown eyes and gleaming white teeth that shone brightly when she smiled. Every man in the bar turned to watch the three women cross the room.

"Wow," Bob said. "I wonder who she is."

"Beats me," Skip said. "Put your eyeballs back in your head, Corky, before they fall out."

Corky said nothing but continued to stare, mesmerized by the mystery woman.

"Here we are, gentlemen. Your dates for the evening," Jan said. "I suggest you move fast, though. We got a lot of offers on our way across the room."

"Yes," Christy said, "and some of them were real interesting, to say the least. By the way, this is Delores. She teaches the class we're taking at the teachers' college. Delores, this is my husband, Skip, Jan's husband, Bob, and Corky.

"Nice to meet you all." Delores smiled as she first shook Skip's hand, then Bob's. "Corky," Delores said, her eyes dancing merrily as she shook his hand, "I've heard so much about you. I feel like we've already met."

Corky tried to say something, but nothing came out. Meanwhile, his face turned beet red.

"Oh, Corky gets around," Skip chuckled. "Also, he's an accomplished actor and, umm, likes animals a lot." He flinched as Bob kicked him in the ankle.

"So," Bob said, changing the subject. "You've come to see the exciting and sinful life we live here at the base, eh?"

"Well, actually, my dad was stationed here when he was in the Air Force. He met my mom here."

That would explain the olive skin and dark brown eyes, Skip thought. I'll bet her mother is Mexican. She sure is gorgeous.

"Well enough of this chitchat," Jan said snuggling up to Bob. "Are you gonna buy me a drink big boy?"

"Sounds like a good deal to me." Bob took his wife by the arm. "Why don't we all go into the dining room and get a table?"

The dining room was not as fancy as the one at Offutt, but it was cozy. They were seated at a table by the window. The sun was setting, and the room was bathed in a soft, pink light. The jukebox in the bar was playing the Kingston Trio's latest hit, "Tom Dooley." Skip was feeling no pain, thanks to the few drinks he'd had at the bar, along with the excitement of the day's flight. This is a good life, he thought, idly squeezing Christy's hand. A day of flying, dinner and drinks with a few friends, and a good-looking wife who loves me. What more could a man ask for?

As soon as they were seated, the ladies left to powder their noses.

"So, Corky," Bob said as soon as they were out of earshot. "What do you think?"

"What do I think about what?"

"About Delores of course! This is a seriously good-looking babe. You need to put some moves on her, and fast."

"Yes, she's beautiful. But I don't think…"

"Corky, Corky, that's always been your problem. You don't think. Listen to your old Uncle Bob, it's time for you to put your five best moves on her and get on with it."

"But why would she be interested in me?"

"Why would anyone do anything? You never know until you try. Look, repeat after me: a faint heart never screwed a porcupine."

"Aww, that doesn't make any sense!"

Skip listened to them in amused silence. Finally he spoke up. "Hey Corky, don't listen to him. Sometimes a woman is just too classy or too smart for that 'if in doubt, whip it out stuff.' If that's the case, she's a keeper, and you have to play it by ear. Do what you think is right. That's what happened when I met Christy."

"Aargh," Bob said disgustedly. "Listen to you guys. What a couple of pussies!"

"Well, maybe you're right," Skip said. "But what happened when you met Jan? You met her in a bar, put a few swift moves on her, and wham-bam, right into the sack?"

"Hey wait a minute that was different. Jan was…"

"I rest my case," Skip said as the ladies returned.

"What were you guys talking about?" Jan asked.

"Oh, just man's talk," Corky said.

"Yeah," Skip said. "Bob was just telling us how you two met."

"Yes, it was quite by accident. I was working in the school library, and he kept hanging around the circulation desk asking me for books he didn't need. It took him three weeks to muster up enough courage to ask me out, and when he did, he was so shy. But he was very sweet and still is, aren't you baby?" she said, pinching Bob's cheek.

"I think that's a wonderful story," Skip said. "Don't you, Corky?"

"Yeah, very touching." They both grinned broadly. Bob squirmed uncomfortably in his chair and glared at them.

"Miss me?" Christy seductively ran her fingers up the back of Skip's neck.

"Big-time."

"Would you hold on to these for me, please?" she said, handing him something under the table.

"Sure." Skip reached under the table to take whatever it was. As soon as he touched the soft silkiness of what she was handing him, he realized they were her panties. "Yes, right. No problem. I'll just, uh…" He quickly dropped them into one of his flying suit pockets and quickly zipped it up.

"I don't think I will be needing them tonight, do you?" she asked, looking at him innocently."

"Definitely not."

"Need what?" Jan asked.

"Oh, nothing." Skip fidgeted in his chair.

As the night wore on, there were more drinks, more laughs, and an enjoyable meal, but Skip scarcely noticed. His mind was focused on just one thing—the pair of panties in his pocket. It was her way of telling him that he had been neglecting her lately, and she was right. But that wasn't going to happen tonight. He couldn't wait to get her home.

The neighborhood was serenely quiet when they got to the house. All that could be heard was the steady strumming of crickets. Walking arm in arm onto the front porch, he opened the door and flipped the porch light off. He maneuvered her inside and up against the wall in the hallway. Then he began to kiss her neck.

"My, my," Christy said, "somebody is certainly eager."

"What did you expect after you handed me your panties under the table? It sure got my attention."

"It got someone else's attention too, I see," she giggled.

He wasted no time getting her upstairs. In the bedroom he laid her on the bed while he turned on a small lamp. He wanted to see everything, which was always the best part. Clothes and underwear were quickly removed and flung aside. Then, he was on top of her in a frenzy of passion. "Honey," she said, clutching his head, "aren't you forgetting something? Shouldn't you…" His reply was muffled. One of her breasts was in his mouth. "Never mind," she moaned, as he plunged deep inside her.

*   *   *   *

"B-52s?" Bob exclaimed. "You want to be a bomber puke when you graduate? Give me a friggin' break!"

"Shhh," Skip said. "Keep your voice down. You don't have to tell the whole club. Besides, I didn't say I wanted to fly B-52s. I just thought…"

"You just thought what? Gee, it might be fun to fly around straight and level all day in this huge piece of crap with eight engines hanging under the wings? Is that what you thought?"

"No, but…"

"Think about it man, they call the B-52 the BUF. Do you know what that stands for?"

"Of course I do. Big-Ugly-Fucker."

"And that's what you want to fly?"

"Not exactly. It's just that Christy and I talked it over and thought it would be a nice stable four-year assignment. There would be very little TDY, and I'd be home every night for dinner."

"Ahh, I get it." Bob slapped his forehead. "You're going to let the little woman decide for you. How could I have been so dense?"

"I didn't say that. It's my decision of course."

Bob leaned over and spoke directly into Skip's face. "I don't want to get into your personal life, but Jan and I have an arrangement that works pretty well. When the baby was born she didn't ask me how to nurse him. Why? Because I am not an expert on that subject. On the other hand, I do not consult with her about flying matters, and I'm sure as hell not going to ask her advice about what aircraft to fly after I get my wings. See what I mean?"

Skip nodded miserably.

"Besides," Bob continued, "I thought we went through all this already. Fighters, it's the only way to go. Fly once or twice a day, go out to the gunnery range, maybe do a little air-to-air combat, then a quick debrief, and we're off to the club for happy hour. It's going to be a sweet life."

"Well," Skip said doubtfully, "it's probably all academic anyway."

"Why?"

"I heard a rumor that there will only be five fighter assignments for our class. Five assignments for a class of sixty. Do you realize what that means?"

"Yeah, it means the Blunderbirds and two other lucky guys will be flying fighters. The rest of the assholes in our class will end up being bomber and transport pukes."

"It also means that I'll have to graduate in the top ten percent of my class to get one of those assignments. It's based on class standings, remember? That's gonna be pretty tough, considering I almost washed out a month ago."

"I know that. But I also know that flying grades only count one third toward the final standing. One third is based on academic grades, and the other third on military performance. Nobody ever figured out what the hell the military part is all about, though. My guess is it's based on how well you suck up to your instructor and the flight commander."

"So?"

"So, who's aced every test in academics? And which student does Robbie think the sun rises and sets on? I'll tell you who. It's Skip, the pink-cheeked, all-American boy who can do no wrong. I've even heard the flight commander talk about Lieutenant O'Neill and what a fine young officer he is. It's enough to make me puke."

"Aww, give me a break."

"I *am* giving you a break. I'm trying to tell you that if everything falls into place the right way, you might be in the top ten percent. It's a long shot, but it could happen."

"I don't know," Skip said stubbornly. "The idea of a nice stable life is kind of appealing too."

"Okay, okay," Bob said wearily. "The way I see it, if you want to run with the big dogs, you have a chance. If you don't, well, that's your decision."

"Hey guys! What's up?" Corky was in a good mood. He had just talked to Delores, and she agreed to have dinner with him on Saturday night.

"Pull up a barstool," Bob said. "We have a major emergency on our hands."

"Well, the doctor is in. What seems to be the problem?"

"Our boy Skip here wants to fly B-52s when he graduates."

"Holy shit!" Corky said, looking at Skip with mock horror. "Are you out of your mind?" Bob said nothing but rolled his eyes back in exasperation.

"I didn't say I was going to fly B-52s," Skip protested. "It's just something we...I mean...I have been thinking about."

"Hmm," Corky said, "this is a problem that requires serious dialogue and all our analytical skills. Bob, I assume you went over the whole deal about the joys of being a fighter pilot?"

"Yep, I covered all the points," Bob responded solemnly.

"And he was still not convinced?"

"Nope."

"Okay Skip, let's hear your side of the story."

Skip was beginning to feel uncomfortable, but he told his side of the story again.

"Well, if that's what you want, why be a pilot at all? Why not work at a bank in a small town? You could have a cozy little white house, with a picket fence, a garden, and the whole thing."

Skip was getting angry. "You guys just don't get it, do you?"

"How's Delores doing?" Bob asked, quickly changing the subject.

"Great," Corky said. "She's a neat lady."

"Get in her pants yet?"

"Aww come on, Bob, how many times do I have to tell you? It's not that kind of deal. She's not that kind of girl."

"That means no," Bob said.

Skip drove home thinking about the conversation he just had with his friends and decided they were absolutely right. He had always wanted to be a fighter pilot and never pictured himself flying anything else. Why was he hesitating now, acting like a loser? Because the odds were against him? They were against him back in primary when Ross was about to shove him out the door and again when he took that progress check here in Laredo. But he had hung tough, and somehow survived. He hadn't been a quitter so far, and he wasn't about to start now. He and Christy needed to have another talk about assignments.

*   *   *   *

Christy was troubled by Skip's decision to be a fighter pilot. They spent hours talking about various assignments, and in the end, she had convinced him that he should go to B-52s. She didn't want to control him, but she knew it was her job to make a stable life for the family. This was important, now more than ever. But Skip didn't know that. How could he? She had to tell him, soon.

She was not feeling well this morning. No big surprise there. Lying in bed with an untouched cup of coffee at her side, she reviewed the options. Assignments were based on class standings, and there would be only a handful of fighter assignments available. Chances are, he won't qualify for one, she thought. She felt bad about that for Skip's sake, but that's the way it was. In that case, the problem will go away. But what if he does? She closed her eyes and tried to think. Her head ached, and her stomach felt queasy. Assignments won't be selected until Friday, so there's still time. The question is how to change his mind. Skip can be so damned stubborn sometimes. Suddenly, her thoughts were interrupted by the memory of Penney's words, "Men like my Tom and your Skip are in the Air Force because they want to be. It is not a job to them; it is a way of life. It's who they are. If you persuade them to change, they won't be happy, and they'll never forgive you." Well, there you have it, she thought. Persuading him not to be a fighter pilot would be persuading him to change, wouldn't it? I have to stand aside and let him do what he thinks is best. I'll wait until he gets his assignment. Then I'll tell him the news.

*   *   *   *

The class standings list was posted the same morning. Skip approached it with dread. He was so pessimistic that he began reading it from the bottom up. To his amazement, he graduated seventh in his class of sixty. He was overjoyed. There was a good chance that he could go to fighters. He couldn't wait to go home and tell Christy.

Christy took the news well and seemed to be happy for him. Still, he could tell something was wrong. Her face was pale and drawn, and there were dark circles under her eyes. She's probably sick, he thought. Maybe she's coming down with the flu.

The next day, sixty students stood anxiously in a small meeting room set aside in the club. The air of excitement was palpable. Today they would choose their assignments.

Skip paced the floor nervously. "What do you think, Bob?"

"I think you've got a good shot at it."

Corky nodded his head. "I agree. Five chances out of seven are not bad odds."

"I don't know…"

"Listen up, guys," a young lieutenant from the school secretary's office said. He was standing by a small curtained partition. "When I call your name, go in and report to the assignment board. They'll ask you for assignment preference. Your flight commander and instructor will be there. If everybody agrees, you've got it. It's as simple as that. Good luck."

"Lieutenant Dunn."

"Don't worry about him," Bob said. "He wants to fly transports in Germany. His wife is German, and she wants to be near her family." Moments later Dunn emerged smiling. "C-118s at Ramstein," he told a friend.

"Odds are looking better," Corky said. "Five out of six now."

"Lieutenant Caldwell." No help there. Everyone knew he wanted to fly F-100s.

"Lieutenant Lewis."

"Oh, oh," Bob said dramatically. "Show time!" Moments later he emerged grinning.

The fellow after Bob also chose F-100s. Now it was Corky's turn. "One more to go," he said when he came out. "Hang in there, Skip."

"Lieutenant Rogers."

Skip looked at Bob and Corky quizzically. Both shrugged their shoulders. Nobody knew what Rogers would choose. Skip was so nervous he could hardly breathe. One man stood between him and what he wanted. His future was in the hands of someone he didn't know. Rogers didn't come out right away. Time seemed to stand still. When he finally came out, Skip asked him anxiously, "What did you choose?"

"Interceptors," he replied. "Didn't think I was going to get it, but I lucked out."

Skip let out his breath in relief. He was almost there. "Lieutenant O'Neill."

He stepped through the curtain and saluted crisply. Three captains sat at a small folding table. One of them was carefully checking a list of names. Robbie and his flight commander sat off to one side. "Well, Lieutenant. What will it be?"

"F-100s, I want to be a fighter pilot, sir."

"Jim?"

"I agree."

"Robbie?"

"I agree."

"F-100s it is then, Lieutenant O'Neill."

"Thank you sir," he said, saluting and doing an about-face. He wanted to let out a cheer when he walked through the curtain. Instead, he clasped his hands above his head in a sign of victory, grinning broadly. The Blunderbirds surrounded him and began to pound his back.

"This calls for a celebration," Corky said.

"Not me," Skip said. "I'm going home to tell Christy. I'm worried about her. She hasn't been herself lately. I think she's coming down with something."

There were no roads from the base worthy of his Le Mans driving skills, but he drove home with reckless abandon anyway. Bounding across the front porch whistling, he burst through the door. "Christy," he started to shout, but she was right there waiting for him.

"How did it go, honey?"

"F-100s." He hugged her and spun her around "I got the last one."

"Oh baby, I'm so glad! I know how much you wanted that. Let's sit down. I want you to tell me all about it."

She seems truly happy for me, Skip thought, yet, there's something in her eyes. Something's not right. They sat on the living room sofa while Skip told her the whole story, about the torturous countdown until he grabbed up the last assignment, and how excited he was that the Blunderbirds would be able to stay together.

"Phoenix, Arizona," she said. "I've never been there. It will be hot, I suspect, especially in July."

"Over one hundred degrees, every day. But it's a dry heat, and hey, it's only for six months."

Christy nodded wanly. The talk about the hot, desert heat had turned her face still another shade of gray.

Skip took both of Christy's hands in his and looked earnestly into her eyes. "Honey, I know flying F-100s wasn't what we talked about, and I'm sure you're disappointed, but it's the right thing to do. It's going to be fine. You'll see."

"I know it will. Anyway, who knows what's right and what's wrong? Only time will tell. The B-52 thing wasn't about your career, it was about our family. I realize that now. It seemed so right, and I figured with the baby coming…"

"The what?" Skip was dumbfounded.

"The baby. I'm pregnant. I found out for sure the day before yesterday."

"But, I mean…I'm shocked. How did that happen?"

There was a sparkle in her eyes, and for an instant the old Christy had returned. "How did it happen? The usual way. You know, man and woman make love. Didn't your dad tell you about all that?"

"Stop it. You know what I mean. We are always so careful."

"Well, not always."

"The night you gave me your panties at the club. Of course!"

"Bingo. That's when you shot the silver bullet, cowboy, and hit a bull's-eye."

"A baby! This changes everything. Why didn't you tell me?"

"Because I didn't want you to choose an assignment based on that. I knew that's just what you would have done if had I told you. We keep calling it an assignment, but it's much more than that. It's a fork in the road. A career path that will decide what our lives will be like for years to come. Besides, fighter pilots' wives get knocked up all the time, don't they?" She smiled mischievously. "Excuse me," she said suddenly, and rushed out of the room. There was the sound of the bathroom door slamming, water running, and finally, the toilet flushing. She returned looking miserable.

"Morning sickness," he said. It all made sense now.

"I don't know why they call it morning sickness," Christy replied. "Twenty-four-hours-a-day sickness is more like it."

"Honey?" Christy said as they lay in bed recapping the day's events. "Are you really glad we're having a baby? It's not something we talked about."

"It's a wonderful thing, and I couldn't be happier. One thing bothers me though."

"What's that?"

"Well, we're always so careful about protection. Did this happen because you wanted it to? I mean, it's not like you to make a decision like that on your own."

"I don't know. I honestly don't. I remember thinking about protection and even saying something. Then suddenly it didn't seem important, and I forgot about it."

"Well, I'm glad you did. It's going to be a beautiful baby."

"Our baby," he said later, placing his head on her stomach. "Listen, I can hear it moving."

"Don't be silly. It's too early to hear anything."

"Really? Oh well, as long as I am down here…" He began to kiss her belly and then moved down between her legs.

"Stop it," she giggled. "We've got to get some sleep and start packing tomorrow."

F-100 Combat Crew
Training

Luke Air Force Base, Arizona
July 1960

The blazing sun beat down on the ramp, causing waves of heat to shimmer above the concrete. Skip could feel patches of melted asphalt sticking to the soles of his flying boots as he walked toward his aircraft. Although it was not yet ten o'clock, the temperature was already over a hundred degrees. It was a typical summer day for Phoenix, Arizona. But it was not a typical day for him. After weeks of waiting, he was going to fly the F-100 for the first time.

The F-100 Super Saber, affectionately called the "Hun," was the first Air Force operational aircraft capable of flying faster than the speed of sound in level flight. Although it was designed to destroy aircraft in aerial combat, its role had changed over the years to ground attack. It was a beautiful aircraft. The wings and horizontal stabilizer were swept back, as was the vertical stabilizer. On the ground, the aircraft sat firmly on its main landing gear, its nose raised slightly, giving the illusion that it was ready to leap into the air at any second. Its most distinctive feature was the scoop in the nose, which fed air to its single engine. He first noted the scoop when he saw an F-100 make a high-speed, low-level pass during an air show. The aircraft was coming straight at him at five hundred knots and two hundred feet above the ground, with dust and debris boiling in its wake. From his vantage point, it looked like a monstrous catfish devouring everything in front of it as it passed over with an ear-splitting roar. It was an incredible sight.

He would be flying with an instructor in the two-seater version, the F-100F, because it was his first flight. Students flew with a different instructor on every flight. Each instructor had a personal call sign, which he chose to reflect his personality or outlook on life. Skip's instructor today was "Rowdy." He had seen Rowdy in action during happy hour and had no doubt he was aptly named.

It was the busiest time of the day at Luke, and by the time they arrived the noise was deafening, as dozens of aircraft started their engines and began to taxi, some singly, others in flights of two or four. The F-100 cockpit sat higher above the ground than any aircraft Skip had flown thus far, and once he got there, he took a moment to look down at the ground crew scurrying around, preparing for the launch. It was a much different view than from the T-Bird cockpit, and he liked the feeling of power and confidence it gave him. After his shoulder harness, lap belt, and oxygen hose were secured, he put on his helmet and started the engine. When he was ready, he released the brakes and increased the power. The aircraft glided easily out of the parking space. He turned down the row of parked aircraft and headed for the main taxiway.

It was a clear day, and as he taxied out, the sky was so bright and blue that it hurt his eyes, even with his sun visor down. The surrounding mountains stood boldly on the horizon, appearing nearer than they really were, their image altered ever-so-slightly through the prism of the shimmering heat waves. As he approached the runway, he saw four F-100s line abreast in the arming area with engines running, their pilots waiting expectantly, as the armament crew dashed around, cocking the twenty-millimeter cannons and arming the practice bombs that hung in racks under the wings. They were off to the gunnery range, and he wanted to be with them. Slow down, he thought. You haven't even learned to fly this beast yet. There'll be plenty of time to shoot the guns later.

It was time to go. Skip had closed and locked the canopy. All was quiet now except for the soft idling of the engine and Rowdy's rhythmic breathing in the back on the intercom. The aircraft glided easily onto the runway, and Skip lined it up on the centerline.

"Rowdy, wind is zero-five-zero at five knots, cleared for takeoff."

"Roger, cleared for takeoff."

He held the brakes and advanced the throttle to full power. The engine responded quickly, accelerating from a soft purring idle to a deafening roar. Glancing into the cockpit, he could see that all of the instruments were in the green. Meanwhile, the aircraft was shaking and straining against the brakes. It wanted to fly now, and he could hardly hold it back. "Rowdy is rolling," Skip called out as he released the brakes and lit the afterburner.

What happened in the next two minutes was reduced to a single blur of activity that Skip could scarcely remember afterwards. The afterburner lit with a resounding crack, pushing his head against the headrest and causing the aircraft to shoot forward like a thoroughbred coming out of the gate determined to lead the pack. Things began to happen quickly. Meanwhile, Rowdy came to life in the backseat, issuing a non-stop barrage of cues and reminders in a crisp and authoritative voice. "Nose wheel liftoff speed...rotate the nose twenty degrees above the horizon! Gear up, gear up...the gear down limit speed is 275, you're already doing three hundred! Watch your climb speed; you're going too fast...the afterburner climb speed is four hundred knots. Get the nose up!" Rowdy grinned to himself. It always starts out this way on the first flight, he thought. His brain is still on the end of the runway. He'll catch up, though.

By the time Skip settled down, the aircraft was passing ten thousand, still in afterburner; nose thirty degrees above the horizon. On the instrument panel, the altimeter was spinning crazily like a gyro gone out of control. The vertical velocity indicator was pegged at its limit—six thousand feet per minute, although he was climbing much faster. At twenty-five thousand feet, the flight controls began to lighten as they bit into the less dense air. It was quiet in the cockpit now. The landscape had fallen away as they climbed and was now reduced to a vast, brown mosaic, whose features were blurred and distant. Even the mountains seemed small and insignificant. This is cool, Skip thought. Must be how it feels to be on the nose of one of those rockets they launch at Cape Canaveral, untethered and free to float away.

"Watch your altitude," Rowdy said sharply.

"Huh?" Skip snapped out of his daydreaming state

"You were supposed to level off at forty-five thousand feet."

He looked at the altimeter and saw they were at forty-eight thousand feet. He couldn't believe it. They had only been airborne for six minutes. He pulled the throttle out of afterburner and coasted back down to the proper altitude. They were cruising high above a vast desert now. "Might as well start with the supersonic bit," Rowdy said. "Everybody needs to break the sound barrier at least once in their lives, just to say they did it. I must warn you though, it'll probably be the last time you do it for awhile. By the time you hang fuel tanks, bombs, and rockets on this baby you'll be lucky to get it up to a decent cruise speed, much less supersonic." Skip eased the nose of the aircraft below the horizon, then engaged the afterburner and quickly shut it down, as it rapidly gained speed. The mach meter read .95...then .98. They were almost there. Suddenly, the altimeter reversed itself, backed up one thousand feet, and then resumed its descent. The mach meter read over 1.0. They were supersonic.

"Not much to that," he said, slowing the aircraft back down. "I could hardly tell it happened."

"There's a bunch of prairie dogs down there that knew it happened," Rowdy chuckled. The sonic boom probably spoiled their whole day.

They remained at altitude for another thirty minutes or so while Skip performed a series of maneuvers designed to demonstrate the handling characteristics of the aircraft. Then it was time to head back to the base. They had only been airborne for forty-five minutes, but the afterburner climb had taken its toll on fuel.

Landing the F-100 was not so much a matter of rounding out and feeling for the runway, as it was breaking the rate of descent just before touch down. He timed it just right, and the aircraft kissed the runway with a comfortable thud. When he deployed the drag chute, it blossomed immediately, and the aircraft slowed down appreciably. There was plenty of runway left when they turned onto the taxiway.

"Good job," Rowdy said.

"Beginner's luck," Skip replied.

After the flight, he went to the club for a quick drink but didn't stay long. Christy hadn't been feeling well lately, and he wanted to check on her. It was 105 degrees when he drove into the carport of their on-base quarters. The small cinder-block house was more than adequate for their needs: two bedrooms, a large kitchen with a dining alcove, parquet floors, and best of all, central air conditioning. They were still in the process of moving in. Boxes were everywhere, while clothing and kitchenware lay stacked on tables, shelves, and the floor. In the center of the chaos stood Christy. Her face was pale and drawn, with beads of sweat glistening on her forehead. Her hair hung in damp strings. She was wearing a nondescript, two-piece maternity outfit with a long top and toreador pants. The khaki material was damp and wrinkled, the drawstring on the pants let out to accommodate her swelling belly.

"Hi honey," Skip said cheerily.

"Hullo," Christy replied.

"You'll never guess what I did today."

"What?"

"I flew the F-100 for the first time, and I broke the sound barrier."

"That's nice," Christy replied dully.

"That's nice?" Skip said laughing. "It was only one of the most exciting days in my life. That's all. How was your day?"

"How was my day? Hmm, let me think. Well, first I played a few sets of tennis in the morning, then had a sauna and lunch at the spa, and…oh yeah, I had tea with the Queen of England after that."

"Geesh, Christy, I just meant…"

"How do you think my day was?" Christy continued, her hand sweeping expansively around the room, as her voice became louder. "Boxes, boxes, boxes…everywhere I look. And the more boxes I unpack, the more I find. I'm hot, I'm tired, and I don't feel good. Meanwhile, you're off flying around the sky having a great time, breaking the sound barrier and playing with your big shiny toys. Does that answer your question?"

"Aww, I'm sorry baby. I didn't realize…"

"And you know what else, Lieutenant O'Neill?" Her voice was beginning to quiver now. "I hate this life. I hate this heat. I hate the Air Force, and I'm never going to move again." She flung the towel she was holding, across the room, where it crashed against the venetian blinds with a rattling thump and fell to the floor. Then she burst into tears and rushed into his arms.

"Hey, hey," Skip began to croon, rocking her in his arms. "It'll be all right. I had no idea things were that bad. Tell you what, let me get out of this smelly flying suit and spend a couple of hours unpacking things. Meanwhile, you can lie down for a bit and maybe take a cool bath afterwards. Then we'll go out for dinner. Would you like that?"

Christy nodded, still sobbing into his chest.

He attacked the task of unpacking with determination. What he lacked in neatness, he made up for in sheer volume of work done. In two hours, more than half of the boxes were emptied, their contents placed more or less where they should be. Meanwhile Christy took a nap and had a long bath.

"Where are we going for dinner?" she asked, coming out of the bedroom. She was wearing a long, crisp white dress with sandals. Her hair was brushed, and she was wearing makeup.

"We'll figure something out," Skip smiled. "Maybe we'll try that little Italian café just outside the main gate."

"Can we? I'd like that."

That night as they lay in bed, Christy asked, "Do you think it will be a boy or a girl?"

"I don't know."

"Well, you must have an opinion. What do you want it to be?"

"I don't know. What do you want it to be?"

"I asked you first," Christy giggled.

"Well, whatever it is he or she will have your looks and brains."

"We need to think of some names, you know."

"I know."

"I bought a book today with a list of names for babies. Can we look at it tomorrow?"

"You bet."

"Honey?"

"Yeah?"

"I'm sorry I was such a bitch today."

"It's okay, baby. You're entitled. You had a rough day."

"And it really *is* going to be a good life, you know?"

Skip laid his head back on the pillow and closed his eyes. In his mind he could see himself streaking across the bright blue sky, high above the Arizona desert. "Yeah," he said. "It really is."

*   *   *   *

Skip didn't have to wait long to shoot the guns. Just ten days after his first flight in the F-100, he was airborne on his first gunnery mission. For the first time since they started F-100 training, the Blunderbirds were all flying together. Bob was in the number two position, flying on the wing of the instructor, and Corky was flying on Skip's wing. "That's a good position for you," Skip had told Corky after the briefing. "Just hang back and watch what I do. You'll learn a lot."

"I think they put me there to keep an eye on you, to make sure you don't get lost or bust your ass," he had replied.

The gunnery range complex was at Gila Bend. It was a small, dusty place in the middle of southern Arizona. In the center was a small airfield surrounded by buildings to house supplies and support equipment. The whole operation was manned by a hundred or so men. The runway was just long enough for a jet to land in case of emergency. Outside the airfield were thousands of acres with gunnery ranges of all kinds. Some were structured, or "conventional ranges," with bombing circles and strafe targets, highlighted by lines of white paint on the ground. At other locations, hundreds of obsolete tanks, trucks, and artillery pieces were nestled in the hills and valleys. These were the "tactical ranges" where pilots could hone their gunnery skills in a more realistic environment.

The rules of the road on the conventional ranges were simple and designed to avoid midair collisions in the frenzied, fast-paced environment in which they were flying. The traffic pattern was an imaginary rectangular box with each aircraft at a different corner. Thus, when one was turning final, another was pulling off the target. Meanwhile, a third was turning base, and a fourth was on downwind. It was all very logical and necessary, considering the aircraft were maneuvering in a tight space at 350 knots or more.

The first event when the flight arrived was skip bombing, a maneuver that required a final attack run at fifty feet above the ground and four hundred knots. The hardest part was deciding when the aircraft was at fifty feet. Instruments were of no use in this situation; it was all done by looking outside the cockpit. Skip decided that when the ground seemed to surround him, and the horizon appeared to be higher than the cockpit, he was at about fifty feet.

Skip rolled in on his first skip bomb pass and descended to fifty feet. Things were moving fast now. Rocks, bushes, and trees were screaming toward him, looking as if they were about to come through the windscreen. Up ahead, he could see the skip bomb target—a large canvas panel suspended between two telephone poles. The idea was to drop the bomb just short of the target so that it skipped through. He was drifting slightly so he made a correction to the right. "Try to drag your ass right across the center of the target," his instructor had said. "When the gun sight reaches the base of the target, hit the pickle button, and let it fly." The pickle button was slang for the bomb release button on the control stick. Skip did as he had been told. As the target streaked by, he released the bomb, and then pulled smartly up and away.

"Three's off," he said.

"Hit on the fly, Three," the range officer reported. This meant the bomb flew straight through the target, which was as good as a skip-hit. It was a good start.

Each aircraft dropped four skip bombs. When it was over, the leader pulled into a steep climbing turn to a 4,500-foot downwind for the first dive-bomb attack. Dive-bombing was tricky and required a lot of finesse. There were no computers or special instruments to help during the attack. It was all done by the seat of one's pants. The target was off to one side—two concentric circles, 150 and 300 feet in diameter. The idea was to roll in at four hundred knots with a thirty degree dive angle and place the aiming point in the gun sight or "pipper" in the center of the target, correct for the wind, and then drop the bomb when the proper release altitude was reached. Every parameter was critical. If any of them were off—airspeed, dive angle, or release altitude—then the bomb would likely miss the target.

When all the bombs had been dropped, the flight dropped to the original pattern altitude for strafing. This was the most difficult event and required the most concentration, because everything happened so fast. There were four strafe targets, one for each aircraft. The target was a ten-by-twenty-foot panel with a bull's-eye in the center, suspended between two poles. An acoustical counter heard the bullets pass through the target and compiled the number of hits. A perpendicular line was drawn sixteen hundred feet in front of the targets. Firing past this line was a foul. Each target was identified by a white lead-in line that extended from the foul line to the base of the target. The lead-in lines were useful for tracking the target and computing the wind drift. As Skip rolled in on his first strafe pass, he set the dive angle at fifteen degrees and accelerated to four hundred knots. The gun sight wandered aimlessly on the ground for a second or two, until Skip eased it along the lead-in line and up onto the bulls-eye. At two thousand feet slant range, he pulled the trigger and fired a short burst. Just as he did, the wind drifted the aircraft to the left. "Zero hits," the range officer said. Shit! Skip thought. There was the faint sound of a Bronx cheer on the radio. That's gotta be Bob. Who else? That asshole!

On his second pass, Bob got sixty-five hits. This was unheard of for a student. In fact, it was a damn good score even for an instructor. Skip sighed. He's going be a pain in the ass at happy hour tonight.

Thirty minutes after they arrived, it was over, and the four aircraft were off the range, and on their way home.

$$* \qquad * \qquad * \qquad *$$

"Sixty-five hits!" Bob crowed, flexing his finger as if pulling a trigger. Is this a golden finger or what?"

"I've got a golden finger for you," Skip replied. "Would you like to see it?"

"Now, now, jealousy doesn't become you. I mean, talent is an awesome thing to compete with."

"Talent, my ass. Luck is more like it."

"Maybe so, but then I have to say that I was very lucky today, considering my stellar performance on the range. This leads me to your performance Skip—zero hits on not one, but two strafe passes. Using your definition of talent I guess we can say you were unlucky today, right?"

"Maybe so," Skip replied weakly.

"Unlucky?" Corky said walking up to the bar. "Incompetent is more like it."

"Ah, Corky," Skip said. "So nice of you to join us. You're just in time to buy the first round."

"Me? Why me? I didn't have the worst scores today."

"You know the rules. A foul automatically qualifies you to buy the first round. And may I say that as fouls go, yours was a beauty."

"Yeah," Bob said, "I understand the range officer crapped in his pants when you almost crashed into the skip bomb target. You see, my man, the idea is for you to hit the target with the bomb, not the aircraft. Anyway, it would have been a tragedy if you had killed yourself out there today."

"Yeah," Skip said solemnly, "A real tragedy. Who would buy the drinks if you were gone?"

"Okay, okay," Corky said. "I'll buy the first round. But I think Skip should buy the second, because he had the worst scores."

"Okay," Skip said.

"By the way, Skip," Bob said, "are you and Christy gonna be able to join us for dinner Saturday?"

"Yeah, I guess so. What's the occasion?"

"What's the occasion? I guess you haven't heard. Our boy Corky is having a visitor this weekend…a very special visitor."

"No kidding! Who?"

"None other than the Mexican bombshell La Senorita Delores, direct from the sunny banks of the Rio Grande River."

"You sly devil, you!" Skip said. "Must be getting serious for her to come all this way just for a visit." Corky shifted uncomfortably in his chair and began to turn red.

"I assume you've finally gotten in her pants," Bob said, leaning over the bar and speaking in a low confidential tone. "I mean, it was not looking promising back in Laredo, but surely by now…"

"Dammit Bob, how many times do I have to tell you. It's not that kind of deal."

"Still no luck, eh? I've got an idea. The first night when she's getting ready for bed, we'll all get under her window and sing a serenade. You know…Aye, Aye, Aye, Aye." Bob strummed an imaginary guitar. "Then we'll leave, and you'll be in like a bunny rabbit."

Corky groaned and slumped against the bar, his head in his hands. "You guys just don't get it."

"Look, if you keep that 'it's not that kind of deal' shit up, you'll end up like my boy Skip here—a newlywed whose wife has a bun in the oven, and Lord knows how many kids there'll be after that."

"The voice of experience," Skip commented.

"Yep, which reminds me, how's Christy feeling these days?"

"Much better. It was a little dicey for awhile, though."

"Women do get a little testy when they're pregnant. Especially in the early months."

"A little testy? That's a gross understatement. A few weeks ago she nearly ripped my head off for absolutely no reason. I swear to God!"

"Well, just hang in there for a few more weeks, and the worst will be over."

"I certainly hope so," Skip said.

*   *   *   *

Looking back on his experience on the gunnery range, it all seemed so easy. But Skip knew that if he were ever called on to apply those skills in actual combat, things would be much different. There would be no shiny circles and bright straight lines pointing to a target so obvious that only the visually impaired could miss it. But this was the Cold War era when the world trembled at the thought of an all-out nuclear exchange between the United States and Soviet Union, and Pentagon planners devoted most of their energies to fine-tuning the Single Integrated Operations Plan or "SIOP," a sequence of events that brought to bear all available aircraft, missile, and submarine forces in a way that would assure ultimate victory.

The F-100 was part of the SIOP, and many squadrons, especially in forward overseas locations, were designated almost exclusively to that mission. Pilots in these so-called "nuke squadrons" rarely practiced strafing and conventional bombing, but instead visited gunnery ranges regularly to hone their skills in the low-angle bombing system delivery, or "LABS" as it was called. This was a crude but effective way to deliver a nuclear weapon slung below the aircraft by performing a half-loop, slinging the bomb far above the aircraft, and dashing to safety while it fell back to earth. Seasoned fighter pilots tried to avoid nuke squadrons whenever possible and derisively refer to the LABS deliveries as "idiot circles." Skip didn't want to be assigned to a nuke squadron either, but he knew that when the time came, he would have no say in the matter.

His training at Luke would be finished in mid-February, but it didn't end there. He and his classmates would be obliged to endure three more months of advanced combat crew training at Nellis Air Force Base, Nevada, often referred to as "fighter town," because it was the home of the fighter weapons school and the Air Force aerial demonstration team, the Thunderbirds. Only then would they be certified as combat-ready F-100 pilots and sent to serve in a squadron somewhere in the world.

*   *   *   *

Madeline Nicole O'Neill made her grand entrance on January 15, 1961, and swept Skip and Christy off their feet. She was a perfect child with bright blue eyes, dark brown hair, and the high-cheeked beauty of her mother. The first time Skip held her, he decided there could be no more perfect testimony to a love between a man and a woman than this wriggling child who stripped away every vestige of his macho, fighter-pilot image, exposing a heretofore unknown sensitive man underneath.

But there was little time to enjoy the moment—just four weeks to be precise. During that time, the respective grandparents traveled to Phoenix to pay homage to the new reigning princess and help Christy with chores. Then the new family of three packed their belongings and drove to Las Vegas.

Fighter Town

The KB-50 tanker lumbered high above the Nevada desert, the massive propellers from its four engines slicing through the night air. The sky above was overcast, obscuring the moon and stars. A solid layer of clouds below left the aircraft and its crew suspended in a black void without visual reference to the horizon.

The tanker was brightly lit. Blinking green and red navigation lights on the wingtips and tail defined its shape, while floodlights bathed the fuselage, wings, and surrounding area in a white glow. The hemisphere of light around the aircraft created the image of a brightly lit arena suspended in midair. Three refueling hoses were reeled out fifty feet behind the aircraft; one directly behind the fuselage, and two from pods mounted on the end of each wing. On the end of each hose was a funnel-shaped steel basket, three feet in diameter. Behind each basket, an F-100 was struggling to refuel, as the hose and basket dangled and whipped in the air erratically.

The KB-50 was a World War II-vintage bomber converted for the refueling mission. It was too slow to refuel jet fighters, but it was the only aircraft in the Air Force inventory available to perform the task. Its refueling speed was only twenty knots faster the landing speed of the F-100. This forced the F-100 to refuel with its nose raised above the horizon, in an envelope that was not optimum for precise maneuvering.

It was a surrealistic scene, the brightly lit tanker, its hoses and baskets swaying in the air, along with the three F-100s, bobbing and weaving, trying to hook up, but Skip had no time to enjoy it. He was behind the basket on the left wing, desperately struggling to refuel. He had tried and failed five times so far. He was getting tired and frustrated.

In class, the subject of aerial refueling evoked a typical "it's gonna be a piece of cake" response from Skip, and in fact, it wasn't a complicated maneuver, not in theory anyway. The F-100 was equipped with a six-foot refueling probe attached to the wing root on the right side. The probe was bent upwards and then straightened at the end, so the pilot could see the tip of the probe. To hook up, the pilot was obliged to stabilize behind the tanker, aim the probe at the center of the basket, and then move forward slowly until it entered the basket and locked into place. After that, it was just a matter of holding the aircraft in position while fuel was transferred.

Each hose and basket was controlled by a boom operator, whose job was to reel the hose in and out, manage the fuel transfer, and call out directions to keep the fighter in position. Corrections were given in terms of direction and distance in feet needed to stay in position. For example, "Up two…Forward one…Down three…"

"The way I see it," Bob once said, "it's just matter of holding your tool steady and sticking it in, then staying there until you get what you want. I mean, we all know how to do that, right? What's the big deal?" This observation had drawn a round of laughter from Skip and Corky.

But Skip was not laughing now. He was too busy. Everything was moving at the same time in different directions. The tanker pitched and bobbled as it struck pockets of turbulent air, while its prop wash swept across the wing causing both the basket and his aircraft to weave from side to side. As he struggled to stay in position, his aircraft seesawed and bucked, sometimes at dangerously low airspeeds. He eased forward for another try. "Receiver's ready," he announced. He was four feet back with the probe aimed at the center of the basket.

"Tanker, ready," the boom operator replied.

Skip inched forward. From the corner of his eye he could see that everything was aligned. Trying to relax, he eased forward. The probe pressed against the rim of the basket, and for a teasing second, he thought he had missed again. Then he felt a slight "thunk" as the hose whipped forward and curved into an S shape.

"Contact, tanker."

"Contact, receiver." He was hooked up at last.

This would be a "wet stick," meaning he would only receive one thousand pounds of fuel, just for practice.

Skip worked hard to maintain his position. It wasn't easy.

"Good connection. You're receiving fuel. Up two…Back one…Left three…"

The boom operator's instructions droned on as Skip tried his best to make the small corrections. He was getting tired. The download seemed to take forever. Actually it took only two minutes.

"Cleared to disconnect."

Skip sighed with relief as he backed away from the basket. "Receiver, disconnect."

"Tanker, disconnect. Your offload was one thousand three hundred pounds."

"Roger."

The disconnect was automatic. He pulled back fifteen feet from the basket and stabilized. It was not over yet. He still needed two more "dry sticks"—hookups without downloading fuel—to qualify.

Skip released the throttle for a second and brushed the sweat out of his eyes. Tired, but determined, he took a deep breath and moved into position to try again.

The second hookup was accomplished in short order. He was getting the hang of it. The third hookup was looking good until he felt himself dropping back and in danger of disconnecting. Without thinking, he snapped the throttle forward abruptly, causing the nose to pitch up, and the airspeed to drop dangerously low. Suddenly...BANG! The sound of the explosion came from directly under his feet. Then...BANG! BANG! BANG! The cockpit filled with an acrid, burning smell, and a bright orange flame shot out of the engine intake.

"Break away! Break away! Break away!" The boom operator shouted. Loosely translated, this radio call meant, "Get the hell away from the tanker before you blow us all up."

Stunned, Skip disconnected and backed away. What the hell just happened? Did the engine blow up? Was he on fire? Looking at his instruments, he could see that the engine exhaust temperature was too high, and the RPM was spinning erratically. He wasn't sure what to do next. Then it hit him. Compressor stall! He had learned about them in ground school.

"I could stand up here and talk about compressors stalls for hours," the instructor had said. "About how they will sound like a bomb going off under your ass, scaring the bejesus out of you, and maybe even blowing your feet off the rudder pedals. They happen when the angle of attack is too high, and the engine is literally starving for air. All the moving parts of the engine grind to a stop during a compressor stall—turbine blades, compressors blades, everything, and then they start turning in the opposite direction, causing the engine to suck the exhaust gases forward and out the intake. You'll probably forget everything I've said, until it happens to you. Then, you'll remember."

He knew what he had to do. Carefully, he lowered the nose and retarded the throttle, giving the engine a chance to "breathe." Fifteen long seconds later, it stabilized and Skip was able to advance the throttle to regain speed. "Very impressive," a voice said on the radio. "Could you do that again so the rest of us can see it?" He wasn't sure who made the sarcastic comment. Some wiseass in his flight probably or maybe in the tanker. He pulled into position to try yet another hookup.

Ten minutes later, it was over. The three F-100s backed away from the tanker and into the pitch darkness to rejoin their leader, who had been holding above and to one side, watching the proceedings.

The leader started a gentle turn to the left so his wingmen could join up. Skip was flying in the number two position and would be on the left wing. In the pitch dark, all he could see of the leader was three lights: a blinking red navigation light on the left wingtip; another navigation light on the tip of the vertical stabilizer; and a white light on top of the fuselage, just behind the cockpit. They formed a triangle, which gave him some perspective of distance.

Keeping his eyes fixed on the leader, he increased his speed and began to ease up the slant line toward the three lights. Soon, the triangle formed by the three lights began to expand. He was getting close. When he was fifty feet away, the dim outline of the leader's aircraft began to appear. Skip dropped down slightly to ensure they didn't collide, eased the power back, and slid into position. The other two aircraft arrived shortly thereafter. It would be close formation the rest of the way home.

The flight throttled back in a slow descent back to Nellis. They had been flying between layers of clouds since leaving the tanker. Fifty miles out, they plunged into a thick layer of clouds below. The gray, soupy mixture streaming across the leader's aircraft added a dimension of speed to its surroundings, and at times Skip's wingtip was below and overlapping the leader's. It had to be that close. He would lose him otherwise. His world was reduced to just two objects: a blinking red light on the leader's wingtip and the dim outline of his fuselage. Nothing else existed or mattered. If the leader was inverted, or going straight up, or even straight down, that was okay. He was going to stay in tight formation.

When the flight burst out of the clouds, Las Vegas was spread out before them, a magnificent collage of blinking, colored lights. Off to the northwest was the rotating, green and white beacon atop the water tower at Nellis. Life was real again. They were almost home.

"What happened, man?" Bob asked. They were walking across the ramp to the ops building.

"Compressor stall," Skip replied. "It scared the shit out of me."

"Me too. I was worried."

"Really?"

"Well, yeah. What if you blew up and torched off the tanker, and the tanker torched me off?"

"Thanks for your concern," Skip said sarcastically.

"You're welcome. What are friends for?"

"The human torch is back," the scheduling officer said, as they walked into ops.

"Bad news travels fast," Skip muttered.

It was after midnight when Skip and Bob walked across the deserted parking lot, savoring the cool desert air. They were exhausted and ready to go home.

"So, what do you think about this night refueling stuff?"

Bob stood in front of his car and thought a minute before answering. "I think it's a lot like trying to stick a wet noodle up a wildcat's ass," he said finally. "In the dark."

"You've got that right," Skip replied wearily.

*   *   *   *

The final weeks at Nellis passed quickly. Meanwhile, the students awaited their next assignment with anxious anticipation. F-100 squadrons were deployed all over the world, and they could be sent to Europe, the Far East, or bases in the United States. Each place had its pluses and minuses, and everyone, wives included, had their opinion about which was best. Skip and Christy favored Europe. "It would be a chance to see another part of the world, and to see what it's like to live in a foreign country," Christy had said. "Wouldn't it be wonderful if we got stationed in Germany? I could visit my aunt regularly and get to know my family there. And I could teach you how to speak German."

"You speak German? I didn't know that," Skip had replied.

"Yep, we spoke it all the time around the house when I was little. There's a lot you don't know about me, baby."

Many favored the Far East, especially the two bases in the Philippines and Okinawa. The weather there was warm, and the culture more exotic than in Europe. There was also Itazuke Air Base near the large Japanese city of Fukuoka, which drew a lot of interest. None of the wives wanted their husbands to be stationed in the U.S., because Stateside squadrons were typically deployed overseas every eighteen months or so for six months, leaving them to deal with the children and problems at home. The purpose of these deployments or "rotations" was ostensibly to train in an overseas environment, but it was really to augment the force structure in the region. "I'm not about to sit at home being the mommy and daddy, while you gallivant around the world playing fighter-pilot games," Christy said, "so don't even think about going to a squadron in the States."

"When it comes right down to it," Rowdy had said, "there's not a bad assignment in the lot. It all depends on where you want to live." Then he paused for a moment, before adding, "Except for Misawa Air Base in Japan."

"What's wrong with Misawa?" someone asked.

"There's nothing wrong with Misawa, except it's a frozen shit hole in the middle of nowhere. There's nothing to do there, except fly and sit around freezing your ass off. Other than that, it's a great place to be stationed."

He just described Presque Isle, Skip thought at the time. Well, we'll cross Misawa off our wish list, thank you very much. I've already done that frozen north scene and I don't want to do it again.

Two weeks before graduation, a sergeant from personnel paid a visit to the class. Everyone waited in hushed anticipation as he sat down and laid a stack of folders on the table in front of him.

"I have your assignments," he began. "Let's get started, shall we?"

The class shuffled uneasily.

"We'll start with the assignments in the U.S."

Skip gripped the edge of his table and held his breath.

"To Cannon Air Force Base in New Mexico: Smith and Douglas. To Myrtle Beach, South Carolina: Hagen and Friedman." There were soft groans and mumbles of, "Oh, shit." Three of the students were married and had children. This was not what they wanted. So far so good, he thought.

"Next, there are the assignments to USAFE," the sergeant continued, which meant U.S. Air Forces in Europe. "Would you believe that every member of the class put down USAFE as their first choice? Fortunately, there were three more than we expected."

Skip smiled to himself. It was looking good.

"To Lakenheath, England: Johnson, Gretchen, and Fielack. To Ramstein Air Base in Germany: Thomas, Groesbeck, Roberts, Wilson, and Thompson."

Scattered cheers broke out around the room as the chosen ones began to congratulate each other. The Blunderbirds looked at each other. There were only three assignments left. That meant they would be going to the Far East.

Skip let out a disappointed sigh. Well, those are the breaks. You can't win them all. There are great bases in the Far East…Okinawa, the Philippines.

Christy's already been to Germany anyway. It will be good for her to see something different."

The sergeant paused for a few moments, shuffling his papers.

"What about the rest of us?" Bob asked. "Where in PACAF are we going?" meaning the Pacific Air Forces.

"The rest of you are going to the 531st TAC Fighter Squadron, Misawa Air Base, Japan."

The Blunderbirds looked at each other in disbelief. Misawa! The very last base on their list. And they were all going there. This couldn't be happening.

"What? No way!" Skip blurted out. "This has got to be a joke."

"I know. I know," the sergeant said defensively. "It's the first time I've ever seen three students from the same class assigned to the same squadron."

The sergeant continued talking about travel orders, methods of travel, and other details, but Skip wasn't listening. The same words kept surging through his mind—531st TAC Fighter Squadron, Misawa, Japan. Each syllable of each word slammed into him like repeated punches to his solar plexus. Rowdy called it a frozen shit hole that made Presque Isle seem like Miami Beach. This was the worst F-100 assignment in the Air Force. And, the 531st was a nuke squadron. That meant flying idiot circles every day…nothing but friggin' idiot circles.

When the meeting was over, the Blunderbirds shuffled out of the building in a daze.

"Look at it this way," Corky said brightly, "we'll all be together. That's something, isn't it?"

Bob's shot him a look that froze the smile on his face. "Jan is going to be pissed. She's going to be big-time pissed."

"Yeah," Skip groaned. "Christy isn't gonna like it either."

Skip walked into the small apartment they rented in North Las Vegas. "We got our assignments today," Skip said. His voice was flat, and he wasn't smiling.

Christy studied his face for a moment and then said, "I guess we're not going to Germany."

"Not even close. I'm really sorry, honey."

"Hey, it's okay. No big deal." She shrugged and tried to hide her disappointment. "I've been to Germany. It's time to see a different part of the world."

"But it is a big deal. I know how much you wanted to go there."

"So, where are we going? Wherever it is, you don't seem too happy about it." She paused, and a look of consternation crossed her face. "Oh my God! We're not going to one of those squadrons in the States, are we? Please don't tell me that. I don't know what I'd do if you were gone six months out of the year. I'd miss you too much."

"No, we're going to the Far East."

Christy let out a sigh of relief. "Well, there you go. That sounds much better. Why the gloom and doom? You told me there were some great bases there. Okinawa, the Philippines…"

"There are. But we're going to Misawa Air Base in Northern Japan."

Christy tried to remember what Skip had told her about Misawa. "That's the place that's like Presque Isle, right? Out in the boondocks, nothing to do, and up to your rear end in snow all winter?"

"That's the place."

"Well, you survived Presque Isle, didn't you?"

"Yeah, but…"

"And this time you'll have me to keep you warm, plus a little girl to play with. What more can you ask for?"

"Nothing, but…"

"No buts about it. Now, enough of this chitchat. What's the deal, Skip? When do we leave? How long do we stay there? Tell me everything."

"There's not much to tell yet. Tomorrow I have an appointment with personnel. They'll go over all the details then. I do know it will be a three-year tour, and there is housing on base. We'll have a month to get organized after graduation before we have to leave."

"Base housing? Perfect. I'll bet it's a lot nicer than the dump we are living in now."

"I have no idea."

Christy's face softened. "I sure am going to miss Jan, though. She's become my best friend."

"I know. But you're not going to get a chance to miss her."

"Why not?"

"Because she and Bob are going to Misawa too. And so is Corky. We're all gonna be in the same squadron."

"Perfect," she said hugging him and laughing. "All of us together. We'll have a great time."

"I hope so," he said doubtfully.

The meeting at the personnel office didn't last long. As it turned out, Skip had a lot of questions, and the sergeant had very few answers.

"We've set up a port call for June 4th," he said. "You'll report to Travis Air Force Base in California and proceed by military air to Tachikawa Air Base near Tokyo. Then, you'll take the next available military flight to Misawa."

"What about my family? When do they leave?"

"That depends."

"Depends on what?"

"Depends on when housing is available. The regulations say that dependents can't travel to an overseas location until there is available housing."

"But there is base housing in Misawa. I already checked."

"That's true, but there's a waiting list. You'll have to go there first and get your name on the list. Then, when something becomes available, your family can join you."

"Why can't we live off base until something becomes available?"

"You can, but the same rule applies. You have to go there first and arrange for the housing."

Skip sighed and slumped in his chair. Christy had taken the news about Misawa very well, but she would come unglued about this. He was sure of it.

Corky was waiting for him when he left personnel.

"Are you doing anything right now, Skip?"

"Not really." There were no classes scheduled for the rest of the day.

"I need to talk to you about something. It's real important." He looked agitated and pale.

"Sure, fire away. What's on your mind?"

"It's kinda complicated. Can we go somewhere where we can sit down, just the two of us?"

Skip looked at his watch. It was almost lunchtime. "Why don't we go over to the club and grab a sandwich?"

"Great!"

It was only 11:30. The dining room was almost deserted. Corky led Skip to a table in the far corner.

This must be really serious, Skip thought.

Corky looked around nervously, as if afraid of being overheard. Then he leaned forward and began to talk earnestly. "Okay, this is about Delores, but before I start, I want you to promise me something."

"Sure...what?"

"No jokes or bullshit about my getting in her pants. This is serious stuff."

Skip smiled understandingly. "I promise. Bob and I do go overboard on that subject sometimes. It's all in fun, you understand."

"Well anyway, I have a serious problem, and I don't know what to do." Corky paused and took a deep breath. "The thing is, I asked Delores to marry me, and she agreed."

"That's great news, congratulations! Christy told me that was going to happen."

"Christy? How did she know? I didn't tell anybody."

"She knew because she's a woman, and women know everything. That's what she told me, anyway."

"Oh."

"Since you'll be joining the ranks of the happily married soon, you might jot down that rule for future reference."

Corky smiled weakly. "Soon to be happily married. That's the problem. Delores wants to wait a few months."

"How can you do that? You're going to Japan in five weeks, for God's sake!"

"I know, I told her that. But her folks are very religious and will insist on a proper wedding, and that takes time to plan. They think I should go to Japan, and then come back when I have housing arranged."

"Well, I see two things wrong with that. One, you have no way of knowing how long it will take to arrange the housing. It might take six months or even a year. Second, you can't be sure they'll even let you have leave to come home and get married. Do you want to take that risk?"

"Of course not. I want to marry her now. I can't bear the thought of leaving her behind."

"And what about Delores? Is she pushing for more time too? Or is it just her parents?"

"I don't know for sure. Maybe just her parents."

Skip leaned forward and grasped Corky firmly by the arm. "Look, here's what you have to do. Tonight, you call her up and tell her you'll be arriving in Laredo the day after you graduate. Don't say anything else. When you get there, you tell her that you want to get married before leaving for Japan. Tell her you can't bear the thought of leaving her behind, not even for a few weeks. That's how much you love her."

Corky nodded and continued to listen.

"She's probably going to be upset at first. She'll argue, cry, and maybe even get mad. But in the end, if you're lucky, it will all come down to one thing: she's afraid to face her parents. That's when you jump in and tell her that she won't have to face them alone, because you will go with her for moral support."

"Go with her to tell her parents? Are you crazy? I could never…"

Skip cut him off sharply. "You not only can do it, but you will do it. It's the only way. They're both gonna be royally pissed and probably assume that you knocked up their darling daughter."

"Oh my God," Corky moaned. "I never thought about that."

"You have to attack that issue first, head-on. Be mad as hell and insulted that they could even think such a thing, and then let Delores do the talking. Daughters usually know how to handle their fathers. By the time you put the pregnancy issue to rest, the mother will be sniffling and crying, saying it's just not enough time to plan a proper wedding. That's when you jump in and suggest that you could get married at the base chapel and have a reception at the officers' club. By the way, what does her mother look like?"

"What difference does that make? She's an older version of Delores. Similar face and figure."

"Perfect. When her mother gets to the part about how it takes time to make a wedding dress, Delores can ask her if she can wear hers. With any luck at all, she'll still have it. Unless, of course she had a shotgun wedding at the justice of the peace, in which case you're screwed."

"I don't know about the wedding dress thing," Corky said doubtfully. "Will that really work?"

"Of course it will. It worked like a charm for Christy."

A wave of understanding swept over Corky's face. "So that's why you have all the answers. This happened to you and Christy, didn't it?"

"Yep, exactly the same thing. Stick with your old pal here, fly the flight plan I filed for you, and you'll be in like a bunny rabbit."

"Will you come to my wedding?"

"Yep. Christy and I both. Bob and Jan will come too, I'll bet."

"Promise?"

"I promise."

"Good, I need all the moral support I can get."

＊　　　＊　　　＊　　　＊

"Where have you guys been?" Bob said. "I've been looking all over for you."

"We've been just sitting here, having lunch and some serious conversation," Skip replied.

"Well, I've got news. There's a guy over in the fighter weapons school that's in our new squadron. I called him, and he agreed to tell us all about Misawa. We're supposed to meet him at his quarters at 1:30."

"That's in twenty minutes," Skip said. "We better get going."

"Yeah," Corky said cheerfully, "Let's rock and roll." He looked like a new man.

"What were you guys talking about so seriously in the corner of the dining room?" Bob asked, as he and Skip walked toward their cars.

"Ask Jan when you get home tonight. She'll tell you all about it."

"Ask Jan? Why?"

"Because she's a woman, and women know everything."

"Huh?"

"Never mind."

First Lt. Stewart "Duke" Christiansen was the kind of pilot who wore his sunglasses everywhere. Even inside. He was a wiry man of medium height with sharp chiseled features, topped by brown hair cut short in a military crew cut. Skip figured they were the same age. His flying suit fit perfectly, and his boots were shined to a high gloss. When he spoke, his voice had a condescending edge, making him seem unpleasant and unlikable.

Duke watched indifferently as the Blunderbirds crowded into his small room. It was obvious from his manner that he was not meeting with fellow pilots; he was holding court. "So," he began, "you guys are all going to be in the 531ˢᵗ, right?" He looked around the room like a drill sergeant addressing new recruits. Everyone nodded his head vigorously. No one wanted to be the first to speak.

"Yes, sir," Corky said. "We were wondering if you could tell us about the squadron and the base."

"The squadron and the base. Let me see…" Duke assumed the air of a college professor giving a lecture, hands clasped behind his back, gazing out the window as if seeking inspiration. "Well, there are four squadrons there—two F-100 squadrons, the 4ᵗʰ Fighter Interceptor squadron, and the 45ᵗʰ Tactical Reconnaissance Squadron. The mission of the two F-100 units is nuclear weapons delivery, and we take our responsibilities very seriously. Anyone who doesn't won't be with us very long." He paused for minute, looking around the room, letting his message sink in. It was hard to tell who he was looking at because of his sunglasses, but Skip had the eerie feeling he was being singled out. The Blunderbirds shuffled uneasily and glanced at each other.

"As for the base," Duke continued, "There's not much there. The base exchange, commissary, officers' club…that's about it. It's bitter cold in the winter, and there's lots of snow."

"What about base housing?" Skip asked.

"There's always a long waiting list. It will take you anywhere from one to two years to get a house. You can build one off base though."

"Build a house?'

"Yep. You go to the credit union and borrow three thousand dollars. There are Japanese contractors off base who will build you a two-bedroom house for that. When it's finished, the base inspects it, and if it's okay, they'll provide furniture, appliances, and an oil heater. The whole process takes about four months." Skip wondered what kind of house could be built for $3,000. Still, it sure beat the hell out of waiting a year or more for base housing.

The question-and-answer session continued in the same vein for another ten minutes. Then, Duke took off his sunglasses looked directly at the men. He was in the drill sergeant mode once more. "I'm probably going to be one of your instructor pilots when you get to Misawa, maybe even your flight commander. If you do what I tell you when we are flying, we'll get along just fine. But if you decide to do your own thing instead, well…let's just say I have no patience for lack of discipline."

He put his sunglasses back on. It was obvious that the meeting was over. Everyone stood up, thanked him for his time, and left.

"Wow," Corky said when they were outside. "What a piece of work that guy is."

"Yeah," Bob replied, "He's a real asshole."

Skip said nothing. He had a gut feeling that Duke Christiansen was going to have a profound effect on his life someday. And it wasn't going to be positive.

Somewhere Over the
Pacific Ocean

June 4, 1961

Skip had been airborne for so long that he'd lost track of time. They told him the flight would take thirty-six hours, including refueling stops. So far they had stopped at Hawaii, Wake Island, and Guam. Each stop was one hour, just enough time for a crew change and for the passengers to stretch their legs. They had just left Guam on the final leg to Japan. Everyone on board was anxious to arrive.

The Super Constellation aircraft was configured in rows of six seats with an aisle down the middle. Every seat was occupied. There were passengers of all descriptions and ages on board—officers and enlisted men from every branch of the service, civilian contract workers, and families traveling to join their spouses. Some of the wives carried infants in their arms. Others had restless children in tow. The cabin was hot and sticky. The passengers tried to keep occupied so time would pass quickly. Some slept or read, while others paced up and down the crowded aisle trying to restore circulation to their limbs. Children cried, squirmed, slept fitfully, and scrambled below their parents' legs to play with toys on the floor. Everyone was on edge and numb with exhaustion after flying for so long.

The Blunderbirds were sitting together. They decided to exchange seats every few hours. It was Skip's turn to sit by the window. Bob was in the aisle seat, and Corky sat in the middle. Skip stared gloomily at the ocean below. Nothing moved. There were no white caps, no ships, nothing to mark their progress. It was as if they were suspended in time and space above a vast bowl of still water.

Occasionally, he would watch the propellers slash through the air, scattering rays of sunlight into bright flashes that danced off the wing. The four engines on the "Connie" were large and powerful and set up a vibration that could be felt throughout the aircraft.

He saw that Corky was sound asleep, and he smiled. The wedding had been a smashing success, even though there had been an awful row when the couple confronted her parents. But in the end, everyone settled down, and as Skip predicted, Delores swept down the aisle in her mother's wedding gown, looking like an elegant Spanish aristocrat swathed in filmy white lace. The reception afterwards was a grand affair. Throngs of relatives from both sides of the Rio Grande attended. There was both American and Mexican food, and drinks of every kind. There was even a mariachi band that played into the wee hours of the morning. With Maddie safely tucked away in Omaha, Christy and Skip partied long and hard, something they hadn't done for months. Saying goodbye to Christy at the airport as she left for Omaha turned out to be a lot harder than either of them had expected. When it was time to board the aircraft, Christy burst into tears and flung herself into Skip's arms, "I'm going to miss you so much, I really am."

"I know baby," he said soothingly, stroking her hair, and kissing the tears from her eyes. "I'm going to miss you too. You have no idea how much."

Christy composed herself, stepped back, and looked into his face. "I want you to promise me something." Her face was stern now.

"Sure, anything."

"I want you to promise me that you'll get us a place to live as soon as you can. We're a family. Maddie and I need you. And we..." She broke up and started sobbing again.

Skip pulled her back into his arms. "I promise, baby. I'll start working on that the minute I get there."

"Promise?"

"I promise." He hugged her tighter.

Christy stayed in his arms until the last call for boarding. Then she tore herself away. She held her head high and looked him in the eye. "I love you, Skip. I'm your woman. Don't ever forget that."

"I love you, Christy, and I'm your man. And always will be."

She turned away quickly and dashed through the gate, her eyes full of tears.

He walked outside the small terminal and began to wave as she crossed the ramp and filed up the stairs with the other passengers. He waved until she disappeared through the cabin door. The aircraft started its engines and began to taxi. After the plane took off, it made a wide turn and started climbing to the north.

He watched until it disappeared into the dusty horizon. He could taste the salt from her tears on his lips. There were tears in his eyes as well. Then he got in his car and started the long drive to California.

"All right, pay attention here. It's chow time." The voice broke into his daydream and brought him back to the real world. "I thought fighter pilots were always steely-eyed and alert, ready to pounce on anything that moved. Here I find you guys dozing off like a bunch of old ladies." The speaker was one of the stewards, part of the all-Navy crew that was operating the aircraft. His name was Steve, and he was a petty officer. The stewards' job was to look after the passengers. They served meals, made the passengers as comfortable as possible, and were responsible for their safety in the event of an emergency. They performed all of these tasks with patience and good humor.

Steve and his friend Brian, who was also a steward, came aboard with the new crew at Guam and immediately began a bantering dialogue with the Blunderbirds about the relative masculinity of Air Force versus Navy men. It was all in good fun, and it helped to pass the time.

"Obviously, you are not familiar with the tactics of professional killers like us," Bob said to Steve. "We have been trained to feign sleep, watching our prey through slotted eyes, waiting to pounce at exactly the right moment; much like the lions on the Serengeti plains."

"I don't know about that. You try that lion stunt in a Japanese hostess bar and the mama-san will think you're drunk and toss you out, I guarantee you."

"Maybe so, and maybe not." Bob was rummaging through his box lunch, tossing aside the plastic utensils and small packages of condiments. Finally he hauled out a sandwich. "Hey, where's that steak I ordered?"

Steve was already serving the next row. "We ran out of steaks. The guy in front of you got the last one."

Bob opened his sandwich and inspected it closely. "Damn! Ham and cheese again. This was the third time in a row. What have you got, Corky?"

"Ham and cheese."

"Skip?"

Skip pretended not to hear.

"Yoo-hoo Skip, I'm talking to you."

"Roast beef," Skip mumbled.

"Roast beef? You always get roast beef. That's not fair. Let's trade."

"But I don't want to trade. I like roast beef. Why should I?

"Because we're buddies, and we take care of each other. That's why."

"All right, here." Skip reluctantly handed the wrapped sandwich over to Bob. "Are you happy now?"

"Very." Bob regarded the roast beef sandwich with a big smile on his face.

After lunch, Skip fell asleep. He slept for five hours, tossing and twisting as various parts of the seat dug into his body. During his sleep he experienced a ragged patchwork of dreams, each one unrelated to the other. First, he was lying in a snow bank at the front gate of Presque Isle. It was cold, and he wanted to get up, but he couldn't. Cactus Jack was there trying to help him. Then he was holding Maddie in his arms and Christy was in front of him saying, "Don't leave, we need you," over and over. As she stood there, she turned into Ross, except there was a T-33 tip-tank in his mouth instead of a cigar. Through it all, he felt certain that the Connie had been descending, and that now it was skimming across the waves, its giant props flicking against the salty spray. They were about to crash. He was sure of it.

He awoke with a start. Something was different, but he didn't know what. He listened carefully. The engines were quieter. There was less vibration. Then it dawned on him, they were throttled back. The aircraft was descending. They must be near Japan. Thank God, it was almost over. The announcement came over the PA system five minutes later. They would be landing at Tachikawa Air Base in one hour. The passenger cabin exploded into a flurry of activity. People stood up, stretched, and straightened their clothing. Everybody tried to use the bathroom at once. Wives rummaged through their carry-on luggage to find makeup and clean clothes for the children. Some hadn't seen their husbands for months, and they wanted to look fresh and beautiful when they arrived. It was an impossible task after thirty-six hours aboard a hot, crowded aircraft, but they tried.

Steve walked up and down the aisle helping people organize their carry-on luggage in preparation for landing. When he stopped at the Blunderbirds' seats, he told them that it was time to put this Air Force versus Navy thing to bed once and for all. "I talked it over with Brian, and we have decided to be your guides for a little soirée off base this evening to explore the nightlife. It will be our way of saying welcome to Japan."

The Blunderbirds hesitated and looked at each other. They were dog-tired after the long trip. The idea of a hot shower and good night's sleep was much more appealing.

"Unless you're not up to it," Steve added hastily.

That did it. Everyone started nodding their heads vigorously.

"Good. We'll be landing at about 3:30. Why don't we meet at the main gate at seven o'clock this evening? Oh, and by the way, don't forget to convert some of your U.S. dollars to Japanese yen. You can't spend dollars off base. It's against regulations."

Skip was getting excited. They were almost there. Looking out the window, he could see the Kanto Plains surrounding Tokyo, the flat surface cut up by a checkerboard of rice paddies, each a neat green square with water glistening below the surface. Then he saw it, off the wingtip some fifty miles away—Mount Fuji. It was a moving sight. A flat layer of clouds hugged the plains, obscuring the base of the mountain, but its torso thrust majestically above it all, a mantle of snow glistening in the bright sun. He couldn't take his eyes off the mountain as they circled to the north of Tokyo in preparation for landing. The visual effect was that of a large turning wheel with the aircraft on the rim and Mount Fuji at the hub, always off the wingtip. It was as if the two were bonded together. I wonder what it's like to climb Mount Fuji, he thought. I read somewhere that the Japanese do it all the time. They say watching a sunrise from the top is a religious experience, and it also brings good luck. I'd like to do that someday. Maybe I will.

When the Connie touched down on the runway at Tachikawa, a round of applause broke out in the cabin. They had arrived at last. The total flight time from California was thirty-nine hours and fifteen minutes. As soon as the engines stopped, the passengers rose up hastily, gathered their belongings, and surged to the doors, eager to disembark and smell the fresh air. Once they were down the boarding stairs, they milled around on the tarmac stretching their legs, grateful for the feel of solid ground below their feet, as they waited for the buses to take them away.

It was almost four o'clock when the Blunderbirds checked into their small rooms in the transient officers' quarters. They talked about taking a quick nap but decided it was too risky. The Navy guys had challenged them. How would it look if they overslept and didn't show up? Better to shower, change clothes, and go to the club. Skip stayed under the shower for as long as he could, letting the hot water coax all the stiffness out of his body. He emerged a new man. They arrived at the club at five o'clock. Happy hour was just beginning. Everyone ordered the special of the evening—martinis served in glasses the size of small fishbowls, for fifteen cents. "There you go, gentlemen, three Tachi-tinis," the bartender said.

"Geesh," Bob said, "Look at the size of these babies. We'll be blitzed before we ever leave the base."

The drinks were chilled to perfection and went down easily. They finished the first and ordered a second. The effect of the alcohol was soothing and laid another level of comfort on top of the hot shower. Skip felt himself slip into a warm, relaxed state. The three of them chatted amiably as they leaned back on their bar stools. They were glad to be off the cramped and noisy flight.

Skip looked at his watch. "It's 6:40 guys. We've got to get going. They'll be expecting us in twenty minutes. We need to convert some currency and get out of here!"

After everyone changed their money, they raced to the main gate, arriving precisely at seven. "Behold, the boys in blue are here," Steve called out. "And just in time, too. You guys remember Brian?" They all shook hands. "Everybody ready? Let's launch the fleet."

Skip was overwhelmed by the scene that greeted him when he walked through the gate. Neither he nor his friends had ever been overseas, thus they had no idea what to expect when they left the comfort and safety of the base. Directly ahead lay a narrow, twisting street teeming with people. Pedestrians rushed in all directions along the crowded sidewalks, pushing, shoving, and sometimes overflowing into the path of taxis and bicycles, who took no notice of their presence. Everyone seemed so small! He felt like a giant transported to a world of little people. Did he look like a giant to them? Were they intimidated by him? He didn't know. As far as he could tell, they were paying no attention to him at all. Even the air smelled foreign, a collage of cooking smells, flowery scents, and an unpleasant stench he couldn't identify. The buildings were different than anything he had ever seen as well, all built entirely of wood and brightly lit with neon signs of all description. Some were adorned with strings of festive Japanese lanterns.

The sight of so many flashing lights, in so many colors, was startling, and it took Skip a minute to gather his bearings. Part of him wanted him to go back the base, back to the comfortable world he was familiar with. But he wasn't about to do that. Instead, he stepped off the curb and hurried after his friends. As he did, a taxi screeched to a stop behind him and nearly hit him. Where did he come from? The left, he thought, they drive on the left side of the road like the English!

It was clear that the neighborhood catered to the needs of American GIs. There were restaurants, tailors, barbershops, and bathhouses all with English names like Eat Good Restaurant, Gentleman Tailor, and Good Shave Barber. But the majority of the establishments were hostess bars, and these had the most creative names. Skip smiled as he passed the Honey Bar, Bar Romance, and Good Time Bar. Steve strode down the sidewalk briskly with the others close behind. It was obvious he knew exactly where he was going. At times, it was hard to keep up with him on the crowded sidewalk. At the second intersection, he turned into an alley lined with smaller bars. It was quieter, and the lights were not as bright. "Here we are," Steve said. The sign above the door said New York Bar.

It was dark inside, and it took a moment for their eyes to adjust. There were at least a dozen young women sitting at tables, laughing and flirting with their customers. Others waited expectantly by the bar. Some were dressed in brightly colored kimonos with silk-brocaded "obis," silk sashes wrapped around their waists many times and tied in an elaborate bow in the back. Others were dressed western style, with tight, short dresses, high heels, and plenty of makeup. An old Elvis Presley song was playing on the stereo behind the bar.

"Holy shit, I'm all shook up," Bob said, thrusting his pelvis in and out, Elvis style.

"Steve-san!" a voice cried from the darkness. A middle-aged woman detached herself from behind the bar and rushed over to where they were standing.

Steve hugged her affectionately. "Good evening, Mama-san. Long time no see."

"How come you no come to my bar anymore? I think you don't love me."

"Now Mama-san, you know that's not true. You're my number one Japanese girlfriend. I've been busy lately."

"Humph, I think you busy with other girls. I think you cho-cho boy-san, Steve." Cho-cho was a Japanese word for butterfly. In bar-girl lingo, it meant men who flitted from one girl to another, never keeping their promises. The conversation continued in the same vein for a few minutes. Then everyone sat down at a long table. There was an empty chair beside each man. Five girls glided across the room and sat in the empty chairs. The Blunderbirds looked at each other uncertainly.

"Lesson one," Steve said. "These lovely young ladies are here to entertain you—to make conversation and drink with you. There are no strings attached. It's the way things are done in Japan. So relax and enjoy yourselves."

Steve ordered three large bottles of Japanese beer. "Lesson two is acquiring a taste for Kirin, Sapporo, and Asahi. They're all good beers. A large bottle is 180 yen, which works out to about fifty cents."

The young girl on Skip's right tugged at his sleeve shyly. She was wearing a white silk kimono richly embroidered with pale blue flowers and a dark blue obi. Her tiny face was carefully made up and framed by rich, brown coils of hair done up in the back and held in place by elaborate pins. The white powder on her face gave her an almost ghostly appearance that contrasted starkly with her bright red lipstick. Skip had to admit that she was very pretty.

"My name is Etsuko. What is your name?" Her English was soft and correct. She chose her words carefully.

"My name is Skip."

"Very happy to meet you, Skip-san." Brian had explained earlier that "san" was an honorific that was added to all people's names, except among family or in very intimate circumstances.

"I'm very happy to meet you, Etsuko-san." They shook hands solemnly.

"How long have you been in Japan?"

"I just arrived today."

"Oh, I see, you must be very tired." Her face showed polite concern.

The hostess brought the beer. Skip reached for a bottle to pour a glass for Etsuko. But she took the bottle from his hand and filled his glass instead. Then she filled her own. The other girls did the same. When all the glasses were full, Steve raised his in a toast. "Compai." That's Japanese for "cheers," or "to your health."

"Compai," everyone responded.

The cold beer was refreshing, coming on the heels of three large martinis. He drank thirstily, and Etsuko poured him more. He began to sink drowsily into his chair. There was a slight buzz in his ears, and the sounds of talking faded into the background. Otherwise, he felt fine.

When the beer was finished, Steve rose from the table. "Okay, gang, time to move on. We've got a lot of ground to cover tonight."

Everyone rose and said their goodbyes.

"I was very pleased to meet you, Skip-san," Etsuko said. "I hope you will come to see us again."

"I will, I promise."

Etsuko-san crooked her little finger in his and tugged gently. "This is how we make promises in Japan. You won't forget, will you?"

"I won't, I promise." He tugged her little finger back.

The second bar was a carbon copy of the first. Only the name was different. The Bar Happy. This time Steve's friend Brian was met enthusiastically by the mama-san. It was apparent that Brian was very popular in the Bar Happy. Several girls gathered around him, teasing and flirting, competing for a chance to sit beside him. Brian had flaming red hair and freckles. Skip figured that was the reason that the girls flocked around him. Red hair was a rarity in Japan. Skip did not protest when a tall girl with copper-colored dyed hair sat beside him. Her tight red dress displayed a generous cleavage when she leaned over. He would soon learn that big-breasted women were also a rarity in Japan. He sat back, intent on enjoying the view. Brian ordered Suntory whiskey for everyone. The Blunder-birds were beginning to look glassy-eyed, but they responded gamely to the toast. "Compai!" Skip couldn't remember the girl's name and had no idea what they were talking about. They drank two whiskeys and left.

As they stepped out into the fresh night air, Skip knew he was in trouble. Mar-tinis, beer, whiskey, and fatigue had all come together to deliver the inevitable mortal blow. It was only a matter of time. He knew that. He could not walk straight, and the world seemed tilted. Stumbling along beside Steve, he tripped and almost stepped into the concrete ditch alongside the curb. Steve grabbed him by the arm and pulled him back on the sidewalk. "Easy there, you don't want to step in there. That's a 'benjo ditch.'"

"What's a benjo ditch?" Skip slurred.

"It's an open sewer from all the buildings on the street. It's basically full of shit. You step in that, and no one will come near you for the rest of the evening, I guarantee you."

This was the stench he couldn't identify earlier. He wanted to puke. But he held himself in check.

Steve ordered a Japanese rice wine called sake in the third bar. "This is a must for your first night in Japan. It's delicious." Skip eyed the small china cup of warm, clear liquid. It seemed harmless enough. Thank God, he thought, we're tapering off. It will be over soon. He downed it quickly and then drank another. Suddenly, the room began to spin. Dinner, he forgot to eat dinner! That's what's wrong. As they stumbled out of the third bar, Corky rushed to the curb and retched. No one noticed. Bob was slumped against the wall, slowly collapsing to the sidewalk. Then the Blunderbirds rallied and continued to follow Steve and Brian. They were not beaten yet.

Skip was confused. He thought they were back at the bar where it all started, but he wasn't sure. Everyone had stopped drinking. Steve was standing at the counter, engaged in an animated conversation with the mama-san. They both turned and looked at the Blunderbirds. He wondered why. Steve returned to their table. "Listen guys, I need three thousand yen from each of you. That's about ten bucks." They handed him the money. Nobody asked what it was for. Then they got up and left. Three taxis were waiting outside, engines running and rear doors open. Steve took Skip gently by the arm and eased him into the back-seat of the first taxi. "Lieutenant, you guys did good tonight. Most don't last near as long as you did. Enjoy your stay in Japan. Good luck."

Skip tried to say, "Thanks for everything," but nothing came out. He slumped in the corner of the backseat, and the taxi drove off. He was vaguely aware that Etsuko was in the cab with him. That's nice, he thought. She's making sure I get back to the base safely. Then he passed out.

Skip could sense the sunlight streaming across his face but was afraid to open his eyes. He was sure the sun would puncture his eyeballs and pulverize his brain. His headache was severe, the worst ever. It felt as if someone had plunged an ice pick between his eyes. He was incredibly thirsty, and when he tried to swallow, the insides of his mouth stuck together. He was a very sick and hung-over man. How did he get home last night? The last thing he remembered is drinking that second cup of sake. Squirming uncomfortably, he realized that something was very wrong. Slowly, he opened his eyes. He was not in a bed. He was lying on a padded quilt spread out on the floor. The floor was covered from wall-to-wall with thick straw mats. There was no furniture in the room, save for a lamp and a small table. His clothes were hung neatly in a nearby closet.

He tried to sit up. It wasn't easy in his condition. "Where the hell am I?" he muttered. One side of the covers had been thrown aside and was in disarray. There was another pillow next to his. It was still warm and gave off a faint scent of perfume. Oh shit! he thought. His thoughts were interrupted by the sound of a door sliding open. Skip froze. He wanted to run but couldn't, because he was wearing only his underwear.

"Ohayo-gozaimusu," a woman's voice said cheerily. It was Etsuko. She was dressed in a simple white robe held closed by a loosely tied blue sash. Her hair hung down to her shoulders, and she wasn't wearing makeup. She looked much younger and even prettier than last night. She was carrying a tray. On it was a bottle of water and a mug of hot, steaming coffee. "'Ohayo-gozaimusu,' means good morning," she said, as she padded across the floor and set the tray down.

Skip tried to repeat the phrase, but it didn't come out right.

The coffee was rich and strong, and the water ice-cold. He was beginning to feel better. Etsuko was kneeling beside him watching him drink. "You were a very bad boy-san last night. I think you very drunk."

"I think you're right. But how did I end up here?"

"No problem. Steve-san is my friend. He say that Air Force guy too drunk to go back to base. Please take care of him."

"That was very nice of him. I have to give you some money then."

"No, no. No money. Steve-san give me enough for everything. Taxi, house stay, everything." He struggled to remember what happened between the time he got in the cab and this morning. They slept in the same bed together. Did they do anything? He couldn't remember. It was all a blank.

Etsuko was gone for a few minutes and then returned. "I call taxi for base on pay phone. He be here in ten minutes. You need to dress now, Skip-san." He rose unsteadily and started to dress. Etsuko stood by his side and held the legs of his trousers while he stepped into them. When he was dressed, they made their way to an outside foyer. His shoes were lined up neatly beside hers. Before he could reach them, Etsuko kneeled down and slid them on his feet expertly.

The taxi's horn blared impatiently. "Etsuko, there's something I have to ask you. Did I…I mean, did we do anything? You know?"

Etsuko smiled but didn't answer. He sighed, kissed her on the cheek, and walked out into the bright sunlight.

"Skip-san!"

He turned back to Etsuko as he opened the taxi door. "Yes?"

"You nice man. You keep promises." She held out her crooked little finger and gestured meaningfully.

"Sayonara, Etsuko-san," he said waving. "You're nice too." I guess I'll never know what really happened, he thought. It's probably just as well. The taxi pulled away.

Bob's taxi arrived just as Skip got out of his cab. "And a happy ohayo-gozai-musu to you," Skip called out. "Looks like you had a late night too."

"I don't want to talk about it," Bob mumbled. He looked weak and pale.

"Where's Corky?"

"Missing in action."

"That figures," Skip said.

He was glad to be back in his quarters. Lying on his bed, he thought of all the things that had happened since last night. It was not a good beginning for his new life in Japan. He wondered if it was an omen of things to come. He didn't think so. But then again, he was not sure of anything.

*   *   *   *

It was snowing outside. Skip was sure of that, although he couldn't quite open his eyes. As usual, the contents of the IV were tugging at him, trying to pull him back into its world of darkness. When he finally managed to come awake, he saw that the sky-line across the East River was obscured by a depressing blanket of dingy, white mist, as large, wet snowflakes splattered on the pane of his window. Snow—he had seen plenty in his life, and he knew that it was a living being with many personalities. There was the snow in Presque Isle, for example, that arrived in a businesslike fashion in the fall, and layered the ground relentlessly throughout the winter, leaving on cue when spring finally arrived. Then there was the snow in Misawa—nasty, unpredictable, and sometimes capricious, it came and went as it pleased, leaving churned muddy ruts and fine layers of soot in its wake. He hated Misawa, and the miserable life he had lived there, even after all these years. It was there that he and Christy had both stumbled and almost lost it all. Misawa was where his dreams were crushed and nearly destroyed. How could that have happened, he wondered, as he drifted back to sleep.

MISAWA AIR BASE, JAPAN

June 7, 1961

A steady rain was falling from leaden skies when Skip and his friends stepped off the C-130 transport that took them four hundred miles north of Tokyo to Misawa Air Base. It was early June, and the rainy season had just begun. It would continue until mid-July. Misawa was near the northeast tip of the main Japanese island of Honshu in Aomori Prefecture. The city of Misawa was small, with a population of about 25,000 people. It sat on the southern shore of picturesque Lake Ogawara. The nearest city of any size was Hachinohe, which was almost a two-hour drive on unpaved roads. It was the winters that gave Misawa the reputation of being an unpleasant place to live and work. The season started in November, and by January, the temperature dropped to between twenty and thirty degrees Fahrenheit during the day. Strong winds often made it feel much colder. Snowfall was erratic and difficult to predict. Typically, snow showers descended from the mountains, passed over the base, and continued to the nearby Pacific Ocean. A passing shower could reduce visibility so quickly that approaching aircraft had to be sent to other bases to land. Quite often, the showers passed, and the skies were clear again within minutes. Other times the bad weather persisted for hours or even days.

The base was strategically located. To the north and west, lay the Soviet Union with its array of military bases, plus the port of Vladivostok, which faced them across the Sea of Japan. All were within easy reach of the F-100s. In particular, there were two large Soviet Air bases just minutes away from Hokkaido, the most northern of Japan's major islands. F-102 interceptors from Misawa routinely scrambled to challenge Soviet reconnaissance aircraft flying east across the Sea of Japan to probe the air defense system. The aircraft usually turned around when challenged, but if the weather was too bad for the interceptors to take off, they continued on, sometimes flying over Japan for an hour or more. Another hazard to flying at Misawa was the Soviet intelligence-gathering ships, which were disguised as fishing trawlers. They were equipped with "faker beacons" that transmitted signals on the same frequencies as beacons used by aircraft for navigation. If an unsuspecting pilot flying at night or in bad weather followed a faker beacon, he could find himself lost and in danger of running out of fuel. Cat-and-mouse games between the United States and the Soviet Union were an integral part of life in Misawa and went on twenty-four hours a day.

There was no one to meet Skip and his friends when they got off the aircraft. "What?" Bob said, "No marching bands? No dancing girls?"

"Obviously, someone didn't get the word," Corky said.

"Wait for me," Skip said. "I'll go into base ops and call the squadron." The young lieutenant who answered sounded friendly enough. "Welcome to the 531st," he said. "Everybody has gone for the day, so I suggest you check in to the BOQ and report back tomorrow morning. Colonel Sullivan, our CO, will want to see you right away. He likes to be the first to greet new pilots. I'll let him know you've arrived."

"Sounds good to me." Skip was still recovering from the fiasco in downtown Tachikawa. "What time should we be there?"

"Well, we usually start at seven AM sharp, but tomorrow, with the funeral and all, you might as well wait until ten. Nobody will be around until then."

"The funeral?"

"Yeah, couple of guys from our sister squadron, the 416th, ran into a mountain while on a formation low-level. They just found them two days ago after a week of searching."

"A week? They must have crashed in a pretty remote area."

"Naw, it was the weather. It was so bad, we couldn't launch the search aircraft, much less see anything on the ground."

"I'm sorry to hear that." Skip didn't know what else to say.

"Yeah," the young man said.

"What's the word?" Bob asked.

"Everyone's gone for the day. We report tomorrow at ten. There's a funeral in the morning."

"A funeral?"

"Yeah, a couple of Hun drivers busted their ass on a low-level."

There were plenty of rooms available at the BOQ. They were simple, but functional—a closet, single bed, chest of drawers, and a small easy chair with a side table. Bob was in the room next door. They shared a small bathroom with a shower. Corky was across the hall. Skip looked around the room and started to unpack. It didn't take long; he hadn't brought much. He placed two photos on his desk, one of Christy and the other of Maddie. Home sweet home, he thought. Hopefully, I won't be here long. He lay back on his small bed and stared at the ceiling, thinking about Christy. He wondered what she was doing right now. He wasn't sure, but he thought it was early morning in Omaha. Maybe she's asleep or, knowing Maddie's disruptive eating patterns, maybe not. It was hard to believe that he'd left California just four days ago. So much had happened since then. He thought about Etsuko. Spending the night with a strange woman so soon after he'd said goodbye to Christy in Laredo was inexcusable. But, he had been drunk, and they hadn't done anything, he was pretty sure of that. He would go to the housing office first thing in the morning and get things rolling. Then he could write Christy a long letter.

His thoughts were interrupted by a loud knock on the door. It was Bob and Corky. "Hey, Skip," Corky said, "if we leave now, we can catch the end of happy hour. Let's go." Skip leaped to his feet. He was ready.

The officers' club was different from Luke and Nellis. The atmosphere was somber and silent. It reminded him of the club at Offutt, except it was much plainer. There was a bar upstairs, with nobody in it, and a large dining room that was almost empty, except for a few early diners. Downstairs, there was a large stag bar and small snack bar. It was inhabited almost exclusively by pilots. There were only a dozen or so customers, even though it was still happy hour. The Blunderbirds found a place at the end of the bar. "Geesh," Bob muttered, "where is everybody? This place is like a morgue." They asked the bartender for a dice cup. It took him awhile to find one, which Skip thought was odd for a stag bar. They ordered a round of drinks.

To Skip's left, an older captain sat slumped over the bar, drinking a double-vodka martini. From the sound of his voice when he ordered his drink, he guessed the captain had been there for awhile. He glanced up at the newcomers dully and went back to his drink. Skip decided to break the ice. Maybe he could learn something about the base, and why it was so quiet. "Hi, my name is Skip, and these are my friends Bob and Corky. We just signed into the 531st today."

"The 531st, eh? That's John Sullivan's squadron. He's good people. You'll like him. I gotta warn you though, he's a teetotaler and a very religious man. And he doesn't like foul language."

"No shit!" Bob said. He laughed and gulped down his drink. He couldn't resist it. The idea of a Bible-toting fighter squadron commander who didn't drink and didn't cuss seemed ludicrous.

The captain smiled weakly but gave no indication that he had been joking.

Skip decided to change the subject. "I understand we lost a couple of birds this week."

"Tell me about it," the captain muttered. "I'm the division flying safety officer. I've hardly slept a wink since they were reported missing."

Skip nodded sympathetically. "I can imagine. What do you think happened?"

The captain shrugged his shoulders. "They were on a low-level when the weather turned to dog shit, and they tried to stay under the clouds. They didn't see the mountain coming. Boom! Boom! Two big holes in the side of the mountain."

Skip nodded. "I take it they were in fairly close formation when they crashed."

"You got that right. Perfect formation."

The captain ordered another martini. He was slurring his words now. "You know what bugs the shit out of me? We've lost a total of four F-100s and four pilots this year, and it's only June. And the hell of it is the boys down in the 8th Wing at Itazuke have matched us one for one. The cause of the latest one was 'pilot error' with weather as a contributing factor. As for the rest of them, we haven't a clue"

The Blunderbirds were gathered around the captain now, listening intently. "What were the other accidents like?" Corky asked.

"Every one was different, but most of them happened during formation flights close to the ground, like on the way to the range, for example, or on a low-level. Everything would be looking good, and suddenly one of the birds would pull up abruptly, roll inverted, and auger straight in. It usually happened so fast that the pilot had no time to make a radio call, much less eject. We think it has something to do with the flight control system, but nobody knows for sure."

Skip and his friends stayed with the captain until he slumped over his drink and stopped talking. Then they went upstairs to eat. Welcome to Misawa, Skip thought.

*   *   *   *

The next morning Skip was up bright and early. After a quick breakfast at the club, he headed straight for the base housing office. He had promised Christy that he would arrange for housing as soon as possible. He intended to keep that promise.

The housing situation was worse than he expected. "You'll have at least a one-year wait," the sergeant said, "probably more like eighteen months."

"Why so long?"

The sergeant shrugged. "Housing is always full. When someone leaves, the next person on the list moves up. It's a very slow process."

Skip felt helpless and frustrated. "How does the list work?"

"It's based on the date you arrived in Japan. If more than one person arrives on the same day, it goes by rank. Of course, there are some people who go to the head of the list, like squadron commanders and other key people."

"What if, say, three lieutenants arrived on the same day?" He was thinking about Bob and Corky.

"Then it goes by date of rank."

Skip sat back heavily in his chair and tried to make sense of it all. Special treatment for key people, date of arrival in Japan, date of rank…how could he be sure someone wasn't going to cheat the system and cut in front of him?

The sergeant read his mind. "Look, sir, nobody screws around with the housing list. The system is just too visible. People at the head of the line usually call once a week just to see how things are going. If anybody tried to pull a fast one, the word would be out in no time, and heads would roll. Trust me."

Skip sighed, thanked the sergeant, and left. As he did he spotted Bob coming up the sidewalk.

"You're too late," Skip said. "I got the last house."

"Yeah, right. How long is the list?"

"You don't want to know."

Bob nodded and plodded up the steps.

"Hey, Bob."

"Yeah?"

"What's your date of rank?"

Bob looked at him suspiciously. "Who wants to know?"

"Never mind."

*   *   *   *

The Blunderbirds arrived at their new squadron precisely at ten o'clock. "Good morning, gentlemen," the captain at the ops counter said. On the wall behind him hung a large board, which depicted the flying schedule, plus all the other activities planned for the day. Several pilots stood in front of the counter studying the board while glancing curiously at the newcomers. "We'll get you introduced around later, but right now the old man wants to see you in his office right away. It's down that hall, last door on the left."

Lt. Col. John Zachariah Sullivan leaned back in his desk chair, folded his hands in his lap, and gazed appraisingly at the new arrivals. He was a man of medium build whose almost total lack of hair made him look much older than he was. A slight deformation on his upper lip suggested that he might speak with a slight lisp. This was true, but it was barely noticeable. When he smiled, the corners of his eyes crinkled, giving him a kindly look. Everyone in the squadron called him "Colonel John." He was born in Kansas and had a strict Baptist upbringing. His father was a minister who taught his family that drinking, dancing, and cursing were mortal sins. By the time he was old enough to make his own decisions about such matters, he saw little reason to change. He glanced at one of his desk drawers uneasily and then back up to the three young men before him. There, was a telex from PACAF Headquarters in that drawer. It came this morning, and he was the only one who had read it so far. When the contents of this telex are disclosed to the rest of the squadron, he thought, these young men will not feel welcome. It's too bad, but that's the way it is. But there was no sense telling them about the telex just yet.

John paused for a moment, then leaned forward in his chair. "Let's begin by having each of you tell me a little about yourself. Lieutenant O'Neill, why don't you go first?"

Skip glanced at the others nervously. "Well, I enlisted in the Air Force in 1954 and became an aviation cadet. Then I went to navigator training and became a radar observer in F-89s. I flew in the 76th Fighter Interceptor Squadron at Presque Isle. After two years, I went to the University of Omaha to get my bachelor's degree under the Bootstrap program and entered pilot training just after I graduated." Not a very impressive resume, Skip thought, but that's all there is.

John nodded his head but made no comment. Then he looked at Bob. "Lieutenant Lewis?"

Bob explained that he received his commission through the ROTC program and then went to navigator training. Like Skip, he had been an RO in F-89s before going to pilot training.

Corky's story was the shortest, because he was the youngest and had the least experience of the three. When he graduated from the cadet corps at Virginia Tech, he went directly to pilot training. That was it.

John remained silent. The newcomers shifted uncomfortably in their chairs. Finally, he cleared his throat and began. "Well, as you know, the 531st has a very important and highly classified mission. We are a nuclear strike squadron and, as such, must be prepared to go to war on a moment's notice, seven days a week, twenty-four hours a day. Unlike the SAC bombers, our targets are minutes away, not hours." The three men were listening carefully, nodding their heads to show they understood. "It can be stressful at times," he continued, "training for a mission that we pray to God will never happen. Meanwhile, there's not much to do here, especially in the winter when the snow sets in. Of course there are bars downtown and Japanese women…but that's not the answer, believe me." He paused and looked at the men significantly. "But there is one answer—families. I notice that all three of you are married, and that two of you have children. Yet no one mentioned their families when they talked about themselves. That concerns me."

He was leaning over his desk now, talking in earnest. "Remember, your families are part of who you are, and they are very important. In particular, wives are often the glue that holds your lives together and keeps you focused on your career. Don't ever forget that."

There was an awkward silence. No one knew what to say. "Speaking of families…" Skip started to say. Then he thought better of it.

"Yes? Go on, son."

"What I was going to say is we went over to the base housing office today, and they told us it would be eighteen months before we could get housing for our families. That's a long time."

John nodded sympathetically. "Yes it is. But there is a solution, and we can help. Several of our men have had houses built off base by a Japanese contractor. He's cheap, and he's fast. It usually takes him about eight weeks from start to finish. I can give you his name." He was making notes as he talked. When he finished, he picked up the phone. "Send Rosie in here, will you please?"

John stood up. "It's time to get off my pulpit and let you gentlemen get back to work. Rosie, our operations officer, will introduce you to your flight commanders so you can get started."

An operations officer named Rosie? Skip thought.

Emmett "Rosie" O'Grady blasted through the door like an unexpected flash of sunlight with a wide smile on his face. Although he was only a captain, he looked considerably older than John. His iron-gray hair was cut short, and he held a smooth, well-used pipe in his right hand. Rosie was a graduate of the Naval Academy and like most "ring knockers"—that is to say West Point and

Annapolis graduates—his career had been on a fast track. But somewhere along way, he had been derailed. The word around the squadron was that if he didn't get promoted to major this year, he would be out of the Air Force.

John smiled at his ops officer indulgently. "Rosie, have you met our new arrivals? These are Lieutenants Lewis, O'Neill, and Myers."

"Indeed I have not. What a pleasure. Welcome to the fighting 531st, lads." Rosie shook hands vigorously, beaming broadly.

"Please show these men around and introduce them to their flight commanders. O'Neill and Myers will be in A Flight, and Lieutenant Lewis will be in B Flight."

"Will do, sir."

The operations building sat adjacent to the flight line, directly in front of the 531st aircraft. It was a standard World War II building, much like the one that Skip's squadron had in Presque Isle. Next door, an identical building housed their sister squadron, the 416th. Rosie gave them a tour of the building, starting from the back where the snack bar was located and ending with the ops counter by the front door. Although the building was not large, the tour lasted a good half hour, mainly because they were introduced to each person they encountered along the way. The pilots were an interesting group, some young and some old. They seemed friendly enough, although somewhat distracted. This was understandable given that they had just returned from a funeral.

When the tour was over, Rosie brought them back to the ops counter. "Well, gents, that's the nickel tour. Unfortunately, both flight commanders are TDY today, so you'll have to meet them on Monday. Meanwhile, the personnel office is expecting you at one o'clock for in-processing, so you might as well grab a bite to eat. As they were leaving, they almost collided with Duke Christensen who was walking in the door.

"Well, we meet again," Bob said cheerily. Duke merely nodded his head and brushed on by.

The three of them walked on outside. "What an arrogant asshole," Skip said.

"Careful now," Corky said. "He might be your flight commander someday."

"My flight commander? Give me a friggin' break. Fat chance of that happening!"

*   *   *   *

Capt. Jim Landry, A Flight commander, was not happy. He had just spent a week in Korea, his second tour this month. This shit of going to Korea every other week has got to stop, he thought. When he got home, his wife bitched the entire weekend about Christ knows what. Flo is a good woman, but I'd rather wrestle a ditch full of alligators than take her on when she's on a tear. Now it's Monday, and I've got a shit-load of paperwork to do. So what happens? As soon as I get in, Rosie walks into my office with two young pilots right out of Nellis in tow, and announces that they've been assigned to my flight. As my old grand-daddy used to say, "It's enough to piss off the Pope."

Jim Landry, or "Big Jim" as he was called in the squadron, was born and raised in Beaumont, Texas. His father was a roughneck in the oil fields, and that's where Jim went to work when he graduated from high school. For a time, it looked like he would follow in his father's footsteps. Then the Korean War sent his life in another direction. His early days of working in the oil fields had taken their toll. His weather-beaten face always looked sunburned, even in the dead of winter, and it had sharp, creased features with numerous scars, the result of "accidents," both on the job and in the bars. Big Jim was a good man, but he viewed the world in black and white and expected everyone to see things his way.

Skip and Corky could tell that Big Jim was not happy. His handshake was per-functory, as his eyes bore into theirs. There was no "Welcome to the squadron," or, "Pleased to meet you," just a blunt, "Have a seat, I'll be with you in a minute." They waited nervously on a small sofa while he finished looking at some papers on his desk.

Jim tossed the telex he had been reading onto his desk. "Shit," he said, and with a look of disgust, turned to the two young men. He began talking without preamble. "The first thing you should know about me is that I tell it like it is. I always have and always will. That's my way. So I have to tell you that I am not happy to see you and don't want either of you in my flight. But I have no choice." He paused. The newcomers looked at him in stunned disbelief. His fea-tures softened and his voice sounded less harsh when he continued. "Right now, you are both wondering why I am talking to you this way, and what you have done to deserve this. It's a fair question, and I'll try to answer it. It's all about this telex." He held it up for emphasis. "Colonel John distributed it this morning. It's from PACAF headquarters. They are concerned about the number of F-100 acci-dents in Japan this year. Nobody knows for sure what's going on, but they've noticed that most of them involved young pilots who recently graduated from Luke and Nellis. Their theory is that those pilots were not adequately trained to deal with the bad weather here. So, in their infinite wisdom, they have decreed that each new arrival has to repeat the entire F-100 training program before he can be certified as combat ready." He paused to let the effect of his words sink in.

Skip and Corky looked at each other with dismay. My God, they thought. It will be as if Luke and Nellis never happened. They're going to treat us like we just graduated from pilot training.

"How many missions did you fly at Luke and Nellis?" Jim asked.

Skip shrugged and looked at Corky. "I don't know…sixty or seventy maybe."

"Let's say sixty for the sake of argument. Now, we have three new pilots on board. That's a total a 180 missions. Many of them are in the F model. We only have two F models in the squadron, and one of them is usually down for maintenance. Plus, there has to be an instructor pilot on every flight. We have only six, when they are available. And you can't always fly a training mission in the shitty weather we have here. What I'm saying is it will be a hell of a long time before you guys get combat-ready. Do you know why that's important?"

Skip and Corky shook their heads.

"Nuke alert at Kunsan, that's why. Every Saturday, six guys fly over there in the C-130 and come back the following Saturday. It's boring work, and it's hard on the family to have them gone that long, especially in the winter. The schedule is rotated among the four flights. When it's A Flight's turn, we provide the six pilots. Since there are four flights in the squadron, and each has eight pilots, this shouldn't be too bad. Each pilot goes once a month, at the most. Maybe less. But we don't have eight pilots in our flight. We have six pilots plus two new heads that won't be combat-ready for several months. That means that if any of my guys get sick or reassigned elsewhere for a few weeks, somebody else has to go in his place, even though he's already been there that month. We've been doing that a lot lately, and it's a crock. Now do you see why I'm pissed?"

Skip and Corky nodded solemnly. There was nothing they could do but listen.

Jim sighed heavily and glanced at the stack of paperwork on his desk. Perhaps he was being too harsh with these young men, but he had to tell them where they stood. Meanwhile, it was time to end this unpleasant conversation and get back to work. "Okay, I have no idea when you'll start flying, but it won't be anytime soon. No matter, there are plenty of things to do around here. Every pilot in the squadron has an additional duty. Lieutenant O'Neill, the flight planning room next door is a mess. The wall chart needs to be replaced, some of the flight planning documents are out of date, and we need more maps. The place looks like a pigpen. As of now, you are in charge of that room. I want you to get it straightened out."

"Lieutenant Myers, you're the most junior officer in the squadron. That means you are the new snack bar officer. Go back there and keep an eye on

Frankie, the Japanese national who works there. Make sure he doesn't goof off and/or steal us blind. You are also in charge of ordering personalized coffee cups, squadron patches, and the like when somebody needs them. In two weeks, we'll be sending you both to Numazu for sea survival school. Now, if you'll excuse me, I've got work to do."

Jim watched Skip and Corky rise hastily and start for the door. "One more thing," he said. The two men stopped and turned around. "Just because you can't fly for awhile doesn't mean you can goof off whenever you feel like it. I expect to see you every morning at seven thirty for the daily briefing, and I expect for you to stick around in the afternoon until everyone else leaves. Is that clear?"

"Yes sir," the two men responded in unison.

*   *   *   *

The next afternoon the Blunderbirds went downtown to meet with Hitoshi Sunabori, a local builder who had built several homes for pilots in the squadron. Although he came highly recommended, there was one small problem. Sunabori could speak very little English, so the meeting was conducted using a mixture of pidgin English, gestures, and pointing. Each man presented him a contract provided by the base and $1,500 in yen as a down payment for his house. Sunabori took the yen eagerly and signed the contracts without reading them.

Sunabori took them to the neighborhood where their houses were to be built. It was less than a mile from the main gate and consisted of twelve homes already built and occupied by Americans from the base. The houses seemed sturdy enough, with stucco walls and tile roofs, but the streets were not paved, and the summer rains had made them muddy and almost impassable. Although the residents did their best to keep things tidy, the neighborhood reminded Skip of slums he had seen when he was growing up. The three houses would be built side by side. As the newest additions, they would be at the back of the development, farthest from the nearest paved road.

That night Skip wrote a long letter to Christy. "Our new house is going to be beautiful," he wrote. "It should be finished by the end of August, maybe earlier. I hope to have you here by the middle of September so we can be a family again." He went to sleep a happy man.

*   *   *   *

In early September, Skip, Bob, and Duke Christiansen were promoted to the rank of captain. Colonel John called them into his office, gave a small speech about how proud he was of them, and pinned a shiny new set of "railroad tracks" on their collars. Skip left the office feeling older and wiser. His six-year apprenticeship was over. He was no longer just a lieutenant. He went to tell his flight commander the good news. Big Jim was about to leave for a meeting. He had already heard about the promotions. "I'll be goddamned if you're going to be the assistant flight commander," he said when Skip walked into the room. "I don't give a shit if you are the next most senior officer in the flight. You just graduated from pilot training for Christ sakes! Hell, you're not even combat-ready. And at the rate things are going, you probably won't be any time soon. By the way, when are you going to unpack those boxes of maps that have been sitting in the flight planning room for a week?" He turned on his heel and strode out the door without looking back.

Skip stood transfixed, staring at the spot where Big Jim had just been, hands clenched at his sides, fighting to suppress the rage that was boiling up inside. I don't believe it, he thought. In less than five seconds this asshole blew away the only good news I've heard since arriving in this place. Is it my fault I had to be an RO for four years before going to pilot training? If it hadn't been for those dip-shits in the Pentagon with their "We didn't say you had to go to observer training, you just assumed…" bullshit I would be an experienced pilot now, and none of this would be happening. He looked around the room in frustration. He wanted to smash something, hit someone, and shout an obscenity. Instead, he turned and walked dejectedly into the flight planning room, hands still clenched at his sides.

*   *   *   *

The weather began to cool. Fall was coming and slowly but surely, the surrounding mountains began to slip into a mantle of bright red and gold. The air became crisp and clear and tasted like fine champagne. Skip watched it all indifferently. He was suspended in a slice of time that moved at a molasses-like pace. As Colonel John had suggested, the Japanese contractor who was building his house was cheap but certainly not fast. His house was taking shape slowly, one board at a time, and at the rate things were going, it wouldn't be ready until

November at the earliest. His checkout program progressed at the same snail-like pace. Some weeks he flew two or three times. Others, he didn't fly at all. It all depended on the weather and the availability of aircraft and instructor pilots. To add insult to injury, all flights were flown in the two-seat model with an instructor on board, as if the new arrivals could not be trusted to fly alone. It was demoralizing and humiliating.

After awhile, the waiting became too much, and Skip started going downtown to the bars. Bob usually went with him. Corky preferred to stay at home and write long letters to Delores. Skip knew that he was playing a dangerous game. His experience in Tachikawa taught him that much. Still, the opportunity to kick back, relax, and forget about his problems was appealing, and as time went on, he went more often. The scene at Misawa was similar to Tachikawa—narrow, neon-lit streets filled with restaurants, bars, and shops twisting and turning in every direction. There was an unwritten rule that three of the bars downtown were patronized only by officers. These were the higher-class places staffed with more educated hostesses. Skip and Bob preferred the Bar Interlude. It was the unofficial officers' club for the 531st and was located just a half a block from the main gate. "I like the place. I can crawl back to the base if I have to," Bob once commented. Many nights he and Skip did just that.

The proprietress of the Bar Interlude was named Jeannie. She had been in the business a long time, although she was not yet thirty-five years old. Rumor had it that she had a brief fling with Colonel John when he first arrived at Misawa without his family. Skip seriously doubted that, given John's strict sense of morals, but it made for a good story. Skip's favorite hostess was Mariko. She was from a suburb of Tokyo and had attended two years of college. She was not the prettiest girl in the bar, but she had a winning smile and a quick, clever wit. Like Jeannie, she had been in the business several years, and her looks were beginning to fade. But this didn't matter to Skip. He enjoyed talking to her and considered her a friend, nothing more. Mariko, on the other hand, adored him. Bob also had a favorite named Hiroko, who happened to be Mariko's friend.

A typical evening started when Skip and Bob went to the officers' club for happy hour. After a few martinis, when both were feeling mellow, Bob would announce that it was time to strafe the machi. "Machi" was a Japanese word for village or town. Skip never objected, and within minutes they would be downtown, their pockets filled with yen. Their first stop was an upscale restaurant next to the Bar Interlude, which specialized in Kobe beef steaks. The steaks were always cooked to perfection and mouthwatering. They usually arrived at the Bar Interlude around ten o'clock. It was seldom crowded on weeknights. Sometimes they sat with friends; other times they sat alone. Once they sat down, they were always joined by Mariko and Hiroko. Sinking into deep, cushioned chairs, the four of them would laugh, joke, and talk, while drinking tall, cold bottles of Japanese beer. Skip enjoyed those times of camaraderie and easy intimacy. They made the stress and headaches of life on the base melt away.

By midnight, a patron was supposed to tell his hostess if he wanted to spend the night with her. This could be arranged for about four thousand yen, roughly ten dollars. At first, Skip always left early and never offered to go home with Mariko. But after a few visits, he relented. After all, he reasoned, this was her livelihood, and she deserved to be paid for all the time she had given him. The first time he went home with her, he explained that they were not going to make love, and he would not be spending the night. "I just can't do it," he said. "I love my wife, and it would devastate her if she found out. Besides, it's not right." Mariko nodded and said she understood. If her feelings were hurt, she didn't show it. They spent the rest of the evening playing with her dog and talking about books and music. He went home with Mariko several times, but it was always the same. It didn't occur to him that she yearned to show her friendship in a more physical way. Nor did it occur to him that she would be devastated when Christy arrived, and he abruptly disappeared from her life. She'll find another guy the minute I leave and forget all about me, he rationalized.

One morning he heard someone moving around in Bob's quarters. He was certain that Bob was not there. Crossing the adjoining bathroom quietly and peeking in the other door, he saw Hiroko, humming softly, making the bed.

"Hiroko-san, what are you doing here?"

"I waiting for Bob-san. We come here last night."

"Did he tell you to stay here and wait?"

"Oh yes. He say no sweat."

Skip was doubtful. "When did he say this?"

"When we left the bar."

Skip was there when Hiroko and Bob left the bar. He doubted if Bob remembered coming home, much less telling Hiroko she could stay with him.

"Well, okay. But be careful. If the air police find you here, you're in big trouble, understand?"

"Okay, Skip-san. I be careful."

Skip caught up with Bob at lunch. He looked like death warmed over, nursing the worst hangover he had ever experienced.

"Hey good buddy, you have a guest in your quarters. Did you know that?"

Bob nodded wearily, unable to focus his eyes on Skip because of the pain. "I know, I know. Just let me get rid of this headache, and I'll take her home."

"Well, you better. Colonel John would not be amused if he found out about this."

Hiroko was still there the next day. One of the maids gave her extra pillows, and she spent the day rearranging Bob's clothes and making his room homier.

"This is bad shit," Skip said when he saw Bob later. "You've gotta do something."

I know. It's just that…"

"Let me ask you this. Have you considered the fact that our wives will probably be here in a few weeks? How are you going to explain Hiroko to Jan? I can see it all now. Honey, this is the maid. She is so conscientious that she stays here twenty-four hours a day, just to be sure nothing gets dirty."

"Tonight after work, I swear to God. I'm gonna take her back to the club and drop her off."

"Good thinking."

Hiroko was still there the third day.

Bob rushed over to Skip immediately after the morning briefing. "Listen man, I've got a problem."

"No shit, Red Ryder."

"I mean, you don't understand. I know I have to kick Hiroko out, but I just can't bring myself to do it. She's so…so…defenseless."

"So what do you expect me to do about it? Throw her out for you?"

"Would you? It would mean a lot to me."

"Let me get this straight. You want me to go to your quarters and throw your Japanese girlfriend out on her ass? Give me a friggin' break."

Bob leaned forward, a look of desperation on his face, and grasped Skip by the arm. "We're the Blunderbirds, right? We stick together and take care of each other, don't we?"

Skip could see Bob was deadly serious. He weighed his options quickly and decided. "All right. I'll give it a shot, but I'm not making any promises."

Skip formulated a plan on his way back to his quarters and moved quickly to execute it. Rushing into Bob's room out of breath and in a panic, he began waving his arms and talking excitedly. "Hiroko-san, you've got to get out of here. The security police are doing a sweep of all the quarters looking for people who are not supposed to be here. We have to move fast. They are just two buildings away. They'll be here any minute."

A look of doubt crossed Hiroko's face for a moment, but then she began to panic and rushed about the room stuffing her belongings in a large tote bag.

When she was ready to leave, Skip held the door for her and began to speak in a quiet, conspiratorial voice. "Okay Hiroko-san, here's what we're going to do. We're going to walk to the car slow and casual-like, like we know what we're doing. If anyone asks what you are doing here, tell them you came to pick up some clothes for alterations. Got that?"

"Hai. I understand."

Five minutes later they glided through the main gate, Skip crisply returned the security policeman's salute, as Hiroko sat primly in the front seat. He drove straight ahead and pulled up in front of the Bar Interlude. "Sorry I have to drop you off like this, but I have to get back to work."

"I understand. You are a very good friend, Skip-san, to do this for me."

"It's the least I could do."

Hiroko slid across the seat and quickly kissed him on the cheek. Then she got out of the car and dashed into the bar, not looking back. He turned the car around and hurried back to the base.

Later in the day, Skip and Bob met at happy hour. "Thanks a lot old buddy. I really owe you one," Bob said.

"Owe me one? Surely you jest. It's going to take more than one of anything to pay me back for what I did for you today."

"Meaning what?"

"Well for starters, I have no intention of paying for a single drink tonight, here at the club or anywhere else."

"Well, that's fair, I guess."

"And then there's the matter of dinner…"

Bob sighed heavily. "Okay, we'll go downtown for a steak later. I'll pay."

"There's one more thing," Skip said later.

"Now what?"

"I think you should follow Corky's example and stay home more often. You know, writing letters to Jan, that kind of thing."

Bob stared at his martini for a moment. "You're busting my balls, aren't you?"

"Certainly not. You need a transition period before she gets here. You've been riding them hard and putting them away wet lately, old buddy. It's time to slack off."

"But what kind of fighter pilot would stay at home every night writing letters to his wife when he could be downtown drinking and chasing pussy?"

"The kind of fighter pilot who doesn't want to get caught and end up paying alimony and child support. That's what kind!"

"You've got a point. We'll talk about it at the Bar Interlude tonight after dinner."

"Okay."

Skip woke up the next morning feeling filled with motivation. He was certain the house would be finished in a week or two. He was scheduled to fly twice, and there was not a cloud in the sky. No weather cancellation today. As he bounded up the steps to the operations building, he was ready to meet head-on whatever the world had in store for him this fine day.

The scene that confronted him when he walked in froze him in his tracks. Six pilots clustered around the ops counter were speaking in hushed tones. Behind the counter the scheduling officer was on the phone listening worriedly, replying only occasionally with a cryptic "Yes sir," "I understand," or "Will do."

"What's going on?" Skip asked.

"Big Jim Landry is down," someone said.

"What happened?"

"We don't know yet. Apparently his engine flamed out while making a practice instrument approach, and he punched out over Matsushima Bay. It took awhile for the base chopper to pick him up. It's on the way home now."

"He's probably okay," Skip said without conviction.

But Jim Landry wasn't okay. When he plunged into the cold water, a twenty-five-knot wind billowed his parachute and began dragging him face down, out to sea. Fighting for his life and slowly drowning, he tried desperately to free himself from the parachute by activating the two quick releases on his parachute harness. It was his only chance to live. But he couldn't grasp the metal releases with his wet, slippery fingers. He was still clawing at the releases when he died. The helicopter chased him five miles before retrieving his lifeless body and bringing it on board.

It was the fifth funeral Skip had attended since arriving in Misawa. After the service he found himself standing with Flo Landry, offering his condolences. Ordinarily a tough-as-nails woman with thick makeup and dyed black hair, she was devastated and sobbing like a child.

"I just feel so bad," she said between sobs. "I gave that man so much grief, and now he's gone before I had time to tell him how much I loved him."

"Oh, I think he knew that, and I know for sure that he loved you very much," Skip said.

"You think so?"

"I know so." Skip gave her a reassuring hug.

It seemed strange consoling Big Jim's widow and giving her comfort after Big Jim had gone out of his way to make him miserable every chance he got. But it was the right thing to do.

The next day, he walked briskly into the A Flight room vowing to start the day on a positive note.

"Ah, speak of the devil," the man behind the desk said. "I was just going over your training records. I have to say that your performance so far has been far from sterling. In fact it's been downright weak. We have to do something about that, don't we?"

The speaker was the new A Flight commander, Capt. Duke Christiansen.

*   *   *   *

Skip paced nervously in the passenger terminal at Tachikawa. Christy's flight was due to arrive in thirty minutes. Outside, dark, gray clouds hugged the tree-tops, and intermittent showers had left the asphalt parking ramp wet and gleaming. The sunless sky made it feel like evening, although it was not yet noon. The waiting room was stifling. Skip stepped outside to get some fresh air, but the raw, biting wind quickly drove him back inside. Even though it was cold, the air was laced with the same fetid, indefinable smell he first noticed when he landed here five months ago. Christy will smell it too, he thought. Five months. It was hard to believe he had been in Japan that long. The first four months crept along from one disappointment to another. Then, almost overnight, everything changed. One day he was looking at his house thinking it would never be finished, and two days later it was done. It took the Air Force just one week to inspect it and authorize Christy and Maddie's travel to Japan. Meanwhile, Colonel John decided the checkout program mandated by PACAF was taking far too long. He needed pilots now, not in three months. After much discussion, the authorities agreed and waived the remainder of the course. One week later, Skip and the other new-comers were given check rides and certified as combat ready.

Not all the changes in the past month were positive. The relationship between Skip and his new flight commander was tense and getting worse every day. Duke Christiansen made it clear both publicly and privately that he didn't like him. As far as he was concerned, Skip was immature and undisciplined, with marginal flying skills. Skip, on the other hand, thought Duke was an arrogant asshole, anxious to make himself look good at the expense of his peers. Unlike Big Jim Landry, Duke never addressed the subject of Skip being his assistant, even though he was the next most senior officer in the flight. It was unthinkable, considering the low opinion he had of him. In meetings, Duke would generally ignore Skip and often assigned important responsibilities to younger officers to "make sure the job got done." These public humiliations made Skip so angry at times that he wanted to invite Duke outside to settle their differences with fists. But he never did, because he was sure that's what Duke wanted him to do—lose his temper and give him a reason to get rid of him once and for all. Duke was Skip's first-line supervisor and wrote his effectiveness reports. One derogatory report, or even one that "damned him with faint praise," would ruin his career. And they both knew it.

He couldn't understand why Duke disliked him so much. It seemed like it all started the day they met at Nellis. He thought about that day many times, trying to figure out what he'd said or done that might have triggered it. But he could think of nothing. Finally, he concluded that if there was such a thing as love as first sight, why not dislike at first sight?

Love at first sight. Christy! The words jerked him out of his somber reverie. She would be arriving any minute. Family...that's what's important. Duke Christiansen can wait. I'll deal with him later. There's always a way. Nervously, Skip dashed into the men's room and combed his hair for the third time since he got there. A scratchy voice on the loudspeaker announced that MATS Flight 5172 from Travis Air Force, California, had landed and would be at the gate in ten minutes. Skip's heart skipped a beat. It was finally going to happen. He thought back to the day he arrived in Japan on the same flight, jammed in a cabin full of sweaty, irritable passengers all eager to leap up and rush out the cabin door like trapped animals. Your ordeal was a piece of cake compared to what Christy just went through, he reminded himself—trapped in an airplane for thirty-six hours with a restless nine-month-old child. Oh God, she's going to be trashed.

The aircraft lumbered into view and turned slowly toward the parking ramp with two of its engines already shut down. The rain had stopped and a few rays of sunshine cast a faint glow on the wet asphalt. When all four engines were stopped, ground crews positioned two mobile stairways to allow for the passengers to debark. The plane was full, and passengers streamed out of both doors for several minutes. He waited impatiently for Christy. What if she isn't on the plane? What if she missed the flight in California? He began to panic. Then he saw her, standing at the top of the stairs looking around anxiously, wearing a rumpled trench coat, shapeless brown slacks, and brown loafers. Her hair was pulled back in a ponytail. She was holding a large, wiggling bundle, capped with a red bonnet. He waved his arms vigorously, "Christy! Christy! Over here!" A look of relief passed over her face. She tried to wave back but couldn't because she was holding Maddie. All she could manage was a weak smile. She's exhausted, he thought. Totally exhausted.

Skip rushed over to his family the minute they entered the terminal, throwing his arms around both of them, hugging them for dear life. "There you are at last," he said, gathering them in his arms. "I have missed you both." Christy looked up and kissed him, her face pale and drawn. "It was awful," she said. "Just awful."

"I know baby, I know."

"No you don't know. Your daughter fussed and cried the entire flight and never fell asleep, even for a minute. Needless to say, I didn't sleep either. I tried to give her away, but there were no takers. She's all yours now, I've had it."

Skip clucked sympathetically and pulled Maddie into his arms. "Is that right sweet pea? Were you a little stinker the whole flight?" As he lifted her into his arms, she began to scream, kicking her feet angrily against his chest.

"Hey, hey, what's going on? I'm your father, remember?"

"No she doesn't remember. You're a stranger, and she's scared. She hasn't seen you for five months, more than half of her life so far."

Skip held on to Maddie firmly but gently and began to walk toward the luggage carousel. "Well, we'll just have to get reacquainted, won't we?" She continued to kick and cry but soon became too tired to go on. Then she fell asleep on his shoulder.

Christy rolled her eyes in exasperation. "Thirty-six hours on the airplane making everyone miserable. Now she falls asleep."

"It's probably my seductive charm."

"Well, don't expect that charm to work on me anytime soon. After what you put me through, I'm not sure I even like you. By the way, what is that disgusting smell?"

"You don't want to know. I'll tell you about it later."

He gathered up the luggage and guided his family to a waiting taxi.

Christy got into the car reluctantly. "Honey, do we have to go to Misawa today? I'm so tired. I'm almost brain-dead."

"Nope. We are booked on a military flight tomorrow afternoon. We have a room at the guest quarters tonight with nothing to do but bathe, eat, and sleep."

Christy sighed with relief and placed her head on his shoulder. "Thank God." She was asleep by the time they arrived at the quarters.

Christy never stirred until nine the next morning. Maddie woke up twice but quickly went back to sleep after drinking the bottles that Skip gave her. By mid-morning everyone was refreshed, rested, and ready to start their new adventure in Misawa, Japan. It was one week before Thanksgiving, 1961.

*   *   *   *

They landed at Misawa in late afternoon. Snow was falling in wet globs like pancakes, sticking to their hair, eyelids, and clothes as they trudged from the terminal to the parking lot. All training flights had been canceled, and the base was eerily quiet. Now and then, a snowplow rumbled by, doggedly trying to beat back the falling snow. Christy looked around her and shuddered. She didn't know why.

"Here we are," Skip proclaimed cheerily, pointing to a large mound of snow. "The old Chevy convertible."

"Oh, wow! I forgot that we had her shipped over here."

"Yep, and she survived the crossing like a trooper."

"I sure hope she'll start, after being covered in all this snow."

"Are you kidding? She spent three winters in Presque Isle, remember? She loves this stuff."

He dropped the luggage and began vigorously brushing the snow off the back of the car. Eventually the trunk appeared. He opened it quickly and brought out a large Air Force parka. "Here honey, put this on. It'll keep you dry. I also brought a baby seat for Maddie." He took a shovel out from the trunk and set about digging out the car. It took about ten minutes, but when he was finished, the windshields were scraped clean, and the engine purred warmly. Maddie watched all of the activity with curiosity, as she lay bundled in Christy's arms. Gazing skyward, she giggled when snowflakes landed on her eyelids and licked her lips when they fell on her mouth.

"You like that stuff, don't you, sweet pea?" Skip said. "That's called snow. You'll be seeing a lot of that here. "

"I'll bet," Christy commented dryly.

Although the base was deserted, the streets outside the main gate were ablaze with neon lights, their sidewalks jammed with people. Many of the young airmen who were sent home from work early had been drinking in the local bars all afternoon. The snow-covered streets took on a festive air, as laughing and singing men thronged from one bar to another looking for new adventures. Occasionally, a hostess ventured outside to say goodbye to a customer, the bright colors of her kimono contrasting starkly with the falling snow. Christy took it all in as the car rolled down the main street. It was a fascinating scene, but at the same troubling. She didn't know what to make of it, not yet anyway.

The unpaved street leading to their house was covered with a thick blanket of snow, the muddy ruts underneath frozen solid. At one point the car dropped into a rut so hard that its frame slammed onto the road with a metallic crunch, throwing Christy against the dashboard. "Yeow," she cried. "Watch what you're doing."

"Sorry," he said sheepishly. The neighborhood looks nice covered with snow, he thought. Like a Christmas card from New England. I wonder what Christy is going to say when it all melts and the place becomes a dump again?

"Well, here we are," Skip said. "Chateau O'Neill." Stepping gingerly across a small snowdrift, he opened a sliding door and ushered her into a tiny foyer with a concrete floor. There was a small wooden bench and a rack for shoes. "Every Japanese house has a room like this. It's where you take your shoes off before going inside." After they removed their shoes, he unlocked the main door and led Christy inside. The kitchen and dining area was just inside the doorway and beyond that was the living room. The kitchen was equipped with a refrigerator, electric stove, and plenty of cabinets. There was a four-piece chrome dining set. The entire house was the size of a modest two-bedroom apartment. All furniture had been provided by the Air Force. Everything was clean and functional. A small table lamp glowed in the living room, shedding light on a beige sofa with matching easy chair and an oak coffee table. There were no pictures hung on the white plaster walls. The windows were covered by dark brown drapes for privacy. Between the kitchen and living room, a large oil stove burned, filling the house with welcome warmth.

Christy looked around appraisingly. "Not bad…not bad at all. This could really be cute when I fix it up."

"Beats the hell out of Laredo," Skip volunteered.

"Who turned on the lights and started the stove?"

"Jan did. Bob's in Korea this week. She said to tell you she'd be over tomorrow around lunchtime."

"Great! I've missed her so much. What about Corky and Delores?"

"Delores will be here in two weeks, thank God! Corky's been like a bear with a sore paw lately. If the weather clears tomorrow, he will take his final check ride. Then we'll be all set. The three of us living with our wives in the same neighborhood. Pretty neat, huh?"

"Yeah," Christy said absently. She was already thinking about how to decorate the house.

They walked down a short hallway to the two bedrooms, one large and one small. "This is the master bedroom," Skip said, sliding open a door made of rice paper in a thin wood frame. The room was sparsely furnished with a double bed and a single chest of drawers. The floor was covered wall to wall with sections of tatami mats, each one measuring four by six feet. They were made of tightly woven straw and were four inches thick.

"The Japanese usually sleep on the floor on top of a padded quilt called a futon," Skip said.

"I'll take an old-fashioned bed, thank you very much," Christy said.

The second bedroom was smaller but furnished much the same. Skip put Maddie on the floor. "And this, Princess, is your room. What do you think?"

Maddie looked around for a moment and then began to crawl vigorously across the floor, laughing with glee.

"I think she likes it," Skip said.

The last stop was the bathroom. "Wow, the bathtub is huge," Christy said. "We could both get in there. I like that. I like that a lot."

"So do I, and I like the way you think."

*   *   *   *

The sun was shining through the small bedroom window when Christy woke up. It was nine o'clock, and Skip had long since left for work. For a moment, she was confused and disoriented. Then she remembered. Misawa! She put on a robe, walked to the window, and looked outside. It was a discouraging sight, even in the bright sunlight. They were surrounded by rows of small, squat, identical houses. The snow was beginning to melt, and water was streaming off the gut-ter-less roofs. Meanwhile, passing cars had turned the streets into a sodden mess, tossing mud onto the snowbanks and sides of the houses. Yuck, she thought. Then she shrugged her shoulders. Not my idea of paradise, but hey, it's not for-ever. What did Skip say? We'd be living on base in six or seven months? I can live with that.

She walked into Maddie's room and found her lying in the crib giggling and cooing, her little feet kicking at the side railings. She was dressed in a clean diaper with a fresh bottle at her side. "Well, look at you. Don't you look bright and chipper this morning? And with a clean diaper yet. Daddies are kinda useful to have around sometimes, aren't they? Stay here for a few minutes while Mommy takes a bath, then we'll play, okay?"

Christy went into the bathroom and started filling the tub. The water burst out of the faucet, hot and steaming. She added lavender bath salts and went into the kitchen to make a fresh pot of coffee. When she returned, the tub was almost full. Slipping off her robe, she stepped into the water. Yeow! The water was ice cold. Impatiently, she put her hand under the tap. The water coming out was certainly not hot anymore, but it wasn't cold. She didn't understand. The water coming out was hot, but the water in the tub was cold. Discouraged, she let the tub drain and took a sponge bath using warm water from the sink. "Not a good start," she said out loud.

At noon, there was a knock on her door. It was Jan, standing in the outside foyer taking off a pair of muddy rubber boots while holding a basket.

"Come in, my dear friend," Christy cried. "How are you? I really missed you."

"Welcome to Misawa," Jan replied, giving her a big hug. "I missed you too."

"What's in the basket?"

"Just a few things for lunch—fried chicken, potato salad, a fresh salad, some cheese and crackers and…a bottle of wine."

"Oh, wow. Just like Las Vegas. I sure miss those days.

"Me too."

The two women sat in the living room and began nibbling on the cheese and crackers. Jan looked around the room. "I see we have the same decorator, same furniture and everything."

"Nothing but the best, I always say," Christy replied. They both laughed.

There were a few moments of awkward silence, then Christy said, "Well, what do you think about this place?"

"This house you mean?"

"I mean everything. The house, the neighborhood, the base, Japan…everything."

Jan chose her words carefully. "Well, for starters, this neighborhood is a dump. I've seen slums back home that looked better. But we won't be here forever. Hopefully, we'll be on base in six months or so. And that's a good thing too, because Bob has only been gone three days, and I hate it already. This is definitely not a good place to be left alone. There's just nothing to do here. And another thing…" Jan started to but changed her mind.

"Yes? Go on. Tell me."

"Well, it's just that whenever I am around the people in the squadron I get a bad feeling, like something is not right. Everyone is depressed, and morale is low. There's no esprit de corps. Not that I blame them, mind you. After all, six pilots have been killed this year. You know that, don't you?"

Christy nodded and shuddered.

"And to make matters worse, who do they take everything out on? Newcomers like our husbands. As if they had anything to do with it. It's just not right."

Jan paused to sip her wine, brightened, and then continued. "On the other hand, a lot of the squadron wives are really nice, and there's always something going on at the wives' club. In fact, there's always something going on at the base, period. That's why we have to make a rule."

"A rule?"

"Yep. Bob and Skip can never take both cars to work. They always have to leave one at home, so we can escape. If we get stuck out here without transportation, we're doomed."

"Sounds good to me. I agree."

The conversation drifted on to other things. After awhile, Christy leaned forward and began to speak hesitantly. "Jan, can I ask you a question?"

"What?"

"When we drove home last night, we passed all those bars and nightclubs."

Jan rolled her eyes back. "Ah, yes. The so-called hostess bars."

"Right. What I was wondering is…"

"What you're wondering is, do the customers take those Japanese girls home and screw them? Or more specifically, did Bob and Skip do that while we were gone?"

Christy blushed and began to stammer. "Well, umm, yes, I guess that's what I'm asking."

Jan sighed and leaned back in her chair. "Look, Christy, let me put it this way. I haven't a clue what Bob did while I was away, and quite frankly, if he did take one of those girls home, I don't want to know about it."

"You don't? I don't understand. Don't you care what he does?"

"I didn't say I didn't care. I said I didn't want to know about it. Those are two different things. Of course I care." Jan's face softened. "Look, there is a lot of little boy in most men. They like to play once in awhile, and there's nothing we can do about it. To make our marriages survive, we have to praise them when they are good and scold them when they are bad. It's like potty training, don't you see?"

The image of potty training Skip made Christy break out laughing. Still, what Jan said made a lot of sense.

Jan looked at her watch and rose to leave. "Geesh, I'm late. Got some errands to run."

"By the way," Christy said, "I had the oddest experience this morning. I filled the tub with steaming hot water and when I stepped in—

"It was ice cold," Jan finished for her.

"Yeah, how did you know?"

"Skip forgot to tell you that our bathtubs are really pits dug in the ground and lined with tile. They work okay in the summer, but in the winter when the ground freezes, it's like pouring boiling water into the refrigerator. There's not enough hot water in the heater to make a difference."

"So how am I supposed to take a bath?"

"The Japanese make these enormous teapots so you can boil extra water on the stove. I'll pick one up for you today."

"Great!"

"Have Skip boil the water for you whenever you want a bath."

"And praise him when he does it, right?"

"Now you're learning."

*   *   *   *

At precisely 1:15 PM, Winchester 22 reached the initial point and started its final run to the target. The aircraft was carrying a two thousand-pound practice bomb that simulated the size and shape of a nuclear weapon. Corky glanced at the stopwatch on the instrument panel. He was only five seconds early at the initial point. Not bad, he thought. Now, if I don't toss the bomb to east Jesus somewhere, I'll be home free. Pushing the throttle up, he accelerated to five hundred knots and checked his armament switches one last time. "Ripsaw range, Winchester 22 is on the final run for a LABS maneuver. This is a check ride," he called.

"Roger, Winchester 22, cleared hot."

In the back seat, Capt. Marty Hale, the check pilot, also thought Corky would be home free. His student had flown an excellent flight so far, and he was already jotting down notes for the grade sheet. Marty was a highly motivated young man whose love of flying was only exceeded by his love of his wife and five children. Marty was a non-drinking, non-smoking Mormon which was a rarity in the fighter squadrons, and his peers loved to tease him. "Hey, Marty," they would say, "you need to loosen up and have a drink once in awhile. It'll help get your head on straight. For example, you're supposed to have a bunch of wives first, then a bunch of kids." Marty always took their teasing good-naturedly.

At 1:18:26, the aircraft yawed violently to the left, rolled inverted, and slammed into the ground. They were traveling at 845 feet per second on impact. The sound of the crash was heard for miles. The range officer, who was watching for their arrival, not only heard the explosion but saw the fireball and the thick, oily column of smoke that rose immediately thereafter. He pressed the mike button on his radio, but there was nothing to say. Oh shit, he thought, and reached for the red phone. It took nearly four hours for fire and rescue teams to slog through snowdrifts in the dense forest to the crash site. Pieces of the wreckage, as well as several hundred acres of trees, were still burning. There were no survivors.

The next day, investigators began sifting through the wreckage seeking clues to the cause of the accident. Pieces of wreckage were scattered throughout a three-mile radius. There was nothing left of the pilots except bits and pieces of body parts in the snowbanks and surrounding trees. These were carefully placed in plastic bags and carried out by the investigating team. Several weeks later, the accident board concluded that an abnormal amount of rudder had been applied just before the crash. The cause of the accident was listed as unknown.

*   *   *   *

"Explain it to me again. I'm just not getting it," Bob said. His eyes were glazed, and he was slurring his words. Both the funeral and the informal wake were over. He and Skip were the last customers in the stag bar.

"I told you before, I can't explain it. Shit like that happens. Maybe it's a random thing."

Bob slammed his hand on the bar, spilling his drink. "Unacceptable answer!" he roared. The bartender glanced at him uneasily and moved farther down the long bar. "Didn't you hear what the chaplain said today? God loved him so much he brought him to heaven to be with him."

"I know but…"

"That's bullshit, Skip, and you know it. How does he do that? Does he look down and say, 'Gee I'm kinda lonely today. I think I'll kill that nice young man in the airplane down there and maybe…I don't know…that whole family driving down the freeway.' It doesn't make sense. He had so much to live for."

"More than you know."

"What do you mean?"

"Christy talked to Delores back in the States today, just before the funeral. She's five-and-a-half months pregnant."

Bob slumped onto the bar and moaned, "Oh, no. Just what she needs." Suddenly he looked up sharply. "Five-and-a-half months?"

"That's right."

"But…they were only married four-and-a-half months ago."

"I know, she mentioned that. Remember the time she came to visit Nellis for a visit, and you were busting his balls about not getting in her pants? You were even going to organize a serenade to get her in the mood, remember?"

Bob broke into a smile.

"Do the math, Ace. It works out."

Bob wobbled to his feet, his glass raised, as he looked skyward. "Yes Corky! Done like a true Blunderbird. I knew you could do it…I just knew it. You did it. You did it. Here's to you, my friend!"

The sight of Bob shouting at the sky, made Skip laugh, and he rose to join him. Standing together, they began recalling funny things they had done together, looking upward all the while, as if Corky were standing beside them. The more stories they told, the harder they laughed.

"I still think we need Corky more than God does," Bob said, wiping the tears of laughter from his eyes.

"Yeah, we need him. Let God pay for his own drinks."

"Right. God can say, 'Bartender, bring another round for my friends.' And poof, they're all lined up on the bar. We can't do that, but we always had Corky." They raised their glasses solemnly.

The moment of joy and laughter passed as quickly as it came. "The hell of it is Delores told Christy she was going crazy waiting for the house to be built. She wanted to get away from her parents before she started to show."

"That fucking Sunabori," Bob mumbled, cursing the builder.

"Now it doesn't make any difference."

There was an awkward silence. "I guess that's the end of the Blunderbirds," Bob said finally.

"No," Skip said sharply and grasped him by the shoulder. "Nobody said the Blunderbirds had to be a flight of three or even a flight of four, did they?"

"No."

"And we're still here, right?"

"Right."

"Then we're still the Blunderbirds!"

"You bet your sweet ass we are."

Skip stood up and drained his glass. "Let's go home my friend. Our wives are waiting for us. This has been a tough day for them too."

Together they weaved through the door and into the darkness. Skip was glad no one could see him crying.

*   *   *   *

Corky's death changed everything. Skip realized that life was more fragile than he thought and should not be squandered recklessly. He had a wife and family and a career. People counted on him, and he wasn't going to let them down. He decided he had been trying too hard to be a nice guy. When people confronted him, he usually backed down. It was easier that way. Besides, he wanted everyone to like him. That was going to change. From now on, when someone got in his way, he would stand up for himself. And if an obstacle couldn't be removed, he'd run over it. He was not only ready, but looking forward to the next challenge. He didn't have to wait long.

Two weeks after Corky's funeral, he walked into the A Flight office to check his mailbox. Duke looked up from his desk and gave him his usual sarcastic greeting. "Well look who's here!" Skip ignored him and crossed the room.

"I was just writing your effectiveness report," Duke continued, as if talking to himself. "Hmmm, seems like I'm forgetting something. Oh yes, I remember." Abruptly, he rose from his desk and left the room. Skip followed him to the doorway and watched as he walked down the hall to look at the LABS ladder.

The LABS ladder was a list that hung on the wall in operations. It was the bane of his existence and a constant source of embarrassment. On it was the name of every pilot, along with the average score of all the LABS deliveries they had made since joining the squadron. At the top of the ladder was the pilot with the best score. Skip was currently third from the bottom. Duke was gloating when he returned to his desk. "What is it you don't understand about LABS bombing, young man?" he sneered.

"I don't know," Skip replied. He didn't know what else to say. Duke continued writing.

The next day Skip was summoned to Rosie's office. It was Major Rosie now, much to the satisfaction of the squadron pilots. Rosie was not happy. Skip saw that immediately, as he walked into his office. There were two chairs in front of his desk. Duke was sitting in one of them, a satisfied smile on his face. Rosie motioned Skip to the other.

Rosie took his time, puffing his pipe and reading a document in his hand. Finally, he spoke. "I called you in here because I have your annual effectiveness report, which Captain Christiansen just prepared. I want you to read it and tell me if you think it is a fair evaluation." He handed it to Skip without further explanation.

Skip glanced quickly at his Officers Effectiveness Report, or "OER" as it was called. The form called for ten leadership and performance areas to be graded on a scale of one to seven. There was a space under each grade for comments. It was common knowledge that the only score that counted was a seven. Promotion boards that saw even one six took it as a subtle sign the officer somehow didn't measure up. Skip's OER was short and to the point: one seven, eight sixes, and one five. The report was devoid of comments and explanations save for the item graded five, which said, "Failed to grasp the concept of weapons delivery." He stared at the report for a long time, fighting back feelings of anger, frustration, and panic. Rosie and Duke were watching him closely, waiting for him to speak. "Well, I don't know. I suppose you could argue that this report is fair..." He was stalling, and they knew it.

Rosie reached across the desk impatiently, snatching the report from his hand. "I'm sorry you feel that way, Captain, because what you are looking at is a one-way ticket out of the Air Force. Not right away, maybe, but for sure if you get one more like this." Duke's smile widened.

Now, he thought...now's the time to make your move. You want a chance to be the new Skip O'Neill? Well, you've got it. He raised his hand in the air as if signifying he was about to say more. "What I was going to say is that it could be fair if you accept the notion that the only leadership quality that matters in the Air Force is the ability to do LABS maneuvers."

"I didn't say that!" Duke snapped back.

Skip remained calm. "Sorry, I must have misunderstood you. I just assumed that, given the only comment on the form was about weapons delivery..."

The smile on Duke's face faded. He was getting angry. He hadn't expected this confrontation. "Comments? Why? The numbers tell it all. What they say is this guy is w-e-a-k. What part of weak don't you understand?"

Skip continued as if Duke hadn't spoken. "Another thing that caught my eye was that last block on the form, the one that says, 'Summary of deficiencies and plan to overcome them.' It's blank. Perhaps you didn't notice it."

"I noticed it. But what's the point? You have so many deficiencies I wouldn't know where to begin"

"Isn't that one of the qualities of a good leader, to take care of his men and help them grow?"

Duke raised half out of his chair. His face was red and contorted with anger. "I don't need you to lecture me on leadership qualities."

"Enough!" Rosie said sternly. "You are Skip's flight commander. You're supposed to look after him. I want you to go back to your office and sort this thing out. Then have a new OER on my desk by tomorrow morning—one that is more reasonable."

Duke was stung by Rosie's words but tried not to show it. As the two young men rose to leave, Skip noticed a faint twinkle in Rosie's eye. Well I'll be damned, he thought happily, he doesn't like the son of a bitch either.

Duke walked grimly down the hall and into his office. Skip was right behind him. Once inside, Duke sat down at his desk and began to read a paper on his desk. Skip locked the door and waited expectantly. Duke ignored him for a minute or two. Finally he spoke. "Well? What are you standing there for? I don't have time for this shit right now."

Skip walked calmly across the room and leaned over so that his face was level with Duke's. "Sure you do, Captain. Didn't your boss tell you to go back to your office and sort this thing out?"

"Oh, I'll sort it out all right, when I'm ready."

"Look, let's cut through all the bullshit shall we? At some point in time, for whatever reason, you decided you were going to screw me the first chance that you got. You knew you were going to do it, and I knew you were going to do it. Now you've done it. What happens next?"

"I'm sorry you're taking this so personally. The bottom line is I consider you to be a weak and undisciplined pilot. I've told you that before. This is a nuke squadron, and we don't have time to screw around with weak-dicks like you. That OER was my way of telling you I don't want you in my flight."

Skip walked away from the desk and gazed thoughtfully out the window, his hands clasped behind his back. When he turned, his face was calm, his voice soft and reasonable. "Well, for the first time since we met we see eye to eye on something."

"What does that mean?"

"It means you don't want me in your flight, and I sure as shit don't want to work for you. It's a piece of cake. Just ask Major Rosie to transfer me to another flight, and bingo, we're both happy."

A malicious smile crossed Duke's face. "There's just one problem. I would never do that."

"Of course you wouldn't," Skip snapped back. His voice cracked through the air like a slap in the face. "Because that would mean admitting that Duke Christiansen, boy fighter pilot and newbie flight commander, has run into a problem he can't handle. And that wouldn't be good for your fair-haired boy image, now would it?"

Duke leaped to his feet, his face contorted with rage, his fists away from his body. "Don't you ever talk to me like that again," he shouted. "I am your flight commander and the senior ranking officer here."

"Oh puleez!" Skip shouted back. "Spare me the senior ranking officer bullshit. Three weeks, Duke. That's all you outrank me by—three friggin' weeks."

"You just don't know when to keep your mouth shut do you? Maybe I should just take you out in the parking lot and..." Duke stopped and didn't finish the sentence.

It was Skip's turn to smile maliciously. Duke wasn't about to do anything physical, and they both knew it. Skip took a moment to calm himself. When he continued, his voice was quieter and more in control. "Okay, I'm a reasonable man, so how about this? I'll go to Major Rosie and request a new flight assignment. I'll even say it was all my fault. Fair enough?"

"I couldn't care less what you do."

"Good, then it's all settled." Skip turned and started for the door. Suddenly he stopped, turned around, and walked back to Duke's desk. "I almost forgot. Going over the head of a superior officer without his permission is not very professional is it? And I am a professional." Skip stood at rigid attention and clicked his heels. "Captain Christiansen, request permission to see Major O'Grady about a new flight assignment."

"I don't give a fuck what you do, O'Neill. Just get the hell out of my office."

"I'll take that for a yes." Skip stepped back, saluted smartly, and left the room.

Skip almost knocked over Bob, who was passing by.

"Did my delicate ears deceive me," Bob said, "or were you just engaged in a minor pissing contest with your esteemed flight commander?"

"Your delicate ears did not deceive you, but I wouldn't characterize it as a minor pissing contest. A major big-time pissing contest is more like it."

"Oh? And how did it all come out?"

Skip grinned broadly. "I busted his balls pretty good."

Bob looked genuinely shocked. "You're joking, right?"

"Nope."

Bob walked away shaking his head. This is not like Skip, he thought. What's gotten into him?

Skip left the building and went for a long walk, thinking about how to present his case to Major Rosie. The cold, fresh air helped clear his mind. He had to do this just right, or he would be in even more trouble. When he returned, he strode resolutely to Rosie's office and knocked on his open door. "Sir, I'd like to speak to you for a moment if I may."

Rosie looked up as if he were expecting him. "Ah, there you are. I was looking for you. Where have you been?"

"Outside, taking a walk."

"I see. Nothing like a brisk walk on a winter day to lower the blood pressure and put things back in perspective."

"Pardon me?"

Rosie smiled. "The walls are pretty thin here, and the A Flight office is next to mine. When I told you two to go back and sort things out, I didn't expect it to result in hand-to-hand combat."

Skip's face reddened, and he started to protest. "But sir, we..."

Rosie cut him off with a dismissive wave of his hand. "Never mind that. I should never have assigned you to A Flight. Assigning an officer to work for another of almost equal rank is not ideal, and in the case of a personality conflict, the result can be disastrous. But I was under some pressure from above to make your assignment work, and for awhile I thought it just might. I had no idea things would get out of control so quickly."

Skip nodded. Things were going his way, and he was not about to say something and screw it up.

Rosie leaned back in his chair and lit his pipe. "So, here's what we're going to do. I'm assigning you to Bud Sexton's flight. I'll explain the situation to him this afternoon, and you'll report to him tomorrow morning. Bud's good people and has been around for awhile. In fact, I hope to see him on the major's list next year. Also, there are two other captains in the flight who are experienced pilots and senior to you. That should take the pressure off about your rank versus flying experience."

"Yes sir," Skip managed to say. He couldn't believe his ears. There was no need for him to plead his case.

"Now, as for your OER, the one Duke submitted was way out of line and would never make it up the approval chain, even if I signed it, which I won't. The problem is, he'll submit another that is reasonable, and I'll have to sign it. And that so-called 'reasonable' OER will stand out like a sore thumb in your promotion folder. The bottom line is your Air Force career will soon have its first strike called against it. But the Air Force is not like baseball. It's not three strikes, and you're out. Generally it's two strikes, and you're out. This means the playing field is no longer level for you. You'll have to work harder and do better than the others just to keep up, much less excel. It also means no personality conflicts, errors in judgment, or screwups of any kind. Understand?"

Skip nodded. He had been relaxed, even beginning to smile, a few moments ago. Now his brow was furrowed with concern. "Yes sir, I understand."

Rosie seemed to read his mind. "On the other hand, it's not an impossible situation. I ought to know. I had a personality conflict with my flight commander several years ago, and as you know, this year was my last chance for promotion. Had I failed, I would have been out of the Air Force by now, but I'm still here and still swinging at the ball."

"Yes sir."

"So here's what it all boils down to. You've been in the Air Force how long now? Seven years?"

"Yes sir."

"Well, the race started a long time ago, and you haven't left the starting blocks yet. So, what are you going to do?"

"Get my ass in gear and keep swinging at the ball until I win or they force me to stop."

"Good man."

Rosie made a sign that the discussion was over. Skip scrambled to his feet, thanked him for his help, and headed for the door."

"By the way, what did you want to see me about?"

"Umm...nothing important sir."

"I thought so."

*   *   *   *

Rosie was right about Skip's new flight commander. He *was* good people. He reminded Skip of Tom Denison, Rowdy, and even Cactus Jack—people he had known and trusted. This made him comfortable and optimistic about his new boss. Bud Sexton was not an imposing man, barely six feet tall with a thin wiry frame. His dark hair was cut in a flat-top crew cut. The flecks of gray hair and the wrinkles around his eyes when he laughed suggested that he might be overdue for promotion. Skip wondered if there might have been a "personality conflict" in his past. If so, he would understand why Skip was now in his flight. Understanding his situation wasn't a problem. When he reported for duty, Bud spent fifteen minutes explaining rules, policies, procedures—the usual things newcomers are obliged to learn. He never spoke of why he was there. Likewise, the other members of the flight took little notice of his arrival, other than to welcome him on board. He did notice that the two captains who outranked him were especially friendly and helpful. Skip decided that was because if they outranked him, they probably outranked Duke, which means one of them should have been A Flight commander. They understood his situation better than the others.

His first day in his new flight went very well, except for one bit of bad news. Bud explained that the flight had been short of pilots for several weeks. His pilots needed a rest and some time off. Skip would be going to Korea at the end of the week. Skip was not happy about that, because he had just returned from Korea the week before. He was sure Christy would not be happy to see him leave again so soon either. She was having trouble adjusting to her new life, and he didn't blame her. The neighborhood they lived in was becoming more confining and depressing as the winter snows moved in. Plus, she was depressed about Corky's death and overwhelmed by the strangeness of living in a foreign country. It was a lot for a young woman to deal with, even one as tough as Christy. Skip was worried about her, but there was nothing he could say to his new flight commander, especially on the first day. He would go to Korea. End of story.

*   *   *   *

The winter of 1961–1962 was the worst anyone could remember. The snow came early and remained until early April. It came in relentless waves, creeping softly down from the mountains, pausing to lay a thick carpet of white over the base, before advancing toward the sea. It was not unusual for a shower to stop just shy of its destination, retrace its steps, and then resume its journey, pausing each time to lay down another coat, like a fastidious painter determined not to leave a spot untouched. Sometimes, a snowstorm would arrive with a vengeance, its howling wind tossing mounds of snow that buried everything in its path. When this happened, all activity at the base ceased, as cars, sidewalks, streets, taxiways, and runways were shoveled and plowed. The worst storm came in January. It left the base paralyzed for three days.

While the effects of the snow were inconvenient to the residents of the base, they were devastating to those who lived in Skip and Christy's neighborhood. Many mornings when Skip was away, Christy opened the door and found snowdrifts that had to be shoveled before Yoko, her housekeeper, could get in. Because the streets were never plowed, she had to wait until neighbors created a path to the main street by battering through the snowdrifts in large cars and trucks. Only then could she gain her freedom. Usually a well-worn path was made by mid-morning. Occasionally, the snow would be too much for even the most adventurous motorist. When that happened, she was a prisoner all day.

As the winter tightened its icy noose around the neighborhood, Christy became increasingly depressed and lonely. When Skip was gone, she felt abandoned and uncared for. She, Yoko, and Maddie spent hours on end trapped in the small house gazing out the window at the bleak, sunless landscape. Depression set in, and sometimes at night, when Maddie was fast asleep, Christy lay in bed crying softly, thinking how much she hated her life. At times, she even hated Skip for bringing her to Japan. But that didn't happen very often, because in her heart, she knew she loved him, and all this was not really his fault.

Christy would not have survived the winter had it not been for Jan and two other squadron wives who lived nearby. The four of them became an informal club of sorts, taking turns hosting luncheons at their homes. Trudging through snowdrifts in boots and parkas, each would bring hot dishes to share, as they laughed, talked, and gossiped. In the beginning, these lunches occurred two or three times a week and were the highlight of Christy's day. It was a chance for her to get out and be with other people. It helped her maintain her sanity. The luncheons seldom lasted over three hours. Everyone brought something to drink, and copious amounts of alcohol were drunk, usually some kind of wine or beer. Christy was not a heavy drinker, but she kept up, although some afternoons she returned home too sleepy to function the rest of the day. But Yoko was there, and there was always an opportunity to take a nap. It all seemed harmless enough. Besides, she was not about to give up this lifeline to the rest of the world.

By February, the luncheons were a daily occurrence and lasted well into the afternoon. Sometimes one of the wives would observe that it was almost time for happy hour. This was the signal to bring out the stronger stuff—bourbon, scotch, and gin for martinis. Christy was over her head then, and many afternoons she would return home downright tipsy, her eyes glazed and her movements uncoordinated, going through the motions of being a caring mother as Yoko watched disapprovingly. When that happened, she could not wait to get Maddie into her crib so she could collapse in her bed and sleep it off. This is not right, a voice inside her would say. You're in trouble. But she didn't listen.

One evening she arrived home at seven, staggering drunk. Concerned for Maddie's well-being, Yoko offered to stay for awhile and look after them both, even though she normally left at five. But Christy refused. "It's late," she slurred. "You need to go home to your family. I'll take care of things here." Yoko reluctantly left. Weaving around the house, Christy was scarcely aware of what she was doing. Picking up Maddie, she muttered some words of endearment and took her to her crib. Then she lurched into the bedroom and passed out on the bed.

Christy woke up at midnight to the sound of painful wailing. For a moment, she didn't know where she was. Her head was pounding painfully, and her mouth was incredibly dry. The wailing was coming from Maddie's room. She immediately became cold sober, her senses sharp and alert. Rushing into Maddie's room, she looked in her crib. She was still dressed in her play clothes from the afternoon. Worse yet, it was obvious that she had messed in her pants hours before. The poor child was miserable, choking in sobs as she looked up at her mother. Christy was horrified. She picked Maddie up and rocked her back and forth murmuring, "Oh my poor baby, oh my poor baby," over and over. Laying Maddie on the changing table, Christy began to undress her. Maddie continued to cry, though not as loudly. When Christy took off Maddie's diapers, she saw that the skin underneath was bright red and chafed raw, the result of lying in the urine and feces so long. Christy took Maddie to the changing table and began to clean her up, still murmuring, "Oh my poor baby, oh my poor baby." When she finished, she wrapped Maddie in a blanket and took her in the living room. Sitting on the sofa in the darkened room she rocked her gently, crooning nursery rhymes until Maddie finally fell asleep. Then she put her back in the crib.

She could not go to sleep for a long time. Lying in bed, staring dully at the darkened ceiling, she reviewed the day's events over and over. What's happening to me? What have I become? she thought. A drunk and a bad mother, that's what I've become. This has got to stop. Things have to change. She cried herself to sleep. But it was too late. The luncheons continued, and things didn't change. Skip knew something was wrong. Each time he returned from Korea he saw the pain and stress in her eyes. But she wouldn't tell him what was going on. Neither would Yoko or Christy's friends. Christy was too ashamed, and her friends were too loyal. Skip was in the dark and feeling very frustrated.

In early March a brief thaw raised Christy's spirits, and her life became more normal. One afternoon Jan called. She sounded happy, and her voice had an edge of excitement to it. "Hey girl, it's time to bust out of this place."

"What do you have in mind?"

"What do I have in mind? I have in mind suiting up and going to the club for dinner, acting like grown-ups for a change." Bob and Skip were both in Korea.

"I don't know," Christy said doubtfully.

"What's not to know? Get a babysitter, and let's do it. You know you want to."

"Well, it might be fun," Christy conceded. "Shall we take your car or mine?"

Jan hesitated just slightly. "Let's take them both. I have some errands to run first. We'll meet there at seven."

"Okay, I'll see you there."

Around three o'clock Christy glanced out the window and saw Jan get in her car. Her hair was carefully done, and she was wearing full makeup. She looked gorgeous. That's why Jan wanted to take two cars, she thought. She must have so many errands to run that she won't have time to come back and change. She put the scene out of her mind.

By six thirty she was dressed and ready to go, waiting for the babysitter. Maddie was playing in her bedroom. Christy had taken a hot bath and spent a long time in front of the mirror checking her hair and carefully applying her makeup, trying to look as feminine as possible. She didn't know why she was doing this. It just seemed like the thing to do. When she finished, she liked what she saw. Her long hair hung to her shoulders, brushed until it gleamed, with short, neatly cut bangs framing her forehead. She was wearing stylish, black wool slacks and a gleaming white angora sweater. Both sweater and slacks clung to her body, tight, but not too tight. There was a gold necklace around her neck, as well as a pair of matching earrings. Skip had given those to her on their first anniversary. In a small bag nearby was a pair of matching pumps, sensible, but at the same time glamorous. She would put these on when she arrived at the club. As a final touch, she put a dab of perfume behind each ear.

When the babysitter arrived, Christy went to Maddie's room to say good-bye. "Sweet pea, Mommy's going out for awhile to be a grown-up. Be a good girl and don't give Tammy a hard time, okay?" She gave her a big hug and walked out the door. Once outside she paused, ankle deep in the wet, gray slush, gazing at her sordid surroundings. Although it was not yet six o'clock the sun was already setting, leaving a cold, damp chill in its wake. "Mommy's going out to be a grown-up." Suddenly, the words made her uneasy, and she felt a momentary surge of panic. Maybe this isn't a good idea, she thought. But the moment of doubt passed quickly. Stepping carefully over the snowdrifts, she slid into the car and drove away, leaving the dreary houses and muddy, slush-filled roads behind her.

*　　　　*　　　　*　　　　*

The club was mostly deserted, save for the usual activity downstairs in the stag bar. The main dining room was empty except for one table along the wall. As her eyes adjusted to the dim light, Christy saw Jan sitting at the table talking animatedly to two young Marine pilots in flying suits. Their conversation was light and familiar, as if they knew each other. Jan didn't see her at first, but when she did, she jumped to her feet and rushed to greet her. "There you are, honey. I was afraid you would be late. I was all alone when I got here, and these gentlemen invited me to join them for a drink. Come and meet them. They're really nice guys." She took Christy by the arm and led her to the table. She followed her doubtfully.

"Jim and Brad, this is my very best friend, Christy. Christy this is Jim and Brad." Jim had dark hair and a moustache. Brad was tall and muscular with a blond crew cut and deep blue eyes. Christy had to admit they were both cute, especially Brad. The two men scrambled to their feet for the introductions. Brad pulled out a chair for Christy, and she sat down next to him. Jan returned to her seat beside Jim. She looked at Jan curiously. Something had changed since this afternoon when Jan left the house. Something about her hair, her makeup, or the glowing, almost flushed look on her face. She couldn't put her finger on it. She's probably been drinking, she thought.

The conversation was awkward at first, but then everyone relaxed. After two rounds of drinks, Christy began to feel that happy glow that always came. But she was determined to keep herself in check tonight. "I hope we can all dine together," Brad said. "After all, we're the only ones here." Christy considered this for a minute. Why not? She thought. It would be fun, and it's all on the up-and-up. After all, it's not as if they had anything to hide. They were in the middle of the officers' club for God's sakes!

It was a splendid evening, filled with good food, good conversation, and, of course, a lot to drink. The men were witty and charming, and she had never seen Jan so bright and flirtatious. Christy was skimming atop a light alcoholic haze. Laughing and talking, she was having fun and didn't care who knew it. Nobody was there to see them anyway. At ten o'clock, as she was talking intently to Brad, Jan gave Jim a significant look. "Gosh, look at the time. I've got to go."

Jim rose hastily. "I'll walk you to the car." A moment later they were gone.

Brad and Christy looked at each other awkwardly. They didn't know what to say. It was obvious that neither wanted the evening to end. Not yet anyway. They ordered an after-dinner drink, then another. Christy told him about Skip and how they met and about their life off base.

"He sounds like a really nice guy."

"He is, and I love him very much."

They switched to coffee. Christy's mind began to clear, and she felt more in control. "How about you? Are you married?"

"Yes, for three years."

"Any children?"

Brad smiled wryly. "Not yet. Linda has this old-fashioned idea that I should be around first to help raise them."

"I can see her point. Where is she now?"

Brad hesitated for moment, and then he looked deep into her eyes. "I don't know."

"You don't know?"

"The last time I saw her she was in North Carolina. That's where I left her when I came over here. Now she's disappeared. Nobody knows where she went. Of course somebody does. Linda is a beautiful woman, and there are a lot of guys back in the States available to help her with her loneliness problem."

"That must be awful for you. I am so sorry." Christy reached across the table and took his hand gently. "Listen to me. Things like this have a way of working out, especially if you love each other. And if you don't, it's probably for the best."

"I know, you're right, and I think about that a lot. Especially the part about whether she loves me. That's the most painful part."

The conversation turned to lighter subjects. They had another cup of coffee. Suddenly, Christy realized she was still holding his hand. She withdrew it awkwardly. Brad pretended not to notice. The little voice inside was saying something, but she couldn't hear it, or perhaps she didn't want to hear it.

Christy reluctantly looked at her watch. "Look at the time. I really have to go."

"I'll walk you to the car."

"That would be nice," she heard herself say.

They stopped at the cloak room. Brad watched as she took the snow boots out of the bag. "Let me help you with that," Brad said, kneeling down. It was a gentlemanly gesture, yet the feel of his strong hands on her foot and lower leg taking off her pumps and putting on her boots, excited her.

They walked into the cold, night air and started for the car. Halfway there she realized they were walking arm in arm, bodies pressed together for warmth. She could hear the small voice now, speaking urgently. "What are you doing? This is not right. You're a married woman!" She ignored it and continued dreamily on. When they got to Christy's car, they paused. Neither knew what to do. Christy felt excited and attracted to this man, yet she knew it was wrong. Suddenly, almost by mutual consent, Brad drew her into his arms and kissed her. It was a long kiss, bodies pressed together, tongue just inside of her mouth. She could feel the rising urgency between his legs. Her breasts were against his chest. Christy's brain was reeling with desire. He smelled good, he tasted good, and he felt good. She didn't want him to stop. When it was over, Christy stepped backed to catch her breath. "Wow! That was some kiss."

Brad still held her lightly in his arms. "I'm sorry. I didn't mean to come on to you like that. It just that…it was something I've wanted to do all evening."

Christy wanted to tell him it was something she'd wanted to do all evening too. But she didn't.

"Look, Christy, I don't want you to take this the wrong way, but this has been a remarkable evening for me, and I just don't want it to end. Not yet, anyway. Why don't you come with me for a nightcap? My quarters have a small living room. We could talk some more."

Christy's head was spinning. To her shock and amazement she wanted to go with him. She wanted to lie in his arms and yes, let him make love to her. She considered her options. The babysitter would not be a problem she knew. It was not that late. Not now anyway. But who knew what time it would be when she finally got home? Meanwhile, the voice was screaming at her, using the most vulgar terms to get her attention. "Are you crazy? Is this what you want to do? Go back to his room and let him fuck you? First it was the drinking and then the lapses in motherhood. Now you're ready for the final challenge…learning to become a cheating slut! How could you do that to Skip? He deserves better." She was torn by conflicting emotions. She didn't know what to do.

Brad stood waiting expectantly, looking helpless and childlike. Christy's mind snapped back into focus. She laid her hand softly on his cheek. "Dear one, if I told you I didn't want to go with you I'd be lying, because I do. You are a very exciting and attractive man, but I am afraid of what might happen if I did…afraid that once we were alone, I wouldn't be able to control myself. Do you understand that?"

Brad nodded, a look of disappointment on his face.

Christy stepped back, easing out of his arms. "You see, I could never be unfaithful to my husband. If I did, what would be the point of our marriage? The romance, the wedding vows, the sharing of our lives? Everything would be trivial and meaningless, like saying that Skip is my husband and the love of my life…until somebody more interesting comes along. What kind of person would that make me?"

Brad sighed with resignation. "When Jim called and asked me to join them for dinner this evening, I didn't want to go. 'You have to,' he said. 'Jan says a very special woman is going to join us.' She was right. I knew that the minute you walked into the room. You are a very special woman, Christy, and I'm glad I met you."

Christy froze as the impact of his words sank in. "Jim and Jan know each other?"

"Well, yeah. For a month or so anyway. Didn't you know?"

Christy felt a wave of anger surging inside of her. *Now I know where Jan was all afternoon,* she thought. *She was with Jim doing God knows what. This whole thing was a setup—the accidental meeting at dinner, everything. I almost committed adultery because of a stupid blind date. A blind date I didn't agree too.* Her anger subsided quickly, and she was back in control. She was pretty sure Brad was not part of this deception, because he seemed as clueless as she was. "It's getting late," she said simply. "I really have to go."

"I know."

"I'm really glad we met tonight. I had a wonderful time."

"Me too."

She kissed him lightly on the cheek, turned, and walked quickly to the car, not trusting herself to look back. He was still standing there when she drove away.

Christy drove blindly, scarcely noticing where she was going. She was overwhelmed with guilt over what she was feeling but was relieved that she had escaped. *What if she had weakened and gone home with him?* The thought that excited her ten minutes ago now sickened her. Mostly she was angry, angry at Jan for what she had done, and angry at herself for what she had almost done to herself. Turning off the main street, she began to slowly navigate the muddy ruts in her neighborhood, bumping along from one to another, as she gazed morosely at the squalid, mud-splattered houses. It was a clear night, filled with stars, and a full moon hung on the horizon as if making a final farewell before disappearing. *I hate this place,* she thought. *I hate it with all my heart. I hate what it is, and I hate what it has done to me.* She looked up at the stars. *God, if you're up there give me a sign that this nightmare will soon be over—just a small sign, that's all I ask. Without it, I'm not sure I can go on.*

She stepped out of the car and inhaled the cold, air. *Spring will be here soon,* she thought, *and then it will be time for planting—human excrement for fertilizer and all.* She wrinkled her nose. *Yuk!* Looking across the street, she saw that Jan's car was not there. *She's probably still with Jim having a "nightcap." Didn't she get enough this afternoon?*

Christy paid the sleepy babysitter and sent her home. Still wearing her coat, she went to Maddie's room. She was sleeping peacefully in her crib. *Thank God,* she thought. She looked tenderly at Maddie's small face. Being grown-up is not all it's cracked up to be kiddo; try to avoid it as long as you can.

She felt better the next morning. The crisis had passed. Jan called at nine, bright and cheerful. "Well?" she asked, "what do you think?"

"Don't ever do that to me again," Christy said.

"You sound upset. I only meant did you have a good time?"

"Being thrust into a situation where I don't know what's going on is not my idea of a good time, and neither is being so tempted that I almost cheated on my husband."

Jan was crestfallen. "Aww, I'm sorry. I really am. It's just that I found something that really made a difference in this shitty life of mine, and I wanted to share it. I thought it might make a difference in yours. We both have the same needs, after all."

Christy began to soften. How could she be harsh with her? "Indeed we do. Let's just say we don't agree on how to fulfill them."

"Are we still friends?"

"Of course we are."

"Good."

"But you're on probation for awhile, kid. Big time"

Skip came home from Korea five days later. By then, Christy had managed to regain control of her life. Before he arrived, she took Maddie to a friend's house. When he got home, they went straight to the bedroom, where a bottle of iced champagne was waiting. They spent the afternoon in bed. It was the best homecoming yet. She never told him about her night out with Jan. And she vowed she never would.

*   *   *   *

The sign Christy was waiting for came sooner than she expected. Two weeks later, Skip dashed happily into the house, a big grin on his face. "I'm tired of this dump," he announced.

Christy looked up from the stove where she was preparing dinner. He's probably had a couple of rounds at happy hour, she thought. "So what else is new? We're all tired of this place."

"No, I mean it. We deserve better than this. Something with class. A dining room, two bathrooms, maybe…sidewalks, a parking space. The whole nine yards."

"Some playmates for Maddie would be nice," Christy added. "But where are you going to find this palace?"

"Base housing, baby!" he crowed triumphantly. "We are now number one on the list, and they told me that we should be getting a house in six weeks."

Christy dropped what she doing and began to dance around excitedly. "Did you hear that, Maddie? We're getting out of here. Will there be a yard for her to play in?"

"Yep. Plenty of grass, both front and back. It's all common area of course, but that makes it better for the kids to play together."

Thank you God, Christy thought. Tears of joy were welling in her eyes. It's going to be okay now. I can feel it. Six weeks? I can do that standing on my head!

*   *   *   *

Winter departed the last week in March, leaving as abruptly as it had arrived. Slowly but surely, the ground reappeared from under its heavy mantle of snow. By early April, the land began to dry, and farmers braced themselves for the dust storms that inevitably appeared that time of year. The weather turned mild as the winds shifted and came in from the sea. From time to time, thick sea fog rolled in, gently obscuring everything in its path, especially in the morning and evening, but it seldom stayed long.

Once the snow departed, the residents of Misawa awoke, as if from a deep slumber. The spring air was filled with promise. It was a time for planting and for starting over. Soon the mountains would be dressed in green, and the fields would explode in a riot of color from plants and flowers of all kinds. Everyone was waiting for May, which would be warm and pleasant. But the old-timers knew that the warmth of May was the calm before the storm. In June, the rainy season would begin and continue relentlessly until late July. The O'Neill's were oblivious to the subtle changes taking place around them and the pleasures nature had in store from them. They were living from day to day, waiting to move on base.

When moving day finally arrived, Skip and Christy loaded their belongings onto a small truck. There wasn't a lot to take, mostly clothes, linens, books, and toys. When they were finished, Christy walked slowly around the house looking for forgotten items. As she did, a flood of unpleasant memories followed her everywhere she went. At the door, she looked back one last time and shuddered. Then they drove away.

Their new home was a corner unit in a two-story, four-family building. By American standards it was modest, if not slightly rundown, although it was spotlessly clean. But it looked like a palace to them. On the main floor, there was a living room, dining room, kitchen, and small bathroom. Upstairs, there were two bedrooms and a full bath. The kitchen was spacious, much larger than the one off-base. The floors were all hardwood. As they started to unpack, Maddie ran happily around her new home, darting in and out of the boxes. Suddenly, she turned a corner too fast, slid across the floor, and landed unceremoniously on her rump. She sat there for a moment, a look of shock and surprise on her face. It was obvious she wasn't hurt, but she started to cry anyway.

Christy walked over and picked her up. "We've got to get some rugs for this place, the sooner the better."

"Either that, or Maddie has to learn that hardwood floors are not like tatami mats," Skip said.

The move expanded Christy's horizons. No longer did she have to rely on a small circle of friends in the neighborhood for recreation and diversion. The wives' club was especially active, and they had something going on nearly every day. There were luncheons, coffees, bridge parties, and even special arts and crafts classes. Bob and Jan moved to the base two weeks after they did, and were living just a block away. She and Jan were still friends, but things were never the same after the incident with the two Marines. For Christy, it was about lack of trust; for Jan, it was about guilt. The couples still did a lot together and, of course, the Blunderbirds were still the Blunderbirds. Skip and Bob never talked about a replacement for Corky, and they always toasted him with their first drink.

In late April there was a dance at the club. The weather had turned balmy, so Christy decided to wear her favorite of all dresses, a black, off-the-shoulder number that fit her exactly right in all the right places. She dressed carefully, deciding to wear black stockings and black pumps with tiny rhinestones on the straps. A tiny diamond nestled just above her cleavage, hanging from a simple silver chain, and she wore earrings to match. She looked spectacular. It was a fine evening. They swirled and mingled among their friends, laughing and talking. When they danced, people watched them with fascination and sometimes envy, especially the men, who took every opportunity to watch her behind. It reminded him of their first date at the officers' club at Offutt. Eat your hearts out, Skip thought happily.

When they sat down for dinner, it was Laredo all over again. The table was crowded, and Christy casually began to rub her leg against Skip's, hiking her dress up slightly as she did. Skip reached under the table while talking to the man next to him and began massaging the upper part of her thigh. It was apparent that she wasn't wearing panties. They weren't in her purse this time, but the effect was the same. The rest of the evening was spent in heated anticipation, waiting for the moment when they would be alone. Unlike Laredo, there was no frantic coupling at the front door, not because they didn't want to, but because they had to send the babysitter on her way first. When she left, their passions exploded. Skip pulled Christy close and began to back her onto the stair landing, kissing the tops of her breasts as he went. On the first landing, he unzipped the back of her dress and let it fall to the floor, kissing her all the while. He unsnapped her bra and took it off. When he released her, she paused for a moment and started climbing the stairs. Skip stood transfixed on the landing, mesmerized by the sight of her swaying slowing up the stairs in her high-heel shoes, garter belt and stockings. It was an incredibly erotic sight. Shaking himself back to reality, he started up the stairs after her. She was almost to the top.

When she reached the top, she turned and posed, one hand on the banister, smiling at the look in his face when his eyes drew level with her waist. Playfully, she moved her hips forward slightly, urging him on. He hurried up the remaining steps, picked her up, and carried her into the bedroom. He was impatient now and took off as few clothes off as possible before starting their lovemaking. They made love several times that night, taking off more clothes each time. They fell asleep nude in each other's arms, exhausted but happy. Thankfully, Maddie slept through the night.

Six weeks later, Christy announced she was pregnant.

Skip placed his head in his hands in mock despair and sighed deeply. "Honey, you have to remember to wear your panties when we go out for an evening on the town, or we're going to have a houseful of kids."

Christy batted her eyelashes innocently. "Did I do something wrong?"

"Not really." Skip pulled her into his arms and kissed her. "I couldn't be happier."

They had lived together off base for five months. During that time, Christy had learned a lot about herself and about Skip. Looking at the joy on his face as they discussed their next child, she realized she loved him more than ever. *I'll need to do something unexpected from time to time*, she thought, *just to spice things up and keep him on his toes.* She smiled and looked down at her stomach. *Skip's right about the houseful of kids, though. I should try something different next time.*

*   *   *   *

For the first time since he arrived in Japan, Skip felt comfortable in the squadron. He was beginning to fit in. He liked his new flight commander and was making more friends. His run-in with Duke Christiansen had been mostly forgotten, except by Duke of course, who still felt Skip had no business flying the F-100, much less being in the squadron. Otherwise, life was good.

The pilots in B Flight were an easygoing bunch, mostly mirroring the personality of their leader. Skip particularly liked one of the older captains, Jack Van Riper. At first glance, Jack seemed dry and uninteresting. In reality, he was intelligent and articulate, with a quick wit. Those who knew him best would tell you that when he was on a roll, he was the funniest man in the squadron. He had a problem with weight, which fluctuated almost daily on his pear-shaped body. For some reason, most of it collected in his rear end. This earned him the nickname of "Buns." Buns believed that Skip had two strikes against him the day he arrived in Japan because of the antipathy the squadron held toward inexperienced pilots. He decided to take Skip under his wing and teach him the ropes.

One Friday morning, Buns grabbed Skip as he returned from running an errand. "Ah, there you are, just the man I've been looking for."

"Well, you found me. What's up?"

"Our fearless flight commander has charged me with a very important mission and gave me full discretion to choose someone to help me. Right away, I thought of my man Skip!"

Skip had to smile at those words. They were almost identical to those uttered by Cactus Jack five years ago in Presque Isle. The ones that drove him into the arms of an older woman named Dottie, followed by a two-week adventure on an aircraft carrier.

"So what's the mission?"

"One of our birds is stuck down at Itazuke. We're going to fly down there in the F model, spend the night, and bring it back the next day."

Skip had never been to Itazuke Air Base, home of the 8th Tac Fighter wing. The boys in the 8th Wing had a reputation of being some of the biggest hell-raisers in PACAF, almost as bad as the Marines. In particular, happy hour at the club on Friday night was supposed to be a wild and wooly affair. This was going to be fun; he couldn't wait. "It works for me."

"Good man."

They took off at two o'clock sharp. The weather was good. Their route of flight would take them south toward Tokyo and then southeast along the Sea of Japan to the southernmost island of Kyushu. The air base was near Fukuoka, a large industrial city. There were four F-100 squadrons in the 8th Tac Fighter Wing. They too had been plagued with fatal accidents during the past year. But that's where the similarities ended. While the Misawa pilots went about their business in a dull, dreary way, those at Itazuke worked and played with joyous abandon. Role models in the fighter squadrons had names like Whiskey Bill, Wee Willie, and Beetle Bailey. Nothing seemed to faze them. They believed being able to fly fighters was a gift from God, better than sex even, and if someone got killed doing it, well, that was unfortunate. The centerpiece of the freewheeling lifestyle at Itazuke was the officers' club. Not the main club—a stuffy place that sat in the middle of the base and was frequented mostly by the wives—but the Top of the Mach, a club just for fighter pilots, that sat on the other side of the base near the flight line.

The main entrance to the club was in the front facing a circular driveway, but everyone used small back doors that lead directly to the bar. Newcomers entering this door were sometimes met with a nasty surprise. One of the house rules was that anyone entering the bar with his hat on bought drinks for everybody. When this happened, the bartender rang a large bell to announce that the drinks were free. Buying the bar could be costly…especially on a Friday night. Sometimes things happened for no reason at all. One afternoon, two Marines walked in, hats off and ready for an evening of drinking. "Hooray! The jarheads are here," a young lieutenant cried. Then he dumped a pitcher of beer over their heads. They took it with good humor, and, in typical Marine fashion, one of them ripped off his flying scarf and began wringing beer into his upturned mouth. "You can't waste this shit," he declared.

Skip and Buns landed at four o'clock. At five, they were standing outside the back door of the Top of the Mach. They could hear the roar of voices through the closed door. "Ready?" Buns said.

"Ready." Skip had already taken off his hat.

"Let's do it." Buns opened the door, and they walked in.

"A couple of Misawa pukes have arrived!" someone shouted. He recognized the 531st squadron patch on their flying suits. Buns saw someone he knew and walked over to say hello. Skip stood uncertainly, unsure what to do next. Suddenly, a dice cup appeared under his nose. "Your roll," one of the pilots at the bar said. Skip took the dice and rolled them. He didn't have to buy the round. Taking the drink that was proffered him he turned to look around. A thick haze of cigarette smoke made it difficult to see more than a few feet. There were at least a hundred people in the room, laughing, drinking, and shouting to make themselves heard. The bar ran the entire length of the room. Men were stacked three deep behind the bar stools, elbowing each other to get a drink. There were empty tables and chairs scattered around the room, and a jukebox was playing in the corner. Skip thought he caught strains of Marty Robbins singing "El Paso," but he wasn't sure.

They stayed in the bar for more than three hours. Skip saw some guys he knew from Luke and started talking to them. They rolled the dice several times for drinks. He wasn't sure how many he drank. He lost count after five. One thing he did know, however, was that he didn't lose a single round. It was his lucky night. When Buns motioned him toward the dining room, he nodded, said goodbye to his friends and left.

It was almost ten thirty by the time they finished dinner. Skip paid his check and started for the bar, intent on buying an after-dinner drink. "Negative, Ace," Buns said. "It's been a long day, and we've got work to do tomorrow." Skip knew he was right. They left the club and went home.

Skip walked into his room and sat down wearily on the bed. The effects of the alcohol were just beginning wear off, and he was tired. How many drinks did I have tonight? he wondered. His thoughts were interrupted by a knock on the door. It was Buns. "Have you got your luggage?"

Skip turned and looked over in the corner where he had tossed his small bag when they arrived that afternoon. It was gone. "No."

"Neither have I. We have to go back to the club."

The bar was still crowded. Nobody seemed to notice their return, although Skip thought he saw some amused smiles when they walked in. "Wait here," Buns said, and walked over to talk to some friends. Skip ordered a drink and waited.

Ten minutes later Buns returned. "Let's go."

"Where are we going?"

"To get our bags."

Mystified, Skip followed him out the door.

They walked two blocks to a row of buildings where the bachelor officers lived. After consulting a scrap of paper, Buns entered one by the side door and started stealthily down a long hallway, reading the name on each door he passed. The building was deadly quiet. Everyone was asleep. Buns stopped and motioned for Skip to be quiet. He had found the door he was looking for. There was no light under the door, but they could hear soft music playing. There was something else, the unmistakable sound of squeaking bed springs, accompanied by moans and sighs. Buns turned the doorknob gently. Satisfied that it was unlocked, he looked at Skip significantly as if to say, "Get ready." Then he flung the door open, turned on the light, and stepped into the room. Skip was close behind.

Whiskey Bill, one of the Itazuke pilots, was mounted atop Michiko, one of the waitresses at the restaurant. They were lying on a small twin bed pushed against the wall, their nude bodies sweaty and intertwined. The girl screamed in terror and tried to get up. But she couldn't, because she was pinned down. Instead, she wriggled partially free and wrapped herself in the sheets like a mummy, sobbing and crying. Whiskey Bill was in a state of shock. He looked like a wild animal ambushed by a hunter. At first he didn't know what to say. "What hell are you guys doing here?" he said finally. "Get the fuck out."

"Where are our bags, Bill?" Buns said quietly.

"What bags? What are you talking about?"

Buns walked slowly to the refrigerator, took out two beers and handed one to Skip. Then he walked to a small writing desk and sat down. "Sure you do, Bill. You're a little distracted right now, but it'll come to you."

"I swear to God, I don't know anything about your bags."

Buns' chair was tilted back, one of his legs thrown carelessly on the desk. He looked totally at ease, as he took a long pull from his beer. Michiko was sobbing under the sheets. "Still can't remember, eh? Well, don't worry, I've got all night. By the way, don't let me interrupt whatever it was you were doing. Feel free to continue…if you can."

Whiskey Bill was in a jam, and he knew it. With Michiko rolled up like a mummy, there was only a small corner of the sheet left to cover his scrotum. The rest of his scrawny, hairy body was exposed. He was totally without dignity and thus, without power to negotiate. "Okay, okay. I didn't take your bags, I swear. But the guys who did…uh…I think they put them in the room next door. There's nobody living there now. The door's unlocked."

"You think they are there?"

"Okay, I know they are there."

Buns motioned in the direction of the other room. Skip left to check it out. He was back in a minute nodding his head. The bags were there. Buns rose slowly from his chair and started for the door. "Well now, looks like a happy ending for all concerned. We'll just be moseying along." Pausing at the door, he tipped the brim of an imaginary cowboy hat. "Y'all have a real nice evening. Sorry to have troubled you ma'am."

They managed to make it outside before they lost their composure. Then they started laughing. They laughed all the way back to their quarters. Sometimes they laughed so hard they had to stop walking to catch their breath. Sitting on the curb, tears streaming down their faces, they recounted every hilarious detail of their adventure. Skip was still laughing when he fell asleep.

News of the great luggage caper traveled fast. The next morning, they were greeted by strangers smiling broadly and giving them a thumbs-up. After breakfast they headed for base operations to file a flight plan and leave. It was a fine day for flying.

As they stood in the flight planning room, a pilot from one of the F-100 squadrons walked up. "Sorry about your CO," he said.

Buns looked up blankly. "Huh?"

"Your commanding officer...wasn't John Sullivan your squadron commander?"

"Was?"

"Sorry. I guess you haven't heard. Colonel Sullivan busted his ass yesterday."

Skip and Buns were stunned. Neither knew what to say. "What happened?" Buns said finally.

"Don't know. He was making a practice approach at Matsushima. The engine flamed out, and he had to punch out. The chute opened okay, but when he landed in the water, he couldn't get free of it. A strong offshore wind gathered it up and took him for a ride. He was drowned by the time they picked him up."

They looked at each other in disbelief. It was exactly what happened to Big Jim Landry last fall. Buns shook the pilot's hand and thanked him. Then he turned to Skip. "Let's go home."

The death of John Sullivan devastated the men of the 531st. To many, it seemed like a vengeful, almost capricious act. Why did God choose him of all people, a good man with so few vices? It was incomprehensible. Still, most pilots felt such accidents would always happen to the other the guy, not to them. They could not think otherwise and fly every day.

The wives viewed the death of John Sullivan differently. Each wondered if her husband would be next. It was a thought they carried with them every day.

The spring of 1962 began with a promise of better things to come. Now it was over, and nothing had changed in Misawa. Optimists were sure things would get better. Pessimists were worried they would not. Slowly, life returned to normal.

But it wasn't over.

*   *   *   *

Two weeks after Colonel Sullivan died, two more F-100s were lost. The flight leader was an experienced F-100 pilot with over a thousand hours in the aircraft. The wingman had several thousand hours of fighter time but very few in the F-100. He was a colonel from the air division headquarters, flying that day to "get among the troops and see what's going on."

The two aircraft had taken off bright and early, the first flight of the day. The leader rolled first, the explosive crack of his afterburner shattering the early morning calm. By the time he reached the middle of the runway, he was airborne, his landing gear starting to retract. His wingman was fifteen seconds behind. The leader was still low to the ground but gaining speed rapidly when he passed the far end of the runway. Easing the stick back, he started his climb. Just as he did, a fuel line burst, spraying raw fuel into the afterburner. The entire aft section exploded, leaving a bright, orange flame streaking behind the aircraft like the tail of a skyrocket. The control tower and the mobile control officer came on the radio at the same time. "You're on fire, lead. Get out of the bird now. Eject!"

The leader was too low to eject. He needed more altitude. Pulling back on the stick, he started a zooming maneuver, trading airspeed for altitude. As the aircraft reached the apogee of the maneuver, he ejected. His chute opened and swung violently twice. Then he hit the ground. It was close, but he made it. The aircraft crashed in a ball of fire two miles off the end of the runway. The colonel saw it all. Rolling abruptly to avoid the stricken aircraft, he began to circle the parachute. He, too, was slow and close to the ground, but he wanted to see if his leader was okay. "He made it," he reported. "I can see him in the chute. It looks like..." He never finished. His left wing struck ground. The aircraft cartwheeled and exploded, send flaming sections of the aircraft in all directions. The colonel's wife and nine children were sent back to the States in a military aircraft, along with his remains.

The latest accident raised the toll to nine aircraft destroyed and nine pilots killed, all in one year. The number was almost the same at Itazuke. The commander-in-chief of PACAF sent a message to the two bases. "Seventy-five percent of all the F-100 accidents worldwide have occurred in Japan," he said. "This is unacceptable. I am particularly troubled by those deemed 'cause unknown' by the accident investigation boards. Every accident has a cause. It is your job to find it. I expect the accident rate to decrease dramatically." The message did not contain the phrase "or else," but everyone knew that's what the general meant.

The pressure was on. Everyone agreed the accidents had to stop, but where to begin? Earlier a pattern was emerging—flight control problems. Now there were aircraft lost from engine failure, pilot error, impact with the ground, and materiel failure. One thing was for sure: all eyes would be on the next accident, if there was one.

Like most pilots, Skip took it all in stride. The death of the colonel was unfortunate, but it didn't affect him personally. Christy was too numb to take much notice. She was busy helping John Sullivan's widow pack for the move back to the States. She was also very pregnant.

The rainy season ended early in the summer of 1962, and in mid-July the weather turned unseasonably warm with bright blue skies. The air was filled with smells of growth and renewal from the rice paddies and gardens surrounding the base. Skip and Christy's life settled into a comfortable routine. Maddie seemed to be growing every day. She was a happy child and a joy to be around. Two more pilots were assigned to Skip's flight, so he was only going to Korea once a month. Meanwhile, Christy, with her expanding belly, always had things to do. Life was getting better.

KUNSAN AIR BASE, KOREA

August 7, 1962

The two F-100s were over the Sea of Japan now, heading due west, on their way to Korea. Their flight leader was Capt. Patrick J. Morgan, a man who had been flying F-100s for several years and was known by one and all at Misawa as "Moose." Skip was flying in the en-route formation position, behind and off to one side; close enough that the leader could see him, yet far enough away that he could maneuver comfortably while watching for other aircraft and navigating.

There was little need to navigate on this flight. The route was simple and direct, down the west coast of Japan and straight to Kunsan. Sitting above it all at thirty-five thousand feet, watching the landscape drift lazily by, it seemed to Skip that it had all been worth it—primary pilot training with that asshole Ross, the struggle to get through basic pilot training, the demanding training at Luke and Nellis, and last but not least, the hassle getting checked out at Misawa. It was worth it all right, he thought. I could stay up here all day. His reveries were interrupted when Moose reported to the traffic control center that he was beginning his descent. Already? Where did the time go? I don't want to land yet. And Moose wasn't ready to land either. When he contacted the approach control at Kunsan, he told them he needed to burn the remaining fuel from his drop tanks before landing. Skip grinned to himself. This was an excuse to play around for awhile before landing. They were going to have some fun.

They turned north toward Osan, another U.S. air base in Korea, and then back to the east, hoping to find some ROKAF F-86s to bounce. But it was Saturday, and none were flying. Turning back to the south, they began to descend, gaining speed as they did. We're probably going down to the deck to buzz someone, Skip thought, or maybe do some formation aerobatics. He tensed with excitement and anticipation. Passing through five thousand feet, Moose signaled for Skip to go to the in-trail position. He slid behind and under Moose and tucked in tight.

By the time they leveled off at five hundred feet above the ground, they were doing five hundred knots and still accelerating. Moose started to climb abruptly, with Skip right behind him. For a second, the forces of gravity jammed him into the seat, and his vision began to gray. But the air in his G suit surged around his stomach and squeezed the blood back toward his brain. He was okay. They were climbing almost straight up now, and Skip was oblivious to everything but the other aircraft, which hovered above him like aluminum overcast. The sound of the engine bathed his cockpit with a throbbing roar. He was so close that he could see every rivet and every detail of its belly. Don't even think about losing me baby…I'm on you like glue, he thought.

They were in perfect sync now, flying together as one aircraft. Soon, they would drift over the top, inverted, losing airspeed rapidly before starting down the back side and gaining speed in a dive. Skip eased back on the stick to move in closer. Nothing happened. Moose started to disappear above his head. He eased the stick back farther. It didn't move. It was frozen. He was in shock. He had no flight controls and was flying straight up. The F-100 couldn't climb straight up, even with full power and afterburner. Soon the airspeed would dissipate to zero, and the aircraft would become uncontrollable. He looked desperately for a way out. There was nothing he could do. Out of the corner of his eye, he saw two flight-system control failure lights on the caution panel. It didn't matter now. Nothing mattered except what the aircraft would do when the airspeed reached zero. If it rolled inverted and fell toward the horizon, he might be able to roll it upright with the rudders and bail out. The rudders were powered by a separate hydraulic system.

The aircraft did not roll toward the horizon. When the airspeed reached zero, it began to buck and shake violently. Then, it tried to nose over to the straight-and-level upright position. He realized his lap belt was too loose. Rendered weightless by anti-gravity forces, he floated out of the seat, along with every loose item in the cockpit. His head and shoulders were jammed against the Plexiglas, arms pinned helplessly against the windscreen. The cockpit was filled with debris, all at the top of the canopy. A navigation book floated up and struck him on the head, cracking the sun visor on his helmet. Desperately, he tried to free his hands so he could find something to hold on to and push himself back in the seat. But the anti-gravity forces wouldn't let him. Blinded by the debris and unable to move, he waited helplessly to see what the aircraft would do next. He didn't have to wait long. Without warning, the aircraft rolled over and snapped into a tight inverted spin. Looking through the top of the canopy he could see the rice paddies rotating faster and faster as the spin tightened. It was time to go, even though it meant ejecting inverted. The thought crossed his mind that he would no doubt be severely injured in the ejection, because he wasn't fully in the seat. It didn't matter. Better to be injured than to die.

He freed his left arm from the top of the canopy. Reaching across his lap, he grasped the right ejection seat handle with his left hand and raised it. It was an awkward maneuver, but somehow he managed. The canopy departed the aircraft with a loud bang as on-rushing air jammed him back into the seat and swept all the loose items out of the aircraft. He squeezed the exposed trigger, and the rocket motor in the ejection seat exploded with a deafening roar. The acceleration forces jamming him into the seat caused him to black out. One second later, he was vaguely aware of tumbling through the air as his lap belt was flung open by a small explosive charge, and the "butt-kicker," a nylon web device in the bottom of the seat, snapped taut like a bowstring and flung him clear. He fumbled to pull the ripcord, but he was too late. The automatic system deployed the parachute, and he was snatched from 200 mph to a dead stop. Exactly two seconds had elapsed since he squeezed the trigger.

Skip's body was numb with shock, his mind unable to comprehend what had just happened. The debris from the cockpit was still with him. To his left, he could see his nylon helmet bag tumbling end over end like a lazy acrobat. He was surrounded by maps, charts, and pages from the maintenance log, all dancing in the air like confetti in a ticker-tape parade. Just seconds ago all was noise, confusion, and chaos. Now it was deadly quiet. Moose was gone, Skip's aircraft was gone, and Skip was suspended six thousand feet above the ground. He shook his head vigorously trying to snap himself back to reality. Looking up, he saw that the parachute canopy was fully deployed, and all its panels were intact. So far, so good. Looking down, he saw his helmet dangling between his feet, hanging by the oxygen hose that was still attached to the parachute harness. It had been ripped off his head during the ejection. He reeled it in and put it back on. A faint, cool breeze swayed the parachute gently. He was feeling better.

Then he saw the river, snaking through the rice paddies like a fat muddy serpent, looking as wide as the Mississippi. He was heading straight for it, but there was still time to avoid it. Grabbing the left riser with both hands, he pulled down on it vigorously. This should have changed the direction he was drifting, but it didn't. He tried again, tugging harder. This time, one side of the canopy collapsed causing a sickening drop before the canopy re-inflated. Skip decided he'd rather land in the river. He pulled a lanyard on his seat pack, and a one-man life raft inflated and dropped to the end of a twenty-foot tether. At the same time, he inflated his underarm life preserver. He was ready, no matter how deep the river was. Things were happening quickly now. From the corner of his eye, he could see a small boy running toward the river, his arms gesturing wildly as he looked up at him with wide-eyed excitement. He was shouting something, but Skip couldn't hear him. The water rushed toward him. He braced himself and hit the water.

The river was only two feet deep. The impact of his fall drove him another foot into the muddy bottom. Dazed, he stood awkwardly until the weight of his survival equipment pulled him backwards, causing him to plop unceremoniously into the water. It was a ludicrous sight, Skip sitting in knee-deep water, surrounded by his survival equipment. His bright yellow, one-man life raft floated nearby, clearly not needed, while his parachute canopy with its alternating orange and white panels had collapsed a few yards away. The pièce de résistance was his fully inflated, Day-Glo orange, underarm life preserver, which remained high and dry because the water was so shallow. The little boy ran to the river breathlessly, his mouth agape, marveling at the scene before him. Skip looked at the boy and then at the colorful collage of unneeded survival equipment that surrounded him. He began to laugh. When he did, the little boy laughed too, although he didn't know why. Skip rose to his feet and waded to shore, dragging his equipment behind him. There was a grassy knoll twenty yards from the bank. He decided to go there to wait to be rescued.

The equipment was hard to drag, especially the water-logged parachute canopy. The little boy grabbed one of the parachute risers and tried to help, and together they labored up the hill like a team of mismatched mules. There was a village nearby, and people came running from all directions. Within minutes he was standing at the top of the hill, surrounded by excited people. There were old folks, children, and farmers from the rice paddies, all talking at once. An arm reached out of the crowd and handed him a bottle of orange soda. Skip took it gratefully and drank it down. It wasn't bad. He said "thank you," one of the few Korean phrases he knew. It sounded something like, "ko-mops-soom-mi-da." The crowd murmured appreciatively. The air was hot and fetid and reeked of human fertilizer from the rice paddies.

Fifteen minutes later, the local constable arrived. He was an irritable little man dressed in a sweaty, rumpled khaki uniform. In his hand, he carried a large bandana handkerchief that he used to swat insects on the back of his neck and to clear a path so he could reach the top of the hill. Skip and the policeman looked at each other. Skip bowed slightly. The policeman did the same and turned to face the crowd. Neither spoke. A small boy reached out to touch the life raft, and the policeman swatted his hand hard with his handkerchief. The boy yelped with pain and jumped back.

The throbbing sound of an approaching helicopter snapped Skip back to reality. He extracted a small survival radio from his parachute harness and turned it on. The helicopter pilot was telling Kunsan tower that he had the survivor in sight but wasn't sure if the surrounding terrain was safe to land on. Skip cut in and assured him that soil along the river bank was solid and firm, and there would be no problem landing. The helicopter swooped in from the south, hovered for a few seconds, and touched down. The downdraft from his blades blew dust and debris everywhere. The crowd watched with fascination, their hair and clothing rippling in the wind. A crewmember jumped out of the door, ducked low to avoid the whirling blades, and raced toward Skip. The policeman cleared a path so that Skip and the crewmember could drag the equipment back to the helicopter.

The crowd gathered around to say goodbye as Skip started to climb aboard. Standing in front, closest to the helicopter, was the little boy who had helped him. Impulsively, Skip turned around, dashed back down the stairs, and put his flight cap on the boy's head. The cap dropped below his ears and almost covered his eyes. The little boy stood straight, the shiny captain's bars on the cap gleaming in the sun, and saluted solemnly. Skip returned the salute, waved to the crowd, and ran back to the helicopter. He was on the ground at Kunsan fifteen minutes later.

The base commander was waiting for him when he landed, with Bob Lewis standing at his side.

"Are you all right, son?" the colonel asked.

"Yes sir, no problem. I feel great." Skip was returning to normal and rapidly assuming the macho role.

"Well, the flight surgeon needs to check you out to be sure. After that, you can expect a visit from the base flying safety officer. He'll want a full statement about what happened. By the way, what did happen?"

"Lost my flight controls. The aircraft went ape-shit, and I had to punch out."

The colonel nodded, but didn't comment. He turned to Bob. "Captain, I want you take your friend over to the base hospital, get him checked out, and then stick with him for a few hours."

"Yes sir." Both men saluted the colonel and walked away.

"Some guys will do anything to avoid spending a week on alert," Bob said, as they walked toward the jeep.

"Trust me. It wasn't worth it."

"I guess not. Are you really okay?"

"So far so good. I'm still a little numb in a couple of places, but I'm sure that'll go away."

"What about your cajones?"

"What?"

"You heard me. I've heard that if the leg straps on the parachute are too tight, there can be some serious damage to the family jewels. You know what I mean?"

"Look, I appreciate your concern. Let me get back to you in a few weeks, after I've had a chance to check them out. Okay?"

"No reason to get huffy. I was only asking."

"By the way, what are you doing here anyway? Didn't you get relieved from alert this morning?"

Bob sighed dramatically. "Unfortunately no. The dipshit who was supposed to relieve me rolled his aircraft up in a ball on the way over from Misawa, so now I have to wait for another replacement. I don't mind though. What are friends for?"

"I can hardly wait to find out what the payback is going to be for this," Skip said sarcastically.

"I have to think about that. Suffice it to say, it will be more than a couple of drinks."

"No shit."

The flight surgeon checked him over carefully and gave him a shot of "mission whiskey," which actually came from a bottle of Old Grand Dad in his desk drawer. "No broken bones or internal injuries as far as I can see. You're a very lucky man, considering it was a downward ejection, and you weren't positioned correctly in the seat. You'll be hurting tomorrow, though. You'll feel like you tangled with the Chicago Bears. I'm giving you some muscle relaxant and a pain-killer. Oh, and by the way, I want you to spend the night in the hospital for observation, just in case."

Skip looked dismayed and started to protest. "The hospital? But I…"

"I know, I know, you'd rather lick your wounds at happy hour tonight. Just think of it as an overnight stay at a BOQ with room service."

After he checked into the hospital, Skip described the accident in detail, while Bob wrote it all down. When he got to the part about the two warning lights, Bob stopped him. "Two lights, right?"

"Right, two lights."

"And what did they say?"

"I told you, Flight Control System #1 Failure and Flight Control System #2 Failure."

"And where were they located?"

"Warning panel on the right side, half way down."

"You're sure it said flight controls?"

Skip was getting irritated. "Of course I am! What are you getting at?"

"Look, I'm on your side old buddy. But as you know, the two systems are totally independent. A lot of people are going to say that it would be impossible to have a double failure. You have to be prepared for that."

Skip calmed down somewhat. "I know, but that's what happened. I swear to God."

The conversation was interrupted by the phone ringing beside his bed. It was the command post at Misawa. They had Christy patched in on another line.

"Honey, are you all right?" Her voice was strong, but it was obvious that she had been shaken up.

"I'm fine, baby. Not a scratch on me. I promise."

"Are you sure? I've been so worried."

"I'm sure. The flight surgeon says there are no broken bones or anything."

"You know what the scariest part was?"

"What?"

"When your new squadron commander called. What's his name?"

"I don't know, baby. I didn't know we had one."

"Well anyway, when he identified himself, all I could think of was Corky and Colonel John. I just went numb, but he was real cool about it. The first thing he said was that you had been in an accident, but that you were okay. I couldn't breathe for a moment I was so scared."

"I can imagine. But it's okay now. Everything is okay." Skip's voice was soothing and reassuring.

"I know. When will you be coming home?"

"In a couple of days I guess. They're sending someone over to take my place on alert."

"That's good. Get back as soon as you can. I need to see you in person to make sure you're in one piece."

"I will. I promise."

"I love you, baby."

"I love you too."

*   *   *   *

Brig. Gen. Trent Davis, commander of the 39th Air Division at Misawa, wasted no time when he learned of the accident. By the end of the day, he had formed an accident investigation board. "Remember what the PACAF commander said," he told the board president, a full colonel who was the division director of operations. "No more cause unknown findings. Do your job and get this thing sorted out. Find out what the hell happened."

The board consisted of five members: the president, a trained accident investigator, a maintenance representative, an engine specialist, and a pilot representative. The latter was a key member of the team. Using his expertise and experience, it was his job to make an unbiased evaluation of the pilot's performance and determine if any of his actions caused or contributed to the accident.

The pilot representative was Capt. Duke Christiansen.

*   *   *   *

The recovery team found Skip's aircraft in a rice paddy five miles from where he ejected. Residents of a nearby village called the police when they heard the explosion. By late afternoon, the crash site was secured by the air police. A long ribbon of bright yellow tape surrounded the area that contained the wreckage. The aircraft was flying straight down when it hit, leaving a scorched crater several yards across. A few pieces of the landing gear, brakes, and tires were scattered around the rim. Otherwise, the surrounding area was untouched.

A captain and a sergeant from the recovery team walked gingerly to the edge of the crater and looked down. The afterburner section of the tailpipe was visible three feet below the rim. The rest of the aircraft was buried in mud.

"Oh shit," the captain said. "That baby is gonna sink like a rock!"

"What do you mean?" the sergeant asked.

"This rice paddy has been flooded for centuries. The water table is so close to ground level that it's like standing on top of a lake. My guess is the aircraft is gonna sink a foot or two every day."

"So, that means we gotta get moving. We need to get some heavy equipment out here on the double and jerk her out before we lose her."

The captain sighed. He had majored in civil engineering in college. "It's not that simple. First we've got to pump the water out of the crater and set up a system to keep it drained, and then we have to remove all the mud and debris from around the wreckage. If all that works, we can talk about yanking her out."

"Headquarters isn't gonna like this," the sergeant said as they walked away from the crater.

The next day a team of experts flew in from Japan. By the time they reached the crash site, the aircraft had sunk another two feet. They estimated the type of equipment and number of man-hours required to drain the crater, remove the mud, and excavate the aircraft. It would be necessary to build a paved road to the site to support the weight of the equipment. Their report was sent to headquarters for review.

The equipment was not available in Korea. It would have to be shipped from Japan. Building a road to the site would be expensive and would require negotiations with the Korean government. It would be a time-consuming and costly project. Meanwhile, the airplane continued to sink at the rate of one foot per day. The authorities reviewed the report and reluctantly decided to abandon it. The base commander at Kunsan was ordered to clean up the crash site, fill in the crater, and compensate the farmer for damages.

The accident board was in a bind. Discovering the cause of an accident without the aircraft was like solving a murder case without a murder weapon or a body. But their instructions were clear. Find the cause, no matter what. They began their investigation using the only tools available to them—Skip's testimony and technical analysis.

Skip's testimony was simple and direct: the two warning lights, the lack of control stick movement; it all fit. But the facts didn't square with technical analysis. An engineer from the aircraft manufacturer was flown in to assist the board. Using wiring diagrams and detailed diagrams of the hydraulic systems, he made a convincing case that it was impossible to have a double flight-control system failure. "I can assure you that not a drop of hydraulic fluid can flow from one system to the other," he said. "They are totally separate. We designed them that way so that if one system is shot up in combat, the other one will get the bird home." Duke smiled knowingly and settled back in his chair. Everything was going his way.

Despite the overwhelming evidence to the contrary, Skip had supporters. Among them was the investigating officer who was none other than Whiskey Bill from the 8th Wing at Itazuke. It was odd that Whiskey Bill would be on Skip's side in light of the famous lost luggage caper. But that had been in good-natured fun, and this was serious business. Whiskey Bill believed that Skip was being railroaded, and he was pretty sure he knew who was behind it. The board president ordered his people to investigate every possibility. This would take time, but he wanted to do the job right. No one was going to get railroaded if he could help it. He was a fair and honorable man.

Meanwhile, Skip was grounded pending the results of the investigation. As the flight surgeon at Kunsan predicted, he was in severe pain for more than a week. For awhile, he had difficulty standing up straight, and his lower back hurt when he sat down. An X-ray revealed two herniated disks in his lower back. Christy did her best to help and comfort him, but it was not easy. He was tired, irritable, and angry that no one believed his story, and the waiting was becoming intolerable. He was greeted with sympathy and good-hearted teasing when he returned to the squadron. Several of the pilots suggested that he teach sea survival at Numazu based on his adventure landing in the river. The fact that Duke was on the accident board did not go unnoticed. "Mark my words," one of the pilots said, "he's going to screw Skip big-time if he gets a chance."

"Knowing Duke, he'll make sure he gets a chance," another said.

*   *   *   *

The board was assembled in a large conference room that had been their home for the past two weeks, writing the final report. It was late, and everyone was tired. The conference table was littered with ashtrays, coffee cups, and documents of all kinds. The air was filled with a blue haze of cigarette smoke. Writing the body of the report was simple. There were relatively few facts to report, and these had laid out in a logical fashion. It was time to select the cause of the accident.

By regulation, the cause had to be selected from a predetermined list that included pilot error, material failure, and mechanical failure. There could be more than one cause—a primary and secondary cause, for example—but each had to be selected from the list. The colonel rubbed his eyes wearily and looked around the table. "Okay, what have we got?"

Duke responded quickly. "Pilot error. Pilot lost control of the aircraft while performing an over-the-top maneuver."

"I disagree," Whiskey Bill responded. "We don't have evidence to support that."

"Look, how tough can it be? The guy tries to stay with his leader during a loop, loses it at the top, and has to punch out. When he gets back on the ground he says, 'Gee, I think I lost my flight controls.' Maybe he really believes that. What do I know? But it's all bullshit."

"There could have been other reasons. Maybe something fell on the cockpit floor and jammed the stick, or maybe there is a possibility we haven't considered."

"Maybe," Duke sneered, "but we can't look at the aircraft, can we? So, we'll never know."

"And we weren't in the cockpit when it happened, were we? So, we'll never know what the pilot did, either."

Duke's voice became icy calm. "There's a difference, though. The aircraft will never fly again and is not a threat. The pilot, on the other hand, is an undisciplined flake who is a threat to himself and those he flies with. And we have a chance to get him out of the air for good, if we do the right thing."

Whiskey Bill sat back in his chair and regarded Duke narrowly. "What I'd like to know," he said softly, "is what's the real reason you're so eager to let this poor guy swing in the wind. It would help me understand why we are doing this. It has to be something serious and very personal."

Duke rose out of his chair angrily and almost shouted. "Goddammit, I resent that implication. There's nothing personal about it. I was his flight commander for chrissakes. He's a weak-dick who has no business flying the F-100, or any other aircraft for that matter. Why can't you see that?"

The colonel slammed his fist on the table. "Enough bullshitting around! Listen up troops. Here's how it is. Cause unknown is not an option. We all know that it has to be pilot error; it's the only one that fits. Captain Christiansen suggests the pilot lost control of the aircraft while performing an over-the-top maneuver. I'm open to suggestions. Let's get on with it!"

"Can't we soften that up a little?" the maintenance officer asked.

"Like how?"

"How about, the pilot lost control of the aircraft while performing an over-the-top maneuver with limited flight control effectiveness."

"What does that do for us?"

The maintenance officer hesitated. "Well, for one thing, it leaves the door open to the possibility there really was a mechanical problem. On the other hand, if he simply lost it, and the airplane was out of the envelope, the flight controls wouldn't be very effective anyway, would they?"

The colonel looked around the table. Everyone nodded their heads approvingly, even Duke.

The colonel chuckled appreciatively. "You've been hanging around fighter pilots too long, Captain." He turned to the board secretary. "You got that, Lieutenant?"

"Yes sir."

"Write it up. That's the way it's going to be."

Duke quickly masked a look of triumph that crossed his face. He had won.

*   *   *   *

General Davis had a problem. His boss, Lt. Gen. Winston Slade, commander of 5th Air Force, wanted him to fly to Tokyo and brief him on the results of the accident investigation. The board's report was lying on his desk. He had read it twice, and he still couldn't shake the feeling that the pilot was getting shafted. But it was hard to tell. There was so little information. If only they had recovered the aircraft, it would have been a different story. He leafed through the first pages of the report idly. "Pilot lost control of the aircraft while performing an over-the-top maneuver with limited flight control effectiveness." What the hell does that mean? It was just a bunch of weasel words as far as he was concerned. But in an odd way they make sense. The board was trying to say something—a message inside a message. Cause: Pilot Error…P.S., but maybe this guy is getting screwed. He leaned back in his chair and gazed at the ceiling. There's got to be a way to do this without getting my dick stepped on. General Slade can be a real son of a bitch when he's in a bad mood, and flying accidents are not one of his favorite subjects. He thought about the pilot. What is his name? O'Neill…Skip O'Neill. That's it. He seems like a bright enough young man. Not the flakey type. I met him at the last squadron party…him and his wife. He thought about Skip's wife and smiled. Now there's a looker. She was the one in the black dress that fit just right, with tits to die for…like two bulldogs straining on a leash. Down boy…you're not a young lieutenant anymore, chasing the Luftwaffe over Europe. This is serious business. What are you going to do?

He thought about Skip again. Then he had an idea. Why not take him to Tokyo and let him tell his side of the story? The worst that can happen is that he looks guilty as hell, in which case, the pilot error cause looks justified. On the other hand, he might convince the general that he really did have a mechanical problem. If he does, I can say that's why the board put the qualifier in the cause. They knew "cause unknown" wouldn't fly, but they had reservations about the young man's guilt. The young man has a fifty-fifty chance of getting out of the crack he's in, and I win either way. Not bad odds! He reached for the phone. "Call the 531st and tell them I want to see Captain O'Neill in my office." He leaned back in the chair and thought about the black dress.

HEADQUARTERS 5TH AIR FORCE

Fuchu Air Station, Japan
August 28, 1962

Two days later General Davis, Skip, and Whiskey Bill stood on the stage of a small amphitheater at Fuchu Air Station near Tokyo facing Lt. Gen. Winston S. Slade, commander of 5th Air Force. Whiskey Bill was there to answer any technical questions that might arise. General Davis spoke first. He described the circumstances surrounding the accident, the methodology the board used to investigate it, and their findings. He emphasized that the board had worked hard and was determined to find a cause for the accident, despite the lack of physical evidence. He did not express doubts about the finding or suggest that the aircraft might have had a mechanical problem. It was up to Skip to speak for himself. That's what he brought him for.

As General Davis spoke, Skip looked at General Slade. He was slightly slouched in his chair, his unbuttoned blouse displaying rows of ribbons, as he listened to the speaker, glancing occasionally at the accident report in his hand. He was wearing reading glasses and smoking a large briar pipe. His face was vaguely familiar. Skip thought he had met him somewhere but wasn't sure because of the glasses. When it was Skip's turn to speak, he stepped to the front of the stage confidently and stood at attention, wincing visibly because of his back. He told his story simply, starting from the beginning, without using notes. He described the maneuver he was flying and the shock of realizing that he was going straight up with no flight controls. He recalled the two warning lights he saw, and what they meant. He also described the chaos in the cockpit just before ejecting straight down, barely in his seat. His voice was strong and sincere. He did not exaggerate, embellish, or defend himself. He simply told what happened.

When he finished, General Slade leafed through the accident report, then asked Whiskey Bill some questions about the F-100 flight control system and about the aircraft manufacturer's assertion that a double failure was impossible. Whiskey Bill answered smoothly and knowledgeably. The room became quiet as General Slade looked at the report again. Everyone wondered what he was going to say. He turned to General Davis first. "What troubles me is that a significant factor in this accident was barely mentioned. Namely, what in the hell were these guys doing flying formation aerobatics with 450-gallon drop tanks on in the first place? Correct me if I'm wrong, but their mission was to ferry those two birds over to the alert pad, right?"

The question took General Davis by surprise. "It didn't seem relevant to the accident itself, sir. That's why it wasn't in the report. We, uh, downgraded the leader from flight lead to wingman status pending further training," he added lamely.

"I think it's damn relevant under the circumstances. If he hadn't been out there screwing around, his wingman wouldn't have punched out of an airplane. I want the flight lead's actions added as a contributing factor before the report is sent to PACAF."

"Yes sir."

The general turned to Skip. He held his breath. "Young man, I think you are lucky to be alive, considering what happened. But you are alive, and that's what counts. I'm glad you survived. We all are."

"Thank you sir."

"On the other hand," he continued, "I imagine you are at least an inch shorter since that rocket went off under your ass." His staff laughed at this. The general's use of colorful language was legendary.

"Yes sir, I imagine so."

The general rose abruptly and turned to leave. His staff did the same. Skip stood on the stage, uncertain what to do next. Did he win the battle or lose it? He wasn't sure. At least he had his day in court. General Davis seemed satisfied, except for the part about hammering the flight lead. Tough shit about Moose, he thought, but that's the least of my problems.

Whiskey Bill walked up and shook his hand. "Good job, Ace. I think he got the message."

"Thanks."

"By the way, are you leaving today?"

"No. We're going back in the morning."

"Why don't we hit the club tonight? Dinner and drinks are on me."

Skip hesitated.

"And I promise nobody will touch your bags while we're there."

Skip laughed for the first time in weeks. "You've got a deal."

Their conversation was interrupted by a young captain who hurried up to Skip. The long silver braid draped around his shoulder denoted that he was the general's aide. "The general wants to see you in his office. Follow me, and I'll take you there."

General Slade was on the phone when Skip was ushered in. He motioned for him to take a seat. Skip settled in a deep leather chair in front of the general's desk and looked around. The general's office was larger than the briefing room at the 531ˢᵗ. The floor was covered with plush, blue carpet. Long, blue-velvet drapes hung on the window. The walls were paneled in rich walnut and were covered with plaques, pictures, and mementos. Skip saw that he had shot down fifteen German aircraft in World War II. There was a picture of him as a lieutenant standing in front of a P-51 Mustang, flying helmet under one arm, his hand draped casually over the propeller. He looked young, confident, and poised. He was sitting at a walnut desk larger than a dining room table. An American flag and a blue flag with three stars on it stood behind him. The general wasn't wearing glasses now. Skip was sure he'd met him, but he couldn't remember where. General Slade put down the phone and turned around. "Good job on the briefing today, son."

"Thank you sir."

"By the way, how is your wife? Here name is Christy, isn't it?"

Skip was startled. "She's fine, sir. How did you know…I mean…" Then it hit him, the bachelor party at Offutt, the night before his wedding! He was the SAC general who came downstairs to quiet them down and ended up drinking with them all night. He tried to recover. "Sorry sir. The bachelor party at Offutt. I didn't recognize you at first."

"I'm not surprised. You were in no condition to remember anybody that night."

"That's true," Skip admitted.

"You're between a rock and a hard place, young man," he said abruptly. "You know that, don't you?"

"Yes sir."

"It's a shame too. That part in the report about it being impossible for an F-100 to have a double flight-control failure was a little too pat for my taste—the kind of thing an engineer would say to cover his ass. It's a pity we couldn't recover the aircraft. But we couldn't, and that's that. Meanwhile, there's at least one person out there who would be quite happy to see you go down in flames, right?"

Skip nodded.

"And you know whose fault that is?"

"No sir."

"It's your fault."

Skip looked puzzled.

"It's your fault because you had a major confrontation with your flight commander, and you didn't handle it right. You didn't cover your backside. As a result, you've got this character parked at your six o'clock taking pot shots at you. It was only a matter of time before he got lucky and scored a hit."

Skip was beginning to understand.

The general leaned forward in his chair, and his voice softened. "Look, I have no idea what General Davis is going to do with you. I'm going to talk to him, but it's his call. But regardless of what happens, try not to lose your perspective. If you have to leave the cockpit for awhile, you'll be back. Hell, the way things are going in Southeast Asia, we'll all be back, getting our asses shot off. In the meantime, don't forget that being a fighter pilot is a matter of attitude, not assignment. And for God's sake, always remember to check your six o'clock!"

"Yes sir."

The interview was obviously over. Skip rose and saluted.

"Good luck, son, and say hello to your wife."

"I will, sir." He turned and walked out the door.

General Davis was the next visitor. The two men had known each other for a long time. General Slade had been an upperclassman when General Davis was a plebe at West Point.

General Slade got right to the point. "Well Trent, you really set that kid up, didn't you?"

"Not intentionally, I assure you."

"Intentionally or not, assigning his former flight commander to the accident board, a man who had been in a major pissing contest with him just a few months before, pretty much cooked his goose."

"I didn't know about that. All I knew was that Captain Christiansen was a highly qualified F-100 pilot with a reputation for getting things done."

"Well, it would have probably ended up the same way if you had appointed someone else."

General Davis saw the opening and took it. "I agree. But it would have taken longer for the board to get there."

General Slade seemed lost in his own thoughts. "What are you going to do with him?" he asked finally.

"Take him out of the F-100. I have no choice."

"I suppose not. Still, it seems like such a waste. As soon as he becomes a ground-pounder, he'll no doubt bail out of the Air Force. Most of them do."

"There's no need to permanently ground him. He can still fly T-birds in the base operations flight."

"He's got a good head on his shoulders, and he's quick on his feet. Give him something challenging to do."

"I have a job in mind."

"That's good. I have a feeling we're going to be up to our ass in a shooting war in Southeast Asia pretty soon, and we'll need all the fighter pilots we can get."

"We're already getting shot at over there," General Davis pointed out.

"Ah yes, reconnaissance squadrons 'training missions.' I understand the sheet-metal shops in Misawa and Kadena are getting pretty good at patching bullet holes on RF-101s."

"So I'm told."

General Slade rose as if to leave. General Davis followed suit. "Coming to dinner tonight? Sally has something special planned."

"Does it include something to drink?"

"Doesn't it always?"

"I'll be there."

"Good. See you at 1900."

General Davis turned and walked toward the door.

"One more thing, Trent."

"Yes sir?"

"Keep an eye on our boy and let me know how he's doing from time to time, will you?"

"I will, I promise." Our boy, he thought. Okay, General, I heard you loud and clear.

*   *   *   *

Major Rosie gave Skip the bad news when he returned. "We just got a call from headquarters. You're being reassigned to the Air Division. I'm really sorry, Skip."

Skip sagged visibly and sank in a chair. "That fucking Duke," he muttered.

"For what it's worth, the outcome would have been the same whether Duke was on the board or not."

Skip was beginning to get angry. "Why? Because nobody believed my story? Is that it? Everyone thinks I'm a liar!"

"No, that's not it at all. Look at it from the board's perspective. They had to come up with cause. The PACAF commander said so. Maintenance or materiel failure was out of the question. They had no airplane, which means no evidence to support that finding. That left pilot error. Essentially, you were screwed the minute Moose decided to have some fun while burning off fuel for landing. Let's face it Skip, you were in the wrong place at the wrong time."

Skip's anger began to subside. His fate had been decided, and there was nothing he could do. He saw that clearly now. "So, what happens next?" he asked, dully.

"Starting Monday you'll be working in the command post. I doubt if you'll stay there long. I have a feeling General Davis has something in mind for you, but I don't know what. Meanwhile, you'll be flying T-birds in the base ops flight."

Skip nodded absently, only half listening. He was still trying to comprehend what had just happened. Finally, he rose and started to leave.

"Remember what I told you a few months ago, Skip? This is not a one-mistake Air Force. It's not over unless you decide it is."

Skip turned and regarded Major Rosie gravely. "I'm not so sure I made a mistake," he said. He walked out the door and didn't wait for a reply.

HEADQUARTERS 39TH AIR DIVISION

Misawa Air Base, Japan
September 15, 1962

Three weeks ago Skip's life was full of hopes and dreams. Now he had nothing. He was no longer a fighter pilot, and that's what hurt the most. The "new Skip" had failed just as badly as the old one, maybe even worse. Depression set in. He started going downhill. His job at the command post was mind-numbing, sitting in a windowless room answering the phone, coordinating meaningless details. There was no one to talk to except the sergeant that sat next to him. They both did the same job. It all depended on who answered the phone first. He worked twelve-hour shifts, sometimes all night, other times during the day.

The new 531st squadron commander soon got wind of Duke's activities on the accident board and didn't like what he saw. Shortly thereafter, Duke was reassigned to the air division. His new job was to give check rides and perform evaluations of F-100 pilots in both squadrons. This change was applauded by most, although one man pointed out that he would be giving everyone shit now, instead of just the pilots in his flight. Buns Van Riper became the new A Flight commander. It was ironic that Skip and Duke were in the same organization. But Duke was still flying the F-100, and Skip was not, and that made all the difference. Skip still went by the club for happy hour now and then, but it was not the same. His former squadron-mates were always friendly, but he had nothing in common with them. He and Bob continued to meet after work, but even they ran out of things to talk about. Occasionally, he imagined he saw a look of pity in

Bob's eyes. When he did, he usually finished his drink quickly and left. It was a sight he couldn't bear to see.

Skip discovered that the pain pills the flight surgeon had given him created a state so mellow that nothing bothered him. The pills were far more effective than alcohol. Often, he would bypass the club and head straight home so he could take one of the pills. Then, he would sit in the living room listening to music and dreaming, oblivious to the chattering of his wife and the pleas of his daughter for attention. Christy knew he was taking the pills, but she said nothing, because she thought he was in pain. After a month, she was fed up. Yoko was gone, and she had her hands full taking care of the house and running after Maddie. Being five months pregnant didn't help. It was time for Skip to get on with his life. If he didn't, she was going to take drastic action. Things might have remained status quo for some time, but fate intervened.

One afternoon Bob called Skip at work. "I gotta talk to you. There's a problem." He sounded tense.

"Sure, let's meet at the club and knock back a couple of rounds."

"Not at the club. We need some privacy. Can you come to the house at six? Jan's taking the kids to a movie."

"No problem. Are you okay?"

"I don't know."

Whatever was going on, it was serious, Skip was sure of that. He was at Bob's house promptly at six. He was shocked when Bob opened the door. He had never seen him look so pale. There were dark circles under his eyes, and his face was creased with worry and fatigue. It was obvious he hadn't been sleeping well.

"Hey, old buddy, you look like shit!" Skip said.

"Thanks, I needed that."

"Always glad to help."

"Have a seat in the living room. I'll be right back."

Skip sat on the sofa and waited. He was more curious than ever. Bob returned with two bottles of beer and set them on the coffee table. They both took long pulls of their beers, savoring the ice cold taste. "So, what's up?"

"What's up? My marriage is in the toilet, that's what's up."

Skip looked shocked. "You're kidding. I always thought you and Jan had a good marriage."

"We did. But not anymore."

"What happened?"

"It all started in January when she found out about the hostess bar scene downtown and that girl I was seeing…Hiroko, remember her?"

"Remember her? I hustled her out of your BOQ room for God's sake!"

"Oh yeah, I forgot. Anyway, Jan was highly pissed, to put it mildly. At first, I thought she was going to come after me with a butcher knife and cut my balls off. When she settled down, she announced sex was a thing of the past and would be for the foreseeable future. She said she didn't know where 'my thing' had been, and she wasn't taking any chances. It got pretty dicey for a few weeks, and she almost packed up the kids and headed back for the States. But after awhile things settled down. Then the other shoe dropped."

"The other shoe?"

"Yeah. One morning I borrowed some lunch money from Jan's purse. I was running late for work and didn't want to wake her up. I didn't think she would mind. When I got to the base, I found a note crumpled up in the bills. It was from some guy named Jim, saying he was flying up from Iwakuni and couldn't wait to see her again."

"You mean she was…?"

"Yep. This Marine pilot was banging her every time I went to out of town."

Skip shook his head incredulously. "So what did you do?"

"I confronted her right away, and you know what she said?" Skip shook his head. "She said that was payback for screwing that little Japanese bitch. She said that now we were even. Of course, I couldn't let it go at that. I hammered away at her until she spilled her guts. Eventually, she told me everything." A look of pain crossed his face. "She told me more things than I wanted to know, actually. It was my turn to swear off sex. I told her it was good thing she cut me off, because I wasn't sure where 'her thing' had been. So there we are…a Mexican standoff. We barely speak to each other and everybody is uptight. The kids are having trouble sleeping at night, and that's not good."

Skip didn't know what to say. I wouldn't want to be in his shoes for all the money in the world, he thought. It's a hopeless situation. "Geez, Bob, I'm really sorry, but you and Jan have been married a long time. Surely you can work something out. It's not as if only one of you is a victim. You both got your hands caught in the cookie jar."

Bob shifted nervously in his chair. "There's more," he said.

"More? My God!"

"Yeah. The note said he was bringing a friend along—some guy named Brad, whom he describes as a big, good-looking, blond guy. The poor guy is separated from his wife and very lonely, the note said. Maybe you could fix him up with one of your friends."

"And did she?"

"Oh yeah. My sweet, innocent wife did a real number on her friend. Picture this: She invited her for a ladies' night out, dinner and drinks at the club. It was a Monday night, and when the friend arrived, the dining room was empty except for Jan, who was sitting at a table with two guys. Jan tells her she just met them and asked her to join them for a drink. They had a couple of drinks, and this Jim character suggested they have dinner together, because the dining room was empty. Actually the dining room was closed, but Jan sweet-talked the manager into serving them from the snack bar kitchen—candlelight and all. Pretty cozy, huh?"

Skip shook his head sadly.

"The girl figures, 'Why not?' It all seemed harmless enough. She was clueless about what was going on, honest to God. It was a setup from the very beginning."

Bob paused to collect his thoughts and continued. According to Jan, everyone enjoyed themselves—good food, interesting conversation, and plenty to drink. Brad and the girl hit it off right away. Before long, it was obvious he was smitten with her. It made sense, him being separated from his wife and all. She was a good-looking woman."

Skip was listening raptly now.

"At ten o'clock, Jan said she had to leave. Jim offered to walk her to the car. It was just an excuse. They had been together all afternoon. They were going to have another go at it before she went home."

This has to be hard for Bob, Skip thought. I guess it's my turn to feel pity. "What happened to the other couple?"

"Brad and this girl stayed in the club for an hour or so, and then he walked her to the car. That's when things got out of hand. When they got to the car, they ended up wrapped around each other with a full lip-lock, hands out of sight, the whole nine yards. It got pretty steamy, and for a minute, it looked like they were going to leave together. But they didn't. Instead, the girl kissed him again, jumped into her car and drove away."

"Jan told you all this?"

"Yep, she gave me a blow-by-blow account."

"I thought she and Jim were gone by then."

Bob's face hardened, and when he spoke, he spit the words out, as if he they were too distasteful to stay in his mouth. "Oh, she knew all right. You see, my beloved wife was so horny when she left, that she couldn't wait until they got to his room. They were in the backseat of her car...in the backseat of my car, I should say…screwing like rabbits…not ten yards from the other couple. They saw the whole thing."

Skip winced as he listened to the words. He was sorry his friend had to say them, but he had to ask one more question. "Where did the other couple go after that?"

Bob shrugged his shoulders. "Jan didn't know."

"What did the friend tell Jan the next day?"

"Nothing, except she was pissed as hell about being set up."

"So she could have gone home," Skip mused, "Or she could have gone around the block and parked behind the BOQ, just for appearances sake."

"I'm sure she went home," Bob said quickly. "She didn't seem like the type who would do such a thing…unlike the slut I'm married to."

"But we'll never know for sure."

Skip leaned back in his chair and tried to picture the scene in the parking lot. What would I do if I were her husband and found out about this? As much as I love her, I'd kill her. Maybe not kill her exactly, but it would be adios, that's for sure. "You know who I feel sorry for?" he said finally. "The friend's husband. He was more clueless than she was and still doesn't know. Who was it by the way? Anybody we know? Somebody from the 531ˢᵗ?"

Bob shifted in his chair and look down at his feet. He didn't reply.

"Come on Bob, I won't tell anybody. Who was it?"

Bob found it almost impossible to look him in the eye. Finally he looked at Skip. "It was Christy," he said in a quiet voice.

It—was—Christy! The words struck him like three quick punches to the solar plexus. He felt sick to his stomach. He thought he was going to throw up. Then a cold numbness spread through his body with an icy grip. He didn't know what to say. "Come on Bob," he said finally, "stop bullshitting around. That's not funny." But he knew it was not a joke. He could tell by the look on Bob's face.

The pain subsided, and so did the numbness. He was getting mad now. Mad at Christy, Bob, Jan, everybody involved in the whole mess. Good God Almighty! He could picture it all. Dry humping under this guy's overcoat, trying to decide whether to go back to his room and fuck…how could she do that to me? He set his beer down carefully before he threw it or did something irrational. "How long have you known about this?" His voice was calm, but he was not.

Bob looked miserable. "Since April."

"Over three months. Why in the hell didn't you tell me before now? What happened to the old 'we're the Blunderbirds and we stick together shit?' Or didn't it apply in this case?" His voice was starting to get louder.

"I wanted to, man. You have no idea how many times I almost did. But I was up to my ass in alligators in my family and I figured...you know...maybe it will all blow over, and you might never find out about it. Then came all that crap with Duke, and after that, the accident. There just wasn't a right time. You didn't need another problem. You had enough on your hands."

"So, why now?"

"You just said it a minute ago. I feel sorry for the clueless husband. Suddenly, I realized that I couldn't let my best friend be clueless anymore. It wasn't right."

Skip rose slowly from his chair. "I've got to get out of here. I need to think."

"Skip, please. Keep your perspective. You are dealing with a one-time, did-she-or-didn't-she deal. I go to bed every night knowing that my wife was getting her brains screwed out by some stranger while I was gone."

Skip paused at the door and patted his friend on the shoulder. "I know my friend. It must be tough. I'll do my best." Then he turned and walked out the door and into the cool, late-summer night.

He stumbled blindly down the street, the words of his best friend still ringing in his ears. Christy had been with another man while he was away! It was hard to believe, but Bob had no reason to lie. After all, his wife had been there when it happened!

His journey took him past the parking lot by the officers' club, the place where it all happened. In the final glow of the afternoon, it looked harmless enough—a small patch of asphalt, bathed in overhead lights that had just come on, a handful of cars carefully parked between painted white stripes. There was a gentle hum of insects coming from a row of bushes beside the building. He took in the scene with morbid fascination. What had it been like that night? His head was a hornet's nest of images and obscene words, all trapped and buzzing around...his wife pressed against the body of another man...the man's hands roaming all over her body...the two of them discussing whether to go to his room. It went on and on. He couldn't make them stop. Damn her! Damn her to hell! How could she do that to him?

Skip was shaking with anger, and that wasn't good. He had to stay cool. Christy has no idea that Bob told him. What did they say in training? The element of surprise is the key to tactical advantage. How to use that advantage? He decided to take it slow and easy and wait for the right moment to confront her.

Christy was in the living room waiting for Skip to come home. She was holding a heavy bar glass filled with a weak bourbon and water. She normally didn't drink when she was pregnant, but it had been a long day, and her lower back was aching. Besides, she had to confront Skip about his depression tonight, and she needed a little extra "courage." Her timing couldn't have been worse.

Skip walked in the door and greeted her diffidently. "Hi, I'm home."

"Work late tonight?"

"Naw, Bob has a problem, and I stopped by to talk to him about it."

"Anything serious?"

"I'll tell you about it in a minute."

He decided to take a pain pill to help him stay calm. He went to the bathroom and opened the medicine chest. The pills were gone. He began to panic, shoving bottles aside, trying to find his pills. He called downstairs. "Honey, where are my pain pills? My back hurts tonight."

"I threw them away today," she replied calmly.

Skip walked down the stairs, shaking with anger. "You what?"

"I threw them away. The flight surgeon said you shouldn't be taking them anymore. They're addictive."

Skip stalked across the living room and flung himself on the couch in front of her. "Let me see if I got this straight," he said, his voice dripping with sarcasm. "You appointed yourself as my personal medical adviser, and then consulted with my doctor. Then, the two of you decided to throw away my friggin' pills?" His voice rose at the end of the sentence.

"Honey, please, Maddie is still awake upstairs. She'll hear you."

"I'm sorry."

Christy took a deep breath. It was now or never. "Honey, this thing about the accident and leaving the squadron has been tough on you. I know that, and believe me, I hurt for you. But it's been over a month now. It's time to move on. You have a wife, and a daughter you scarcely notice, and another child on the way. You need to be a man again, the head of the family. Take charge of your life. We need you."

It was the opening Skip had been waiting for, and he attacked. "Be a man. What a splendid idea! Why didn't I think of that? Let me see…where to start? Hmmm…yes…I saw a recruiting poster the other day. Join the Marines. We'll make a man out of you. The very thing! I'll join the Marines. Maybe I'll dye my hair blond and change my name to something macho like…oh…I don't know…Brad, maybe. A big handsome blond Marine named Brad. I'll bet that will get the women attacking my body in the parking lot, trying to get in my pants. Don't you think so, Christy baby?"

His words cut into Christy's heart like cold steel. Her faced turned ashen and she started to cry. "What are you saying? You're talking like a crazy man!"

"I'm merely saying that if I need to change, I might as well go for something tried and true. And it certainly worked for you, didn't it?"

"Necking with a Marine in the club parking lot. That's a juicy piece of gossip. Where did you hear that? From someone in the wives' club?"

"You might say so. Bob told me, but the real source was your dear friend Jan."

"In that case, you must know that the whole thing was a cheap trick. I was invited to dinner with Jan. I had no idea there were going to be two guys there. Did I have a good time at dinner? Sure I did. Brad is a nice man."

"Nothing wrong with having a good time at dinner. But I do have a problem with the good time you had groping this guy in the parking lot. It was a mighty long good-night kiss, and your hands were out of sight under his overcoat the whole time. What were they doing?"

Christy stepped into the trap. "That's ridiculous. You weren't there. How would you know that?"

"I wouldn't know, except Jan was there the whole time."

A look of surprise crossed Christy's face.

"You didn't know that did you? She was in the back seat of Bob's car with her Marine, not ten yards away. Thanks to her, Bob gave me a blow-by-blow account."

Christy was getting angry. He was making her feel like a slut. It was time to fight back. "Okay, time out. You want me to say something, and you're not going to stop browbeating me until I do. Did I kiss him good night? Yes, and it excited me. Did I want to go back to his room? You're damn right I did! Not to get laid—my husband is very good in that department, or at least he was until he started popping pills, but to be with someone...so I didn't have to go home to that dump we lived in with snow up to my rear end. I needed someone to listen to me, to comfort me, and yes, to put their arms around me. But I didn't go. You know why? Because I love my husband and would never be unfaithful to him. There. Are you satisfied?"

Skip continued calmly, as if she hadn't spoken. "Tell me something, and try to be honest...if you can. Are you still doing this guy?"

"'Doing' this guy? Haven't heard anything I said? I never did him. I saw him once. That's it. Period. End of discussion."

"It's important, because you are carrying a baby, and I need to know if it's mine."

A red curtain of rage enveloped Christy. She lost control. Mindlessly, she picked up the whiskey tumbler at her side and flung it blindly toward the wall in front of her. It struck Skip squarely in the middle of his face. Bellowing with pain and surprise Skip fell over and grasped his head between his hands. He could feel the blood flowing between his fingers. Christy gave a cry and rushed to his side. "Oh my baby, my sweet baby, I'm so sorry. I didn't mean to do that. Are you all right?" She tried to pull his hands away so she could survey the damage.

Skip pulled roughly away. "Don't touch me! Don't ever touch me again!" He rose unsteadily to his feet and stumbled to the downstairs bathroom.

Maddie began crying hysterically upstairs. The noise and commotion raised by her parents had scared her. She sensed something was terribly wrong but didn't know what. Christy rushed upstairs to calm the frightened child.

Skip looked at his face in the bathroom mirror. The glass missed his eye by a half inch. The cut wasn't serious, though. Placing a wet towel over his eye, he returned to the living room. When Christy returned he was lying on the couch, holding the bloody towel in place.

"Honey, I…"

Skip raised his hand dismissively. "No more talk. I've heard quite enough for one day."

"You're right about that. So have I. Let's go to bed and make a fresh start tomorrow. Shall we?"

"I'm not going anywhere. I'm staying right here."

Christy sighed, stood up, and held her aching lower back. "Suit yourself," she said, and wearily climbed the steps.

*   *   *   *

At nine o'clock, Christy called Jan. "We have to talk," she said.

"Oh hon, I've got a pretty busy day today. There's a bridge tournament and…"

"We have to talk now. The sooner the better."

"I suppose we could meet at the club for coffee."

"No, it's private. You can come to my house or I'll go to yours." Her voice was cold and hard.

Jan hesitated. She'd never heard her friend talk that way. It scared her. "Okay. Why don't you come over to the house now? Bring Maddie if you want to. She can play with my kids."

"I'll be right there."

"What's going on, Christy? Please tell me."

"When I get there."

Jan's hand was shaking when she hung up. *Whatever is going on, it's serious, and it involves her,* she could tell. *It can be only one thing—that damned night at the club last March! Oh God, she wished it had never happened!* She waited anxiously for Christy to arrive.

Christy arrived ten minutes later. She walked in, gave Jan a perfunctory "hello," and sent Maddie off to play with Jan's children.

"How about a cup of coffee?" Jan said, as they went to the living room. "I've got some Danish too."

"No thanks, I've eaten breakfast."

There was an awkward silence as the two women faced each other across the coffee table. Jan looked frightened. Christy could see her hands shaking as they sat in her lap. Jan saw that Christy looked tired and distressed. There were dark circles under her eyes.

"Skip knows everything," Christy said without preamble, "about Brad, about what happened at dinner, and what happened in the parking lot."

Jan turned pale and started to cry. "Oh Christy, I am so sorry. I never wanted that to happen. Believe me." She was sobbing uncontrollably now, her eyes flooded with tears. "But how did he find out? I never told him. I'd never do that to you. I never told anybody, for that matter."

"That's not true. You told your husband, and being the good friend he was, he told Skip. He didn't think it was right for him to be in the dark. He was probably right."

Jan's face hardened. "That's my dear sweet husband, always faithful…to everyone but me, of course. Damn him! He promised he wouldn't tell Skip!"

Christy sat back in her chair, trying to control her anger. "Help me understand why you did this to me, your best friend. Why did you tell Bob? Did you think, oh gee, one marriage is down the tubes, I might as well try for two? Is that it?"

Jan squirmed miserably in her chair looking like a trapped animal. "It wasn't like that at all. You don't understand. Bob went berserk when he found out. He wouldn't let it go, not even for one day. He wanted details. He even made me tell him intimate things about Jim and me." A look of pain crossed her face. She choked up, as if she couldn't go on. "It went on for weeks. I became numb after awhile, and somewhere in the middle your story came out."

Christy didn't say anything.

"Oh, Christy, it's all my fault," Jan continued. "I did a stupid thing. I should never have done it. But when I found out about the Japanese girl I…"

"What Japanese girl?" Christy interrupted sharply. "Skip didn't say anything about a Japanese girl."

"Well, he should have. That's how this whole thing started." Her face was set hard now, and she spoke bitterly. "I found out that while I was back in Ohio trying to keep the family together, my beloved husband was screwing a hostess from one of the bars downtown. A little tart named Hiroko. Not just one time, but for weeks on end. I went nuts when I found out. I wanted to cut his balls off with a butcher knife. Then, I thought of a better way. Why not do the same thing to him? I saw Jim walking in the door of the club one night and picked him up. It was easy, and it did a lot for my ego. The rest is history."

Christy's mind was racing. There was more to this story. She was certain. Skip and Bob, she mused. Inseparable buddies. The two musketeers. No wonder Skip left that part out of the story! She considered what to say next. Whatever it was, it had to catch Jan by surprise. She looked Jan straight in the eye. "And what about Skip's girl? What was her name?"

Jan's eyes widened and immediately broke Christy's gaze. Her voice faltered when she started to talk. Christy knew.

"Skip? I didn't say anything about Skip. This is about Bob."

"Are you saying Skip didn't have a steady girl, that he was playing the field?"

"No. I mean yes," she stammered. "I mean, I don't know."

"I don't believe you. Why are you trying to protect my husband when you ratted on your best friend? It doesn't make sense. By the way, you think Bob tormented you? You haven't seen me in action. I can be a real bitch, if I have to."

Jan gave up. "Okay," she sighed. "I think he did have a special girl."

"You think, or you know?"

"I know. Her name was Mariko. She was Hiroko's friend. They worked in the same bar."

"What was the name of the bar?"

"The Bar Interlude. It's right out the main gate, about half a block on the right."

Christy was shocked and angry, but in the midst of her torment she saw a ray of light. Maybe this could be used to save her marriage, but she needed more information. She rose and gathered up Maddie to leave.

Jan followed her to the door, looking miserable. "I guess I'm not your best friend anymore, huh?"

For the first time, Christy felt sorry for Jan. Jan was in a tough spot, and Christy pitied her. "Probably not," Christy replied. "Still, this is not a good time in your life. I'll try to help you if I can. Meanwhile, you could do me a big favor today."

"Anything."

"I need to leave Maddie at your house from two-thirty to around eight this evening. Can you do it? It's important."

"Of course I can."

Christy knew what she had to do.

*   *   *   *

Christy arrived at the Bar Interlude at three in the afternoon. She was dressed sensibly for the time of day. She didn't want to attract attention. A yellow sundress and white sandals, not too fancy but not too plain. The dress was getting tight, clearly showing her belly. That was okay. It added to the image she wanted to project. Her hair was brushed and pulled away from her face. She was wearing very little makeup. She took a deep breath to steady herself and opened the door. It was dark inside, and for a moment she couldn't see. The bar was not yet open for business. The porter was still taking chairs off the tables, setting them down on the newly vacuumed carpet. The girls were arriving in ones and twos, chattering and giggling, checking themselves in the mirror, getting ready for the evening.

If Jeannie was surprised to see an American woman in her club, she didn't show it. She walked up courteously and bowed slightly. "May I help you?"

"Yes. I am very sorry to intrude. I am Mrs. O'Neill, Captain O'Neill's wife. I need to speak with one of your hostesses. Mariko is her name."

The polite, helpful expression on Jeannie's face did not change. "May I ask what this is about?"

"It's personal. Please understand, I am not here to make trouble. I just need to talk to her for a few minutes."

"Oh, I see."

Jeannie hesitated. Such visits were not uncommon in her business. Years of experience taught her it was wise to be courteous and helpful to women like Mrs. O'Neill. Otherwise, things could become unpleasant very quickly. She turned and motioned for Mariko. "Mariko-san," she said in Japanese, "Mrs. O'Neill would like to speak with you."

Mariko walked toward them, hands tucked in the sleeves of her blue-gray kimono. Tied around her waist was a plum-colored silk obi, intricately embroidered with a single band of flowers in lozenges. Her hair was done up in the back and held in place by large pearl comb. Tiny glass teardrops hung along the sides. Her tiny, slippered feet scuffed quietly on the carpet as she walked. "Good afternoon, Mrs. O'Neill. How may I help you?"

"I would like to talk to you for a few minutes. I have a problem perhaps you can help me with. I won't take a lot of your time. I promise."

Jeannie led them to the back of the room. The other girls watched the unlikely trio out of the corner of their eyes. None dared to look at them directly or speak. Tucked unobtrusively just beyond the end of the bar was a tiny room. Jeannie drew back a beaded curtain and ushered them in. "You can talk privately here." She turned and walked away. The room was sparsely furnished with two chairs and a small table. The walls were bare except for two Japanese prints, pastoral scenes of nearby Lake Towada. A large white, ceramic ashtray with the words "Suntory Whisky" sat in the middle of the table. There was a faint odor of incense in the air.

Christy sat down. Mariko remained standing. "Please allow me to serve you tea."

"No thank you. I won't be staying long."

"I insist. It would be rude of me not to do so." Her voice was soft and melodious.

"Well, okay."

Christy watched as Mariko brought a pot of tea and two small cups and set them on the table. Leaning over, Mariko carefully poured the tea. Her movements were charming and graceful. She's really very pretty, she thought, but hardly a young girl. Judging by the creases in the corners of her eyes, I'd guess she's over thirty. Christy also noticed that as she bent over, her kimono parted slightly, hinting at generous breasts underneath. That's my Skip. Always a sucker for big boobs. Suddenly she was self-conscious about her size. She was at least a head taller than Mariko and much heavier because of the baby. She felt like a large, sluggish whale swimming beside a graceful carp. But that wasn't important now. She was sitting across the table from her husband's lover. There was work to be done.

They talked for over an hour, and Mariko told her everything. She spoke softly in lilting, proper English. Her tone was not defensive or apologetic, and it didn't appear that she was holding anything back. Christy interrupted her occasionally to ask a question or clarify a point.

Mariko told the whole story starting from when she and Skip first met. She explained that Skip waited weeks before agreeing to go home with her. "Agree to go" was the proper term, she said, because she told him in the subtlest way possible that this was how she earned her living. Skip was nervous and uneasy when they arrived at her apartment the first time, but after awhile, he relaxed as they talked about things that interested them both—art, literature, and music. He was fascinated by her little dog, and asked her to teach him some Japanese words of endearment for pets so he could play with him. When it became late, he rose to go. "I'm sorry, Mariko," he explained, "you are a very sweet person, but I love my wife and could never be unfaithful to her." He paid her and left. He returned several times but never spent the night and always paid her.

When her story was finished, Mariko leaned forward and looked directly into Christy's eyes. "Mrs. O'Neill, your husband is a fine and honorable man. He has a good heart, which is something we Japanese treasure. What drew us together? Loneliness, I think. We were both lonely, especially late at night. I won't tell you that I didn't try to entice him into my bed, because I did. Any woman would, especially a woman in my profession." She blushed slightly at this. "But he never touched me, at least not in that way." She paused, and a mischievous twinkle appeared in her eye. "In fact, I can promise you that the only one in my flat who received his kisses and loving caresses was my dog." Christy had to laugh at this. She couldn't help it.

Christy had no reason to believe Mariko's story. It could be full of lies to protect Skip. But she believed her. She liked the way she told it, without alibis or embellishment, looking her in the eye all the while. She decided that Mariko was a good and decent person, trapped in a demeaning profession.

She rose to leave. "I have to go Mariko. My husband will be home soon and will wonder where I am. Thank you for talking to me. I feel a lot better. And thank you for the tea."

"You're welcome. I was glad to be of service."

Mariko parted the curtain and ushered her back into the lounge. The hostesses glanced at the pair furtively, wondering what had happened inside the small room. Nothing exciting, they decided, judging from the amiable looks on the two women's faces. They turned their attention to other things. The customers would be arriving soon.

"Let me show you a more discrete way to leave," Mariko said. She led Christy to a small door at the back of the bar. Motioning for Christy to stay where she was, she opened the door and looked out. The door opened to a narrow, twisting alley, lined with shops of all kinds that catered to Japanese and foreigners alike. Mariko looked carefully down both sides of the alley. There was no one in sight. She held the door wider and motioned for Christy to leave. For an instant, they stood in the doorway together. Mariko bowed. Christy did the same. It was not easy, but she knew it was the right thing to do. They had shown each other respect during an awkward encounter. It was a good way to end.

"Are you all right?" Jeannie asked after Christy was gone.

"Yes, I am fine," Mariko responded. "Thank you for asking, Mama-san."

Jeannie sighed. "It often happens in our business. Sometimes it leads to unpleasantness."

"I know."

Christy decided to window-shop before leaving, just for appearances. She wandered aimlessly for twenty minutes, pausing now and then, scarcely looking at merchandise. Then she bought a toy for Maddie and strode briskly out of the alley, the small package displayed in her hand for all to see, and hurried home.

*   *   *   *

It was five o'clock. Skip would be home in an hour. Maddie was still at Jan's. They would pick her up later—when it was over. As she waited, Christy sat at the kitchen table thinking about Mariko's story. "You are a very sweet person, but I love my wife and could never be unfaithful to her." That's what Skip had said, according to Mariko. The words were painfully familiar, almost exactly the same words she used when she said goodbye to Brad in the parking lot that night.

The idea that Skip spent several innocent nights in an apartment with a pretty woman, who obviously desired him, seemed absurd on the face of it. On the other hand, was it any more believable that a lonely woman caught up in a moment of passion and desire would run away before she got into trouble, especially when she had no reason to believe that her husband would ever find out? We're both in the same boat, she thought, trapped in a morass of anger, doubt, and jealousy. We need to talk, to put this thing behind us. The sooner the better. He won't want to at first. He's too busy playing the role of the betrayed husband. But he'll come around. Especially when I tell him about my little chat with Mariko.

Skip came home at six, wearing a bandage over his eye. His face was sullen. "I'm home," he said dully. "What time is supper?"

"It depends."

"Depends on what?"

"It depends what we say to each other in the next hour or so. We have to talk."

Skip sighed wearily. "Aww Christy, I don't want to talk about that shit anymore. It seems we talked quite enough last night." He turned and started for the door. "I guess I'll get a sandwich at the club."

"Oh, but you'll want to talk when you find out what I have to say. I have important news. News that will change everything."

Skip stood at the door uncertainly, his hand the knob. Then he returned to the living room and sat down on the sofa wearily. "Okay, what's this important news?"

"We're getting a divorce."

Skip startled. "What? I didn't say I wanted a divorce." He hadn't expected this.

"I know you didn't. But that's what I want."

"Why for God's sakes? It's bad enough I have to live with those sordid images of you groping in the parking lot with a strange man while I was in Korea. It's a nightmare. It should be me wanting a divorce, not you. I'm the injured party here."

"Not anymore."

"What is that supposed to mean?"

"It means that I don't trust you anymore."

"Surely you're joking," Skip said sarcastically.

"Nope. You see, you left out a very important part of Bob's story. The part about a bar hostess named Mariko at the Bar Interlude."

Skip turned pale. How did she find out? Surely Bob didn't tell her. Jan, it had to be her.

"She is a very nice woman by the way. We had a long talk. I can see why you like her. I can also see why you like the bar too. Quite cozy, and all those pretty girls."

"You went to the Bar Interlude?" Skip couldn't believe his ears.

"Yep, I went there this afternoon."

"If you talked to Mariko you know it was all platonic. We didn't do anything, and that's the God's own truth."

Christy rolled her eyes mockingly. "Ah yes, long evenings in her apartment, having intellectual conversations, playing with her dog. That's what she said. That's what you say. But how can I believe that? There's no way of knowing what really happened. Meanwhile, I have to live with sordid images of you rolling in the hay with a little Japanese girl while I was back in the States. It's a nightmare. By the way, how does that work? Did you do it in a bed, or on the floor on top of futons?"

Skip's face was flush with anger. But he held it in check.

Christy lowered her voice and spoke softly. "Skip, I have to ask you something. It's important, so answer me truthfully, if you can. Are you still screwing her?"

Skip almost jumped out of his seat. "Goddammit, aren't you listening at all? I never screwed her, and I haven't seen her since you arrived."

"It's important. What if she is carrying your child? What am I going to tell the kids?" It was a cruel thing to say, but he had said those identical words to her last night.

Skip got the point. He slumped into the sofa, looking defeated.

The two of them sat looking at each other across the coffee table, exhausted, like two animals that had just been in a long, ferocious fight. "So, where do we go from here?" Skip asked finally. The cut over his eye was throbbing.

"I don't know. We're in a bind here. Marriage is based on trust. It's an all or nothing thing. Both partners have to have it, otherwise, it doesn't work. You don't trust me, and I don't trust you. We've got nothing."

Skip nodded.

"Do you want a divorce, Skip?"

"The thought did cross my mind. But you're the love of my life, my best friend. I could never live without you. It's just that…"

Christy didn't let him finish. "Is that a yes or a no?"

Skip hung his head miserably, and for a minute he couldn't look her in the eye. "It's a no," he said finally.

"No what?"

"No, I don't want a divorce."

"Are you sure?"

"I'm sure."

"In that case I suggest you come over here and hug me, before I change my mind."

They put Maddie to bed early and sat downstairs talking until one in the morning. When they finished, they rose wearily and walked arm in arm upstairs, secure in the knowledge that at least they still loved each other. They had no illusions about what was yet to come. It would take months, perhaps years, to restore the bond of trust they once shared. Perhaps it would never be restored. But they were willing to try.

*   *   *   *

Cameron Michael O'Neill was born on January 23, 1963. He was a bright, energetic child with a full head of dark curly hair, the spitting image of Skip. Skip was secretly relieved that "Cam" favored him but wouldn't admit it, even to himself. Meanwhile, General Davis had promised General Slade he would give Skip something challenging to do. He kept his promise. Two weeks after Cam was born, Skip was given a new job. His days in the command post were over. His new job gave him more responsibility than he'd ever had in his life. He was in charge of planning all the missions to be flown in the event of an all-out nuclear war. It was demanding and highly classified work. Most of the time he worked alone with little or no supervision. To his surprise, he enjoyed his new job and was soon transformed into a happy, energetic man brimming with self confidence. Christy was delighted with the change. The man she had fallen in love with was back, but this time he was much more poised and mature. Surely, she thought, the worst is over, and his career will get back on track. Skip was not sure his career would ever get back on track, but he decided to wait and see.

The year drifted by the O'Neills in slow motion. Their lives were happy, although sometimes it seemed like everything important happened on the other side of the world while they were asleep. There was no television in Misawa, so news was fed to them without comment or analysis on Armed Forces Radio and in the Stars and Stripes newspaper. Civil rights demonstrations, the Beatles tour of the U.S., the Cuban missile crisis, even President Kennedy's assassination were events occurring in another time and place and, therefore, did not seem real.

By the end of 1963, there were nearly fifteen thousand U.S. military advisers in South Vietnam. President Lyndon Johnson declared that he was totally committed to winning the war there and would do whatever was necessary to assure victory. Most of the fighter pilots in Misawa viewed the conflict as a minor counterinsurgency operation best left to the special operations types to straighten out while they continued to train for the big shoot-out that was bound to occur someday with the Soviet Union. Skip, if he thought about it at all, viewed the Vietnam conflict as a minor distraction, something that was not part of his life—and never would be. After all, he was no longer a fighter pilot.

*   *   *   *

Skip shifted uneasily in his chair as the colonel studied his personnel records. The room was quiet save for the dry rustle of pages turning one by one. The wait was agonizing. The meeting, which had been arranged by General Davis, was unofficial and off the record. It could never have happened had Skip not been sent to Hawaii to attend a planning conference. He had worked hard for the past year and had done an outstanding job. But he was haunted by the notion that his experience in the 531st had done irreparable damage to his career. He needed to know the truth. The colonel reading his records was the director of officer personnel at PACAF headquarters. In a few minutes he was going to tell Skip how matters stood.

The colonel continued to read, noting the substandard effectiveness report Duke had written and the terse language describing his abrupt departure from the 531st. Meanwhile, Skip gazed idly through the open window at the manicured lawns and flowered bushes at Hickam Air Force Base. Off in the distance, he saw a partially submerged submarine traversing the channel leading to the sub base at Pearl Harbor. The tropical air smelled lush and sweet. The colonel closed the folder carefully, laid his glasses on the desk, and uttered an audible sigh. Skip leaned forward in his chair expectantly.

"To begin with, the effectiveness report your flight commander wrote is a killer. It seems to me he went out of his way to make it very personal."

Skip nodded grimly but said nothing.

"Also, the records don't say why you left the 531st, but the promotion board will pick up on that and draw their own conclusions. Quite frankly I don't think you will make major the first time you are eligible and probably won't make it for a long time. If there is a reduction in force in the next ten years, you'll be one of the first to leave. Otherwise, I predict you will be forced to retire as a major after twenty years."

Skip took the news stoically. He had expected something like this. Still, he was stung by the colonel's blunt appraisal. For a moment, he sat quietly, letting the words sink in. He was overcome by a wave of dull anger, but he held it in. After all, he had asked the colonel to be honest, hadn't he? It wasn't the colonel's fault. It all seemed so unfair. He realized there was nothing left to say, so he rose slowly with as much dignity as he could muster, thanked the colonel for his time and left.

He walked out of the headquarters building and started down the sidewalk, scarcely noticing where he was going. His mind was ablaze with thoughts and emotions. His career meant everything to him, but the scenario the colonel described was not acceptable. They might as well tattoo 1-O-S-E-R on my forehead, he thought. I need to wipe the slate clean and start over. If that means getting out of the Air Force, so be it. Getting out of the Air Force. It was a shocking thought, yet one that made perfect sense. Just thinking the words made everything fall in place, and he knew it was the right thing to do. It was a simple as that.

Getting out of the Air Force would be easy. He was free to leave when his tour in Misawa was over, but what to do next? Go to graduate school and get a master's degree, he supposed, and then get a job in industry. But what kind of job? He had no idea. One thing he did know, however. Christy would not be happy with his decision. He decided not to tell her right away. He needed a plan first. It was September 1963. His tour of duty in Misawa would be over in June 1964. He had ten months to get ready.

*   *   *   *

The letters began to arrive near the end of the year. They came from math and physics departments at large universities all over the United States. The University of New Mexico, the University of Colorado, and the University of Florida were the first three to arrive, followed by a half-dozen more. The mail usually arrived while Skip was at work. Christy said nothing about the letters at first, placing each one on his desk when it arrived. Finally she could contain her curiosity no longer.

"What's going on?" she asked.

"Oh nothing," Skip replied vaguely. "I'll probably have to get a master's degree one of these days to stay competitive, and I want to find out what's out there."

"That's a sensible idea, but why math and physics?"

"You know the Air Force…getting more high-tech every day. I thought it might be a nice fit for the space program or something like that."

"But you never took any undergraduate courses in math and physics."

"Well no, I'll have to take some foundation courses first, but after that, it should be no sweat. In fact, I've enrolled in some correspondence courses from the University of Maryland just to get started."

Christy shook her head in head in disbelief. She couldn't picture Skip as a mathematician or physicist. It just didn't add up. But she decided not to say any more. Their life had been on an even keel for the past year, and she was not about to rock the boat.

Skip began to study in earnest during the Christmas holidays. The courses were surprisingly easy. In a matter of a few months he finished several introductory courses in math and physics. I can do this, he thought. Now, if I can just make the rest of the plan work.

The next wave of letters began to arrive after the first of the year. Like the previous ones, they came from all over the United States, but this time the envelopes bore return addresses like: the 150th Tactical Fighter Group, Kirtland Air Force Base, New Mexico; 140th Tactical Fighter Wing, Buckley ANGB, Colorado; and the 125th Fighter Interceptor Group, Jacksonville, Florida. The names seemed foreign to Christy. She couldn't remember Skip mentioning any of them, but she noticed each address contained the same three words: Air National Guard. She knew very little about the "Guard" as it was called, except it was a form of the Air Force reserves. But reserve units normally weren't on active duty, so why would he be writing to them? It didn't make sense.

Skip read each letter as it arrived and then placed it in a special file folder without comment. It bothered Christy that he did not talk to her about the letters. It was not like him to be secretive. Something was going on. She was sure of it. Why won't he share it with her? She began to feel nervous and insecure.

Skip felt guilty about keeping Christy in the dark. He wanted to tell her everything, to seek her advice, to share his dream. But he needed more time, time to gather all the facts, to finish his plan. He was certain she would oppose him, unless he could show her that what he was about to do would lead to a better life for the family.

By late February, the file folder was bulging with letters, and he was studying every night and on weekends. His spirits were high, and he was behaving like a man obsessed. Several evenings he went to the command post where he persuaded a friend to place calls for him to the States. He never mentioned the calls to Christy. Things were falling into place. He was almost ready.

One day in early March, Christy decided enough was enough. When Skip came home that night she met him at the door. Out of the corner of his eye he could see the file folder lying unopened on the coffee table. "Welcome home, sweetie," she said with a hint of sarcasm. "I thought we would have a drink and a little chat before dinner." Her message was clear, time had run out. He knew he had to tell her everything. The couple sat facing each other, the unopened folder between them. For a moment, neither spoke.

Finally, Skip took a deep breath and began to talk. He told her about the meeting in Hawaii and what the colonel had said about his chances for promotion. He spoke passionately about his need to have a successful career, one that would provide for his family and make them proud of him. Under the circumstances, he concluded, he could see no other way. He needed to get out of the Air Force and start a new life.

Christy was stunned. Get out of the Air Force and go to college? It was a preposterous idea. "You can't do that," she blurted out finally. Her voice was shaking, and she started to stammer. "It's your whole life. It's our life. What happened to all the promises you made? All your dreams? Are you just going to walk away like a spoiled little boy because things aren't going your way?"

"It's not like that, Christy, and you know it. The colonel said…"

"Oh screw the colonel. What does he know? General Davis told me at the Christmas party that you had a promising future. He said that General Slade had been impressed by you when you briefed him on your accident, and that he was keeping an eye on you. He also said you will probably be assigned to PACAF headquarters when you leave Japan."

Skip groaned sarcastically. "That's just what I need, another staff tour…three more years sitting behind a desk. I need to get back where I belong, in a fighter squadron. Christ almighty, don't you see what's happening here? The guys in the squadrons will be flying combat in Southeast Asia in another year or so, while I'm behind a desk shuffling papers. And when they come home, they'll be so far ahead of me, I'll never catch up."

Christy was getting angry. It was Skip's pride talking, not him. The whole idea of leaving the Air Force was ridiculous and very wrong. "Tell me something. When had you planned to share this idea of quitting?" Her voice was cold and icy. "As we were about to leave Japan perhaps?"

Skip shook his head doggedly. "I knew you were going to be angry about that, but I didn't want to bother you until I had all the details worked out."

"Oh, I get it. You didn't want me to worry my pretty little head over small details, like how you planned to support your wife and two kids while playing Joe College. By the way, how do you plan to support us?"

"Well I…"

"Ooooh, I know, I know," Christy said, waving her hand sarcastically like a child in a classroom. "You want me to get a job in the school cafeteria to support us, right?"

Skip had had enough. "God damn it, Christy, if you'll just shut up for a minute, I'll tell you all about it."

Christy fell back in her chair and became quiet. But she was still angry.

"Okay, here's the deal. Two nights ago I talked to the commander of an Air National Guard squadron in Jacksonville, Florida. A very nice man. His unit has four aircraft on active air-defense alert twenty-four hours a day, seven days a week. He needs pilots with flexible schedules who can fill in whenever they are needed. He pretty much guaranteed me twenty days of active duty every month, just for being on alert. That's in addition to two regular training days, plus I am eligible for the GI Bill. Hell's bells, Christy, we might end up making more money than we are now."

Christy remained unconvinced. "Let me see if I have this straight. You're going to sit on alert all night and on the days you don't have classes, and then go to school when you are not working? That doesn't sound like much of a life to me. You'll never see the kids."

"But it's not going to be like that forever. I talked to the chairman of the math department at Jacksonville University, and he said that he could have me ready for graduate school in about eighteen months. After that, we can move to Gainesville, and I will enroll in graduate school at the University of Florida. Maybe I can get a teaching assistantship, and I won't have to spend so much time on alert. All I know is that this is a chance for us to start a new life, a life where we live where we want, make our own choices, and not be bothered by idiots like Duke Christiansen."

Christy couldn't sleep that night. Everything was happening so fast. It was all so unexpected. She was angry at Skip for not sharing his plans. She felt blindsided and betrayed. Most of all, she was afraid. It was the fear of the unknown. She was sure that what he was about to do was a mistake. She was also sure he was going to do it, no matter what she said. At least he will still be flying, she thought. Maybe someday…she tried to hold on to that thought as she finally fell asleep.

Things happened quickly in the final three months. Skip went to personnel and requested a release from active duty. There was no discussion. No one tried to change his mind. The personnel officer said his request would most likely be approved. His request was approved in early May. Two weeks later, Skip and Christy were given a farewell party at the officers' club. It was a low-key affair filled with kind words and wishes of good luck. Everyone was sorry to see them go. But they were not able to say goodbye to Bob and Jan. Bob was in Southeast Asia on temporary assignment. Meanwhile, Jan had taken the children and had gone to the States. No one expected her to return. Not being able to see his friend saddened Skip greatly. They had been through a lot together in the past four years, and in all likelihood, his departure meant the end of the Blunderbirds. Christy was still not sure they were doing the right thing, but she was glad to leave Misawa. So many unpleasant things had happened there. Maybe Skip is right, she thought. Maybe a new start is what we need.

To their delight, they flew back to the States on a chartered Boeing 707—sixteen hours from Tokyo to California, with a stop in Anchorage to refuel. The children were well-behaved and slept much of the way. It was a far cry from their trips to Japan. On June 4, 1964, Skip parked in front of a nondescript, two-story building at Travis Air Force Base, California. As Christy and the children waited in the car, he walked into the building carrying a large manila envelope containing all of his personnel records. Thirty minutes later, he returned with a forced look of cheerfulness and got in the car.

"Well, that's it. It's done. From now on I am Mister O'Neill. Did you hear that everybody? Mister O'Neill." Maddie giggled appreciatively. Christy nodded and said nothing. A large pair of dark glasses covered her red, tear-swollen eyes. Skip drove through the main gate and headed east without looking back. Christy sat beside him, her hands folded in her lap. What have we done? she thought. This is all wrong.

Jacksonville Florida

1964 to 1967

Skip was warmly welcomed to the squadron at Jacksonville. They were good guys, laid back but business-like at the same time. It didn't seem to bother them that he had not flown a high-performance aircraft in two years. They didn't even send him to school to check out in the aircraft. He checked out locally with one of the instructor pilots. The F-102, or "Deuce" as it was called, was a dream to fly. Long and sleek with a large delta wing, it was painted light gray. Seen from the air, it looked like a large graceful dart, which is no doubt why its formal name was the Delta Dart. It could turn on a dime too, and Skip loved to dogfight with his squadron mates, often "waxing their asses" with tactics he learned at Luke and Nellis, tactics that were not taught in interceptor school. As for the mission, it couldn't have been simpler—air defense just like the old days in Presque Isle, except this time, he was both the pilot and RO, flying the aircraft with his right hand and operating the radar hand control with his left.

His transition to college life was equally smooth. The chairman of the mathematics department at Jacksonville University took a liking to Skip, because he was more mature than the other students. He spent many hours working with him one-on-one, and Skip in turn graded papers for his professor, sometimes even grading test papers from his own class. The professor was a quiet, gentle man who was easy to talk to. Some afternoons they closed the door and spent an hour or two discussing some exotic mathematical theory that was in vogue. When that happened, the professor would open his desk drawer and pull out a bottle of bourbon, pouring healthy drinks in chipped coffee cups kept there for that purpose. Then he would explain in sonorous tones why the theory was a "crock of shit."

Skip loved it when he did that. "You would have made a hell of fighter pilot," he told his professor during one of their academic drinking sessions.

"And you're gonna be a hell of a mathematician," the professor responded.

Skip was surprised at how easily Christy adapted to their new life. They rented a cozy ranch-style house in the sleepy town of Mandarin, which was an easy drive from both the airport and the college. It was surrounded by bushes of all kinds as well as elegant cypress trees festooned with Spanish moss. There was an old barn and storage shed in the back, and the children delighted in scrambling around them playing hide and seek. Insects and frogs serenaded them every night. The air was always heavy with the sweet scent of flowers.

Christy moped around for the first few weeks and then sprang into action. "We're going to need more money starting next month," she said one night.

"Money? What for?"

"For the babysitter. I signed up for two classes at the university. I'm going to finish my degree and be a kindergarten teacher, remember?"

Skip remembered. It was a reasonable request. Besides, they were making more money than when they were on active duty. This pleased him, because it proved that he had made the right decision.

He was admitted to graduate school at the University of Florida in the fall of 1965, majoring in mathematics with a minor in physics. The family decided to stay in Jacksonville, even though it was an hour-and-a-half drive to Gainesville. It made for a grueling schedule, especially on the nights when he was on alert and had to make a nine o'clock class the next morning. But somehow he managed. It was for a good cause after all, and he expected to get his masters degree in eighteen months, or maybe sooner.

But one of his physics professors had other ideas. "You need to be physicist, not a mathematician," he said. "Mathematicians create theories, proofs, and formulas—abstract stuff. They don't care what becomes of them or what they are used for. They do it just for the hell of it. Physicists adapt them to their needs and do useful things with them."

Skip decided his professor was right; it would be more interesting to be a physicist. "Sounds good to me," he said, "I'll change my major next semester."

"One more thing," the professor said, "it's a waste of time to stop at a master's degree. I propose to put you in an accelerated program to your Ph.D. Instead of writing a thesis, you'll do a warm-up dissertation that can be expanded later for your doctoral dissertation."

"How long would that take?"

"It's shorter than getting a master's degree first. You can do it in about three years."

Three years. That's a long time to pull alert and drive back and forth to Jacksonville. "I'll have to think about that," Skip said.

Skip talked it over with Christy. "You have to do it, honey. If you want to be a physicist, you have to have a Ph.D." He decided to go for the three-year program.

By the time Skip returned for his second year of graduate school, his professor had arranged a research assistantship for him. "The pay is not much, but you have access to more research materials and will be able to attend all our seminars. Let me show you your office."

The office was tiny and had no windows. A single fluorescent light in the acoustical-tile ceiling was the only source of light. It was unfurnished save for a metal desk and chair.

Skip eyed the room skeptically. "What am I supposed to do in here?"

"Think about the hydrogen atom."

Skip look at him to see if he was joking. He wasn't. "Think about the hydrogen atom?"

"Yes. I want you to start building theoretical models of quantum energy levels of its orbiting electron. Also, you have to learn to read two foreign languages before you graduate. You might as well get started on that."

Skip sighed and said he would do his best.

Something unexpected happened in late 1966. His squadron commander called him into his office one day and said, "You're being promoted to major."

Skip was shocked. "What? Why me?"

"Beats me. The state headquarters says we have a slot in our unit for a major, and we'll lose it if we don't fill it this year."

"But there are a lot of guys in the squadron who have been here for years."

The squadron commander shrugged. "Maybe so, but you are the most senior captain, and that's the way the system works."

He was uncomfortable with the idea at first. It didn't seem fair. But after awhile, he decided, why not? It was not like he promoted himself. It took a few weeks for the Pentagon to process the paperwork. Then he became Major O'Neill. So much for the colonel at PACAF who said it would take years for him to get promoted. It felt good to put the gold oak leaf on his hat and flying suit.

In his second year of graduate school, Skip made his first new friend since leaving pilot training. Ken Foster was a squadron mate at Jacksonville and was working on a master's in political science at Gainesville. He was a quiet, unassuming man with a wry sense of humor. Ken's wife, Jodie, was a pistol, a real free spirit. They lived on a lake in a rural area a few miles from Gainesville.

Skip and Ken were always doing things together. They met between classes for coffee and played tennis on the school courts. At Jacksonville, they tried to be on alert together whenever they could. They spent many evenings in the alert hangar discussing politics and world affairs. Skip was a Republican, and Ken was a Democrat, which made for lively discussions. They never missed a chance to tease or play a practical joke on each other. Ken wanted to go to the State Department when he graduated. Skip told him he would spend the rest of his life drinking tea and eating cookies. Ken was sure Skip would blow up his laboratory some day.

The years 1966 and 1967 were restless on the campus of the University of Florida. Long-haired students dressed in love beads, sandals, and headbands flaunted peace signs and smoked pot openly. Raucous antiwar rallies became almost daily occurrences. The faculty seemed powerless to enforce discipline and at times, appeared to side with the students.

Skip watched the demonstrations from afar, looking out of place with his short hair. The other students were not part of his world, and he was not part of theirs. As for the war in Vietnam, that was part of another life, a life he didn't think about anymore. He was happy where he was, doing what he was doing.

*   *   *   *

Everything changed the night Skip arrived at the alert hangar angry and frustrated. Final exams for the spring semester were starting in a week, and he had been working for three days on a mathematical equation that he couldn't solve. It was a lengthy equation that took most of a large blackboard. There was an incorrect term in it somewhere, but he couldn't find it. Ken, on the other hand, was on top of the world. He would be graduating in three weeks and had already been accepted by the State Department.

The two friends put their parachutes in their aircraft and returned to the hangar. "We have to fly one sortie this evening," the ops officer said. "It's your turn Skip. I've scheduled you for a six o'clock takeoff, okay?"

"Dammit, why me? I've got this assignment to finish by tomorrow morning, and it's driving me nuts. Can't someone else do it?" The ops officer shrugged and walked away.

"Hey," Ken said, "don't sweat it. I'll fly if you like."

"Are you sure?"

"Absolutely. What have I got to do this evening? Final exams are over, and I've got the world by the ass—unlike some dumb-shit physics student I know who can't solve a simple equation."

"I really appreciate it, man."

"What are friends for?"

Skip walked out to mobile control and watched his friend take off. The aircraft thundered down the runway, climbed steeply, and turned gracefully to northeast. Skip stayed in mobile for five minutes listening idly as Ken left the tower frequency and switched to departure control. Soon Ken was out of sight. He won't be back for at least an hour, Skip thought. I'll work on that problem for awhile and then come back.

Mobile control was just fifty yards from the alert hangar. Skip walked back slowly, taking time to smell the fresh air and admire the rich, red glow of the clouds in the deepening sunset. He scarcely noticed the greasy, black column of smoke to the northeast of the city. Rubbish fire, he thought, and went inside.

Phones were ringing off the hook when he walked in. The ops officer stood in the middle of the alert center talking on one phone, while holding another in his hand. Pilots and crew chiefs stood around nervously, listening as he spoke. Finally he hung up.

"What's going on?" Skip asked.

"Kenny's down."

"That can't be. I just watched him take off."

"I know. He crashed five minutes ago…about twenty miles from here."

"Did he get out of the bird? Is he okay?"

"We don't know. He crashed near a state highway. The state police are on their way now."

"What happened? Did he say anything?"

"Just one sentence: I've got a problem. That's all."

The room grew quiet. Nobody knew what to say. Ten minutes later, the phone rang. The ops officer answered it and listened for awhile. "I understand," he said finally and then hung up. "That was the state police. The bird crashed along the side of the highway. He was trying to land on the road but changed his mind at the last minute. The landing gear was down, and there was no fire and very little damage. Kenny was still in the cockpit. He's dead."

Everyone looked at Skip, wondering what he was going to say. He had just lost his best friend. Skip's face was contorted with pain, and for a minute it looked like he was going to cry. But he didn't. "It was all my fault," he said softly. "If I had flown that flight like I was supposed to, this wouldn't have happened."

"It was nobody's fault," the ops officer said, "nobody in this room anyway. If you had flown that flight instead of Kenny, you would probably be dead by now."

Skip slammed his hand down hard on the desk, scattering papers everywhere. "Why didn't he get out of the fucking bird? Just tell me that will you? Why did he try to ride it in? Surely he had time to punch out. It doesn't make sense."

The ops officer shook his head wearily. "How should I know? It just happened. He didn't punch out, and he's dead. Look Skip, shit like that happens sometimes. Nobody knows why."

Skip fell silent. Shit like that happens. That's what he told Bob in Misawa after Corky bought the farm. Shit happens.

The squadron commander arrived thirty minutes later. After talking to the ops officer, he walked straight to Skip. "You know what we have to do, don't you?"

Skip nodded miserably.

"How about Christy? Can she handle it?"

Skip nodded. He thought back to all the funerals in Misawa—Corky, Big Jim, and Colonel John. "She can handle it."

"Good. We'll caravan down to his house. I'll take the flight surgeon and chaplain. You and Christy can show us the way."

It was almost midnight when they arrived. They drove the final two miles along a narrow, black-asphalt road covered by a canopy of interlocking cypress trees. There was no moon, and their headlights were absorbed by the enveloping darkness. As they turned into the driveway, a dog began to bark furiously in the garage. The air was humid and still as they got out of the cars. There was no sound except for the steady barking of the dog. The house was dark.

The five of them walked somberly toward the front porch. Nobody wanted to be there. As they climbed the steps, the porch light came on. Jodie looked out the window and saw the entourage. She opened the door and Skip stepped forward.

"It's Ken, isn't it?"

Skip nodded.

"He's dead, isn't he?"

"I'm afraid so." He drew her into his arms as she began to sob. Christy moved quickly to her side. Together they walked her into the house. The others followed her awkwardly.

They led her to the living room sofa. Skip and Christy sat on either side, while the squadron commander told her all he knew about the accident, which wasn't very much. The chaplain and flight surgeon looked nervous, like they wanted to do something but didn't know what.

The couch, Skip thought, the wife always sits on the couch. He thought back to Presque Isle. What was her name? Pattie, that's it. Charlie Wilson's wife. He ran into the mountain. Pattie sat in the living room on the couch too.

The flight surgeon suggested that Jodie take a tranquillizer. Her face hardened. "No way, you're not going to dope me up like a horse." She turned to Skip. "But I could use a drink."

Skip squeezed her arm reassuringly. "Bourbon and water, right?"

"I think I'll have mine on the rocks tonight. Put water in yours if you like. Ken always said you were a pussy." Skip smiled weakly and went to the kitchen. He fixed her drink and made one for himself and Christy. The others didn't ask for a drink, and he didn't offer them one.

Jodie finally fell asleep at four AM. Skip and Christy took turns watching her as she slept fitfully. It was twenty-four hours before she was ready to talk about Ken's funeral.

Skip accompanied Ken's body to his home in Birmingham, Alabama, and arranged for a military funeral. He also visited Ken's parents, who were still in shock. They didn't understand why their son had died, and neither did Skip. It was an awkward visit for everybody. Christy drove Jodie to the funeral. As Ken's body was lowered into the grave, an honor guard fired a volley of shots, and the bugler played taps. Then, four F-84s from the Alabama Air National Guard swooped low and flew over the cemetery in tight formation. As they passed over the grave site, the number two man pulled up abruptly and climbed skyward until he disappeared from sight. The rest of the flight continued, leaving a gap in the formation for the "missing wingman," a tribute to their fallen comrade.

Jodie stood quietly between Skip and Christy as the roar of the aircraft subsided. "That was beautiful," she said finally.

"Yes it was," Skip replied.

"I kept waiting for Ken to sit up in the casket and flip everyone the bird. You know how he hated mushy stuff." They both tried to smile.

Everyone turned and walked slowly back to their cars. "It's all right if you cry, Skip," Christy whispered in his ear.

"I know," he said and put on his sunglasses.

*   *   *   *

Skip spent hours brooding in his small office, unable to study or think about anything. It all seemed so trivial. The hydrogen atom, getting a PhD...who gives a fuck? He felt like a man trudging up a mountain he didn't want to climb. On alert, he kept to himself. He never did solve the equation, the one that killed his friend. The pain was unbearable sometimes. If only he had flown that night!

"The airlines are hiring," a young pilot said one evening as he walked into the alert hangar.

"Which ones?" another pilot asked.

"All of them—TWA, Pan Am, American, Eastern. They're hurting man. The Air Force isn't releasing pilots from active duty any more because of the war. The airlines have to get pilots from somewhere."

Skip felt a sudden surge of boyish, devil-may-care enthusiasm. The airlines, why not? It would be a classy way to make a living—good pay and travel to interesting places. It beats the hell out of the hydrogen atom, that's for sure. The whole idea was irrational, but it appealed to him nonetheless.

He talked to Christy and then called Pan Am. She didn't try to dissuade him. She could never picture him as a physicist anyway. They invited him to New York City for an interview. Six weeks later he was hired.

"I sure hope you know what you're doing this time," Christy said when they got the word.

"It'll be great. Pan Am flies all over the world, and we'll be able to get employee tickets. Paris, Rome, Germany. Do you remember how you wanted to be based in Germany?"

Christy groaned. "I remember. But listen, there are strings attached to this deal."

"Strings?"

"Yep, the kids and I aren't going anywhere until I get my degree and teacher's certificate, and that will take six more months."

"No problem. My training will last that long. Meanwhile, I can come home on weekends using employee passes."

The squadron commander was not surprised to see Skip leave. Pilots in his unit came and went all the time. The day Skip stopped by his office to say good-bye, the commander reached in his desk and handed him a letter. "I thought you might like to take this with you. It's the only copy."

The letter strongly advised the commander not to let Skip join the unit and fly the F-102. "Captain O'Neill is undisciplined, unreliable, and a poor pilot," it said. "I firmly believe that he crashed an aircraft due to pilot error and fabricated a story about a flight control failure." The letter was signed, "Stewart Christiansen, Major USAF."

Skip read the letter slowly, feeling the familiar glow of anger rise to his face. "You had this letter, and you let me join the squadron anyway. Why?"

The squadron commander smiled. "I worked for an asshole like that back in the Korean War. That's why I'm in the Guard and not in the regular Air Force."

Finding a Guard unit to join in the New York City area was not easy. Nobody wanted a major. The squadrons would rather promote their own pilots. After several weeks of searching, Skip found a billet in Atlantic City, New Jersey. He would be the plans officer, not a squadron pilot, the commander told him, but he could fly anyway. The unit was equipped with F-100s. Skip was ecstatic. He would be a Hun driver again!

PAM AMERICAN FLIGHT

OO2

Somewhere over the Atlantic Ocean
January 25, 1968

It was midnight, and they were high over the cold, dark North Atlantic, rushing toward the sunrise that would soon greet them. A light, choppy wave of turbulence rocked the wings gently and rhythmically. The cockpit door opened, and a flight attendant walked in bringing breakfast trays filled with eggs, sausage, croissants, orange juice, and plenty of fresh, rich coffee, a fine meal that would hold them until they landed in Paris. She was a young Swedish girl, a tall, cool blonde who looked like a model. That was Pan Am's style—wholesome and attractive flight attendants from European countries like Holland, Germany, and Sweden.

Skip watched with fascination as the girl leaned over and lowered the trays onto the pilots' laps, wondering what she would be like in bed. Abruptly, he swiveled his chair back toward the engineer's panel and turned his attention to the instruments. Smiling wryly, he thought back to Mariko and the trouble he got into when Christy found out about her. It was dangerous stuff. Besides, Christy takes care of my needs very well thank you, and, as Bob used to say about extramarital affairs, "The screwing you get is not worth the screwing you get." He thought about Bob and wondered how he was doing. It had been a long time since he had talked to him. Did he even have a wife to cheat on these days? He doubted it. I'll send him a postcard from Rome, he thought.

The stop at Paris was brief, just enough time to refuel, take on catering, and load the passengers. Skip walked around the big aircraft conducting the preflight inspection on the big Boeing 707. It felt good to stretch his legs after the long flight. The area around their gate at Orly Airport was awash in sounds and furious activity, as aircraft from all over the world arrived and departed. Skip stood for a minute taking it all in. Jet engines whined and roared, and the wake from their exhaust blew his necktie askew and nearly blew his hat off. It was all so new and exciting. Then they took off for the short flight to Rome.

It was a bright, sunny day when he stepped off the aircraft in Rome. Skip couldn't wait to take off his uniform and strike out to see the city. He had never been to Italy. The ride downtown to the Hotel Metropole was insane. The driver weaved and careened crazily around traffic circles, engaging in a modern chariot race with other cars and taxis. These Roman taxi drivers are crazy, he thought. They make New York cab drivers look like a bunch of old ladies. The neighborhood around the hotel was exciting and colorful, a mixture of ancient and modern buildings. People were everywhere; some rushing off as if late for an appointment, others sitting lazily in sidewalk cafes sipping espressos or wine as if they had all the time in the world. As he left the hotel for a walk, he watched a young man drive his Lambretta motor scooter onto the sidewalk and deftly pinch the derriere of a well-dressed lady before speeding away. This is my kind of place, he thought exultantly. If only Christy were here to see this. She would love it.

The crew ate dinner at a small restaurant near the hotel. It was a modest place with marble floors and colorful tile walls. Works of art hung everywhere. The food was simple but mouthwatering. A trio of musicians strolled from table to table playing Italian folk songs. Skip took it all in—the sounds, sights, and smells—and was filled with happiness. This is the life, he thought. I should have done this a long time ago.

After two glasses of smooth, rich Chianti, the check engineer leaned over and spoke to Skip confidentially. "As far as I'm concerned, you have passed the check ride. I'm going to ride in the cabin on the flight back to New York." Skip was relieved. The last obstacle had been removed. He was about to be a full-fledged, Pan Am flight engineer.

The first officer was a former Marine fighter pilot. Over dessert and coffee, he and Skip fell into the usual Air Force vs. Marine banter. At one point, Skip mentioned that he had joined the Guard unit in Atlantic City and would be flying the F-100 again.

"You're crazy. That was a dumb thing to do."

Skip looked at his face to see if he was joking. He wasn't. "I thought Marines were always hot to fly fighters."

"I was, when I was on active duty. But I'm not in the Marine Corps now. I'm an airline pilot."

Skip didn't know what to say. The first officer leaned over the table and began to talk earnestly. "Listen to me, if you screw around with the Guard or Reserve, you're going to get recalled to active duty someday, sure as hell. It always happens. And when you do, the world is going to move on without you, and things will never be the same."

Skip felt himself tense. This guy is raining on my parade, he thought. Then he relaxed. He probably means well. "All I know is once a fighter pilot, always a fighter pilot. And if flying fighters in the Guard means a risk of being recalled to active duty, I'm willing to take that risk."

"Do you know what that tells me?"

"What?"

"It tells me you haven't broken your ties with the Air Force. You may think you have, but you haven't."

"You may be right," Skip conceded.

It took a long time for Skip to fall asleep that night. It had been a long day. Tomorrow it all starts, the beginning of a rich and productive new life. A life that will provide travel, excitement, and comfort for Skip and his family. He could hardly wait to call Christy and tell her the news. For a second, a cold, clammy thought gripped his mind. What if the first officer is right, and I am risking my future in order to fly fighters? He brushed the thought away and fell asleep.

THE PUEBLO CRISIS

January 26, 1967

At five the next morning, the crew met at a small espresso bar next to the hotel. Standing elbow-to-elbow at the marble counter, they drank strong, hot coffee and savored fresh croissants. The bar was not crowded, just the four men and a half dozen ladies of the night. The men were dressed in their Pan Am uniforms, their luggage nearby. A car would take them to the airport in thirty minutes. The women were still dressed in their "uniforms"—micro-miniskirts, low-cut blouses, net stockings, and spike-heeled shoes. They were a tired and defeated lot, their makeup smeared, their bodies smelling of cigarettes and cheap perfume. The fluorescent light in the ceiling was not kind to them.

"It's always the same this time of the morning," the check engineer grumbled. "Nobody in here but Pan Am pilots and hookers."

"Six of one, half a dozen of the other," the captain observed. "We're all hookers. We just do different things for money than they do."

"So true. That's what I like about you, Jim. Always the philosopher, even at five AM."

"I try."

Skip smiled to himself. We're all hookers...I'll have to remember that one.

They took off at eight and climbed quickly to cruise altitude. The aircraft seemed more eager to fly than yesterday. It was a spectacular day, not a cloud forecast between Rome and New York. Once again, the stop in Paris was brief. Skip supervised the refueling while the rest of the crew went into the terminal. They returned with newspapers and fresh loaves of French bread to take home with them.

The flight to New York would take an hour longer than normal because of seasonal headwinds. Skip worked at the engineer's panel efficiently and with confidence. He was no longer a student. He was a full-fledged engineer, or at least he would be when the check engineer signed the paperwork in New York. He thought about the small house in Queens he had rented last week. It will be perfect for us. There is an elementary school just three blocks away. That's important, because Maddie will be starting third grade in September and Cam will be in the first grade. Gosh they were growing fast! He missed them so much. But it's okay; it was all worth it. What a great life we are going to have!

When the aircraft leveled off at cruise altitude, everyone settled in for the long day ahead. Checking the autopilot one last time, the first officer eased his seat back and opened the Paris edition of the International Herald Tribune. He gave a low whistle of surprise. "I don't believe it! They're calling up the Guard and Reserves."

Skip's chain had been jerked by experts. He was not about to be taken in by something so obvious. Extending his raised middle finger in the direction of the first officer, he didn't bother to look up.

"I'm not kidding man, see for yourself." The first officer passed the paper back to Skip. NORTH KOREA SEIZES U.S. SPY SHIP PUEBLO, the headline screamed. Below that, 14,500 RESERVISTS CALLED TO ACTIVE DUTY. The date on the paper was January 26, 1968.

The article went on to list the units recalled to active duty. The first one on the list was the 177th Tactical Fighter Group at Atlantic City. This can't be. There has to be a mistake. But the newspaper offered no hope of a mistake. The truth was Skip was in the Air Force, even as he sat in the cockpit of a Boeing 707 wearing his Pan Am uniform.

The cockpit grew quiet. The others felt sorry for him, even though they barely knew him. No one knew what to say. What can you say at a time like this? The first officer was embarrassed. It was the wine talking last night, he thought. Besides, I was talking in generalities. How did I know things would get so intensely personal just twelve hours later? "I'm really sorry, man," he said finally.

Skip smiled gamely. "All I can say is you're one hell of a fortune-teller. Do you have any tips for the stock market?"

"Unfortunately no. I wish I did."

"So do I," the captain said. Everyone laughed and went back to work.

The shock was beginning to wear off, and reality was setting in. It would be six hours before they landed in New York. Skip tried to concentrate on his work, but it was not easy. His mind was awash in swirling currents and eddies of thoughts, thoughts propelled relentlessly by anxiety, fear, and uncertainty. Maybe it was all a mistake…maybe they didn't recall his unit at all…maybe they only recalled part of his unit…or maybe they didn't recall him. After all, he wasn't combat-ready in the F-100. What do they need him for? Maybe, maybe, maybe. He could sit there and play maybe games until the cows came home, but the truth of the matter was he was back in the Air Force, and that's all there was to that.

He thought about Christy and the kids and about the house he had just rented in the Queens. What about my deposit? Will I get that back? What about my job at Pan Am? How will Christy react to all of this? The questions swirled through his mind. Many of the answers would be waiting for him when he landed in New York.

The crew stood up and gathered their things as soon as the engines stopped and the cockpit was secured. They seemed anxious to distance themselves from the dejected young man sitting slumped at the engineer's console filling out the maintenance log. The first officer was the last to leave. Pausing at the cockpit door, he turned and shook Skip's hand. "Remember what I said about you still being committed to the Air Force?"

"Yes."

"That's an advantage now. It's going to give you an edge over the run-of-the-mill weekend warriors. I have a feeling you're going to do good things."

"Semper Fi, right?"

"Yeah, something like that. Good luck."

Skip slowly stood up, buttoned his uniform coat, put on his hat, and walked through the aircraft exit, his large, leather flight bag in his hand. A passenger service representative rushed forward to meet him. "Are you *Major* O'Neill?"

"Yeah, I guess I am…now."

"Your unit has called three times already today. They want you to report to Atlantic City immediately."

Skip sighed and started walking away. "Oh, and Major, the chief flight engineer wants to see you in his office before you leave. It's important."

"I'll bet he does."

The chief flight engineer was politely sympathetic in a detached sort of way. "Nasty break about this recall business. What's it all about?"

"Beats the hell out of me. All I know is what I read in the papers." You might try reading the papers yourself, Skip thought. You'd be surprised what's in them sometimes.

The chief flight engineer was all business now. "Your employment with us will end at midnight tonight. So will your insurance and other benefits. I need your company ID card and all your flight manuals. Please sign these papers that signify that you understand all this. Oh, and you have to return the wings and other insignia from your uniform."

Skip did as he was told.

"Good luck and give us a call when you get out of the Air Force. We will, of course, retain your seniority number."

Skip walked out the door, his black uniform shorn of all insignia save for the three gold stripes on the sleeves of his jacket. It's like a scene from an old movie, the one where the cavalry officer in the Old West is drummed out of the corps, his saber broken in half and flung out the gate of the fort.

Skip went into the men's room, changed into a pair of slacks and a sweater, and then went to a pay phone to call Christy in Florida. She answered on the first ring. "Well you've really done it this time, Skip." She was trying to be humorous, but her voice was strained and filled with concern.

"Did what? Start a war with North Korea? It wasn't me. I was in Rome the whole time."

"What does it all mean?"

"I haven't a clue. For starters, my career with Pan Am is on hold until further notice, and so are our plans to move to New York City."

"What do you want me to do now?"

"There's nothing you can do. Stay there, keep going to school, and take care of the kids. Things will sort themselves out eventually."

Christy paused, and her voice began to break with emotion. "It's all my fault," she blurted suddenly.

"All your fault? You started the war with North Korea?"

"Listen to me. I'm serious. All the time we were in New York, I kept dreaming that we were back in the Air Force, and you were flying F-100s. I've always felt that's where you belonged."

Skip laughed. "Well, your dream certainly came true. I'm in the Air Force, and I guess I'll be flying F-100s very soon." His voice became gentle and reassuring. "Look baby, this thing is nobody's fault. It just happened. In a few weeks it will all blow over, and our life will get back on track. Meanwhile, I'll call you every day and let you know what's going on."

"Promise? I love you so much you know."

"I promise. I love you too."

177TH Tactical Fighter Group

Atlantic City, New Jersey
The same day

The scene at Atlantic City was one of chaos and confusion. The 177th was a tenant on an FAA research facility. Fifteen hundred men now occupied a few square blocks of hangars and administration buildings. There were not enough billets for so many people, and the unit had already contracted with local motels to handle the overflow. The men of the 177th came from all walks of life. There were airline pilots, lawyers, stockbrokers, and school teachers, as well as store clerks, and day laborers. Many had joined the Guard to avoid being drafted and sent to Vietnam. Nobody was happy, and nobody wanted to be there. Some complained loudly about the abrupt and inconsiderate way their lives had been interrupted. Skip had the feeling that most had forgotten that the mission of the Air National Guard was to be mobilized in the case of war or national emergency.

Skip was one of the last to arrive. He was quickly processed in and sent to his squadron. "Ah, our fearless plans officer has finally arrived," the operations officer said cheerily. "You're just in time. This telex just came in. Read it and make us a plan."

The telex was stilled rolled up and had not been cut into pages. When Skip unrolled it, it was over seven feet long. It was a plan to deploy all the aircraft to the Far East. It listed the route of flight, stopover bases, navigational frequencies, and tanker call signs, everything needed to move the aircraft quickly and efficiently to their destination. The last leg of the deployment ended at an airborne refueling point off the coast of South Korea. The final destination would be determined later. He had prepared several deployment plans at Misawa. It was not a difficult task. The first order of business was to transcribe all the information in the telex onto maps, flight plans, and briefing cards that would be placed in deployment folders, one for each pilot. It was a big job, but he had several squadron pilots to help him. Another telex would provide details for moving support personnel and equipment. They would deal with that later. They had to make sure the pilots were ready to go first.

They worked all night. By 5 AM, the deployment folders were finished. The aircraft could be launched that day if need be. There was nothing left to do but wait. Skip was too exhausted to find a bed. Instead, he crawled on top of the planning table and fell asleep. A lot had happened since he had left the espresso bar in Rome. The captain said we are all hookers, we just do different things for money, he thought drowsily as he drifted off. What am I doing now? Whatever it is, it's not for money.

*   *   *   *

The men of the 177th waited for weeks, ready to deploy at a moment's notice. The order never came. It was obvious that the unit would not be deploying to South Korea. Everyone was puzzled and frustrated. "If they're not going to use us, why don't they release us from active duty?" one of the pilots asked.

"Because they want to use us somewhere else," the squadron intelligence officer responded.

"Where for God's sake? The Pueblo crisis is over. It's time for us to go home."

"Vietnam."

"Vietnam? You're crazy. They can't do that. You can only call up the Guard in the case of a war or national emergency. We've never declared war on North Vietnam, and it's hardly a national emergency."

"It depends on how you look at it. Several F-4 squadrons were deployed from Vietnam to South Korea in response to a bone fide national emergency, and they're going to stay there until we get the Pueblo back. This leaves us short-handed in Vietnam."

"So?"

"So, the Air Force now has six, fully combat-ready F-100 squadrons on active duty. What would you do if you were in their shoes?"

"But there's not enough time."

"Of course there is. They can hold us on active duty for twenty-four months. A Vietnam tour is only twelve."

The pilot didn't have an answer for that. "Aw, you're full of shit!" he said finally and walked away.

The intelligence officer was right. In early May, quietly and with little fanfare, four Air National Guard F-100 squadrons deployed to South Vietnam. They came from Albuquerque, Denver, Niagara Falls, and Sioux City. Everyone wondered if the 177th would be next.

The prospect of being involved in the Vietnam conflict polarized the unit, much as it had the rest of the nation, but for different reasons. Many of the pilots viewed the war with distaste, an inconvenience to be avoided at all costs. Others felt that flying combat was what being a fighter pilot was all about. They were willing to go if sent. Few took the time to debate the war on moral grounds. For some, the desire to escape from active duty became an obsession, and every loophole in the regulations was explored. Three pilots developed a scheme they believed was foolproof. They had never signed a "reserve agreement," which stated that they were subject to recall to active duty in the event of war or national emergency. Although it was clearly an oversight, the pilots argued that they had never intended to be recalled and, hence, should be released immediately. The Air Force denied their request. It was an absurd notion, the Air Force said. These men have been flying in the unit for several years, treating it as a flying club, a club that paid them to fly high-performance aircraft.

The three pilots hired a lawyer and took their case to federal court. The case drew little sympathy from the Air Force and had no priority in the court system. It would take weeks, if not months, to be resolved. Meanwhile, the Air Force sent the three men to Korea to work in the command post. Skip was secretly pleased with the decision. They tried to pull a fast one, he thought, and they didn't get away with it. By the time they get back from Korea, we'll all be released from active duty. They should have done the right thing to begin with. He resolved that he would do the right thing when the time came. No matter what.

He wasted no time getting checked out in the F-100. The squadron needed all the F-100 pilots it could get. This time there was no letter from Duke. Maybe he didn't know Skip was in New Jersey, or maybe he decided not to bother. Anyway, as far as the squadron was concerned, he was just another F-100 pilot who needed to be re-qualified. It had been five years since he last flew the aircraft. What if Duke was right, and he was not good enough to fly the F-100? He thought about that when he strapped into the cockpit for his first flight. But his fear quickly passed. By the time he landed, he felt confident and eager to fly again.

Skip hung around the scheduling board whenever he could, making himself available as a substitute for last-minute changes. To be combat ready, he needed to re-qualify in gunnery, air-to-air refueling, and all the skills he had learned at Luke and Nellis. This would take time, but he was determined to finish before the squadron deployed. He finished the checkout program the same week the other Guard squadrons were deployed to Vietnam. If his squadron deployed, he would be able to go with them. He still had a desk job, but he was certain he could get rid of it when the time came. There were plenty of squadron pilots who would take his job just to avoid combat.

*   *   *   *

Shortly after Skip became combat ready, he flew a cross-country to Jacksonville. Although he talked to Christy every day on the phone, it was the first time he had seen his family since mid-January.

Christy and the kids were waiting in front of base operations waving excitedly as he taxied in. Christy looked cool and glamorous in a white summer dress, her dark hair flowing luxuriously in the wind. As usual, Skip got a lump in his throat when he saw her. God, she was beautiful! He could see men admiring her as they walked by. He didn't care. He wasn't jealous, just proud that she was his wife. He eased the F-100 slowly into the parking space in front of base ops, its engine idling in a low whine. The aircraft was painted in camouflage greens, browns, and tans from nose to tail. Even his helmet was camouflage painted. He waved from the cockpit, his oxygen mask still attached and sun visor lowered. The kids watched it all in wide-eyed amazement. They had never seen their daddy "at work" before.

Skip shut the engine down and wasted no time securing the cockpit. By the time he reached the bottom of the ladder, Christy and the kids were running toward him. He said something to the crew chief, quickly handed him the maintenance log, and rushed to meet his family. They met halfway, in a joyous, scrambling huddle, everyone laughing and trying to talk at the same time. It had been almost five months since he'd seen the kids. He was amazed at how much they had grown. Maddie was eight now and in the third grade. She was taller and thinner than the last time he saw her. She looked like a miniature version of Christy in her yellow sundress and white sandals. Cam was a husky six-year-old, dancing around and hugging Skip's legs, begging for attention. Both children looked tan and healthy.

"Welcome home, Skip," Christy said when everyone settled down. Skip picked up a child in each arm and followed her to the car.

"Wow, these kids are heavy! What have been you been feeding them anyway?"

Christy laughed. "Nothing special. They're like plants you know. Feed and water them regularly, and they'll grow like weeds."

Skip hefted the kids higher and bounced them up and down. "Is that true you guys? Are you like little weeds?" Maddie and Cam giggled hysterically. They were happy to see their daddy.

Pandemonium broke out when they got home. Everyone had something they wanted to tell Skip, and they all tried to talk at once. Finally the children ran off to their rooms to find something special to show him. Skip glanced around to make sure they were alone and pulled Christy hungrily into his arms and kissed her. "What do you think? Should we try the old ninety-nine pennies trick?"

"The what?" She looked puzzled.

"Didn't I teach you that one in Misawa? You toss ninety-nine pennies out the front door and send the kids out to pick them up. Tell them there are a hundred of them, and they can keep every one they find. It's the hundredth one that gets them every time. Meanwhile there's plenty of time to fool around."

"Oh my God, that's so bad! But I don't think it will work today. They're too excited to see you."

"How about sending them outside to play and greasing all the outside door-knobs? That usually works."

Christy smiled and shook her head.

"Help me out here, I am a man in need."

Christy reached down and slowly raised the lower zipper on his flying suit and then lowered it. "Relax Skip, there'll be plenty of time for…umm…extracurricular activities after the kids go to bed."

"I hope so, because you certainly have my attention."

"So I see." The kids rushed back in the room, and Skip and Christy broke apart hastily.

The morning sunlight cascaded through the bedroom window. Christy was lying in the crook of Skip's arm, stretched like a lazy, contented cat as Skip ran his fingers through her long silky hair. "Wow, what a fantastic night," she said. "I almost forgot how good it can be."

"I haven't forgotten."

Christy giggled mischievously. "Now I know why you guys always liked to go on cross-countries. Is this what it was like?"

"Nope. First of all, we always left before dawn, usually with a God-awful hangover."

"Oh, so that's how it worked, was it?"

"Yeah, well, that's what the old heads used to tell me anyway," Skip added lamely.

"That doesn't sound very romantic. Slinking off in the night. Didn't you even say goodbye?"

"Oh sure, I…I mean they…always said goodbye, what a fantastic evening it had been, and how they intended to call the next time they were in town, which, of course, they never did. They always said goodbye, unless the woman was a coyote."

"A coyote?"

"Yeah, that's a woman who is so ugly that when you find her asleep on your arm, you'd rather chew it off than wake her up."

Christy was laughing hysterically by then. "You are so bad. Please tell me you're making all that up."

"You never know."

"Tell me the truth, Skip. Am I a coyote?"

"I still have both of my arms, don't I?" He pulled her close and began kissing her.

"You certainly do."

Suddenly the door burst open, and Maddie and Cam rushed in, clad in their pajamas. Whooping and shouting like wild Indians, they flung themselves on the bed in a squealing, squirming pile. "Hey, hey," Skip said. "What's going on here?"

"Get up, Daddy. We have to do something fun today," Maddie said.

"Something fun? Why don't we sleep some more? Sleeping is fun."

"No, No…something really fun."

"Okay, you win. What'll it be?"

"The zoo!" the children cried.

Skip frowned and pursed his lips as if considering the matter. "Okay," he said finally. "The zoo it is."

"Hurray!" they shouted.

"Now get out of here so I can get dressed."

"Will you wear your flying suit to the zoo, Daddy?" Cam asked.

"Not a chance."

The weekend disappeared in a blur of family activity during the day and love-making at night. During one of their quiet moments together, Skip talked to Christy about the recall and the morale in the 177th. He told her about the three pilots who went to court to win their release, and how they were sent to Korea instead.

"It serves them right," Christy said. "It was a sleazy thing to do."

"It goes deeper than that, honey. This whole Vietnam thing…everyone is taking sides. A lot of the pilots are saying that they shouldn't have to fly combat there; that it's a waste of time and an unnecessary risk. Others say it's part of being a fighter pilot. You don't get to choose which war you're going to fight."

"Is there a chance the 177th will be sent to Vietnam?"

"I have no idea. There are four Guard squadrons there now. They arrived a week ago."

"What will you do if the squadron is sent there?"

"I'll go, of course."

"Even if there's a way to avoid it?"

"Yes."

Christy thought for a moment. She sensed that there was more to his answer. Something he didn't want to say. "What if the squadron is not deployed to Vietnam? Would you volunteer to go anyway?"

"That's not likely to happen."

"But what if it did?"

Skip looked down at his lap for a moment, struggling to compose a reply. "I don't know," he said simply.

*   *   *   *

Two days later, the men of the 177th stood in formation in front of the hangar. All eyes were fixed on the microphone and loudspeaker in front of them. They had been hastily summoned, because the group commander had an announcement to make.

The buzz of excitement and anticipation was palpable. Finally they were going to learn their fate. Most of the men were optimistic. "This is it," one of the pilots said cheerfully. "Release from active duty. I'm out of here, baby! Then, some training to get re-current, and I'm back flying the line at TWA, playing grab-ass with the flight attendants in the forward galley."

"I'm not so sure," someone said.

"Are you kidding me? Of course we're going to be released. The Pueblo deal is under control and four Guard F-100 units are in Vietnam. What's left?"

Suddenly the men were called to attention, and all became quiet. Every eye was on the group commander as he walked slowly to the microphone, a telex in his hand. He adjusted the microphone and looked at his men waiting in hushed anticipation. Then he began to speak.

"Well gentlemen, we have finally received our orders. The 177th and our sister squadron in the D.C. Air National Guard will deploy to Myrtle Beach Air Force Base, South Carolina. Once in place, we will form a replacement training unit to train F-100 pilots for combat in Vietnam."

A collective groan emanated from the men.

"I know this is not the news you wanted to hear. But that's the way it is. Our orders are to clear the base and have all men, aircraft, and equipment gone in one week. We have a lot to do, so let's get to work. Dismissed!"

In just thirty seconds, the mood of excitement and anticipation turned to despair and disappointment. It was a preposterous idea. It would take weeks, if not months, to set up the school and train the first student. They would be lucky if they trained two classes before it was time to be released from active duty. No one was happy.

Skip trudged away from the formation lost in thought. He felt disappointed, let down somehow. Why did he feel that way? Because deep inside he wanted the squadron to be deployed to Vietnam. It would have been much simpler that way.

MYRTLE BEACH AIR
FORCE BASE

Myrtle Beach, South Carolina
June 5, 1968

The deploying aircraft began to arrive at eleven AM, twenty-four in all, approaching the field in tight, four-ship formations. As they taxied to their new home, the pilots could see that Myrtle Beach Air Force Base was mostly deserted. The ramp was bare except for one forlorn F-100 sitting beside a hangar, obviously in no condition to be moved. Parking lots at nearby buildings were empty. The four F-100 squadrons based there had long since left and were now in South Korea and Vietnam. The last to leave, the 355th TAC Fighter Squadron, was deployed to Phu Cat Air Base, Vietnam, the same week the Pueblo was seized. Most of the 355th pilots had just returned from combat tours in Vietnam. No one knew how long they would stay in Phu Cat.

Twenty-four more aircraft arrived the next day from the D.C. Air National Guard, followed by a stream of cargo aircraft delivering equipment, supplies, and support personnel. The base began to come alive. Everyone was eager to get started, but no one knew what to do next. Advisers were on their way to help them set up the training unit. Meanwhile, there was nothing to do but wait. Although the grumbling continued about the inconvenience of being held on active duty, some of the men looked at the bright side. Myrtle Beach was a resort city, blessed with bright, sandy beaches and an abundance of good seafood restaurants. Better still, with all of the squadrons deployed, there was no shortage of base housing. Some acted quickly to secure housing and were soon joined by their families. "This could be a sweet life," one of the pilots said. "Just one long beach party with a little flying thrown in for diversion."

The advisers quickly concluded that the two squadrons had too many people for the mission. Everyone wondered what would happen to those who were not needed. The young pilots were especially worried. They were too inexperienced to be instructor pilots. What would happen to them? Where would they go? The rumor started just two weeks after they arrived. TAC Headquarters was looking for volunteers to replace the 355th pilots, so they could return home. It would be a simple arrangement. The volunteers would go to Phu Cat and fly combat with the 355th until a permanent solution could be found. The rumor widened the rift between the pilots who were unwilling to go to Vietnam and those who were. One night at happy hour, tempers flared, and a debate on the issue degenerated into a shouting match. "Anybody, who volunteers for Vietnam is fucking stupid!" one of the pilots shouted over the din. He was an unpleasant looking man whose face was mottled from too much drinking, the kind of man who thought outspokenness and lack of tact were qualities to be admired. Skip stood and watched the scene from afar. He didn't know most of the participants, and, right now, he wasn't sure he wanted to know them. It's getting ugly, he thought.

Skip felt himself gravitating toward a group of pilots who were willing to go to Vietnam. They were small in number but equally outspoken. In their opinion, anyone who wasn't willing to go was a pussy who didn't have the balls to fly combat with the big boys. They repeatedly referred to their critics as "flower children," sometimes to their faces. The leader of the group was Maj. Ivan "Boris" Karlov. He was an abrupt and sometimes unpleasant man, given to communicating in snarls and clipped sentences. After a few martinis he could be downright mean. But Skip liked Boris, because he was a no-nonsense, dependable kind of guy. Boris could care less if Skip liked him or not, which was all right with Skip. Besides Boris, there was Lt. Charles "Slick" Brennan. Slick was from the hills of West Virginia and was still sowing his wild oats. He had no use for the flower children and told them so every chance he got.

There were two airline pilots in the group. Capt. Dave Sanders was a captain with Eastern Airlines. He was an easygoing man, always smiling, always looking on the bright side of life. Dave had been on active duty for seven years before leaving to work for the airlines. Like Skip, he still felt ties to the Air Force. The other airline pilot was Lt. Steve Miller, a tall, urbane, handsome man who liked to smoke a pipe. Of the five men, including Skip, he seemed the least likely to be in the group. Eventually, the men in the group began to think of themselves as the "Fearless Five." It was nothing official, just the way they looked at things, and night after night, it was "us against them" when the subject of Vietnam was discussed at the bar.

A month passed, and the two squadrons were still struggling to set up the training school. Sometimes the pilots flew, but most of the time they sat around the squadron looking for things to do. Technically, Skip was still the plans officer, but there were no plans to write. One morning Skip walked into operations and was greeted by unexpected news.

"Have you heard about Boris and Slick?" the scheduling officer asked.

"No."

"They're gone, man."

"What do you mean gone? Where did they go?"

"To Vietnam. They left in the middle of the night. TAC Headquarters came down late yesterday with a call for two volunteers to fly with the 355th at Phu Cat, and they were out of here in a flash. Didn't say goodbye or anything." Skip was stunned by the news. He had expected something like this but not so soon. He couldn't sleep that night. Tossing and turning, he was tormented by the same thought that repeated itself over and over: *That's what I want to do—go to Vietnam. If they ask for more pilots, I'm going to volunteer.*

Skip rose early the next morning. He had made a momentous decision, one that would affect Christy and the kids as well. He had to tell her what was going on. How would she react when she heard the news? Angry and upset, he supposed. She had every right to be. It was an unfair thing to do, running off to fight a war he didn't have to fight. Still in his underwear, he sat on the side of his small bed and reached for the telephone. His mouth was dry, and his hand shook slightly as he picked it up. *Damn! I wish I were a smoker. I could have a cigarette first. That's what smokers do before an execution don't they?* He smiled at his own joke and picked up the phone. *Might as well get it over with.*

Christy answered on the first ring. Her voice was bright and cheerful. "What a pleasant surprise. I was just thinking about you. Up kinda early aren't you?"

"Yeah, well, I have a lot to do today." That was a lie of course. He had nothing to do today, except maybe volunteer for Vietnam.

"Well, I'm glad you called. I have some good news."

"Really?"

"Yep. I finally received my teaching certificate. It's official now. I 'are' a teacher."

Skip laughed at her joke. "That's wonderful news, baby. You worked hard for it. I'm proud of you."

"I even have a job offer, teaching kindergarten here in Mandarin, but I don't know what to do. I wish I knew what was going to happen next. New York City, Myrtle Beach, Jacksonville…it's so hard to plan. Anything new there?"

"Actually, there is. Two of my friends were sent to Vietnam yesterday."

"Oh my God! That's terrible. How did they get picked?"

"They weren't picked. They volunteered."

There was a pause, then Christy spoke in a soft voice, filled with resignation. "You want to volunteer too, don't you?"

He paused and took a deep breath. This was so hard. "Yeah, I really do, honey. I know it will be hard on you and the kids. But it's the right thing to do."

"Do you think they will be asking for more volunteers?"

"Probably so. That's the rumor anyway."

"Then I guess you're going, and that's that."

"I guess so."

Skip could tell that Christy was starting to cry, and he felt helpless. He didn't know what more to say.

Finally she regained her composure and her voice took a hard edge. "I want you to do me a favor."

"What's that?"

"If you're going to do this thing, do it quickly and get it over with. I have a life to live too, and all this uncertainty is driving me crazy. And for God's sake, let me know what's going on."

"I will, I promise. Do you still love me?"

"Yes, but you're pushing it, Skip."

"I know."

He went straight to the operations officer when he arrived at work. "Has TAC called for any more volunteers since Boris and Slick left?"

"As a matter of fact, they have. I have a telex on my desk requesting three more."

"Good, I'm thinking about going."

"Well, you better think fast. Your two asshole buddies Sanders and Miller came by early this morning and took two of the slots."

"How long would I be there?"

The operations officer shrugged his shoulders. "Beats the hell out of me. The orders say 179 days, but it will probably be less. You would just be filling in until the Air Force digs up some active-duty pilots to send."

Skip paused to consider this.

"Well, what's the deal? Do you want to go or not?"

"Okay, I'm in. When do I have to leave?"

"Two o'clock this afternoon. You'll be going military air to Seattle and then on to Saigon the next day."

"Two o'clock? You've got to be kidding me. That's only six hours from now. I've got to pack, and…"

The operations officer cut him off with a dismissive wave of his hand. "Then I suggest you get your ass in gear, Major."

Skip raced back to his room and started packing. He wanted to call Christy, but he knew she was at school. He would have to call her when he landed in Seattle. He felt bad about that, but she wanted him to move quickly didn't she? At precisely two o'clock, the last of the Fearless Five—Skip, Dave, and Steve—boarded a C-141 transport to begin their journey. Each carried a parachute bag containing their flying gear and a nylon suitcase. The latter contained flying suits, underwear, socks, and toiletries. No one took uniforms or civilian clothes. They didn't need them.

Skip called Christy as soon he landed and checked into his room.

"What's the deal, Skip?" she asked without preamble.

"I'm in Seattle. We leave for Saigon in the morning."

Christy let out a low gasp. "So soon?"

"You asked me to move quickly didn't you?"

"Yes, but I didn't expect…well, never mind. It's probably for the best. How long will you be there?"

"It's hard to say. I'm going there TDY. Figure three months, maybe more, maybe less."

Christy paused and chose her words carefully. "I've been thinking about this a lot since you called this morning. Things aren't going to get back to normal until you get released from active duty, and that's not going to happen anytime soon, right?"

"Probably not."

"I'm going to take that job in Mandarin and stay right here with the kids. Why disrupt everybody's life when nobody knows what the future holds? We can always change our minds when you get back."

"That's probably a good idea."

Christy had been speaking in a calm, reasoning voice, very much in control. Suddenly, she burst into tears and began to sob uncontrollably. "Oh Skip, I am so scared."

"Scared? Scared of what, honey?"

"Scared of this whole thing. Don't you see? You are going to fight in a war. People will try to kill you. What if something happens? What if you die? I couldn't live without you. I really couldn't. Why are you doing this? Why is it so important?"

"Hey, hey...what's with all this tears stuff? Is this the same woman who wanted me to stay in the Air Force, who'd rather be a fighter pilot's wife?"

"I know, but that was different. I didn't realize..."

"You didn't realize I might actually have to do this combat stuff, right?"

"Right."

"Listen baby, I'll be fine. It's no big deal. Meanwhile, you have to keep a stiff upper lip. You're the head of the house now."

Christy started to laugh, in spite of her tears. "Head of the house? Where have you been? I've been that since we got married."

"That's my girl."

Skip hung up the phone with a sick feeling in the pit of his stomach. "Why am I doing this? Why is it so important?" The pain in her voice when she asked those questions made him want to reach out to her, to comfort her and tell her the truth. But he didn't. How could he, when he could barely face the truth himself? The truth is, this is all about Misawa—about Duke, the accident, and the shameful way his peers branded him as a liar and an incompetent pilot. It was all about starting all over with a clean slate, about showing the world who he was and what he could do.

He looked at the phone sadly. He wanted to call her back. There was so much he wanted to say. But he didn't. Finally, he rose to his feet, placed his flight cap squarely on his head, and walked slowly out the door. Dave and Steve were waiting for him at the club. They would have dinner and few drinks tonight and get up early tomorrow for the long flight to Saigon.

*   *   *   *

Skip gazed dully out the window of his hospital room at NYU Medical, watching as a steady stream of airliners converged on Long Island and lined up for final approach at Kennedy Airport. Pan Am...It would have been a wonderful life for him and his family; a life filled with travel, adventure, and comfortable living. But he chose another path, and somewhere along the way, did something unthinkable. He betrayed those who loved him, and in the end, lost everything. How could that have happened? Tears began to well in his eyes as he thought about those days. At the sound of Nancy's approaching footsteps, he rolled over quickly and pretended to be asleep, hoping she would not see that he had been crying.

Phu Cat Air Base

Republic of South Vietnam
June 27, 1968

Skip jerked awake with a start when the small C-7 "Caribou" transport settled on the runway at Phu Cat. He and his two friends had been dozing fitfully on hard, side-mounted bench seats. The trip from Seattle took nearly twenty-four hours counting stops at Tokyo and Saigon. They were hot, tired, and thirsty. It took a few minutes for the aircraft to taxi to the terminal building. Meanwhile, the travelers groaned, stretched, and tried to restore the circulation in their limbs. No one spoke. Everyone was lost in their own thoughts, wondering what was coming next. Finally, the aircraft was parked, and its engines were shut down. As they collected their baggage, the loadmaster lowered the loading ramp in the tail of the aircraft. A stifling blast of hot, muggy air rolled into the cabin. Skip walked slowly down the ramp into the steamy heat. Dave and Steve followed close behind.

Skip looked around, trying to get his bearings, squinting through a haze of red dust that hung in the air. The base sat on high terrain, surrounded by lush, green mountains about five miles away. Between the base and the mountains, lay a shrub-filled plain dotted with rice paddies. It was a picturesque and peaceful scene, except for the thousands of shell holes that pockmarked the plain in every direction. He would later find out these holes were the result of harassment and interdiction, or "H and I," a nightly routine of intense artillery fire to discourage infiltrators.

The base seemed ordinary enough, with its rows of neat buildings and paved, well-maintained streets. But Phu Cat was not an ordinary base in the Central Highlands by any means. Until 1966, it and the surrounding mountains had been in the hands of the enemy, the Viet Cong, or "VC," as they were called. In fact, the ground on which Skip stood was the site of a VC training camp. That all changed when a combined force of the U.S. and the Republic of Korea (ROK) armies swept in, drove the VC deep into the mountains, and secured the area. The Air Force moved in close behind with a team of construction engineers to build the base.

Skip's thoughts were interrupted by the sight of twelve little boys dashing across the ramp to a waiting C-130. They were dressed identically in black silk trousers and shirts. They ran in single file, clutching a nylon rope that seemed to keep them together. Judging by their size, he guessed them to be fourteen, maybe fifteen years old. Perhaps they were from an orphanage.

"Where are those Vietnamese kids going?" he asked.

The loadmaster looked at Skip to make sure he wasn't joking, then broke into a laugh. "Those aren't kids. They're VC prisoners of war. They're being taken to an interrogation center somewhere I imagine."

Skip was stunned. POWs, he thought. These little runts are the enemy? Impossible! I wonder what's taking us so long to win the war?

A camouflaged step-van drove up behind the aircraft and parked. The driver leaped out of the open door and hurried toward them. It was Boris. "It's about time you assholes showed up. Where have you been anyway?"

"Why, I'm fine," Skip replied. "It's nice of you to ask. How are you?"

Boris ignored Skip and gestured impatiently to the others. "Put your shit in the truck, and I'll drive to your hooches."

"Hooches?"

"Yeah, meaning your quarters." Everyone loaded their bags and piled into the van.

"Where's Slick?" Dave asked. "Too lazy to get off his dead ass and meet us? That sounds like him."

"Slick is flying right now. He just took off."

"Flying? As in a combat mission, where you actually kill people? You gotta be kidding me. You guys have only been here, what, forty-eight hours? What's the rush?"

"The 355th doesn't have enough experienced pilots, and the ones they have just returned from a combat tour. They'll be going home as soon as they can be replaced. That's why we're here, to hold the fort until things get sorted out. It's also why they are in a hurry to get us checked out. The sooner we start flying, the sooner they can go home."

"Christmas help," Skip said absently.

"What?"

"Christmas help...my dad works in the post office. That's what they call people who worked during the holidays when they were short-handed."

Boris nodded his head slowly, and a trace of a smile crossed his face. "Christmas help...yeah, I like that."

"I could sure go for a cold beer right now," Dave groused.

"Don't get your bowels in an uproar. We have a bar in our hooch, plus there is always the club."

"What's the woman situation?" Steve asked. He was known as a world-class skirt chaser.

"Let me put it this way," Boris replied, "there are no women on the base right now...none, zip, nada...although there is a rumor we may get a nurse and eventually a woman to work at the base library."

"But..."

Boris cut him off and continued. "And before you ask, the area outside base is off limits, no exceptions."

Steve slumped in his seat in despair. "That's just great. How am I supposed to get my ashes hauled? Everyone deserves that."

"There are ways," Boris said mysteriously.

"Is it really that dangerous off base?" Skip asked.

"Yes and no. The ROK army 'Tiger' division is responsible for security in the valley, and they are mean sons of bitches. They usually don't take prisoners, but when they do, they usually entertain themselves by torturing the poor bastard until he gives them the information they want, then they kill him. On the other hand, VC infiltrators do come and go in the village, especially in the middle of the night. That's why it's off limits."

The hooches consisted of a group of metal trailers arranged in an expanding series of squares. In the middle, the pilots had built a concrete patio covered with a flat, wooden roof. The top of the roof was supposed to be used for sunbathing and even had a set of stairs leading to the top. But the roof's real purpose was to cover the elaborate wet bar built underneath. The pilots liked to refer to the bar as the 355th annex to the officers' club.

It was three o'clock when the newcomers drove up to the hooches. Everyone was trashed by then. It had been a long day. Boris pointed to the trailers and told each man which one to go to. "Go take a shower, then meet me at our bar. We'll have a few drinks and go to the mess hall for an early dinner...if you pussies can handle that." Everyone agreed that they could.

"By the way, there is a steel helmet and flak jacket in your locker. If the base siren goes off, that means we are under a mortar attack. In that case, put them on, and get your asses in that shelter." Boris pointed to a dugout surrounded by sand bags twenty yards from where they were standing.

Skip walked into the end of his trailer, opened the door, and walked into his new home. Looking around, he could see that it was neat, if not cozy. There was a cot, a chair, a small desk, and a locker. An air-conditioning unit was purring in a small window over his head. I'll bet this baby stays on all the time, he thought. There was a common bathroom that separated the two halves of the trailer. It was clean and functional. Stepping inside, he saw that the door to the other room was wide open. Mostly out of curiosity, he looked in.

A young captain sat half-sitting and half-slouching in a chair, his feet propped on the desk. He was reading a well-thumbed copy of Playboy. It was obvious that he had just returned from flying. He was still wearing his flight cap, which was cocked casually over one eye, revealing a full head of carefully combed dark hair. He was a fit and wiry young man, and although the room was dimly lit, he was still wearing his sunglasses. He scarcely looked up when Skip entered the room.

"Hi, I'm Skip O'Neill. I guess I'm your new roommate."

The captain half rose in his chair and extended his hand. It was obvious that he wasn't intimidated by the sudden appearance of a strange major in his quarters. "Reed is my name, Bill Reed. But you might as well call me Willie. Everyone else does." They shook hands, and Willie settled back into his chair.

Skip gazed for a moment at the cocky young man before him and began to smile. "You aren't by any chance in the Guard are you?"

"Nope, regular Air Force. I just got here from Lakenheath. Why do you ask?"

"No reason, just wondering."

"Oh I get it. The Guard pukes are a pretty casual bunch, aren't they? They're my kind of people. That's why I like to be around them."

The conversation flagged for a moment, as the two men sized each other up. Finally, Skip said, "Well, I'm going to take a shower and meet the others at the bar. We'll probably have a few drinks, eat dinner, and maybe go over to the club afterwards. I'll probably see you there, right?"

"Nope."

"Why not?"

"Because I've been banned from the club for two weeks, that's why."

"No shit. How did that happen?"

Suddenly, Willie came alive. Rising in his chair, he began to speak in an animated voice. "How did that happen? It happened because the people who run the club are a bunch of dipshits…a bunch of dipshits with zero sense of humor. I mean, we used to stand on tables and drop our flying suits and drawers in the stag bar at Lakenheath all the time, and nobody said anything. Here it's a friggin' federal offense. What's the big deal?"

Skip smiled sympathetically. "Banned from the club for two weeks? That does seem a little harsh considering it was only a childish prank."

Willie raised his hand to cut him off. "That's not what got me banned from the club. It was the fight afterwards."

"The fight?"

"Yeah. Slick and I invited a couple of ground-pounders outside to settle our differences. We would have beaten the shit out of them except the air police showed up and broke it up. It was lucky for the ground-pounders that they did."

Skip shook his head in amazement and began to laugh. "Are you sure you're not in the Guard?"

Willie grinned back. "I'm sure. Maybe someday."

It was after four when Skip arrived at the bar in the hooch. Pilots were beginning to arrive after a day of flying. They were a relaxed, congenial bunch and quick to make the newcomers feel welcome. If anyone was stressed from flying combat every day, it didn't show. Liquor was cheap on the base, so the bar was fully stocked. A quart of Canadian Club, for example, cost just five dollars at the liquor store. In the hooch, everyone mixed their own drinks behind the bar and placed a mark behind their name for each drink they mixed. The marks were tallied up periodically, and everyone paid for what they drank. It was all on the honor system.

Skip found Boris at the end of the bar talking to Dave and Steve. "It's about time," Boris said. "We thought maybe you fell asleep."

"No such luck. I was just talking to my new roommate. Is he for real?"

"As far as I can tell. He just got here a few weeks ago. They say he flies a good airplane when he's not off getting in trouble. By the way, he is in A Flight, the same as you."

Skip grinned and tossed back another drink. "All I can say is his fearless flight commander is going to have his hands full trying to keep him out of trouble. By the way, I'd like to meet the flight commander. Is he around?"

"You can if you want, but it would be a waste of time."

"Why?"

"Because he is a dumb shit who is clueless about what's going on."

"Really? What's his name?"

"Skip O'Neill."

Skip paused for a minute to let that sink in. He wasn't sure if Boris was serious or not. "Come on Boris, stop busting my balls. How can I be a flight commander when I just got here?"

"The same way I got to be the ops officer. The squadron is short of pilots, and the senior people are rotating home. We're the Christmas help, remember?"

Skip shook his head in bewilderment. This was all happening too fast.

Skip returned to his hooch at eight o'clock, his body and mind numbed by fatigue and the drinks he had at the bar. After stripping off his flying suit and boots, he flung himself into his cot and fell asleep. An hour later there was a loud explosion, followed by the whistling sound of something flying overhead. Skip bolted upright in his bed, his eyes wide open. There was a second explosion. We're under attack, he thought. I've got to get out of here. Dazed and half asleep, he leaped out of bed, stumbled across the dark room, crashing into furniture as he went, and found the flak jacket and helmet in the locker. Just as he was putting them on, the door to the bathroom opened, and Willie walked in. He was still wearing his sunglasses.

"Relax, it's outgoing."

"It's what?"

"Outgoing…you know, as in friendly fire. It's coming from the ROK artillery battery just across the fence. They usually lay on a few rounds of H-and-I fire this time of night."

Skip stopped to consider this. "How will I know if it's incoming?"

"Trust me, you'll know. It's an entirely different sound."

After Willie left, Skip took off his helmet and flak jacket, tossed them in the corner, and crawled wearily back in bed. He felt foolish and disgusted with himself. Not a good start, Ace, he thought.

*   *   *   *

The late afternoon sun smothered the arming area in a blanket of hot, sticky air. Skip squirmed uncomfortably in the cockpit, waiting impatiently for the arming crew to finish. On top of his usual flying gear, he was wearing a bulky survival vest containing rescue flares, a .38-caliber revolver with tracer ammunition, an emergency radio, and several pockets filled with food and other survival items. It was a lot of clothing for a tropical climate. No wonder he was hot and miserable.

He brushed the rivulets of sweat from his eyes with one gloved hand and gazed absently at the aircraft lined up beside him. A steady breeze blew the exhaust from their idling engines into the open cockpit. The pungent smell of kerosene caused his eyes to water and made him sweat even more. There were four aircraft in the flight, and he was the leader.

Eight weeks ago, he could barely find his way around the base. Now he was leading a flight of four into combat like a seasoned veteran. Hell, he was a seasoned veteran compared to some of the guys who had just arrived from the States, fresh out of gunnery school. But what really made him grin was that he was a flight commander. He had come a long way since the days of Big Jim and Duke in Misawa. But it was different over here. There was no time to bullshit around. You told the troops what had to be done and let them run with the ball.

Skip was certain that today's mission would be boring as hell. This was probably for the best, considering that two of the pilots in the flight were relatively inexperienced. "It's going to be a piece of cake," he had said in the briefing. "We go up, flatten a few trees, check out the local area, and head home." Officially, the mission was called landing zone preparation, or "LZ prep," but the pilots liked to call such missions "tree-busters." The idea was to flatten selected hilltops so the army could land safely on them in helicopters and build fire-base camps. Most pilots considered LZ prep missions dull, uninteresting, and a waste of time. Skip tended to agree.

He much preferred to fly "close air support" missions, which helped troops in contact with the enemy. Rolling back a mortar attack from the perimeter of a fire-base camp, or rescuing a reconnaissance patrol or convoy after being surrounded by bad guys, those were missions worth flying. The cavalry to the rescue—that was more his style.

The arming crew stepped back from the four aircraft and displayed all the safety lanyards from the bombs, signaling that they had finished their work. The pilots closed their canopies and followed Skip onto the runway for takeoff. Show time, he thought, looking around the cockpit one last time. He was ready. The four aircraft rolled down most of the runway before struggling into the hot, humid air. It was slow going at first, but finally they gained speed and started to climb. At three thousand feet, Skip made a slow, lazy turn to the north and started toward the target. The others followed in loose formation. They were on their way.

The air-conditioning system finally kicked in at five thousand feet, and the sudden rush of cold air over his sweat-soaked flying suit felt refreshing, like a plunge into cool water. The cockpit was quiet now, and the exhaust fumes were gone. He was breathing 100 percent oxygen, and it tasted good. With the tinted visor clamped over his face to ward off the glare from the sun, he gazed at the terrain below. They were twenty miles west of the Phu Cat Mountains, which hugged the coast of the China Sea. Everything was lush and green, like a scene from a travel brochure. This is really a beautiful country, Skip thought. It's a shame that…

His thoughts were interrupted by an urgent call from the airborne command post. Their mission was about to change. The flight was directed to reverse course and proceed south to a rendezvous point near the Cambodian border. There were no details about the target. That would come later. Troops in contact, he thought. This is more like it. He could feel a rush of adrenalin surging through his body.

The FAC's voice was calm and professional, but Skip could tell he was stressed. He got right to the point. "Okay Icon Flight, here's the deal. I am circling an Army patrol that was ambushed on the corner of an old Michelin rubber plantation. They are surrounded and outnumbered. So far, they've lost three men and have several wounded." He paused abruptly to talk to the Army on another frequency. Skip waited impatiently. "The only way we can get them out of there," he continued, "is to lay a string of bombs around their position. This will give them a chance to break out if one part of the circle folds."

"Understand," Skip said tersely, sensing there was more to come. There was.

"Icon Flight, the bad guys are within fifty meters from the friendlies. You'll have to drop your bombs that close to do any good."

Fifty meters. That was half the length of a football field. He had dropped plenty of bombs within fifty meters during training. But they were not back in the States dropping on some fancy gunnery range with white lines and circles to mark the target. A small error in the direction of the friendlies could get someone seriously hurt or even killed.

"Understand the friendlies will be only fifty meters away, is that correct?"

"That's affirmative, Icon Lead. The ground commander says that's their only chance. In fact, he says he doesn't give a shit if the bombs fall twenty meters away from him, if that's what it takes."

Skip's bombing skills had improved vastly in the past eight weeks. He was sure he could do it. Slick was flying on his wing. He wasn't worried about him either, but what about the others? Number Three was a captain who had just arrived from a TAC squadron in Arizona. He'll probably be okay, but Number Four was a lieutenant fresh out of gunnery school. Christ knows what he's going to do! He'll probably overcorrect to the safe side, if nothing else. Skip hoped so.

"Okay Icon Flight," Skip said, "check your armament switches hot. We'll be running south to north with a left-hand pattern and dropping one bomb at a time. Acknowledge."

The flight members repeated the information, one after another.

The flight peeled off over the target and began to set up for the first pass. On downwind, Skip looked over his shoulder, waiting for the FAC to mark the target. The mark appeared just as he turned onto the base leg, a bright, white plume of smoke rising sharply from a dense stand of trees.

"Icon Lead, that's a good mark. The friendlies are fifty meters to the left. Hit my smoke!"

"Lead's in hot. I've got the smoke in sight."

*   *   *   *

Skip rolled his aircraft into a lazy wing-over, and entered a steep dive for the final run. There was no time to think now. He had only a few seconds to do this right. Airspeed, dive angle, wind correction, everything had to be perfect. The pipper on the gun sight moved lazily toward the target, as if he had all the time in the world. Finally, it drifted up to the base of the smoke. He held it there, glanced at his airspeed and altitude one last time, and hit the pickle button. As the bomb hurtled toward the ground, he rolled sharply to the left and looked anxiously over his shoulder.

To his relief, the bomb obliterated the mark. It was right on target.

"That's a good bomb, Lead," the FAC said. "Icon Two, move your bomb a little to the left and farther north."

"Icon Two, understand. Move it up around the circle." Slick's voice was laced with an exaggerated West Virginia drawl.

"That's affirmative."

Skip laughed appreciatively. *He sounds like he's moseying off to slop the hogs and in no hurry to get there.*

It was exacting work—sixteen bombs dropped one at a time, stitching a circle of smoke and fire a hundred or so meters in diameter. As expected, some of the bombs erred to the side of caution, but none came closer than within fifty meters of the friendlies. Twice the attack was halted, while the FAC discussed the situation with the ground commander. Each time the response from the ground was the same: "Keep it coming." When it was over, the flight circled the target in case they needed to strafe the area with their cannons. But the FAC reported that the patrol had found a place to break through and was on its way out with their wounded.

Back on the ground, the pilots sat down to debrief, congratulating each other on a job well done. Skip quickly brought them back to earth, pointing out that they had made several mistakes that were not acceptable in combat. These had to be discussed in detail, so they would not be repeated. But before he could continue, he was called away to take a phone call in operations.

The voice was garbled, and the line was filled with static. "This is Major…of the…battalion…Tay Nin. Were you the flight leader of Icon 51…this afternoon?"

Skip was seized with a momentary feeling of panic. Had something gone wrong? He paused a moment to collect himself. "Right. I was the flight leader. I'm Major O'Neill."

The voice was clearer now. "Well, I just called to say that you guys saved our asses big-time today. We got everybody back in one piece. Everybody who was still alive when the shit hit the fan, that is."

"That's great. I'm glad it worked out."

"By the way, the patrol leader is over here on his second tour. He's seen a lot of combat. He said you guys really had your shit together. I guess you've been doing this for awhile, right?"

Skip thought about lying but thought better of it. "Nah, my wingman and I just got here two months ago. We came here from the New Jersey Guard to help until the squadron gets some more pilots, sort of like Christmas help in the post office. The other two pilots are new arrivals."

"Christmas help, eh? Well…whatever. You got us out of a crack, and we owe you one. Tell your guys that for me, will you? And another thing…"

"Yes?"

"Buy them a round or two on me. I don't know how I'll be able to pay you, but…"

"No sweat, I'll take care of it."

Slick and the other two pilots were standing behind him, waiting expectantly. "What did he say?" Slick asked.

"He said they got everybody out okay, and you guys are shit hot."

"All right!" they chorused. They were back in the self-congratulatory mode, but Skip didn't care.

"He also said I should buy you guys a couple of rounds."

"So what are we waiting for?"

"What about the debriefing?" the lieutenant asked doubtfully.

"We'll finish it at the bar," Skip replied.

*   *   *   *

Skip's life settled into a steady routine, much like a nine-to-five job. By September, more than a dozen pilots from the New Jersey and D.C. Air National Guard had arrived, and the term "Christmas help" was now a fact of life, rather than a joke. It was a system that worked extremely well. The squadron commander and executive officer were in the regular Air Force and provided the discipline, leadership, and guidance to accomplish the overall mission. The Guard pilots, all highly experienced, with hundreds, if not thousands of hours in the F-100, ran the day-to-day operations as flight commanders and instructor pilots. They also mentored the young pilots newly arrived from gunnery school.

Skip wrote Christy every day. It was hard, because he never knew what to say. He wanted her to know what he was doing in Vietnam, but he didn't want her to worry. Christy also wrote regularly. Mail delivery was sporadic, and often her letters arrived in packets of three or more. Like Skip, she kept her letters loving but light, masking the fear she felt for his safety. Her letters almost always included pictures of her and the kids. These, Skip would paste on the wall alongside his bunk so he could look at them every night before he went to sleep. It was a strange situation. He loved them and missed them so much. But on the other hand, he was exhilaratingly happy in Vietnam, doing what he was doing. He wondered how it was all going to end.

In early September, an envelope arrived from Myrtle Beach addressed to the pilots from the New Jersey Air National Guard. It contained a photo of their squadron mates, all in flying suits, standing or kneeling in three rows. Each stared at the camera with defiant eyes, gesturing with an extended middle finger. Across the photo, someone had written, "To our brethren in Vietnam, for all you are doing for us." The photo was posted on the squadron bulletin board. Some found it amusing, some annoying. Others, like Boris, were highly pissed. "Typical of the flower children," he said. "A bunch of assholes. Their time is coming, and payback is gonna be sweet." Skip didn't know what to think. He was extremely disappointed in them. It was a childish thing to do.

Payback time came quicker than anybody expected. One afternoon in late September, Boris spread the word for all the Guard pilots to gather in his trailer after the afternoon missions landed. Something was up, but he wouldn't say what. By the time everyone arrived, twelve people were crammed in a trailer designed as living quarters for four. They were sitting on beds and chairs, leaning against walls. There was scarcely room to breathe.

Boris got right to the point. "Okay guys, here's the deal. The Air Force doesn't have any more pilots to replace us. They want us to stay here for a year like everybody else."

A collective groan issued from the group. "Fuck that," someone muttered. "They're trying to screw us."

"A typical regular Air Force dick dance," said another. "That's why I got out and joined the Guard in the first place."

Boris waived his hand dismissively, and everyone fell quiet. "There's more. We're all here TDY, right?" Everyone nodded. "Well, it so happens that they can't change our status from TDY to PCS (Permanent Change of Station) without sending us home to get our families settled. It's against regulations."

A collective sigh of relief swept through the crowded room. "Then we're okay," someone said from the back of the room. "We just tell them we don't want to stay, and they'll have to send somebody else."

"But Boris just said they don't have anybody else to send, remember?" another said. "So how are they gonna replace us?"

"I said the *Air Force* doesn't have any guys to send. But the *Guard* does, and TAC already has a list of non-volunteer pilots standing by, waiting to find out what we decide. In fact, I have the list right here." With that, he opened a large envelope and displayed its contents with a flourish for all to see. It was the group photo of the Jersey Guard pilots gesturing with their extended middle finger.

The pilots in the small trailer exploded in a gale of hoots, jeers, and laughter.

"The flower children? You gotta be shitting me! They couldn't find their way over here, much less fly a combat mission."

"They're probably crapping in their pants waiting to find out if they have to go or not. We've got them by the balls."

"Talk about payback. How sweet it is! Maybe we could send them a group photo giving them the finger and sign it, 'We're coming home assholes. Have fun.'"

It took a few minutes for the group to settle down. When it was quiet, Slick raised his hand from the back of the room. "What if I want to stay for a year? I mean, I feel good about what I'm doing here, and I sure as hell haven't left anything back at Myrtle Beach."

The pilots looked at each other uneasily. That thought had crossed many of their minds, but they had been afraid to say it out loud.

"In that case, you go back to Myrtle Beach for a couple of weeks and then return," Boris responded. "For what it's worth, that's what I intend to do."

Everyone started talking at once, heatedly discussing the merits of volunteering for a one-year tour. All agreed such a move would not be popular with their families. They did miss them after all, and a year would be a long time to be without them. On the other hand, many, like Skip, hadn't brought their families to Myrtle Beach, so they would be without them for at least a year anyway.

Boris let the discussion go on for a few minutes and then moved to cut it off. "Okay guys, I'm not running a friggin' New England town hall meeting here. We don't have a lot of time to sort this out. Just for the hell of it, how many guys think they want to stay here for a year?"

More than half the pilots, including Skip, raised their hands. Some looked as if they were about to, but then changed their minds.

Boris nodded. "This is serious stuff. You have to be sure. I want everyone to meet here tomorrow, same time. We'll take a final count then."

The pilots rushed out the door gratefully, relieved that the pressure was off, at least for a day. They had much to talk about in the next twenty-four hours.

The next day, another poll was taken. This time, everyone raised their hands.

"How much time do we have before we let them know back at Myrtle Beach?" Skip asked.

"I told you," Boris responded. "We don't have a lot of time."

"I know that, but how long? A week? Two weeks?"

"Beats the shit out of me, Skip. A week for sure. Maybe two. Why?"

A smile of satisfaction crossed Skip's face. "I was just thinking, we ought to draw this thing out as long as we can."

A murmur of approval rippled through the crowd. "Yeah," someone said. "Let them sweat it out." Heads nodded all around.

"Good idea," Boris said.

Maj. Tom Adams, D.C. Air National Guard, stood quietly in the back, puffing reflectively on his pipe. He was a lawyer and judge in civilian life, and his jurist mind was racing in high gear. "It seems to me," he said, "that we have an unprecedented opportunity here."

"How's that?" Boris asked.

"You said that we'll all have to return to Myrtle Beach for a week or so, right?"

"So?"

"Well, we can't all go back at the same time now, can we? Half the squadron would be gone, and there wouldn't be enough pilots left to fly all the missions."

"This is true."

"So wouldn't it be logical to stagger the schedule and send the people back one or two at a time? Figuring two weeks at Myrtle Beach plus travel time, it would take us until after the Christmas holidays to cycle everybody through. And, of course, I presume that we would be entitled to one week R&R like everyone else. Those of us with families could meet them in Hawaii if we wanted to. That gives us two opportunities to see them during the tour. It's a better deal than the regular Air Force guys are getting, don't you think?"

The mood of the group became decidedly upbeat. This wasn't going to be so bad after all. The wives would definitely be pissed, but a chance to be with their husbands during the holidays, plus a trip to Hawaii, would soften the blow. Besides, most of the men had already been at Phu Cat for three months, so it was a nine-month tour they were volunteering for, not a year.

The squadron commander balked at first about sending the pilots back in pairs. But he knew they were right. "Guard pukes," he said finally, shaking his head. "You guys wouldn't get away with half this shit if you were in the regular Air Force. Work out a schedule and make sure it's fair to everyone, okay?"

Boris promised that he would.

Looking back, it was hard to see why everyone chose a path that was not in the best interests of their families and would put them in harm's way for another nine months. For some, it was a matter of peer pressure, pure and simple. Others thought it was the right thing to do. For many, although they would not admit it, even to themselves, it was simply a macho, in-your-face gesture to their squadron mates in Myrtle Beach. A gesture that said, "You stay there and play with the kiddies on the beach. Meanwhile, the big guys will stay over here and fight the war." In any case, they sealed their fate, and for many of them, the decision they made that day would change their lives forever.

*   *   *   *

Skip sat on the edge of his bunk staring at the phone. In a few a minutes, he would be talking to Christy. That was the plan anyway. It was hard to make personal phone calls to the States but not impossible. Everyone wanted to talk to their families, so calls were placed on a space-available, first-come-first-serve basis. Sometimes people waited hours for their turn. But he had pulled some strings with a friend at the command post who put him at the head of the line. His turn would come soon, any minute in fact.

He licked his lips nervously in anticipation, and then reached for a half-finished glass of bourbon and water on the bedside table but changed his mind.

After he finished the call maybe—he would probably need it then. But not now. He had been drinking too much lately, far too much. But so had everybody else. After all, what else was there to do around here when they weren't flying?

He fell back on the bunk, stared at the ceiling, and waited. The trailer was quiet save for music coming from Willie's room. The Kingston Trio was playing something vaguely familiar. Where had he heard that song? The club at Laredo, that was it. The night Christy handed him her panties under the table. He smiled with pleasure at the thought of that night, and many others like it. Lord knows, if she were here now she'd have more than her panties off, he'd see to that. As for the telephone, they'd never hear it ring.

He had a feeling it was not the stress of combat that caused everyone to drink like fish over here, but the lack of sex. There were no women on base to look at, much less do something with. It was not healthy.

Of course, there were opportunities for the pilots during their occasional soirees to Okinawa and the Philippines. Just last week, for example, he had spent two mind-numbing days in Manila eating and drinking nonstop, during which one of the pilots ordered a bunch of girls to their motel, much as one would order takeout pizza. He had managed to dodge that bullet, but he didn't know how much longer he could hold out. For the rest of his tour, he hoped, but nine months was a long time.

An hour passed, and he grew tired of rehearsing over and over what he was going to say to Christy. How many times had he told her things she didn't want to hear, things that made her unhappy or insecure? He couldn't remember. Sometimes it was not his fault, like the assignment to Misawa. That was pure fate, and they could do nothing but share their frustration and anger. But his decision to get out of the Air Force or volunteer for Vietnam—those decisions were Skip at his unpredictable worst.

Of course, Skip was not the source of all the surprises in the family. There was the Brad thing, for example. But this was not a good time to think about that, not with Skip in Vietnam and Christy on the other side of the world. Anyway, what he was about to tell her was the biggest yet, and he was sure she wasn't going to like it. Christy seemed to have an unlimited supply of patience and understanding, but could this be the last straw? He didn't know.

Another hour passed. Impatiently, he reached for the drink and drained it. Then, he poured another, stronger than the first, and drank it too. When he finished, he fell into a shallow and uneasy sleep.

The phone rang just after midnight, its burring, metallic sound jarring him awake. For a minute, he was dazed and unfocused. "Hullo," he said sleepily. The operator informed him that his party was on the line.

"Did I interrupt your beauty sleep?" Christy said. Her voice was bright and cheerful, but at the same time had an edge he couldn't quite identify.

"Yeah…you know…I need all of that I can get. How are you, my love? Gosh I miss you!"

"More importantly, how are you?" Christy replied.

"I asked you first. How is school coming along?"

"School is great. I've been teaching about a month now, and the kids are a bunch of sweethearts. Just little people waiting to be told about the world."

"Yeah, you said it would be like that."

"Oh there are a couple little stinkers in the class, what the older teachers call 'little shits,' but I love them all."

Skip laughed at this. "What about our 'little people,' Maddie and Cam? I certainly miss them too."

"They are at a friend's house right now. They'll be so sorry they missed you. Maddie is becoming quite a little lady now and has more than her share of admirers. Cam does too, but they don't get anywhere with him. The minute a little girl gets close, he runs like hell."

"That's wise. Women can be trouble at any age."

There was an awkward silence. Finally, Christy spoke. "Speaking of trouble, what's going on over there, Skip?" The edge in her voice was more evident now, and he had a feeling she already knew what was going on.

"Well…umm…there has been a change in plans."

"I know. You volunteered to stay there nine more months. So did everybody else. All for one, and one for all, something like that."

"How do you know about that?"

"Oh, I keep in touch with the wives at Myrtle Beach, and the word is already out. And I don't mind telling you, some of them are royally pissed."

"I can understand that. But honey…"

Christy had already thought things out and was prepared for this conversation, much more so than Skip. She wasted no time. "Let me see if I understand this," she interrupted. Her voice was cold as steel. "If you decide to come back, instead of volunteering to stay, you still won't be released from active duty, right?"

"Right. I would just…"

"Which means that you would be in Myrtle Beach, and I would be in Jacksonville, right?"

"Well yeah, unless you and the kids wanted to…"

"But I don't want to move to Myrtle Beach. We have a deal, remember? I teach school, raise the kids, and keep the family together. You run around doing your thing until you are out of the Air Force, and we can live a normal life."

"But…"

Christy continued as if he hadn't spoken. She was on a roll now and didn't intend to stop. "So, it really doesn't make much difference, does it? Me in Jacksonville and you in Vietnam, or me in Jacksonville and you in Myrtle Beach. It's all the same thing."

Skip decided to say nothing and let her continue.

"Oh, I forgot, there are a couple of differences. For one thing, in Vietnam, people are trying to kill you every day, which means I'll be lying awake every night wondering if I'm going to wake up the next morning a widow, with two kids to raise on my own. And, of course, I won't be able to see you for nine months. Nine months! Do you realize how long that is, Skip? Apparently you don't, because it doesn't seem to bother you."

Skip saw a chance to deliver some good news during the conversation, and he moved quickly to do so. "It seems to me the wives at Myrtle Beach don't know everything, because if they did, they would have told you it won't be nine months, or anything like that."

"Oh really? Why not, may I ask?"

"Because, we all have to return to the States to get our families settled before continuing our tour. We're going to do that one or two people at time, so the squadron won't be short-handed. We've already made up a schedule for that."

Christy paused for a second or two, letting this news sink in. "When will it be your turn? Six months from now? Seven?" There was still a hint of sarcasm in her voice.

"Thanksgiving," Skip replied promptly. "I'll be home for the Thanksgiving holidays."

"Thanksgiving? That's just two months away."

"Seven weeks, to be exact. And I'll be home for two weeks, give or take a day or so."

"Will you be able to come to Jacksonville?"

"Of course. I figure it will only take a day to out-process at Myrtle Beach, and then I'm on my way to be with you and the kids."

Christy became excited, in spite of herself, and her voice began to brighten. "Thanksgiving holidays at home, just the four of us. It will be so lovely."

Things were finally going Skip's way, and he wasted no time dropping the other shoe. "By the way, everyone in Vietnam is entitled to one week of rest and recuperation, or R&R as they call it. Most people meet their families in Hawaii. I figure you could join me in Honolulu sometime in the spring. What do you think?"

"What do I think? I think it would be fantastic. I've always wanted to go to Hawaii." She was becoming her old self now. Her voice was bright and happy.

"We'll have a wonderful time at Thanksgiving," Skip continued. His voice was soothing and reassuring. "We can...umm...what did we do on Thanksgivings in Jacksonville? I don't seem to remember."

"That's because you were always on alert," she replied dryly. He didn't see that one coming.

"Oh yeah, right. Anyway, we could go out in the woods and shoot a turkey, or something."

Christy had to laugh at the preposterousness of this idea. "Shoot a turkey! Why? That's what we have grocery stores for."

"Well you know, to get us out of the house, away from the kids."

"Oh, I get the picture. Well, we'll have to wait and see. The way things are now, I'm not sure there will even be a need for that." The edge in her voice was back.

There was another awkward silence. Time was growing short. Calls to the States were limited to ten minutes. Soon they would be cut off. Suddenly, Christy's voice began to tremble, and he could tell she was about to cry. "Skip, you have to be careful. I don't think you realize what you've gotten yourself into. You're fighting a war, not playing some macho game. And you are surrounded by people who want to kill you just as badly as you want to kill them, maybe more so."

She was crying for sure now, but she continued talking, spitting out words between broken sobs. "Oh Skip, I know you...you are not lucky about such things. When I heard about the crash in Misawa...I almost died. How could I live without you? You are my life. I...I...I love you too much." Unable to continue, she hung up.

Skip sat back and breathed a huge sigh of relief. The crisis was over, at least for now. Looking back on the conversation, two things became abundantly clear. First, he had betrayed Christy, and not for the first time, by choosing a path that seemed good for him, without considering what was best for her and the family.

How could he do that to her? Could it be that he didn't love her as much as he thought he did? Of course not. Then why? He didn't know.

And the other thing. Why did he feel out of harm's way when he flew combat? Because he couldn't see anybody shooting at him, that's why, and you don't fear what you can't see, right? That was bullshit. The pilots had been briefed time and time again that when under air attack, the Viet Cong usually lie on their backs, point their AK-47s toward the sky, and shoot at the aircraft as they pass over. The AK-47 was no match for the F-100, and with no tracers to see, the ground fire was almost invisible. But, as Boris liked to say, it only takes one round, the "golden BB," and it's all over. Was there a golden BB in his future? He had no idea. He hoped not.

Skip closed his eyes and tried to sleep. You are an immature and selfish man, he thought. A man who does what he feels like doing, with little regard for others. A man who has betrayed his wife more than once and will probably do so again. You are also a stupid and careless man, flying combat every day, impervious to the dangers around you. Clearly you have a death wish, or perhaps a false sense of immortality, or maybe both. What's it all about anyway? Why are you here? To stem the tide of Communism in Southeast Asia and preserve democracy for South Vietnam? Yeah right! That's a lot of political crap, and you know it. C'mon, you can't bullshit a bullshitter. You're here for just one reason. To show "them"—Duke, your former squadron mates in Misawa, everybody, that you are as good as they are, maybe better. Is that worth risking your life for? Of course not.

Skip decided that the guy at the bar at Myrtle Beach was right—the one with the red face and big ears who shouted for all to hear: "Anybody who volunteers for Vietnam is fucking stupid." It doesn't matter. Skip was here now, and he intended to finish this thing that he started…no matter what.

*   *   *   *

So far, all of Skip's missions had been flown in South Vietnam. But the real challenge lay across the border in North Vietnam, a far more hostile and dangerous environment. F-105 and F-4 fighter bombers flew there daily, braving waves of surface-to-air missiles and antiaircraft fire to bomb strategic targets in places like Hanoi and Haiphong. Many who flew those missions were shot down, captured, or killed.

Although most F-100 pilots never went north, a few were there almost every day. This was an elite group who flew as FACs in the two-seat F-100. They worked in high-threat areas too dangerous for the slower, propeller-driven aircraft FACs normally flew. Their area of responsibility was just north of the demilitarized zone in "Route Pack One," as it was called. Everyone referred to them by their call sign, "Misty." The Misty pilots were all volunteers, although they took far more risks than the other F-100 pilots. Flying low and fast in a hostile environment and looking for gun sites, supply convoys and other enemy activity, they were an inviting target, and so far, 25 percent of their number had been shot down. This number remained constant throughout the war. At one time or another, almost every F-100 pilot at Phu Cat was tempted to volunteer for the Misty program. Even Skip thought about it. This was before he had that heart-to-heart chat with Christy about staying out of harm's way. At the moment, Skip's mind was on his family, as he headed north for a mission somewhere near Da Nang. In less than a month, he would be going home to see Christy and the kids. Thanksgiving at home. It was going to be a fantastic experience. He couldn't wait.

He had the first team with him today. Slick was on his left wing, and Willie was on the right. To Skip's amusement, Willie was slightly out of position, oxygen mask hanging off his face for God-knows-what reason, wearing his ever-present sunglasses. Like he needed them, when he had a perfectly good sun visor on his helmet. But that was Willie, always doing something different, pushing the envelope.

Boris had been right about Willie. He was a good pilot, and to Skip's surprise, he hadn't been in trouble for awhile. He was even allowed back in the officers' club, which for Willie was an accomplishment. Skip was certain that his leadership abilities had nothing to do with Willie's new, improved behavior. He didn't have time to play Boy Scout troop leader. Nevertheless, he was pleased that things had changed. It was one less thing he had to worry about.

When they were fifty miles south of Da Nang, he got word that the mission was about to change. He assumed the new mission would be troops in contact. He was wrong. The rendezvous was in Route Pack One, fifty miles north of the DMZ. He would be working with a Misty FAC. Shit, he thought, my first mission in North Vietnam. This does not bode well for the new, cautious, don't-hang-your-ass-out Skip. Putting aside his misgivings, he turned north and set course to the new target. The Misty FAC was already there, waiting for them. The FAC and his partner had discovered an antiaircraft gun site, whose location had been previously unknown. The gun site was in their territory, and it didn't belong there. They were going to take it out, and Skip's flight was going to help them do it.

The gun was a Russian-made, .50-caliber weapon called a ZPU. Skip had seen a picture of one while in training at Nellis. It could be fired rapidly by the gunner, who sat on a seat and used a mechanical crank to point the barrel. It was not much of a weapon compared to the arsenal of large guns and missiles deployed further north. But it was still dangerous. This is not going to be about one "golden BB," Skip thought. This sucker can throw out clouds of "golden BBs," all at the same time. The gun site was in a small clearing beside a bombed-out rice paddy. From where he was, he could see tracers spitting out, as Misty circled above. Technically, the strike pilots were not supposed to duel with antiaircraft gun sites, but that was exactly what they were about to do.

"No need to mark the target," Skip said. "I have him in sight."

"Roger that," Misty replied, and pulled high above the target to watch the attack. He wasn't about to mark the target anyway. He knew better.

The three aircraft began to descend over the target, circling in loose trail formation, like wolves surrounding an angry bear. The gun was silent now—had been ever since Misty climbed high above him. Maybe he doesn't know we're up here yet, he thought. Yeah right! He knows.

"Okay Icon Flight, check armament safety switches and set them up to drop in pairs. Let's try to take this guy out on the first pass." Skip's voice exuded a cool confidence he didn't feel.

They were in position now. Keeping his eyes fixed on the target, Skip took a deep breath and rolled in on his first attack. The gun site opened up immediately, even before he could align the pipper on the target. Out of the corner of his eye, he could see tracers streaming by his right. They were not particularly close, but close enough to distract him. Consequently, the pipper was slightly off the target when he released the bombs. He didn't have to see where the bombs hit. He already knew he had missed. What did the hunters called that—"buck fever?"

Skip pulled up to downwind and watched as Slick rolled in for the attack. The gun wheeled around and was on him quickly. He descended into a shower of tracers that seemed to engulf him. His bombs were also off the mark.

The gunner was really pissed now, and Willie got the worst hosing of all. For a second, Skip thought Willie's aircraft had been hit. But it hadn't, and Willie sent two more bombs hurtling toward the target. The gun site was engulfed in clouds of boiling smoke and dust caused by the bombs. But somehow it survived. Skip knew that for sure, because it was still firing at Willie's retreating aircraft. This was not good. They had to go back in.

The gunner was all over him as he started his run. He had the range, and he was mad as hell. Who wouldn't be after having six, 750-pound bombs dropped right on top of him? I don't want to do this, Skip thought, as he rolled in. The tracers were coming straight at him now, flying past his canopy, feet, if not inches, from his face. They were nasty looking buggers, spitting, red-hot points of fire that looked like something flying from hell. And they were just place-markers for the rounds he couldn't see. For the first time since he starting flying combat, things got personal. And he too, was mad. Mad at himself for missing the target on the first pass, mad at Slick and Willie for getting spooked like he had, and most of all, mad at this guy on the ground who was trying to kill him. "I'm going to stick these two bombs right up your ass," he declared.

His mind and body were engulfed in an icy layer of calm during the final five seconds of the run. Time was moving in slow motion. The tracers were still close, but he pushed them out of his mind. Putting these two bombs on target was all that mattered. After what seemed like an eternity, he hit the pickle button and pulled up, banking sharply to the right, and then to the left. "Take that asshole," he cried out exultantly. The bombs were spot on target. Skip could see that right away. The gun fell silent and remained so while Slick and Willie made their passes. Satisfied, he took his flight high and dry to wait for Misty to check things out. The Misty FAC circled the target twice, then swooped down and flew straight across it at a thousand feet. "You got it," he said finally. "There's a huge crater where the site was, and the gun is lying outside the rim in four pieces. Shit-hot job, guys!" Skip thanked him, rounded up his flight, and headed for home. It was over.

Later that afternoon, he slouched on a chair in his trailer, a cold beer in his hand. The others were waiting for him in the bar, but he wanted to be alone for a few minutes to reflect on the day's activities. It had been a remarkable day, a day filled with excitement, success, and self-discovery. Christy was right. People were trying to kill him every day. He hadn't realized that before, but now he did, and although his life had clearly been threatened today, he somehow found the courage to do what he had to do. He didn't flinch, and he didn't back away. This is what he came to Vietnam for, to find how he measured up against his peers. Now he knew the answer—he was a man of courage, a man with balls. He could hang with the best of them. But he was scared today. He supposed it was normal under the circumstances, although it was not something he was willing to admit. Could he walk up to Slick and Willie later and say, hey guys, guess what? I was scared shitless today, how about you? No way, not in a million years! The thought of him doing that made him chuckle.

Enough of this touchy-feely stuff, he thought. It was time to join the others. He was back to his old self, the relaxed, I-don't-give-a-rat's-ass-about-anything

Skip. I can't tell anybody how scared I was today, he thought, but there is something I can do, namely, walk up to Boris and tell him he's full of crap. Tell him that the "golden BB" isn't golden at all, but bright red…and there is a shit-pot full of them. Laughing to himself, he stepped out of his trailer and headed for the bar. It's all downhill now, pal, he told himself. I hope.

*   *   *   *

What's wrong with this picture? Skip thought. Two weeks ago I flew over North Vietnam for the first time, and now, I'm going there again. Christ almighty! Is there such a thing as a death wish by proxy? As in, someone else wants me to die? If so, that someone has to be Boris. He was the one that scheduled me for this mission. "It's a very special mission, Skip," he had said. "Right up your alley." I have a feeling this deal is going to be right up my something, but alley is not exactly the word that comes to mind.

His flight leader, the major sitting across the table from him, was a stranger who came all the way from the Fighter Weapons School at Nellis. His cohort was a young captain from wing intelligence, who was wearing the kind of serious look that usually spells trouble for the pilots being briefed. The major was about to explain what they were going to do, and how they were going to do it. Skip sat back in his chair, reached into his flying suit pocket, and pulled out a pack of cigarettes. He had just started smoking a couple of weeks ago, right after his encounter with the ZPU site. Christy would not be thrilled to know he was smoking. He definitely planned to stop before Thanksgiving.

"The weapon we will be carrying today is new," the major said, "so new, that it is still being tested. The project is classified, so I'm going to skip the details and tell you only what you need to know to deliver it. We'll be carrying two pods of them today, one on each wing. Each pod holds several hundred mines, each one the size of a softball. The mines are ejected in level flight so they are spread around. When they hit the ground, they arm themselves and eject trip wires in all directions."

"How long do these mines stay armed?"

"It depends. Each mine is set on a timer. It could take up to thirty days for all of them to detonate."

Skip tried to picture hundreds of these mines scattered about, waiting for someone to stumble on one of their trip wires, each programmed to detonate at a different time if no one did. It was a nightmare. "This mission is certainly going to spoil somebody's whole day isn't it?" he commented.

"That's the idea. That's why it's called an area-of-denial weapon."

The intelligence officer laid a series of maps and photos on the table and began to describe the target. "The area we want to shut down is a trans-shipment point located here, along this river. Barges filled with ammunition and supplies come up there from the port city of Dong-Hoi and are offloaded onto trucks. Then the supplies are driven south around the DMZ, through Laos, and into South Vietnam where they are used to support the Viet Cong.

The mines have to be laid along the river just right to be effective. Those that land in the river or on the other side will be useless, while those that land too far away from the target on the other side will cause needless civilian casualties. You'll need to make a straight run west to east, like so."

"What altitude are we dropping these things from?" Skip asked.

"Between one and two thousand feet," the major replied.

A wings-level pass at two thousand feet over North Vietnam, Skip thought. Why don't we just hand-deliver the mines to them in a truck or something? It might be less dangerous.

"There will be a FAC for the mission," the intelligence officer concluded, "just in case you need help finding the target. His call sign will be Misty 41."

"One more thing," the major said, "if you have a problem on takeoff, do not, I repeat, do not, jettison those pods on the runway or anywhere near the base, for that matter. Understand?"

Skip nodded. It doesn't take a rocket scientist to figure that one out. Closing down Phu Cat for thirty days would be a good way to piss everyone off, from the Pentagon down to his squadron commander. He was not about to jettison those puppies on the runway. No sir!

When the briefing was over, Skip stayed at the table for a few minutes, reviewing the maps and photos, trying to get everything sorted out in his mind. It seemed complicated, especially the part about finding the target. In fact, he wasn't so sure he could find the target if he had to do it on his own. But what the hell, he was a lowly wingman today. He could always follow his fearless flight leader there and dump his load where he did. That's what he'd end up doing anyway, probably. Stick with his leader like glue, that's the plan. Dong Hoi was a lot farther north than where Skip was two weeks ago. By the time they crossed the DMZ, a solid undercast had developed at ten thousand feet. He couldn't see any holes in the undercast and wondered how they would be able to get below to find the target. The Misty FAC was already circling Dong Hoi at fifteen thousand feet, wondering the same thing. For sure, he wouldn't be able to mark the target.

But if he could just find a hole for them to slip through, maybe they could find it on their own.

*   *   *   *

The North Vietnamese surveillance radar operator watched the circling aircraft intently. His equipment was Russian-made and barely functional. But it was working fine today. The aircraft continued to circle the city. Probably part of a hunter-killer team, he thought. It was an F-100, judging by its speed. But what is he doing up here? Such aircraft normally spend their time farther south, harassing his colleagues near the DMZ.

As if to answer his question, two more targets appeared at the bottom of his scope, heading directly toward the city. It was all becoming clear. The radar operator turned in his chair and motioned for his boss. The older man leaned over the scope and peered at it intently, a foul-smelling French cigarette smoldering in his hand.

"It appears," the radar operator said, "that we are about to have some visitors to our esteemed city."

His boss nodded.

"It would be a pity if they were not given an appropriate welcome, don't you think?"

His boss took a long drag from his cigarette. "Yes it would."

The radar operator picked up a field phone and began to turn the crank vigorously. Within minutes, air-raid sirens cried out in the city of Dong Hoi.

The Misty FAC found a hole in the clouds. It wasn't very big, just enough to slip through. But he could clearly see the ground. They should be okay once they got underneath. He hoped so anyway. The flight leader saw the hole too, and began to circle it, preparing for the attack. Skip was not far behind. He wasn't about to lose him now, especially with the weather so bad, and there would be no mark for the target.

Arming the weapon was more difficult than usual. There were two extra steps, and these involved switches that were difficult to see and awkward to reach. His hand fumbled when he flipped the last switch. Did he get it right? He wasn't sure. Taking his eye off the leader for a second, he leaned over and peered under the canopy rail to check. "Icon Lead is in hot!" Skip heard the leader say. Skip looked up just in time to see him plunge through the hole and disappear. Shit. I've lost him. Instinctively, he rolled inverted and followed. The cloud layer was not thick, and when he returned to straight and level flight, he found himself over the center of Dong Hoi. It was not a pretty city. Tired, gray buildings and muddy streets lay all round him. But he had no time for sight-seeing. He had to find his leader. It was his only chance to reach the target. But the leader was no longer in sight. Where in the hell was he?

Then he saw the puffs of smoke—blackish, gray mushrooms exploding all around him. Antiaircraft fire! It was big stuff, 57 mm, at least. He had to get the hell out of there. It was not a matter of outrunning it; it was already there. It was more like dashing out of a mine field, hoping he didn't trip on something on the way out. "Dashing out of a minefield." The irony of it was not lost on Skip. The hunter had become the hunted.

Scanning the horizon anxiously, Skip spotted the dim outline of a river, a few miles south of the city. That had to be the place. There were no other rivers around. Turning sharply, he pointed his nose at the river and cracked the afterburner to gain speed. In a few seconds, the antiaircraft fire fell behind him.

Skip wasn't sure what he was going to do when he reached the river. He still had to find the target once he got there. Suddenly, a sprinkle of tiny explosions flashed along the river bank just ahead. That had to be the mines. "Icon Lead is off hot," Skip heard, confirming what he already knew. He had it made now, as long as he didn't lose the target, like he lost his flight leader a few minutes ago. Keeping his eyes fixed on the spot where he saw the flashes, he started to descend, turning to the west as he did so. He would make a descending turn onto the final run, spending as little time at low altitude as possible.

The F-100 was smoking along now, more than five hundred knots. This was probably not the best speed for delivering the mines, but he didn't care. Survival was the name of the game. He needed to dump the load and get the hell out of there. He was level at two thousand feet on the final attack run and would be dropping in a few seconds. A ZPU site opened up ahead and to his right, but his eyes never left the target. Straight ahead, he saw some boats tied up in front of an old building, with a few trucks parked behind. Was this the target? He had no idea, and at this point, he didn't care. He pressed the pickle button and felt the reassuring clunk-clunk-clunk as the mines were ejected from the pods, followed by a yellow light indicating the pods were empty. He pulled the nose up sharply, cracked the afterburner, and disappeared into the clouds. "Icon Two is off hot," he said.

Boris was standing behind the ops counter when he returned. "Have fun today?"

"Oh yes. I had a great time," Skip replied sarcastically. "Thanks ever-so-much for inviting me. I almost got my ass shot off."

"No need to get huffy about it. I thought you were a logical choice. After all, you're the resident expert on antiaircraft guns these days. Some of the guys have even given you a new name, 'magnet ass.'"

Skip shook his head in disgust and turned to walk away.

"By the way," Boris said, "There's a squadron party next Tuesday night. It's A Flight's turn to plan it."

"Another one? We just had one last month. Why so soon?"

"Because it's good for morale. Our fearless squadron commander thinks so, anyway."

"Good for morale but bad for our livers is more like it," Skip groused. "What are we suppose to be celebrating?"

"You'll think of something. And make it look good. The wing commander's going to be there."

"Colonel Gilbert? He never comes to our parties. He doesn't even drink for God's sake!"

"Well, he's coming this time."

"Shit," Skip mumbled, as he headed downstairs to hang up his parachute and helmet. "Just what I need, a party to plan." Then he brightened. Willie, he thought, I'll have Willie plan it. That's right up his alley.

*   *   *   *

Skip gave Willie and Slick Tuesday afternoon off to set up the party. They took their time doing so, drinking copious amounts of alcohol along the way, but by five o'clock, everything was ready. Skip was impressed. The area around the bar was swept clean, all trash was picked up, and the lounge chairs were arranged neatly. There was enough booze behind the bar to keep the Russian army blitzed for a week, plus gallons of ice. Over in the corner, a charcoal cooker stood waiting, piles of freshly thawed steaks (provided by the Army in exchange for a few bottles of Canadian Club whiskey) at its side. The steaks, with baked beans and baked potatoes purloined from the mess hall, would provide ample nourishment for those who chose to eat while they drank.

Slick was leaving early the next morning, returning to the States to sign in at Myrtle Beach. He would be the first in their group to do so. Willie decided it was as good a reason as any for a party. After all, Skip had told him to think of something to celebrate, hadn't he? A large sign over the bar said, "Adios Guard Puke! Get some for me while you're there!" Skip looked at the sign and smiled wryly. Sex. It all came down to that, didn't it? He wondered if there would be any entertainment tonight. Sometimes they would drag out an old, beat-up projector and watch pornographic films. These were brought in from Hong Kong or Manila and placed in the care of the "squadron porn officer." The films were usually crude and amateurish, more comical than erotic. But they watched them anyway, more out of boredom than anything else, and eventually traded them to other squadrons for something different.

Skip doubted if there would be any porn films tonight, because the wing commander was coming. Willie was too smart for that. But there were boxes of old glasses standing by, ready for a frenzy of glass throwing against the fake fireplace, which had been built for that purpose. This usually took place at the end of the party when everyone was too drunk to know what they were doing. He always tried to stand behind the throwers when this took place. It was safer that way.

It was still early, so Skip decided to go back to his trailer and record a message for Christy. Everyone was doing that these days. It was much easier than writing a letter. The machine of choice for recording was the Sony TC 100, a device the size of a hard-cover book that weighed as much as a small brick, and was considered a marvel of technology. The base exchange could never keep them in stock, and whenever a shipment arrived, it usually sold out the same day.

Skip recorded his messages carefully, mindful that kids would probably be listening. He kept his sexual innuendos to a minimum and watched his language. He also made it a point to record such messages when he was sober. God forbid that Christy would think that he did nothing but drink in his spare time, although this, of course, was true.

Willie was in his room in the other end of the trailer. "Hey, Ace, you and Slick outdid yourselves this time. Everything looks really good out there, and the sign is pretty cool."

"Thanks coach," Willie said. His voice sounded slow and artificial, as if it was difficult to talk. He's probably been drinking all afternoon, Skip thought, and the booze finally got to him. He started to return to his room but decided to look in on him, just to be sure. The reason Willie had trouble talking was because his lower lip was more than twice its normal size and was split in the middle. Evidence of a large shiner seeped out from under his sunglasses.

Skip leaned against the door jam, and regarded Willie gravely. "This is just a wild-ass guess on my part, but is it possible that you've been in another fight?"

"Yeah, something like that."

"Well, would you mind filling me in on the details, so I will be prepared when the shit hits the fan over this, like it usually does? I know that's asking a lot, but you know, I would really appreciate it." His voice was dripping with sarcasm.

Willie became animated and began to talk excitedly, which was not was easy to do with his lip. "Hey man, it wasn't our fault. Slick and I were over at the club last night minding our own business, when…"

"Ah, the officers' club…otherwise known as the coliseum, the home of the gladiators."

"Yeah, so Slick and I were there minding our own business, when this fight broke out, and the next thing I knew…"

"You were thrown out, right? And are probably gonna get banned again, I suspect."

"Probably."

"And who threw you out this time?" Skip continued in his best prosecutorial voice.

"Colonel Williams."

"Colonel Williams? The wing vice commander? Christ almighty, Willie, he was the one who threw you out the last time. Couldn't you have been a little more creative and waited until a different senior ranking officer was around? You know, just for variety."

"I know. That's what he said too. In fact, the first words out of his mouth were, 'You again, Reed?' But what the hell were we supposed to do? Somebody else started the fight, and he was getting hammered pretty good, so we jumped in to defend him."

"Defended him. That was very admirable," Skip said dryly.

Skip walked into the room and sat down on the bunk across from Willie, shaking his head wearily. "You know what I don't understand? Why didn't Boris jump in my shit about this earlier today? He loves to point out what a shitty job I'm doing as a flight commander. 'You're too easy on your troops,' he always says. 'You've to be tougher. Kick some ass once in awhile, just to get their attention.' I guess I'm gonna get an earful tonight."

"I don't think so."

"Why not?"

"Because Boris was the one who started the fight. He was the one we were defending."

"Well, that's some consolation," Skip admitted grudgingly. "But that still doesn't make it right."

Willie nodded absently, gingerly stroking his lower lip.

"Does that hurt?"

"Not too much. Except when alcohol gets on it. Then it hurts like a son of a bitch."

"Which means it's been hurting all afternoon, right?"

"You might say that."

"I thought so."

Skip leaned forward and began talking earnestly. "Look man, we've been through all of this before. Fighting…well, that's combat, which is what we do when we fly. You know—bombs, rockets, strafing—remember? The idea is you get in fights when you are flying, that way you don't have to when you're wandering around the base. See? Hell's bells, man, you treat the officers' club like it was Route Pack One or something, just one big, target-rich environment."

Willie looked unconvinced. "I hear what you're saying, but this shit always seems to happen to me. I mean most of the time it isn't my fault."

Skip could see that he was getting nowhere, so he decided to change the subject. "Did you remember to make the name tags?"

Willie brightened at this and was back to his old self. "Right. I've got them right here. Wait until you see them. They're really cool." He walked over to his locker, pulled out a small box, and dumped the contents on his desk so Skip could see.

Each name tag consisted of a three-by-five-inch index card with a clip to attach it to the wearer's flying suit. The name of the guest was carefully hand printed in neat, block letters. A few of the names were not so neatly printed, but Skip figured these had been done last, when the effects of their afternoon of drinking had impaired the skills of the writers. But there was something else on the name tags, something that caused Skip to burst into a gale of uncontrollable laughter.

Willie and Slick had wanted to do something special with the name tags. Something that had never been done before. But they couldn't figure out what. That's when Slick remembered the two nudist magazines he had stashed in his trailer. Poring over the magazines with a quart of Canadian Club at their side, they had an inspiration. Their plan was simple. Working together, each with a pair of scissors, they cut out the pubic area of every female nudist in the two magazines. The cut-outs, in turn, were pasted on the name tags, one beside each name. It had been precise and intensely laborious work. Skip was amazed they were able to do it, considering the condition they were in at the time.

Skip riffled through the pile of name tags, unable to stop laughing. There were pubes of every size, shape, and color there—black, blond, red, brunette, and all shades in between. Mindful of protocol, they had singled out group photos of two or more women. These were set aside for the more senior guests. But the piece de resistance lay on the top of the pile. Pasted on this tag was a long rectangle that included the pubic areas of four women who had been posing side by side. Above the picture was the guest's name, "Colonel Gilbert." Their wing commander! It was too much.

"Nice touch," Skip said.

"I thought so."

The name tags were an instant hit at the party. Everyone crowded around the table where they were displayed, hooting and laughing. The first hour was spent milling around the room looking at each other's name tags, making lewd comments about what they saw. It was great entertainment. Skip was worried about how Colonel Gilbert would react to the name tags, and so was the squadron commander. To their surprise, he took it with good humor, laughing with all the rest. He was also the first to step up and fling a glass at the fireplace, as the party came to a drunken end. By one in the morning, the bar area was empty. The floor was covered with broken glass, empty paper plates, and discarded plastic cups. The farewell sign for Slick had fallen and lay draped over the bottles behind the bar. Soon, everything would be cleaned up, by a select few who were sober enough to do so. Meanwhile, Slick was passed out on his bunk. He would be leaving for the States in four hours, if he didn't oversleep. There were no name tags to be found in the debris, however. Everyone had taken his home as a souvenir, even Colonel Gilbert. The party was a roaring success, by any measure.

Boris did not mention the fight at the club the next day. Skip didn't expect him to, ever. But he did have something to say two days later. "Skip," he said, "Slick called me last night from Hawaii, and he was pissed as hell."

"Pissed? Why?" He could tell that Boris was struggling to keep a straight face.

"Well, it seems that when he landed in Honolulu, the customs officer pulled him aside for a random check of his luggage. When he opened his B-4 bag, a whole bunch of paper pussies flew out. There must have been a hundred of them. They went everywhere, on the conveyer belt, on the floor, everywhere." A group of grinning pilots gathered around Boris and Skip, waiting to hear the rest of the story. "It was a full flight out of Tokyo. Not just grunts from Vietnam, but military wives and children. Everyone was staring at Slick. Some were giggling, others were embarrassed. Nobody knew what to say."

"The custom officer didn't know whether to shit or go blind," Boris continued. "Nothing like that had ever happened to him before. 'You pervert!' he finally managed to say. 'I ought to bust you for importing pornography. Now pick all this stuff up, I mean every piece, and get the hell out of here, before I send you to the back room for a body cavity search.' Slick said he was afraid the guy might change his mind, so he worked as fast as he could. But it wasn't easy. Some of the pictures were hard to reach under the conveyor belt, and it was embarrassing, crawling on his hands and knees while everyone stared. When he was done, he got out of there fast, not daring to look behind."

After the laughter subsided, Skip gave Willie a hard look.

Willie shrugged his shoulders elaborately. "What can I say? It seemed like the thing to do at the time. I mean…we had so many of those things left over, and it was a shame to waste them. Besides," he added brightly, "the last thing Slick said at the party was, 'The first thing I'm gonna do when I get back to the States, is chase some pussy.' So I just…you know…gave him a little head start. Hawaii is in the States, right?"

Afterwards, it occurred to Skip that he, himself, would be leaving for the States in less than two weeks. He made a mental note to check his bags very carefully before he left.

*   *   *   *

When his departure day finally arrived, Skip gathered a few things that he would need for the trip, packed them in a bag, and boarded a C-141 military transport. He was on his way to the States for Thanksgiving. The C-141 stopped to refuel in Tokyo and then flew on to Seattle. It was midnight when he arrived, this much he knew, although he wasn't sure what day it was. It didn't matter. He could have spent the night in Seattle, but he was in a hurry. He decided to wait for another C-141 that was leaving for Charleston, South Carolina in three hours. It would be an easy drive to Myrtle Beach from there.

The trip from Vietnam to Myrtle Beach took well over twenty-four hours, counting refueling stops and the short layover at Seattle. Skip did what he could to pass the time, reading, sleeping, eating, and talking to other passengers, but it was a long, boring trip nonetheless. It was nearly ten o'clock in the evening when he arrived at Myrtle Beach, exhausted and ready for bed. But he had to call Christy first and let her know he was back in the States. She answered on the first ring. *Woman's intuition*, he thought, *she was waiting for me to call.*

"Hey baby, you better get rid of your boyfriend. I'm at Myrtle Beach and heading home."

"My boyfriend? No way. He's in Vietnam, remember?"

"Oh yeah, I forgot. But he's a tricky character. You never know when he's going to show up."

"This is true. I have an idea. Just to be safe, why don't you both come?"

"Both of us? Your husband and boyfriend, in the same bed? You kinky little devil."

"It could be fun."

"It certainly could."

Christy paused, as if struggling with a thought. "Honey, are you really at Myrtle Beach?" She sounded concerned.

"Of course I am. Why do you ask?"

"I had this dream the other night…a really bad dream. Someone called to tell me you weren't coming home, ever."

"Well, last night I dreamed that we were screwing our brains out in Jacksonville."

Christy brightened. "I like your dream better."

"So do I."

"When will you be here?"

"The day after tomorrow, if all goes well, probably in the afternoon. I'll call you when I have an arrival time."

"Hurry home, baby. I miss you. We all miss you. Your family is waiting."

Myrtle Beach had changed since Skip left in June. It was more organized now. Over the past three months, the Air Force had methodically stripped the unit of excess personnel, sending them to Korea, Vietnam, and other places where their skills were needed. Those who remained were hard at work training students. Another change was taking place, as well. A large contingent of crew chiefs, armorers, and other maintenance personnel were about to be sent to Skip's squadron in Vietnam. He was not sure the guys at Phu Cat knew that yet, but it was certainly good news. Their maintenance organization was undermanned and woefully inexperienced.

His reception at his old squadron was polite but reserved. He hadn't expected a hero's welcome, and he didn't get one. Some were curious about how he was doing in Vietnam and what it was like to fly combat, but none of them asked. Not directly anyway. No one mentioned the exchange of photographs or the crisis that was avoided when he and his friends volunteered to remain in Phu Cat. That was okay with him. He had strong feelings about those subjects, but now was not the time to express them. Maybe someday he would. Personnel processing took less than three hours. After signing in from TDY, he was given new orders assigning him to Phu Cat until June 1969. He also requested ten days leave, which was approved.

At five o'clock, Skip went to the club for happy hour, more out of habit than anything else. Lord knows, he had drunk enough alcohol at Phu Cat to last him the rest of his life, but it was a way of killing time. The bar was crowded, filled with people he knew and many that he did not. Once again, the conversation was polite but not especially warm. During the evening, several people came up to invite him to dinner. He could sense that it was a pro forma thing, not something they really wanted to do. In each case, he politely declined, citing other plans. He was in bed by eleven. He had an early flight to catch in the morning.

Skip's arrival at Imeson Airport in Jacksonville was a spectacle that warmed the hearts of all who witnessed it. As he walked into the terminal, Christy and the kids rushed at him headlong, covering him with a mass of hugging, squirming bodies, everyone talking at once. The kids were too heavy to pick up one in each arm, and no one wanted to let go, so he just stood there. Finally, they began to move as one amorphous, wiggling body, inching their way to the parking lot. Everyone was laughing or crying or both.

Christy decided to drive, so Skip could get reacquainted with the kids. Maddie and Cam eyed him speculatively. He looked different somehow, but they weren't sure why. His hair was certainly different, closely cropped in a crew cut that was less than an inch long. Maddie ran her hand over his head and giggled.

"Do you have to go back to Poo Cat?" she asked.

"Yes I do, honey, but not for awhile."

"How long is awhile?"

"Ten days, honey. I don't have to go for ten days."

Maddie nodded. She was satisfied. Ten days was a long time to a little girl.

"What does the Poo Cat look like anyway?" Cam asked.

Skip thought for a moment. "Well…he's pretty hard to describe, but he's really special. He's big…bigger than I am, and really furry, with bright green eyes."

"Bright green eyes?" Cam's eyes widened at the thought of a human-size cat with bright green eyes. "He sounds scary."

"Oh, but he's not. He's my friend, and he stays with me every night."

"Does he have his own bed?"

"Nope. He curls up on the floor in front of the door and stays awake all night to make sure nobody tries to come in and hurt me."

"How do you know he stays awake?"

"Because sometimes I wake up, and I can see his green eyes staring at me in the dark."

"Wow," Maddie said. "He sounds really special. You're lucky he's there to look after you, Daddy."

"You're right, sweet pea, and I'm lucky to have you, Cam, and your mommy, to look after me too."

"I'll always look after you, Daddy," Cam said, nodding his head gravely.

Skip felt a lump in his throat when he walked into the house. Everything looked so warm and cozy. Nothing had changed, except for his study. It was Christy's office now, and the rolltop desk he loved so much was covered with school books and papers. The tape recorder she used to send messages sat in the corner, piles of tapes she had received from him stacked neatly beside it. The walls were covered with pictures her children had drawn, colorful scenes filled with stick figures, houses, trees, and a sun shining brightly. That's the way it seemed when I was in kindergarten, he thought. The sun was always shining. He walked into the living room, arm in arm with the children. A large sign hung suspended over the fire place. "Welcome home Daddy!" it said. The words were surrounded by drawings of airplanes and a stick figure that looked like he was wearing a flying helmet.

"Wow, this is really cool. Who made this sign anyway?"

"I did!" the children shouted simultaneously.

"We all did," Christy said. "I helped with the lettering."

"Well, you know what? I think I am just about the luckiest daddy in the whole wide world. Umm, maybe we should have ice cream for dessert tonight?" He looked tentatively at Christy. She smiled and nodded.

"Yeah!" the kids cheered.

It was late before they could get the kids to bed and settled down. The kids had so many questions to ask, so many things to tell their daddy. When the kids were finally asleep (or pretending to be), Skip and Christy went downstairs to the living room. The evening had turned crisp and cool, and they had built a fire to ward off the chill. Sitting on the floor, propped up by pillows, they sat staring at the fire, each with a glass of brandy.

The brandy went down smoothly, causing a warm glow to radiate in Skip's stomach, much like the schnapps had done the day her father teased him into proposing. He thought about that day. It had been on Thanksgiving, ten years ago to be exact. Ten years! Where had the time gone? He felt like his life was moving in fast-forward, and he was helpless to stop it. What would the next ten years bring? The conversation evolved at a slow, dreamy pace, as they sat in front of the fire. Each described the thoughts, feelings, and frustrations that were part of their everyday lives. Christy loved her job, no doubt about it. The twenty-five children in her class could be a handful at times, but it filled her with joy to see them learn and grow. But teaching school, raising her own kids, and being the head of the house—that was too much. And she didn't like it one bit. But she would continue to do so, at least until Skip got home.

Skip was less than forthright when talking about his life in Vietnam. He described the combat missions as routine, almost boring events, with little or no danger associated with them. She was not fooled by his evasiveness but did not say so. She didn't want to know more. She was worried enough about him as it was.

The brandy, the warmth of the fire, jet lag, and travel fatigue all began to wear him down and he found himself drowsing off.

"I think it's terrible what you guys did to poor Slick," Christy said suddenly.

Skip was instantly awake. "What? You gals really do know what's going on all the time, don't you?"

"That one was pretty hard to miss. Everyone knows about it."

"Well, it was one of my guys that did it. It was only a joke."

"Some joke."

"I don't know. I think it's a hell of a deal, suddenly being surrounded by a hundred naked pussies."

"You already have a hell of a deal, honey. Your deal is one real naked pussy, in your bed."

"Then why are we lying on the floor in the living room?"

"I thought you'd never ask."

Their lovemaking was tentative, almost shy at first. It all seemed so strange. But their need was great, and there would be no chance in the morning. The kids would be up at dawn, that was for sure. Slowly, the pace quickened, evolving from slow, sensuous moves, to urgent, driving passions that culminated in a perfectly timed, climactic finale. When it was over, they lay back satisfied and exhausted.

Skip didn't fall asleep right away. Jet lag had a lot to do with it, of course, but there was something else. Something he couldn't quite identify. Then it dawned on him. It was too quiet. There was no thumping of outgoing artillery fire, no droning of the AC-47 gunship circling the base, dropping flares and laying down suppressive cannon fire. These things had become woven into the nightly fabric of his life, and without them he felt distracted and strangely disconnected. He rose up on one elbow and watched Christy, as she purred gently in her sleep, her hair fanned out on the pillow. Anyone who volunteers to go to Vietnam is fucking stupid. The words returned once more to haunt him. You're probably right, he thought as he drifted off to sleep. You're probably right.

Ten days may seem like a long time to a little girl, but to Christy and Skip it seemed like a passing moment. They did everything together as a family, spending every waking hour together. It was not a normal life, of course, because Christy had arranged for a substitute to teach her class and took the kids out of school for a few extra days after the Thanksgiving holiday. They lived life to the fullest, as happy as they had ever been. But time chased them hard and soon overtook them.

Two days before he was scheduled to leave, a sergeant from TAC headquarters called. "Major, I understand you are leaving for Vietnam in a couple of days," he said.

"That's right. Why?"

"Because I have a deal for you. There are three F-100s just out of overhaul at the depot in Sacramento ready for delivery to Vietnam. We'd like you to ferry one of them for us."

Skip didn't have to think long about this offer. He was not looking forward to the long, boring flight back. "Sounds good to me."

"Good, we'll amend your travel orders and book a reservation to California. You can pick up the ticket at the airport."

"Do I have to go back to Myrtle Beach?"

"Nope, that wouldn't be cost effective. We'll book your trip from Jacksonville."

There was no joyous spectacle at the airport when Skip left. Everyone spoke in sad, muted tones, as if the family were attending a funeral. The kids were restless and constantly misbehaving, the way kids do when something they don't like is about to happen. Christy's eyes were red and swollen from crying. The wait in the departure area seemed interminable. They had run out of things to talk about.

Skip had held up well so far. They announced that the flight was ready for boarding. He gathered up the kids and hugged them hard, so hard that they almost cried out. It was as if he didn't want to let go of them, as if he were never going to see them again.

It was Christy's turn next. Tilting her chin upward, he blotted the tears from the corners of her eyes with his thumb, like he used to do at Misawa when he was about to leave for Korea. "It's going to be okay, sweetie, it really is."

"I know. Just be careful Skip, okay?"

"I will. And don't forget, we still have R&R in Hawaii. Remember? I'll try to set it up for sometime in March. After that, it will be all downhill."

"We'll have a wonderful time in Hawaii, won't we?"

"Indeed we will."

Suddenly, Skip couldn't take it any more. Gathering his family up, he kissed them one last time, then turned and strode quickly out the door, so no one could see that he was crying. They were still waving as the plane taxied away.

*   *   *   *

The weather in the San Francisco Bay area was miserable. Skip and the other two ferry pilots waited four days for it to clear. On the fifth day they launched with a tanker and flew to Honolulu, and on the sixth day on to Guam. The flight to Guam took over eight hours, but Skip didn't mind. The weather was clear all the way, and he was a wingman on that leg. This afforded him the luxury of sitting high and wide, admiring the vast expanse of the ocean below. Seeing all that water reminded him of his first trip to Japan on the Connie with Bob and Corky. So much had happened since then. He wondered what Bob was doing these days.

The flight split up at Guam. Skip accompanied a tanker that was headed for Okinawa. As they approached the Gulf of Tonkin, he refueled one last time and flew to Phu Cat alone. He still had seven months left on his tour in Vietnam. It was time to get back to work.

The man marshaling him into the parking revetment looked vaguely familiar, but Skip couldn't place him. He was a husky man, with sandy hair and blue eyes. He was a master sergeant, which in itself was unusual for a crew chief at Phu Cat. Then he remembered. He was from the New Jersey Guard. The rest of the Christmas help has arrived, he thought happily.

The sergeant was waiting for him when he came down the ladder.

"It's about time you got here," Skip said, shaking his hand warmly.

"Well, you know, we thought we'd let all the hotshot pilots do their thing first, and then come over after you've broken all the aircraft."

"It must have been quite a shock when they shipped you over."

"Naw, we had an idea this was coming. It wasn't something I was thrilled about doing, but hey, what are you gonna do? You just make the best of it, that's all. Of course, my wife is pissed, but she's always pissed about something."

Skip nodded sympathetically. He thought about the ruckus the flower children had made when they thought they were about to be sent here. All that whining and complaining—what a difference in attitude!

"So, what do you think so far?" Skip asked.

"What do I think? I think you are damned lucky one of these aircraft hasn't fallen apart on you. They're in shitty shape."

"That bad, huh?"

The sergeant shrugged. "It'll take awhile for us to get them in shape, but we're getting there."

Skip looked around and realized that there were dozens of new faces on the flight line, older men, wearing four or more stripes on their arms. The rest of the Christmas help had indeed arrived. He slapped the sergeant gently on the back. "I'm glad you guys are here," he said finally and walked away.

Skip walked into ops steeled for the verbal abuse he was about to receive from Boris. He was not disappointed.

Boris was in his usual position, perched on a stool next to the scheduling board. When Skip walked in, he looked up in mock surprise. "What do we have here? A new guy in the squadron? The face looks vaguely familiar, but I can't place the name."

Skip grinned broadly. "Miss me?"

Boris ignored that comment. "Now that you are back, I have a few questions to ask."

Skip put down his parachute and walked over to the ops counter. "Shoot!"

"Well, for openers, you were supposed to return on a civilian contract flight. Instead, you drag in here a week late in an F-100. What's that all about?"

"Hey, it was a TAC-directed mission. They asked me; I didn't ask them. Besides, the bird I brought was for our squadron. If we'd waited for some TAC puke to ferry it over, we would have waited three weeks for it, and we're short of aircraft, remember? As it is, you got the bird and me in only one week. I think that's a hell of a deal, don't you?"

Boris grunted and continued. "And what's this shit about staying in California for four days?"

"Weather. Fog from the San Francisco Bay. We were socked in the whole time."

Skip was having fun. Technically he didn't work for Boris, so he didn't have to put up with all this. But he didn't mind. It was a game they liked to play called "bust each other's balls." And they both enjoyed it.

Their conversation was interrupted by the squadron commander. "Skip, come in to my office a minute, will you? I want you to meet the new vice wing commander. He says he knows you from the old days."

Skip walked into the office filled with curiosity. Sitting in a chair, puffing on a pipe, was Rosie O'Grady.

Rosie's eyes lit up when Skip walked into the room. "Skip my lad," he beamed. "What a pleasure! When they told me there was a 'Major' Skip O'Neill in the squadron I thought, could this be our boy from Misawa? Then I thought, no way. That rascal is long gone from active duty, living in Florida or somewhere the last time I heard. And a major? Highly unlikely. Then I heard he was in the Guard, and I thought, well, maybe."

Skip laughed heartily. "I know what you mean sir. If someone had told me a 'Colonel' Emmett O'Grady was our new vice wing commander, I would have had the same reaction."

"Touché!"

For a moment, neither spoke. They were thinking about those days in Misawa, when they were both struggling to keep up with their peers. But they were here now, and things had changed. As far as Skip was concerned, he had caught up with his peers and was maybe pulling ahead. Obviously, Colonel Rosie had too.

"How's Christy doing?" Rosie said finally.

"She's teaching kindergarten in Jacksonville. Needless to say, she's not thrilled about me being over here, especially since I volunteered."

"Tell me about it. I have the same problem at my house."

"Do you ever see any of the gang from the 531st?" Skip asked.

"Not very often. They're pretty much scattered to hell and gone. I do talk to Bud Sexton from time to time. He's a lieutenant colonel now and works in TAC headquarters."

"Excellent. He's a good man. How about my old buddy Duke Christiansen?"

Rosie shrugged his shoulders. "He's in the fighter weapons school, doing something. I really don't know."

"How about Buns Van Riper? I always liked him."

Rosie shook his head sadly. "He was shot down over North Vietnam in 1966. As far as we know, he's in a prison camp near Hanoi."

Skip thought about this for a moment. "Do you think we'll ever get those guys back?"

"Hard to say. If we do, it won't be for a long time. This war is just getting started."

Rosie quickly changed the subject. "The 531st is in Vietnam these days, did you know that?"

"Yeah, I heard. Down at Bien Hoa, right?"

"Right, and the ops officer is an old asshole buddy of yours, Bob Lewis."

"You gotta be shitting me. Bob's in Vietnam? I haven't seen him since I left Misawa. I hope I get to talk to him while he's over here."

"I'm sure you will."

Rosie looked at his watch and rose to go. "Gotta run, Skip. Things to do, you know."

Skip got up also. "I know. It was great seeing you again, sir."

"It was great seeing you too. By the way, are you ready for wing's new mission?"

"New mission?"

"Guess you haven't heard. The code name is 'Commando Hunt,' or some such thing. We'll be doing interdiction bombing along the Ho Chi Minh trail in Laos."

"I guess that was announced while I was back in the States."

"Probably. Anyway, you better get yourself up to speed on the mission. It's going to be more demanding than busting trees in South Vietnam and a lot more dangerous."

"I will, sir."

Skip turned and started to leave.

"Oh, and Skip?"

"Yes sir?"

"They tell me you are doing a damn good job over here. I'm proud of you."

"Thank you, sir."

*   *   *   *

The next day, Skip wasted no time collaring the squadron intelligence officer. "Tom, can you brief me on this Commando Hunt operation? I was in the States when it started."

Lt. Tom Hunt was from the New Jersey Guard. He was a bright young man, a professor at Rutgers University before being recalled to active duty. Skip liked Tom a lot, but in his opinion, he had one major character flaw. As his father used to say, "Ask him what time it is, and he will tell you how to build a watch." But that was okay. By the time Tom finished briefing him, he would know everything he ever wanted to know about interdiction bombing in Laos, and more.

They went into an empty room and sat down at a small table. Tom hesitated for a moment to collect his thoughts and then began. "Okay, a little background first. As you probably recall, earlier this month, President Johnson halted all bombing in North Vietnam. The idea was to draw them to the bargaining table to negotiate an end to the war." Skip recalled nothing about it. He had been too busy flying and thinking about going home for Thanksgiving. But he nodded anyway.

"So far, the North Vietnamese have shown no interest in entering peace talks, but they have taken advantage of the bombing halt to step up their shipment of troops and supplies down the Ho Chi Minh trail to South Vietnam." He paused and pulled out a sliding board, showing a large map of Laos.

"Most convoys depart from three major loading areas inside North Vietnam's panhandle region and proceed toward the Laotian border, following three paved highways built by the French back in 1945.

The boundary between Laos and North Vietnam is defined by the Annam Mountain Range. This is rugged terrain, and the trucks can only traverse it at major passes, principally this one, the Mu Gia Pass.

The road network extends from the Mu Gia Pass, southward along the western slopes of the Annam range, to a series of exit points stretching from just below the demilitarized zone between the two Vietnams, to the tri-border region of Laos, Cambodia, and South Vietnam, about five hundred kilometers to the south. The roads themselves are primitive by our standards, mostly eighteen-foot wide tracks carved out of the jungles. Some are reinforced by gravel and corduroy surfaces, but most are made of dirt and nearly impassable during the wet season.

So, in a nutshell, the mission of Commando Hunt will be to interdict the traffic moving along the trail, i.e., shut it down entirely or severely limit the flow."

Tom paused while Skip studied the map carefully. "Doesn't sound that difficult to me," Skip said. "Bomb the shit out of the Mu Gia Pass, that's where I would start. Get them where they can't detour. Then I would attack everything that moved along the rest of the trail and crater the road in so many places that it would take them the rest of their lives to fix it."

"That's not as easy as it sounds," Tom replied. "First of all, the roads through the passes are normally concealed in clouds, which makes them very difficult to bomb, and beyond the passes, the tropical forests of Laos provide an almost continuous roof of natural concealment. In that environment, it's difficult to find the road, much less trucks on it. As for repairing the roads, they are surprisingly efficient. We estimate that they have between forty thousand and fifty thousand people dedicated to keeping the route network up and running. They are organized in geographic area units called 'Binh Trams.' Each Binh Tram has the necessary transportation, engineering, and "AAA" (meaning anti-aircraft) battalions to defend itself and keep traffic flowing in its sector."

"AAA?" Skip was all ears now.

"Yeah, mostly ZPU and 23 mm, but we're getting reports that after the bombing halt, the North Vietnamese are started moving bigger stuff down there as well."

"How are they deployed?"

"Mostly on high ground, looking down on the roads. There's one place that's particularly bad, though," Tom said, pointing at a place on the map, "and that's here, at Tchepone. This is a place you want to stay away from if you can. They have AAA deployed all around it. We've already lost a couple of birds there."

"What about FACs?"

"There are O-2s working in Laos, but it's hard for them to see anything because they have to stay above the AAA fire. Otherwise, they'd be sitting ducks, as slow as they fly. Most of the time, you will be working with Misty FACS. The area between the Mu Gia Pass and the tri-border region, which is called 'Steel Tiger,' by the way, is their area of responsibility, now that they are no longer working in Route Pack One."

Skip smiled to himself. Mistys! What is it about those guys? You can't get away from them no matter what. He thought back to his encounter with the ZPU site in Route Pack One, and the special weapons drop near Dong Hoi. A Misty FAC had been there both times, circling the fight, egging him on. After those two missions, flying in Laos should be a piece of cake. How tough can it be?

Tom seemed to read his mind. "One thing you should know. If you get shot down over Laos, all bets are off. It's a nasty place, with North Vietnamese Army troops, Laotian guerillas, and God knows who else, running around everywhere. And they all share something in common: they hate American aircrews. Chances are, if you get captured, they'll kill you on the spot. It's much simpler that way, because they don't have to haul you all the way up to North Vietnam to turn you in. Besides, they enjoy killing 'Yankee Air Pirates.'"

For a second, Skip felt a cold chill, and the small hairs on the back of his neck stood up. "Guess I'll have to watch my ass over there, huh?"

"You got that right."

Boris was waiting for him when he walked out of the briefing room. "Hey Skip, will you be ready to fly tomorrow?" For a change, there was no sarcasm in his voice.

"Sure, why not?"

"Okay, 0900 takeoff. You'll be leading a four ship on a strike mission in Laos. Oh, and by the way, I'm sending Slick and Willie along to keep you out of trouble, just in case you forgot how to fly while you were back in the States getting your ashes hauled."

"J.O.G.F.D.A.O," Skip replied. This was an acronym the squadron liked to use in situations like this. It stood for "just one good fucking deal after another."

"Whatever."

*   *   *   *

Skip and his flight took off, made a wide, climbing turn to the northwest, and headed toward the Laotian border. It was a typical day for the dry season. Only a few small, puffy clouds floating high above the Central Highlands marred an otherwise perfectly blue sky. The target was less than thirty minutes away. The mission was simple: four aircraft with sixteen bombs to destroy a section of road forty miles south of Tchepone. Once they arrived, it would take no more than fifteen minutes to do the job. LZ prep, Skip thought; this is nothing but an LZ prep mission. Only this time, we'll be trashing a road instead of flattening trees.

They entered Laos sixty miles north of the tri-border area and proceeded along the main road leading to Tchepone. Skip decided that the terrain didn't look all that different from South Vietnam—lush tropical forests, rolling hills, and winding rivers. It appeared peaceful enough, although he hadn't forgotten Tom's briefing about the AAA sites that lay hidden along the road. But they were flying at twenty thousand feet, so they were safe, at least for the moment.

The rules of engagement in Laos were different. Low-level attacks were discouraged, and the goal was to remain above five thousand feet at all times. Dive-bomb passes tended to be steep, with high-release altitudes, usually around 4,500 feet. To minimize exposure to ground fire, flights were encouraged to drop all their bombs on the first pass, whenever possible. The pilots referred to this tactic as, "one pass and haul ass." It made sense, but he wondered if all those precautions were necessary, just to dig a few holes in a dirt road in the middle of nowhere.

The FAC was in an O-2, holding well off to the side of the road at eight thousand feet. But there was no need to mark the target, it was well-defined. The section they wanted to render impassable lay at the bottom of a long descending hill where trucks forded a small river. They would cut the road on both sides of the ford as well as at the point where the trucks actually crossed the water. That should do the trick.

They were over the target now, circling it like a big, lazy wagon wheel. Skip decided to do it by the book. Each attacker would roll in from a different direction, just to keep everyone on the ground off balance. He doubted if there actually was anybody on the ground to keep off balance, but that was what he was going to do anyway.

"Okay Icon flight, set them up hot," he said. "We'll drop in pairs and release at 4,500 feet." Checking his switches one last time, he rolled in on the first pass.

Bravo Foxtrot Delta, he thought. It was another of the squadron's favorite acronyms. It stood for "Big Fucking Deal."

It was over in twelve minutes. Twelve minutes and eighteen seconds, to be exact. The FAC eased over the target at eight thousand feet and surveyed the damage through a pair of binoculars. "Good job Icon flight," he announced. "That should put them out of business for awhile."

Skip wasn't so sure. All he could see was a mess of roiling brown smoke and mud.

The flight returned to Phu Cat and landed. They had only been gone an hour and fifteen minutes.

Skip stomped into operations and tossed his parachute and helmet down in disgust. Slick and the others were close behind. "Attention everybody," he said in a loud voice. "I am pleased to announce that today my fearless flight created sixteen…that's right…sixteen potholes today, without a single casualty, how about that?" Some of the pilots laughed.

Slick sighed and rolled his eyes in exasperation. "I keep telling you man, it's not always like that. There's a lot of bad shit in Laos. I mean, guys are getting hosed down there almost every day."

"Maybe so, but as far as I can see, this whole operation should have a different code name. It should be called Commando Crock of Shit, not Commando Hunt."

Slick shrugged his shoulders, and walked away.

*   *   *   *

No one was looking forward to the Christmas holidays, and then something incredible happened. The Bob Hope USO Christmas show came to town. Rumors that the show might visit Phu Cat had been circulating for days. Finally the wing commander made it official. Bob Hope would perform with a bevy of starlets, comedians, singers, and dancers at eleven AM on Christmas Day. Best of all, the main attraction would be movie star Joey Heatherton. She was everybody's sweetheart. Everyone was in love with her. Even Skip admitted that although Christy was still his main lady, he wouldn't turn Joey Heatherton away if she showed up at his door. The thought that she would be seen live and in person at Phu Cat Air Base raised morale on the base to an unprecedented high. It seemed almost too good to be true.

A week before Christmas, President Johnson announced a twenty-four-hour bombing halt, starting at noon on Christmas Eve. This was even better for the troops. Only a handful of them would be needed to launch aircraft and perform other duties the morning of the show. Skip walked into operations the afternoon of Christmas Eve. Flying was finished for the day, and the building was quiet. Boris was standing by the ops counter staring morosely at the flight schedule for the next day. As expected, the board was blank for the morning, except for one flight, a two-ship flight with an 11:30 takeoff. Boris had already written his own name on the board as the flight leader. The other name was blank.

"What's going on?" Skip asked cheerfully.

Boris shook his head sadly. "The White House wants the first bombs to start falling precisely at noon. To make a point…you know, no more mister nice guy."

"So, what's the problem?"

"The problem is, to do that, I have to schedule at least one flight for an 11:30 takeoff, right in the middle of the Bob Hope show. And that means I have to screw somebody by putting them on the schedule. The question is, who?"

Skip laughed. "Boris, Boris, no wonder we're winning the Cold War. You Russians turn everything you do into a big friggin' drama."

"I'm not Russian," Boris observed, "my parents were born in the Ukraine."

"Whatever. Look, it's real simple. All you have to do is pick the guy in the squadron you dislike the most, the guy you always take great pleasure in shafting."

"That would be you, of course."

"There you go. Now wasn't that easy? Put my name on the schedule. I'll fly with you tomorrow."

Boris looked doubtful. "Are you serious?"

"Of course I am. What do I need to see the Bob Hope show for? I already screwed Joey Heatherton when I was in California waiting to ferry that bird over here. That's why I was late. Let someone else have a chance, although I have to admit that I am a very tough act to follow."

Boris snorted derisively. "Yeah right. And I have Sophia Loren waiting for me back in the hooch."

"The only thing you have waiting for you is Madam Palm and her five daughters. Meanwhile, I'm going downstairs to do my laundry. Afterwards I will be at the bar waiting for you to buy me a drink, or even two."

Boris started to say something sarcastic but changed his mind and merely grunted.

At precisely eleven o'clock on Christmas Day, Les Brown and his Band of Renown began to play, as Bob Hope walked onto the stage with the self-assured swagger of an old song-and-dance man. He was wearing a golf hat and a pair of fatigues, with an oversized patch on his breast that said "United States Air Force." His ever-present golf club was in his right hand. Behind him, the supporting cast of men and women stood swaying and clapping to the music, ready to start the show. The women were young and beautiful. Most of them were starlets and winners of beauty contests. They were an eyeful, clad in short skirts and calf-high boots. The audience, an undulating sea of bodies packed closely together, went wild, whistling, cheering, and stomping their feet in anticipation.

Less than a mile away, Skip walked around his aircraft, preparing for the mission. He could hear the roar of the crowd and tried to imagine what they were seeing. Something good, that was for sure. Probably the girls in the chorus line. He smiled as he examined the bombs he would be dropping. Each had been painted with decorative Christmas messages, mostly addressed to Ho Chi Min. The artwork was quite good, although the messages were grossly obscene. They left no doubt about how the boys in the ammo dump felt about Ho Chi Min, the Viet Cong, and the war in general.

The parking ramp had been peaceful until Boris and Skip started their engines. Now the distant sounds of the show were gone, replaced by the persistent whine of the ground power equipment. Skip wondered what was happening at the show. He felt like a child who had been sent to bed early, so the adults could participate in some joyous mystery. Suddenly, he remembered the radio compass, or "bird dog" as it was called. It was a crude piece of navigation equipment of World War II vintage, but it could receive commercial radio stations just fine, so why not Armed Forces Radio? He turned the power switch and began to crank the frequency dial. The needle pointed sharply to his left and the station came in loud and clear. Bob Hope and Rosey Grier, the professional football player, were doing a comedy skit about athletes. He could hear the crowd laughing uproariously. He could also hear the sound of their idling engines in the background.

As they taxied out to the runway, the pace of the show began to pick up. The band was playing a rocking song from the Beatles, and it was obvious from the steady clapping and chanting by the audience that it was a dance number. The sound of their engines was louder now as they passed abreast the site of the show. They arrived in the arming area at 11:25. Five minutes to go. The arming crew began to scurry around the aircraft pulling the arming wires from the bombs and cocking the cannons. The crowd at the show fell silent. Something was about to happen.

Joey Heatherton began to sing "Silent Night." Her voice was sweet and pure, like the sound of an angel. He had no idea she could sing like that. In his mind's eye, he could picture her standing in front of the rapt audience, her long blond hair cascading over her shoulders, her eyes bright and shining. Skip felt a lump in his throat. Suddenly, he felt bad about the smart-ass comment he made yesterday about screwing her in California. It was just a joke, of course, and she would never know he said it. Still, it seemed so inappropriate, so wrong, right now.

The arming crew stepped smartly in front of the aircraft, signaling that they were ready to go. Boris closed his canopy and called for takeoff clearance. Joey Heatherton was still singing as they taxied onto the runway. He lined up on his leader and waited for the signal to run up his engine. Boris hesitated. Skip looked at him quizzically, and Boris shook his head. He's listening to the show too, Skip thought, and he doesn't want to spoil the ending. The final words drifted over the hot, cloying air and hung there as the audience listened in rapt silence. No one was in Phu Cat anymore. Everyone was at home, with families or somewhere else. "Sleep in heavenly peace, sleep in heavenly peace."

When the song was over, the audience began to applaud, quietly at first, then with enthusiasm. "Joey Heatherton, folks," Bob Hope said. "How about that?" Suddenly, his voice was drowned out by the steady roar of two jet engines followed by the resounding crack of their afterburners. He took an elaborate swing with his golf club, the head swooping gracefully toward the departing aircraft, as if urging them off the runway. "Go get 'em boys," he said. The audience cheered loudly.

Skip was still hanging tight in formation as they turned out of traffic. So much for peace on earth, goodwill toward men, he thought. It's time to go kick some ass.

*   *   *   *

"I've always wanted to be a Misty FAC," Skip heard himself say. The words just popped out, as if another person had spoken them. The minute they did, he wanted to reel them back into his mouth like a balloon over a cartoon character and pretend he hadn't spoken. But it was too late. Colonel Rosie finished his beer and set it on the bar. "I had no idea you wanted to be a Misty. It's a great idea, though. After a few missions with them, you'll find out who you are. Not who you are exactly, but what you're made of. Besides, it will be a good thing to have in your records, especially if you decide to stay on active duty."

Skip started to mumble something in protest, but Colonel Rosie ignored him and continued talking. "Getting you into the Misty unit will be easy. I'll take care of it personally."

Say something, Skip thought, before it's too late. Tell him you're joking. Tell him you'll think about it. Tell him anything. But he remained silent. He was trapped, and he knew it. It was a matter of pride and ego. Backing out now would make him look like a total dipshit, and he was not about to do that, especially not in front of Colonel Rosie.

Colonel Rosie looked at his watch. "Look at the time. I've got to go." He slapped Skip on the back. "Good luck lad. I'm proud of you!"

Skip was appalled by what just happened. How could he have done such a stupid thing? It was as if some evil being had taken over his body. It was certainly not something he planned to do, that's for sure. Especially after he had promised Christy that he would play it cool and not hang his ass out too much. And he hadn't been drinking all that much either. That was his usual excuse. Twenty-five percent of all Mistys were shot down sometime during their tour. Twenty-five percent! That should give him a clue about how much trouble he was in. He sighed and headed back to his hooch. Maybe Colonel Rosie will forget all about our conversation. Maybe the whole thing will blow over. Somehow he didn't think so.

Skip walked into operations the next morning, expecting the worst. Boris saw him immediately. "Is there something you want to tell me?"

"Something I want to tell you? I don't think so. Like what?"

"Like you are going to be a Misty and won't be flying with us for awhile."

Skip laughed nervously. "Where did you hear that rumor?"

"From our squadron commander. You're being transferred to the Misty detachment, effective tomorrow, by order of Colonel O'Grady. I assume you volunteered, right? The last time I heard they weren't drafting anyone over there."

"Yeah…well, I guess I did, sort of."

"Christ almighty, Skip, you either did or you didn't! It's that simple."

"Okay, I volunteered. Are you happy now?"

Boris nodded and turned back to the scheduling board. "Just as I thought, not only are you a dumb shit, but you have a death wish as well."

"Thanks for those warm words of encouragement, Boris. And good luck to you too."

The Misty operations area was small and crammed with tables and chairs. Maps and target photographs occupied every available inch of wall space. A long table sat along one wall, filled with the radios, telephones, and other equipment needed to conduct the mission.

The ops officer got right down to business. "Your first mission will be tomorrow morning. I want to spend some time with you today, though, explaining what we do." They poured themselves some coffee and sat down at one of the tables.

"The Misty mission is to interdict men and materials headed to South Vietnam along the Ho Chi Minh trail. This means putting in air strikes on trucks, bulldozers, anything that moves, and a lot of things that don't move, like truck parks as well as fuel and ammunition storage areas. Sometimes we are given specific targets to strike, but most of the time we have to find them on our own by doing low-level visual reconnaissance. The aircraft are configured the same for every mission—two 335-gallon fuel tanks, two pods of marking rockets, and 220 rounds loaded in two 20 mm cannons. We try to discourage strafing in Laos, because you're hanging your ass too much when you do that, but the guns are handy for rescue missions and for that occasional target that pops up when there's nobody available to bomb it.

We try to keep two Misty aircraft airborne at all times, one working the southern end of our area and the other at the northern end. The missions normally last about three and a half hours, which means you will be hitting a tanker two or three times during the flight. They could last a lot longer though, if there's a rescue mission going on, or something else real important is happening. In that case, you'll be staying airborne as long as it takes to get the job done. Some missions have lasted more than eight hours."

Skip winced and thought about the misery he felt on his ferry flight from California to Hawaii. No sweat, he thought, I'll probably be too scared to pee anyway.

"It will take at least ten missions for you to get checked out as a fully qualified Misty FAC. You'll fly the first five in the back seat. This will give you a chance to get oriented and figure out what's going on. Then you will start alternating between the front and back seat. In general, the guy in the front marks the targets and controls the air strikes, just like a regular FAC. The guy in the back handles the navigation and radio communications. There's also a strike camera in the back for photographing targets from time to time."

The ops officer paused, collecting his thoughts. "There are rules to follow while flying over Laos, rules designed to increase your longevity. Rule number one is the most important, namely, speed is life. You need to stay fast, 400 to 450 knots, at all times. If you're in the front seat and the airspeed drops below 400 knots, you're going to hear about it from the guy in the back, real fast. That's how we take care of each other. Rule number two is altitude is your friend. We try to stay above 4,500 feet at all times, except when marking a target, working a rescue mission, or checking out something on the ground that merits a closer look. Rule number three is keep the aircraft moving around at all times, especially at lower altitudes. When flying down a road, for example, we try to jink, or change direction every five to seven seconds. That, by the way, is the approximate time of flight of a 37 mm round.

The problem with rule number three is it often conflicts with rules number one and two. Let's say you're ripping down a road doing visual reconnaissance. Every few seconds you bank the aircraft sharply to change direction. The minute you bank, the aircraft loses lift, and you start losing altitude. This violates rule number two. When you pull back on the stick to maintain altitude, you put Gs on the aircraft, and the airspeed starts to bleed off, which violates rule number one. It's a constant battle; moving the aircraft around, while maintaining airspeed and altitude. But it's important. There are a lot of gunners up there who want a piece of you, and you have to do everything you can to spoil their aim."

"Speaking of AAA," Skip said, "how much stuff is there in Laos? We hear a lot of war stories, but the intelligence guys aren't very specific."

"Nobody knows for sure. We've seen everything from small arms stuff up to 100 mm AAA. Hell, a couple of our guys have even reported being fired at by a shoulder-launched, infrared missile. The problem is these 'war stories' you referred to. Strike pilots report 23 mm guns as 37 mm, 37 mm as 57 mm, and so on. We're trying to keep track of the AAA in our area, so we can give everybody an accurate count."

"An accurate count? That's not going to be easy."

"No, it's not, but we have to try. Some of the gunners are very cooperative, and they shoot at everybody that passes by. It's like saying, 'Hey, I'm over here. Don't forget to count me.' Others are a lot smarter, and we have to do something special to coax them out to play."

"Special? Like what?"

"One of our favorite tricks is to approach an area where we think there is a gun site, and circle it once or twice at five thousand feet or so, like we're getting ready to put in an air strike. Sometimes, that's all it takes, and the guys starts firing right away. If he doesn't, we make two marking passes, one after the other. The gunner usually panics after the first pass, because he knows some real heavy shit is about to come down. If we're lucky, he'll open up on us when we roll in on the second pass."

"If you're lucky?" Skip could scarcely believe his ears. "Sounds like a pretty dangerous move to me."

The ops officer looked Skip straight in the eye. "Everything we do here is dangerous," he said finally. "Just keep that in mind, and you'll be all right."

The next morning, Skip walked across the ramp, lugging his flying gear, plus a large book containing maps and target photos, and the twenty-five-pound strike camera. He was wearing a brand new bush hat with a Misty logo on its upturned brim. Walking beside him was a young captain who had already flown sixty missions as a Misty. Skip was about to fly his first mission.

The Misty detachment had no assigned aircraft. They borrowed F-100s from other units. Skip's first flight would be flown in an aircraft from the Jersey Guard. It was a coincidence of course, but he felt that it was a good omen. The crew chief was a man he had gotten to know very well in the past few weeks. He was a good man, and Skip liked him a lot. The crew chief's eyes widened in surprise when he walked up to the aircraft, but he said nothing, at least not right away.

Skip climbed the ladder and settled into the back seat. It took him a few minutes to stow the strike camera and all the extra gear, but finally he managed. The crew chief climbed the ladder and leaned forward to help him strap in. "What the hell are you doing, Major?" he asked. His voice filled with concern. "You're in the Guard, for God's sakes. You'll be going home in a few months, back to your family and your job at Pan Am. You screw around with this stuff, and you'll get shot down, bigger than hell."

Skip looked up and gave him a patronizing smile, not patronizing exactly, but more like an I-know-what-I'm-doing smile. "It's no big deal, Sarge, really. I'm going to be fine."

The engine was running, and they were ready to taxi. Skip looked at the crew chief and gave him vigorous thumbs up. "What does he know?" he thought.

The first five missions were the toughest. Sitting in the back seat during the reconnaissance runs, looking down at the road as the aircraft banked vigorously left and right, he saw nothing. It was hard enough just keep from getting sick, as his head slammed from one side of the canopy to the other, much less spotting truck parks and the like. And taking pictures with the strike camera? Forget about it. It already weighed twenty-five pounds, and when the front seater put a few Gs on the aircraft, it felt like it weighed a hundred pounds or more. At times, he could scarcely lift it, much less take a picture with it. But after fifteen missions or so, he got the hang of it and was thoroughly enjoying himself. He hadn't told Christy about being a Misty yet, but that was okay. He figured what she doesn't know won't hurt her.

On the sixteenth mission he was in the back seat. The front-seater was a young lieutenant named Troy Roberts. Troy was an Air Force Academy graduate, or "zoomie," as they were called. Bright and quick-thinking, he was a damn good pilot. Skip had flown with him before and was happy to fly with him today.

The two of them strode out to the aircraft walking side-by side, looking a little cocky, like the Magnificent Seven, ready to take on the bad guys.

"What do you think?" Skip asked. "Are we gonna kick some ass today?"

"Probably," Troy said.

Skip nodded his head in satisfaction, then shouldered his equipment and climbed up the ladder to the back seat. "It's going to be a helluva mission," he said. "I feel sorry for those poor assholes on the ground over there in Laos."

TCHEPONE, LAOS

April 1, 1969

They took off at three in the afternoon. There would be plenty of time to get back before sundown. After a short flight to the tri-border area, they crossed into Laos and dropped down low to do visual reconnaissance on the trail. There had been very little truck activity the night before. This was evident from the lack of tracks on the road and the absence of muddy ruts where they usually forded small rivers. Not much going on here, Skip thought.

They were approaching Tchepone now, and both pilots tensed, waiting for the inevitable barrage of AAA. It rose up, as if on cue, as they approached the edge of town. It was mostly ZPU and 23 mm, and they barreled past it, made an abrupt ninety-degree right turn, and headed east toward the Mu Ghia Pass. The gunfire subsided quickly, the last rounds floating harmlessly across their wing from the six o'clock position. "Nice try dipshits," Troy cried exultantly. "Better luck next time!"

They followed the trail beyond the pass and into North Vietnam. Troy pulled up sharply, did a wing-over, and headed back the way they came. "All's quiet on the western front," he said.

They were almost back to Tchepone. "Damn," Troy said suddenly, "I never noticed that before."

"What?" Skip said.

"I think there's a truck park down there."

"I didn't see anything."

Troy was climbing now, putting the road behind him. "Let's go away for a minute or two, and then mosey back over there, like we're just screwing around. When we get back over the road I'll show what I mean."

Troy crossed back over the road, and rolled into a ninety-degree bank. "There," he said. "Look just past the bend in the road on the right side."

"I still don't see anything."

"Damn it, look at the tree tops. They're too symmetrical. There's a net over them with branches tossed on top, to hide the trucks, bigger than hell."

Skip was not entirely convinced, but he decided not to argue. "Okay, big guy, what do you want to do?"

"Let's put an air strike in on it. If I am right, the trucks will be like sitting ducks."

"Okay, but we need to finish the south bound leg of our road recce, and after that, hit a tanker and refuel. Meanwhile, I'll call Hillsboro and see if I can scare up a strike flight to put on the target." "Hillsboro" was the airborne command post that managed the air war in that area of Laos.

"Excellent." Troy was excited.

They were in luck. Four Air Force F-4s were about to take off from Da Nang Air Base and could be diverted to the target. Everything was falling into place.

The F-4 was not the weapon of choice for most Mistys. There were several reasons for this. For one thing, there were very few experienced pilots left who hadn't been to Vietnam by 1969. The Air Force was beginning to train multi-engine pilots to fly the F-4. Most of them had no fighter experience and were being sent directly into combat after training. In many cases, their bombing accuracy was, to put it mildly, atrocious. For another, the F-4 carried a crew of two—a pilot in the front and a navigator in the back. There was something about eight people milling around a target in four aircraft that was not conducive to an efficient operation, especially when things got hairy. Often an F-4 pilot would miss a crucial radio transmission because he was talking to the guy in the back. Nevertheless, if F-4s were all they could get, they would use them.

The F-4s arrived shortly after they returned from refueling. Skip guided them to their position, and then Troy took over to put in the strike. The F-4s circled high and dry and waited for the mark.

Troy rolled in directly over the target. The aircraft was going almost straight down at five hundred knots when he fired the rocket. The crush of the G forces during the pullout caused Skip to black out momentarily, and he vaguely remembered thinking, I hope he pulls this sucker out before he hits the ground. He did, and they passed over the target low and flat, before banking sharply to the left and starting a steep climb.

A ZPU site opened up quickly and with deadly accuracy just as they started to climb.

"Shit!" Troy exclaimed. "Where did he come from?"

"Beats me," Skip said. "Maybe we should take him out first and then put another strike on the truck park."

"It's too late for that. We're already committed."

Skip had an uneasy feeling about what would happen next, but he didn't say so.

The smoke was dead on the target. "That's a good mark Gunfighter 41," Troy said. "Hit my smoke and be advised we took some ZPU fire about two klicks to the west." Klicks was a shortened term for kilometers.

The flight leader acknowledged but did not roll in right away. He hesitated for a minute, maybe ninety seconds, just enough time for the wind to blow the mark away. "Uhh, Misty 51, I've lost the mark. Can you put another one in?"

Troy cursed under his breath and set up for another pass.

The gunner was on them the minute they came in range. But the aircraft was moving too fast and turning too quickly for him to track it. The rounds flew harmlessly behind them. "That's a good mark," Troy said again. "Hit my smoke."

The F-4s made one pass, dropping two bombs apiece. Afterwards, Troy told them to hold high and dry. He wanted to take a look and see if there was indeed a truck park underneath the trees. They flew away and then returned from an entirely new direction, jinking rapidly as they passed over the target at four thousand feet. The gunner was on them the minute they approached, trying gamely to track them through their jinking maneuvers. The tracers were flying dangerously close.

"This guy's good," Skip commented.

"Roger that!"

Troy caught a brief glimpse of a tear in the foliage and the gleam of metal underneath. There were three oily fires blazing nearby. "Bingo!" he cried exultantly. "It's a truck park all right. Let's finish it off."

Let's finish it off and get the hell out of here, Skip thought. I have a feeling that some bad shit is about to happen.

The F-4s made their second pass, and all hell broke loose. The entire target area erupted in a series of secondary explosions. It was obvious that it was a fuel storage facility, as well as a truck park. Fires blazed everywhere, and the trees became engulfed in a blanket of greasy, black smoke.

Troy and Skip were ecstatic. They had hit the jackpot. But in their excitement, they forgot all about the ZPU. That was a big mistake.

The F-4s held high and dry and waited for the bomb damage assessment, or "BDA." The BDA pass was always tricky. To make an accurate assessment, it was necessary to fly lower than usual over the target and to stop jinking for at least a second or two. It was dangerous business. Those who were still alive would be firing with everything they had left, even if it was only small arms.

Troy made a turn wide of the target and got set up for the BDA pass. Skip checked the fuel. "We're getting low on fuel," he said. "We should already be heading to the tanker." Troy agreed. Their approach to the target was flat and too slow. Troy thought about lighting the afterburner but decided not to. The afterburner would make their low fuel situation much worse. Keep jinking, move the aircraft around, he thought. That's the best defense.

The ZPU gunner watched them carefully. Their slow, flat approach made things easy, almost too easy. He came up quickly, bracketing the aircraft with a deadly tattoo of tracers. It was too late to turn back. They were committed. The aircraft plowed through the hail of deadly fire, straight at the target, jinking madly. It was a deadly duel between the aircraft and the gunner. It would be over in seconds, and one of them would prevail. As they crossed over the target, Troy rolled the aircraft abruptly into a ninety-degree bank and held it in this position for a second while he and Skip took a quick count of the damage. Then, he rolled quickly back the other way and started to climbed. The tracers followed them for a few more seconds and abruptly stopped. "Holy shit!" Troy said. It was all he could think of to say. They both breathed a sigh of relief and started to relax.

Skip called the F-4s and gave them the BDA: twelve trucks and a fuel storage area destroyed. It was only a rough estimate of course, but it was close enough. The F-4s departed and turned toward Da Nang. Seriously low on fuel, Troy and Skip turned directly toward the tanker and began to climb. They never made it.

*   *   *   *

The yellow warning light came on as they were passing through five thousand feet. "Engine Oil Overheated," it said. Skip was puzzled. He had never seen this light before in all of his hours in the F-100. What does it mean? He thought back to his training at Luke and Nellis. His mind drew a blank.

"What's that all about?" Troy asked.

"I don't know. Let's open the checklist and find out."

There were many lights on the F-100 warning panel. Some were important, others were not. Sometimes a light would come on for no reason at all. There was no cause for panic. Skip was sure.

He found the emergency procedure section of the checklist and thumbed through it until he found Engine Oil Overheated. "Here it is. I found it."

"What does it say?"

"Step one: Retard the throttle and see if the light goes out." Troy did, and the light remained on.

Skip was still not concerned. "Step two: Check engine RPM and oil pressure. Okay, the RPM is steady as a rock and the oil pressure is uh…uh…" Skip could not believe what he was seeing. The needle on the gauge was dropping slowly in front of his eyes. "Oh fuck! We're losing oil."

"I get the picture," Troy said. "We need to get this puppy on the ground ASAP. Meanwhile, I'm going to get as much altitude as I can, in case we have to punch out or glide the rest of the way home."

"I agree, but hopefully it won't come to that. One of the instructors back at Luke told us that sometimes a jet engine will run for thirty minutes or even an hour without a drop of oil left."

"We'll see," Troy said grimly. He lit the afterburner and started to climb. Skip tuned in the TACAN to the Da Nang station. The needle swung toward it and held steady…085 degrees at eight-five miles. Da Nang was their best bet. Troy turned to a heading of 085 and continued climbing.

The engine ran for five more minutes and then erupted into a series of violent compressor stalls that shook the aircraft so hard that Skip was afraid that the airframe might break apart. The cockpit became engulfed in billows of acrid, gray smoke that burned his eyes and made it difficult to breathe. The noise from compressor stalls was deafening, and they could scarcely hear each other on the intercom. "Shut it down!" Skip screamed. "Shut it down!" But Troy had already retarded the throttle.

The engine wound down quickly, and soon all was quiet in the cockpit. For a few seconds, neither spoke. They were both numb with shock.

"That fucking gunner," Troy said finally. "The son of a bitch hit an oil line when we made that BDA pass."

"Probably so."

"We should have taken him out first, huh? Just like you said."

"Not necessarily. It was a tough call. Anyway, it's done, and we have more important things to worry about."

Skip switched the radio to "Guard" channel, the frequency everyone monitored, regardless of what channel they were on. He paused for a second to collect his thoughts, and then punched the mic button. "Mayday, Mayday, Mayday. This is Misty 51. We're eighty-five miles west of Da Nang at twenty-five thousand feet. We took a hit a few minutes ago and had to shut the engine down. We'll definitely be punching out of the aircraft."

The response was almost instantaneous. "Misty 51, this is Hillsboro. Copy your position. We're contacting search and rescue now. How long before you have to bail out?"

It was a good question. It all depended on the engine, or what was left of it. If the compressor blades were free to "windmill," or turn in the stream of air coming into the intake, it would be able to turn a hydraulic pump and an electrical generator. In that case, they could control the aircraft and ride it down to a comfortable ejection altitude. If not, they would be leaving soon.

"What do you think, Troy?"

"The flight controls are working okay so far. My guess is we have windmill RPM."

"We probably won't make it to Da Nang or any kind of friendly territory, right?"

"No way."

"That's what I think too."

"Hillsboro, this is Misty 51. We'll probably stay with the bird for another ten minutes or so, then eject."

"Understand."

"Misty 51 this is Gunfighter 41. We copy your position and are heading your way." Gunfighter 41 was the F-4 flight they had just controlled. This was good. They needed someone to be there when they punched out, so they could mark their position.

The cockpit was quiet now save for the throbbing hum of an electric motor somewhere in the cockpit. The aircraft was drifting down slowly. It was a peaceful, almost surreal scene. *It's like being in a glider,* Skip thought. He laughed, in spite of the gravity of the situation. *Of course it's like being in a glider, dumb shit. You are in a glider. You have no engine, remember?* He looked around taking stock of the terrain. They were over a range of lush, green mountains that stretched forward as far as he could see. It was rugged, isolated country, with no roads and no villages. Here and there, he could see a few slash and burn areas halfway up the mountainsides. As the name implied, "slash and burn" described patches of land stripped of trees in an attempt to reclaim it for agriculture. *Slash and burn,* he thought. *That means there are people down there.* He wondered if there would be anyone waiting for him when he got on the ground. *He hoped not.*

His thoughts were interrupted by the arrival of the F-4s. Their leader had grossly misjudged the Misty's speed and had his speed brakes out, desperately trying to slow down before he overshot. It was too late. They flashed by with at least fifty knots of overtake and ended up several hundred yards out in front.

"Our rescuers have arrived," Troy said. "Gives you a warm feeling, doesn't it?"

Skip laughed. They still had their sense of humor. That was good.

"Misty 51, this is Hillsboro. Rescue advises the Jolly Greens and Spads launched from Da Nang and are on their way." The Jolly Greens and the Spads, the cavalry was on the way to save the day. They were the good guys, the ones in the white hats. "Jolly Green," as in the Jolly Green Giant, was the call sign of the CH-53 rescue helicopters. The CH-53 was not a state-of-the-art helicopter, but it was sturdy, with two powerful engines that could do the job. The crew consisted of four men—a pilot, copilot, flight engineer, and pararescue man. The flight engineer doubled as a gunner for the .50-caliber machine gun that was mounted in the door. The pararescue man was responsible for operating the winch that hauled the survivor into the helicopter. If necessary, he was prepared to descend to the ground and assist if the survivor was injured or unable to get on the hoist. His was the most dangerous job on the crew.

The "Spads" were the other half of the team, flying the Douglas A-1E Skyraider, a World War II-vintage prop fighter. The Spads job was to escort the helicopters to the rescue area, locate the survivor, and protect the helicopters while they were making the rescue. They were also prepared to "sanitize" the area if the survivor came under attack from enemy forces on the ground. They carried a variety of weapons to do the job, including bombs, rockets, napalm, and a .50-caliber machine gun pod. The A-1E could fly slow at treetop level and stay on the target for hours at a time. It was also susceptible to ground fire.

Skip checked the altimeter. They were passing fifteen thousand feet. "The tops of these mountains are five thousand," he reminded Troy.

"I know. We've gotta punch out pretty soon. Shit! He got us in the fucking oil line. Can you believe that? We really stepped on our weenies this time, didn't we?"

"Yeah we did." He thought about Christy. Would he ever see her again? He pushed the thought out of his mind.

They were all together now, the F-100 and the four F-4s, locked in a slow-moving tableau. The radio was silent. Everyone was waiting to see what would happen next. Troy was still mumbling "shit," over and over again. Suddenly, he was all business. "The flight controls are getting mushy. I think the engine has stopped windmilling. It's time to step over the side."

"I'm ready when you are."

"Okay, don't forget the drill. You eject first. If for some reason the seat doesn't go, I'll initiate the sequence from the front seat, and you will be ejected whether you are ready or not. Take care, buddy. I'll see you on the ground."

"You too. See you on the ground."

Skip looked around the cockpit one last time, making sure that the strike camera was tucked securely under the canopy rail. If that puppy hits me in the head on the way out, it will squash it like a grape, he thought. He pressed the mike button. "Misty 51 is about to eject…Misty 51 is ejecting."

"Here goes," he said to Troy.

He braced himself in the seat, raised both ejection handles, and waited tensely for the canopy to jettison. Nothing happened. What the fuck? He remained in the ejection position uncertain what to do next. Two seconds later, Troy initiated the ejection sequence. The canopy left with a roar, and Skip was crushed unconscious by the rocket seat.

It was Kunsan, Korea, all over again: the sensation of tumbling end-over-end while only partially conscious, the jarring, bone-rattling snap as the chute opened, and snatched him from 250 mph to a dead stop in a fraction of a second, and the eerie silence as he hung suspended two miles above the earth, immersed in a swirling ménage of cockpit debris dancing insanely around him. But the land that lay beneath his feet was not Korea, but Laos, and there would be no little boy running up in wide-eyed wonder to greet him, or a group of friendly villagers to offer him a soft drink. He wondered what was waiting for him when he hit the ground. Death? Serious injury? Capture and torture? He was scared, and it was all his fault. He had promised Christy he wouldn't be a Misty, hadn't he?

Skip snapped out of his dazed, self-reflection. This was no time for self-pity. Things were happening fast. He looked up at his parachute canopy. All the panels were in place. So far so good. He could hear the sound of the F-4s circling somewhere in the distance. He hoped they would be able to keep him in sight. He was descending directly toward the top of one of the many mountains in the area. There was a large clearing down the mountain to his right, but he would never be able to steer the parachute there. The wind was blowing from the wrong direction. Landing on top of the mountain would be okay, though. As far as he could tell, there were no roads leading there. This would make it difficult for potential captors to reach him. The mountain was covered with a dense layer of trees. He had no idea how tall they were, but he had a feeling they were immense. The trees were rushing toward him now, a forbidding, dark green barrier that looked ready to swallow him. He reached across his face, grasped the opposite parachute riser, and crossed his feet. This would help protect his eyes and genitals on impact.

Skip landed on top of a tree with a tearing, splintering crash. For a second or two, he remained standing, engulfed by the top branches, which were holding him upright. He struggled to maintain his balance, reaching around to find a limb strong enough to support him. He wanted to stay where he was and not fall out of the tree. It would be a perfect place to wait for the helicopter, high above the ground, and out of harm's way. But the laws of physics were working against him. His parachute and seat pack, both heavy items, began to fall, and pull him backwards. Frantically, he reached to a nearby branch to resist the fall. But the branch was too fragile and broke off in his hand. Slowly, his upper body began to settle, and he found himself sprawled on his back on a layer of limbs, his legs hooked over a fork near the top of the tree. After a few seconds, the bow of branches he was lying on began to settle, and he found himself hanging upside down, his legs still hooked over the fork. The position was almost comical, like an acrobat, fully attired in flying gear, suspended upside down from a trapeze.

Skip was desperate to stay where he was. With a mighty heave, he tried to pull himself to the sitting position, grabbing anything within grasp for support. But this time it was the legs of his G suit that conspired against him. Their slick, nylon surface began to slide along the smooth bark on the fork. Suddenly they slipped, and the aviator/acrobat was left hanging from the trapeze by only one leg. It was all over, and he knew it. But he gave it one last try. Groaning with a mighty heave, he tried to pull himself up. The second leg slipped free, and he began fall. He plummeted quickly, his legs and arms thrashing wildly, grabbing at anything that might slow his fall. Layer after layer of branches passed, some slowing his descent, but none able to stop him. The final layer was ten feet off the ground. When he broke through it, his head was pointed straight down. He had just enough time to fling one arm above it to cushion the impact. He hit the ground and became very still.

He rose unsteadily to his feet, shocked and dazed. His face and arms were covered with cuts and bloody scratches from his encounter with the tree. His flying suit was ripped in numerous places. He moved his legs and arms gingerly. Nothing seemed sprained or broken. It was a start. Breathing heavily, he looked up. An unbroken green canopy stretched all around him, blocking his view of the sky. This would make it difficult for his rescuers to locate him. The terrain was choked with trees and bushes, all intertwined, as if determined to imprison him. Long vines turned, twisted, and hung from trees everywhere, like large snakes. He wondered if there were snakes around. He hated snakes. There was scarcely a sound in this dark and forbidding place, save for the chattering of a few birds some distance away. The heat and humidity were oppressive. Small insects buzzed hungrily around his sweaty face, eager to taste the blood from the scratches. He wasted no time ridding himself of his parachute and survival gear, stashing them under a large bush. He was still wearing his flying helmet. The visor was broken by the impact of his fall. He started to take it off, but thought better of it. It would protect his head when it was time to egress back through the trees.

Suddenly, there was a loud "crack," as if someone had stepped on a branch. It came from behind him, and not very far away. He spun around, stepped behind a tree, and drew his .38-caliber revolver, training it in the direction of the sound. He held his breath and waited. It was quiet, and he could see nothing moving. It was probably an animal, or perhaps a limb that had fallen from a tree.

He had been on the ground no more than five minutes, but it seemed like he had been there forever. He drew a small radio from his survival vest and turned it on. A comforting buzz came out of the speaker. He began to speak, hoping that someone would hear him. "This is Misty 51 Bravo. I am on the ground and am okay. I repeat…Misty 51 Bravo is on the ground." The "Bravo" signified that he was the second crewmember on the aircraft. Troy's call sign was now Misty 51 Alpha.

Troy came on the radio immediately. "This is Misty 51 Alpha. I'm on the ground too and am okay." Skip was relieved to hear his voice.

The F-4s came on line. "Misty 51, this is Gunfighter 41 flight. We are circling overhead. The rescue force is on its way. An airborne rescue command post will coordinate the effort. His call sign is Crown. We're getting pretty low on fuel now, so our plan is to hit a tanker, then lead the rescue force to your position. That'll take about forty-five minutes. Meanwhile, I suggest you turn off your radios to save the battery. We're gonna get you out of there guys," he added, "Not to worry." Turning off the radio was a good idea, but he wanted to find Troy. Maybe they could get together. It would make the rescue easier. Besides, there was safety in numbers.

"Alpha, this is Bravo," he said guardedly into the radio. "What's your position?"

"In a clearing, to the east of you."

Skip rolled his eyes and looked at the dark canopy of trees above him. Lucky dog, he thought bitterly. "How far away?"

"Not sure…a hundred meters or so…maybe."

"Stay there, I'm going to try and reach you."

"Roger."

He pulled a compass from his vest, raised the sight line, and pointed it to the east. Then, he started walking. Vines and bushes reached out right away and began to tangle his legs. Tree branches slapped against his face, adding more scratches, and making it impossible to see. By the time he walked five yards he was hopelessly ensnared. Frustrated, he pulled out the bayonet knife he carried in a sheaf on his G suit and began hacking methodically to break free. Fifteen minutes later, he stopped. His body was bathed in hot, sticky perspiration. Insects had found every scratch on his body and were feeding on his blood with a frenzy. He had traveled just twenty yards. He decided to give up and return to the small clearing where he had landed. It was better than nothing. He switched on the radio. "I can't get to you. I'm turning back."

"Understand. Let's turn our radios off for awhile. We'll be needing them soon."

"Roger that. I'll talk to you in half an hour."

Skip turned around and began hacking his way back to where he started. He wondered if they would ever see each other again. When he returned, he sat down on a fallen log with his back against a tree. He found the first aid kit in his vest, took out some antiseptic pads, and began rubbing them on cuts and scratches on his leg. The pads weren't very effective, and the bugs scarcely moved aside as he did so, but it gave him something to do.

It took all the willpower he could muster, to wait thirty minutes before turning on the radio. As he waited, he thought about Christy and the kids. Most of all, he thought about the incredibly stupid decisions he had made in his life, and how those decisions had affected his family. What could he have been thinking when he volunteered to be a Misty, or go to Vietnam, for that matter? Look at the pain and suffering he had caused them already. And what would their lives be like if he didn't come back? He couldn't bear to think about it. This was a defining moment in his life. If he can get out of this mess, things will be different. A new, more responsible Skip was waiting in the wings, ready to be born. Thirty minutes finally passed, and he switched on the radio. Troy was already on, trying to call Gunfighter 41 and Crown. Nobody was answering. "What's up Alpha?" he said.

"Beats me. Nobody is answering."

"Let me try. Maybe you're in a dead spot."

"Go ahead."

He called Crown and Gunfighter several times. There was no answer. At one point, he thought he heard the distant sound of engines growing louder, then softer, as if aircraft were circling but never approaching their position. He wasn't sure.

He tried calling again. This time Hillsboro answered. "Misty 51, this is Hillsboro. I can read you loud and clear, and I'm also talking to Crown. I can relay for you."

"That's affirmative. Ask them what's going on. They should be here by now."

"Roger. I...uh...thought they were working your rescap, even as we speak. Let me check."

Hillsboro called back five minutes later. He tried to sound calm, but his voice sounded agitated. "We have a small problem, guys."

"Small problem?" Skip's heart sank.

"The F-4s brought the rescue force to another mountain thirty miles away. They're on the other side of that mountain, looking for you. That's why they can't hear you. Crown advises the force will be there in fifteen minutes."

Skip looked at his watch. It was five thirty. It would be dark in another hour or so. He didn't want to spend the night in Laos. Those who did usually didn't survive. He slumped back against the tree and waited. What else could he do?

Ten minutes later, he heard the distinctive rumble of a prop-driven engine. The sound was getting louder. It was heading toward them. A voice came on the radio, calm and businesslike. "Misty 51, this is Spad 11, how do you read me?"

"Misty 51, loud and clear," Skip and Troy answered, almost simultaneously.

"Roger, I'm about twenty miles west of your position with two A-1s and two Jolly Greens. I should be there in ten minutes."

Skip was on his feet now, the survivor radio glued to his ear. He was energized and excited. This guy knew what he was doing, he could tell. Everything is going to be okay.

"Misty 51 Alpha, what is your location?"

"Alpha is in a clearing, a slash and burn area, a hundred meters from the top."

"Roger, are you injured or unable to get on the hoist for any reason?"

"Negative. No injuries."

"Are any bad guys in the area, or any signs of human activity?"

"Negative. There's nobody around. It's quiet here."

The Spad driver asked Skip the same questions. Skip explained that he was on top of the mountain and under dense foliage that blocked his view of the sky. He started to mention the crack of the limb but decided not to. There was no sense bombing some poor animal into oblivion, just because he was a little nervous.

The two A-1s were circling overhead. He could tell that by the sound of their engines. What next? He was anxious to get started.

"Misty 51 Alpha, I think I have you in sight. Pop a flare for me in ten seconds."

Troy counted to ten slowly and lit the flare.

"Roger, I see the flare. Alpha, we're going to pick you up first. Bravo, we'll locate you and make the pickup after we get Alpha on board. Now, everyone stand by while I go back and get the Jolly Greens."

A wave of panic swept over Skip. Once they rescued Troy, he would be alone, on top of this God-forsaken mountain in Laos. It was bad enough when Troy was nearby, even though they couldn't reach each other. Could they get him on time? Could they even find him under all these trees? He didn't know.

The two A-1s returned, the throbbing roar of their engines blending with the steady "wop, wop, wop" of the helicopter. They were flying in a straight line, on the final run for the pickup. "Misty 51 Alpha, standby to pop smoke on my count." It was a new voice, the voice of the Jolly Green pilot. "Ten, nine, eight, seven, six, five, four, three, two, one."

"Got the smoke in sight."

The chopper was hovering now. He could tell by the sound of the engines. The radio was quiet. Skip waited anxiously. Suddenly, the sound burst into a growl as the pilot advanced the throttles. The sound changed direction and began to fade away.

"Misty 51 Bravo, this is Spad 11. We've got Alpha on board. Now it's your turn."

✳   ✳   ✳   ✳

Skip was alone on the mountain. There was no sign of Spad 11 and the rescue force. He looked around nervously. Long deep shadows slashed through the trees, making a dark and gloomy place seem even more foreboding. The sun was low on the horizon, casting long, dark shadows. It was perceptively cooler. Where was everybody? They were running out of time.

Then he heard it. The sound was unmistakable, a loud metallic, squeal of brakes on a truck or large vehicle. This was no animal or falling branch. He was not alone after all. Adrenalin surged through his body creating a rolling shockwave of numbness. The sound was coming from the west, on the opposite side from where Troy had been. Could there be a road down there? He didn't remember seeing one on his way down in the parachute. He stood perfectly still, facing the direction of the sound, his ears straining to listen. All was quiet for a moment, and then he heard the faint sound of voices. Several people were shouting back and forth in the singsong language he remembered from the Vietnamese civilians who worked on the base. He thought perhaps they were farmers. But farmers arriving in a truck, to climb an isolated mountain at sundown? It was not likely.

The voices seemed to be spreading out and getting closer. How far away were they? He wasn't sure. Two hundred, maybe three hundred meters. It didn't matter. He was in trouble and had to act fast. He put the radio to his lips and called softly. "Spad 11, this is Bravo. I've got a problem."

Spad 11 was just turning back to search for him. He answered immediately. "Roger Bravo. What's your situation?"

"Sounds of a vehicle and people talking, down the mountain about three hundred meters west of my position. I can't see them, but the sound of their voices is getting closer."

"Okay, Bravo, we'll have to find these guys and take them out, or at least sanitize the area. Find yourself a place to hunker down until this is over."

The Spad leader wasted no time. Circling wide over the mountain, his eyes scanned the area Skip described. At first he saw nothing, and then he saw a dull metallic gleam of sunlight bouncing off a flatbed truck. The truck was parked in a clearing at the end of a dirt road. The road climbed the mountain and stopped a few hundred meters from the top. There were six people in all, fanning out from the truck, heading to the other side of the clearing and toward Skip's position. He caught a glimpse of their uniforms, black silk shirts and trousers and conical straw hats. They were carrying AK-47s slung over their shoulders. Viet Cong, he thought, or maybe Laotian guerillas.

He was pretty sure they had seen them flying overhead. If so, he had to move fast. Rolling back quickly, he set up for the attack. He decided to strafe first, to get the guys by the truck, and then sanitize the area with bombs. "Set 'em up hot," he said to his wingman, "we're gonna strafe the troops first." The six guerillas had indeed seen them and were running desperately toward the other side of the clearing. The leader framed them in his gun sight and prepared to fire. Three of them hesitated, as if deciding whether to return fire with their AK-47s. It was a fatal mistake. A burst of strafe cut them down in a hail of bullets. The wingman swooped in seconds later and struck the remainder as they tried to cover the last few yards.

When the Spads finished strafing, they laid a string of bombs with meticulous precision along the tree line and another, closer to Skip's position. On the final pass, the leader fired two rockets into the truck. It disintegrated in a fiery ball of flame, parts flying everywhere. It was over. They had done what they could. It was time to get on with the rescue.

Skip burrowed under a large log and stayed there during the attack. It was hot, sweaty, and uncomfortable there. Bugs and worms were crawling everywhere, even inside his flying suit, but he didn't care. He wasn't about to go outside until it was over. At times the sounds were deafening, especially when they laid the string of bombs closest to his position. His ears were ringing, and he could scarcely hear. The air was filled with acrid smoke and the smell of explosives.

The sounds finally stopped, and Skip crawled cautiously out from under the log. He was caked with dirt and mud, covered with insects. He put the radio to his ear just in time to hear Spad 11 call. "51 Bravo, this is Spad 11. We're ready to make the pickup. I think I know where you are, but I want to make one pass to be sure. Listen to the sound of my engine and give me directions if you need to. When I move over your position, say Bingo, got that?" Skip said he did. He stood in the small clearing and waited. The two A-1s went away, and when they returned, they were coming straight at him. The noise of their engines grew louder, until it grew into a deafening roar. He could no longer hear the radio, but he kept talking into it anyway. "Looking good…keep it coming…keep it coming…turn left ten degrees…that's good…keep it coming."

The A-1s were low, so low that the tips of their props were almost biting into the trees. The prop wash whipped them into frenzy, with branches and leaves falling everywhere. For a second, Skip caught a glimpse of the sky as the trees swayed and gyrated wildly. "Bingo!" he shouted over the radio as they passed. "Bingo!" Then he hunched over, shielding his eyes from the falling debris. The A-1s wasted no time returning with the rescue chopper.

It was up to him now. Because he was unseen to those in the air, he would have to talk the chopper to his position, using his compass and the sound of its engines. It was like a radar approach in bad weather, except there was no radar, and he was his own controller. He had practiced this procedure once during jungle survival school, and the system worked very well. But this was the real thing, and there were no instructors watching and no second chances.

He could hear the chopper approaching. Holding the radio to his ear and the compass in his right hand, he took a quick sighting. He was looking good. But steering a heading of 275 degrees would be even better.

"51 Bravo, this is Jolly Green 11. How do you read?"

"Loud and clear. Turn right to 275 degrees."

"Roger, 275."

"Looking good…keep it coming…turn right five degrees…that's good…keep it coming."

The chopper was almost overhead now. Frantically, he looked for the cable and the jungle penetrator that he would ride when they hoisted him up to the chopper. Where in the hell was it? Suddenly he spotted it. The penetrator, a torpedo shaped object about four feet long, was dragging slowly through the brush. The cable it was attached to had mingled with the vines and was almost invisible. No wonder he hadn't seen it.

He made one last call. "Bravo's got the penetrator in sight." Then he stowed the radio and compass in his survival vest and dashed straight ahead to where the chopper was waiting, unseen above the trees.

The penetrator continued to slither along the ground at the pace of a slow walk. It was obvious that the chopper wasn't hovering. He wondered why. He thought about the men in the truck. What if some of them survived the attack? They would be mad as hell and would most likely head for the chopper. He had to get out of there. When he reached the penetrator, he reached down, unlocked three long, metal blades on its base, and spread them like petals on a flower. These would serve as his chair for the ride. He straddled the blades and snapped a restraining belt around his waist, and then he tugged on the cable vigorously. This was a signal that he was ready to be hoisted aboard.

He was pulled into the air immediately and began to move forward as the chopper accelerated to depart the area. The ride was smooth until he reached the first layer of branches. Just before he collided with them he covered his face with both arms. There was nothing he could do, but ride it out and hope for the best. The branches cut, slashed and scratched at him with a fury as he continued his ascent. The forward motion of the helicopter made things worse. Why didn't he hover, at least until he got on board? It didn't make sense.

He was rising faster now, plowing through the foliage like the bow of a speed boat. A few more seconds, and he would be clear. Then things went wrong.

The penetrator slammed into a large, thick limb, jamming his head into a fork near the trunk. The sound of the chopper's engines changed immediately as the pilot tried to slow down and go into a hover. The hoist operator let the cable go slack, and then reeled it back in quickly, like a fisherman trying to free his hook from an old tire at the bottom of a lake. It didn't work. He tried again. No luck.

Skip was stuck. He wasn't going anywhere. What next? He looked around frantically. To his horror, sharp lines clipped through the foliage directly over his head, chopping branches and leaves as they went. Ground fire! Oh shit! The bullets were not particularly close, he decided. Like as not, the gunner was firing up through the trees toward the sound of the chopper. But that didn't matter. The chopper was his life right now. Kill the chopper, and you might as well kill him.

Within seconds, tracers slashed back down through the trees as the gunner in the chopper returned fire. Meanwhile, chopper's engines roared to life. It was leaving and so was the hoist. Would Skip go with them? That remained to be seen. The cable was pulled taut now, as the limb strained and groaned. He was hunched over the penetrator, his eyes covered, expecting the worse. For a second, he thought he wasn't going to make it. Then, there was a loud "crack," and he was free. Free from the tree, that is, but not from the limb. It remained lodged around his neck, as he continued his ascent. Seconds later, he popped out of the foliage into the fading sunlight. Cautiously, he uncovered his eyes and looked around. The ground fire had stopped. He looked down. He had no idea how high he was, but high enough to scare the hell out of him. Dangling securely in a parachute was one thing, but hanging on to a long metal tube below a bouncing helicopter, that was altogether different. He didn't look down again.

The pararescue man, secured by a harness, leaned out the door, removed the limb from Skip's head, and tossed it away. It was over six feet long. Another pair of hands reached out of the doorway. Together, they spun him around and pulled him into the chopper.

Skip rose to his feet unsteadily. He was a mess, his flying suit shredded and caked with mud, his face and arms covered with bloody cuts and scratches. He saw Troy sitting on a bench along the bulkhead. Troy was grinning, looking relatively unscathed. Skip walked over to him and shook his hand warmly. "Hey Mister Spic-and-Span, where were you when the shit hit the fan?" It was a line from an old joke. They both laughed heartily.

He slumped onto the bench beside Troy, savoring the feeling of being alive and safe. The pararescue man asked him if he required any medical attention. He replied that the only attention he needed was a drink.

"I can't help you there, sir," he said. "But the flight surgeon will probably have some mission whisky waiting, and afterwards, there's always the club."

Skip grinned broadly. Yes, there's always the club.

The chopper was bouncing and weaving, probably from the turbulence. He scarcely noticed. After a few minutes, Troy got up and walked to the door of the cockpit. He returned quickly, shaking his head as if to say, "You're not going to believe this."

Skip walked forward to have a look. The chopper was sitting behind a refueling basket reeled out behind a C-130. The pilot was struggling to get hooked up, as both the basket and the chopper bobbled erratically in the turbulence. He turned and looked at the flight engineer quizzically. He cupped his hand in Skip's ear and shouted, "The mountain we picked you up on was too high for us to hover. The air was too thin. As it was, we had to dump almost all our fuel to make the pickup. We don't have enough left to make it back to Da Nang."

Skip gave him his best "you gotta be shitting me" look. The flight engineer shrugged and spread his arms wide, as if to say, "What can I tell you?"

The rest of the flight was uneventful. They taxied in and stopped in front of rescue operations. As the blades whirled slowly to a stop, two young airmen jumped on board. One was carrying a large video camera on his shoulder, the other held a bank of high-intensity lights. The lights were harsh and blinding. Startled by the intrusion, Skip and Troy stood up and started for the door. Skip mumbled something like it was good to be there. It was all he could think of to say.

A reception committee was waiting for them in front of rescue operations. The man in the center, a lieutenant colonel, was obviously in charge. Suddenly, Skip remembered the card. Did he still have it? He fished through the pockets of his survival vest and finally found it. It was crumpled and sweat-stained after carrying it for eight months. On it was the rescue squadron's logo and the words, "Jolly Green Giants." Underneath, in smaller type, was written, "Good for one free ride." A Jolly Green pilot had given it to him the first time he went to Okinawa for a break. They had gotten drunk together, and Skip had carried it with him ever since, never dreaming that he might need it someday.

Skip walked up to the colonel, saluted, and handed him the card. "Sir, I would like to redeem this." The colonel was startled and, for a minute, didn't know what to say. Hundreds of these cards had been handed out since the war started, but as far he knew, no one had ever asked to redeem one. The crowd broke out in applause and started to cheer. Cameras flashed all around them.

The applause died down. "One more thing," Skip said, jerking his head toward Troy. "Could we possibly include my son on this ticket? You know, like half-fare or something?"

"I think we can work something out. Captain, take these men to the flight surgeon and get them a place to sleep in our hooch. Oh, and by the way, make sure they get new tickets, just in case. You never know."

The flight surgeon at Da Nang checked Skip out and gave him a clean bill of health. "No sprains, concussion, or broken bones," he said. "You should be able to fly in a few days, a week at the most. Meanwhile, your body is going to feel like a bunch of guys worked it over with baseball bats."

Skip thought about the last time he ejected. Been there, done that.

The surgeon wanted both Skip and Troy to spend the night in the hospital for observation, but they vigorously declined. They wanted to treat themselves, which meant, of course, a night of serious drinking. They went to the club for dinner. By the time they finished, every bone in Skip's body was hurting. He could scarcely walk. They went back to the hooch and began drinking with the Jolly Green guys. He was too full of adrenalin to sleep.

They talked until three AM. The copious amount of bourbon he drank had absolutely no effect on the pain, and did not make him sleepy. He decided to go to bed anyway, hoping to get a little rest before the new day started. There was nothing in the closet-size room but a bed, nightstand, and a small dresser. The air was dank, and the walls smelled of mold. Exhausted, he lay back on the thin mattress and prepared to sleep. As he did, fresh pains rose up to torment him. He tried to get comfortable, rolling from one side to the other, then onto his stomach and on his back. The pains followed him wherever he went. After two hours, he gave up. Sleep was impossible. Reluctantly, he rose and went to the common bathroom to take a hot shower. The warm water felt good, especially on the cuts and scratches, but the pain didn't go away. It was going to be a long day, he decided.

PHU CAT AIR BASE

Later the same day

Skip returned to Phu Cat that afternoon. He was a pathetic sight when he walked into operations. He was still wearing his torn, muddy flying suit, although he had cleaned it up somewhat in the shower at Da Nang. The cuts and scratches on his hands and face were plain to see. But it was his posture that was the most compelling. He walked slowly and stiffly, his upper torso bent slightly, putting one foot carefully in front of the other, like an old man. Worse yet, his neck would not move in either direction, so when he was obliged to turn and look at something, he did so with his whole body. Fighter pilots are not known for their sensitivity, but the most jaded of them felt pangs of sympathy for his plight.

Everyone wanted to hear his story about being shot down. He suggested that he would be more than happy to oblige them at happy hour, in exchange for a few drinks, of course. But he had other things to do first. His first stop was to the wing commander's office. He and Troy had been summoned there to brief him on the accident. As far as Colonel Gilbert was concerned, the loss of an aircraft during combat was acceptable. It was part of the cost of waging war after all, but an aircraft accident due to material failure, or even worse, pilot error? That was different. If it was an accident, things would get complicated. An accident board would have to be formed, and there would be a lot of messy paperwork. He didn't have time to worry about such things. He needed to find out how things stood.

Skip and Troy described their encounter with the ZPU and offered their theory about the oil line being hit. They couldn't prove that's what happened, but it was the most plausible explanation. Colonel Gilbert agreed and sent them on their way.

Skip's next stop was to the flight surgeon. "The pain is killing me, Doc," he said. "I hurt all over." The flight surgeon wrote a prescription for a muscle relaxant and a pain killer. "This is heavy-duty stuff, Skip," he said. "Do not...I repeat...do not, drink alcohol while taking this and do not drive or operate heavy machinery."

Skip made a mental note not to drive the squadron jeep for awhile. The part about not drinking alcohol, he shelved for consideration at a later time. No sense rushing into things.

He returned to the hooch just in time for happy hour and fulfilled his promise to tell his story. Before he began, he popped a muscle relaxant and a pain pill in his mouth and washed them down with a bourbon and water. Then he took another of each, for good measure. That should do it, he thought. In less than an hour, the lights went out. First, there was a buzzing in his ears, and the voices around him began to dim. His vision was blurred, and he was slurring his words. The images around him began to lose their sharpness and soon faded into a collage of light and shadows. A hand grasped him firmly by the elbow. "It's time to call it a day, boss," Willie said. Together, they turned and walked unsteadily toward his hooch.

The pilots watched him walk away with amusement. "Boy, has he got a load on!" someone said.

"I don't blame him," said another. "I'd tie one on too if I were in his shoes." Everyone laughed, and returned to their drinking.

Skip undressed and lay on top of his bed. It was much more comfortable than the one in Da Nang. The muscle relaxant was really kicking in now. He felt as if all the flesh on his body was oozing off his frame and into large blobs on the mattress. Getting up was no longer an option. He hadn't talked to Christy yet. His friend in the command post was trying to book a call for him. It probably won't go through tonight, he had said, maybe tomorrow morning. This was good. He had no idea what he was going to say to her. How much did she know? If she knew that he was a Misty, she would be madder than hell. Maybe the grapevine hadn't picked up on that news.

For some reason, he thought about his old mentor on matters involving women, Captain "Fletch" Fletcher. What would he advise in a situation like this? Deny everything, he would say...deny, deny, deny. It was all too much to think about right now. When she calls, he'll play it by ear.

His eyes were unable to focus, and his vision was reduced to two tiny pinholes of light. He felt himself falling into a black void, and he went to sleep.

The light beside his bed snapped on at midnight. Startled, he tried to open his eyes, but it wasn't easy. He was in a foggy, confused state. Everything was blurred and unsteady. Willie was standing over him, his head hanging suspended like a bloated balloon. "It's your wife," he said. His voice sounded strange and hollow, like he was talking in a barrel.

Skip reached for the phone, but it seemed impossibly far away. Willie put it in his hand and positioned it over his ear.

"Hullo?" he said groggily.

"Honey, it's me. Oh my God, are you all right? They told me what happened."

"Yes, I'm all right. I'm fine."

"Why does your voice sound so funny?"

"I took a muscle relaxant. I'm pretty sore. You remember how it was after the accident back in Misawa, don't you?"

She did indeed. First there were the pain pills, and then all the things that happened afterwards, things she didn't want to think about right now. "What happened to you, anyway?"

It was the moment of truth, and he knew it. His mind was alert, and his voice came out steady. "No big deal. I was in the back seat of the two-seater, checking out some new guy, got crosswise with a AAA site...and we lost."

There was a slight pause, then Christy continued. "What did the doctor say?"

"He said I'm fine, no broken bones or anything. I have a lot of cuts and scratches, though. But they'll heal soon enough."

There was another pause, this time much longer. "Are you still there?" Skip asked finally.

"Yes honey, I am. Listen, we don't have much time to talk, and I know my timing is lousy, but there's something I have to tell you."

Skip was finally awake, and he could here the edge of anxiety in her voice. "Is everyone all right? What's wrong?"

"Oh we're all fine. It's just that...well...my principal won't let me take time off to go to Hawaii." She blurted the last part of the sentence out, as if relieved to get it off her chest.

"What? No way! We've been planning this for weeks. How could she do that? More importantly, why did she do that?"

"Why? For one thing, I used all my vacation time during the Thanksgiving holidays, and for another, she felt that having me gone for a week would be too disruptive for the class."

Skip was getting angry. "That's bullshit honey, and you know it. You should tell her that."

"I'm on probation this year, remember? Besides, the war is not all that popular here right now, especially in academic circles. Quite frankly, this whole R&R thing seems like an extravagance to her, an extravagance paid for by the taxpayers."

"But it's just not fair. We…"

Christy cut him off and continued. "Listen sweetie, there is a rumor here that everyone is going to be released from active duty in early June. That's less than three months from now. After that, you will be out of the Air Force, and we can be a family again. Three months, that's not so long to wait is it? For me? I'm worth it, aren't I?"

"I guess it's not," he admitted grudgingly. "Speaking of families, are the kids there? I haven't talked to them in awhile."

"They sure are. I'll…"

A strange voice cut in. "Sorry, I have to cut you off. I have a priority call coming in." There was a loud "click" and the line went dead.

Christy put the phone down. Her hands were shaking, and her eyes were full of tears. The children looked up at her expectantly.

"Are you through talking to Daddy?" Maddie asked. "I want to talk to him."

"So do I," Cam chimed in."

"I'm sorry, honey. Something went wrong with the phone. He's gone"

Maddie began to cry. "But I want to tell him I love him!"

Christy knelt down, gathered them in her arms, and hugged them tight. "Listen dear ones, I am very sure that he knows you love him, and he loves you too. By the time you get out of school for the summer, Daddy will be home, and we will be a family again. Then you can talk to him all you want. Okay?"

"Why are you crying, Mommy?" Cam asked.

"Because I am so glad Daddy's all right," she lied.

She sent the children outside to play. Then she walked into the living room, closed the shades against the bright spring day, and began to sob uncontrollably. He lied to her. He lied to her easily, in a clear, steady voice, without a trace of guilt. He had volunteered to be a Misty two weeks ago and had flown God knows how many missions before he was shot down. Didn't he think she knew that? How could he not?

She paused to consider the impact of all this. How many times had he lied to her in the past? Unwillingly, her mind shot backwards through the tangled road of their life, recalling people…places…the ever-so-slight scent of perfume when he returned from a graduation party at Laredo…Mariko, the hostess at the Bar Interlude. It was a dizzying journey that made her sick to her stomach. She bade herself to stop.

Skip had crossed the line. A precious bond had been broken. Could she ever trust him again? She wasn't sure. She could feel her heart harden. She mourned for their loss.

*   *   *   *

Three days after he talked to Christy, Skip was back in the air. Flying was awkward at first, especially with all his aches and pains, but he felt no fear or anxiety. It was business as usual.

The future was clear enough. It was already approaching mid-April. By the time he finished his Misty tour, it would be almost time to go home. He wasn't sorry to go. Flying combat in Vietnam had been a challenge, and he didn't regret the experience. He was sure he was a better man for it. But he had pushed the envelope more than once since he arrived, and as Bob Lewis liked to say, "Never tug on Superman's cape."

There was another reason he was anxious to go home. He had lied to Christy big-time about not being a Misty, and quite frankly, he was shocked at how easy it had been. But he wasn't sure that he had convinced her, and if he hadn't, he had some fences to mend at home. He loved her far too much to risk losing her. He would make it up to her when he got back. Perhaps they would take a long vacation before he returned to Pan Am. God knows they both needed one.

*   *   *   *

As usual, things didn't work as planned. It all started on his sixth mission. It had been a particularly long one, over six hours by the time they landed. An F-4 had been shot down, and the crew had landed within a hundred yards of a AAA site. The Misty was part of the rescue force. After the three hours, Skip noticed a tingling in his right leg that seemed to be spreading, but he paid no attention to it. He was too busy. By the end of the flight, his leg was numb, and he couldn't move it. The back-seater flew the aircraft home and landed it. It was no big deal. Back-seaters often landed the aircraft after a Misty mission, just for the fun of it. The same thing happened on the next mission, and on the two after that. There was definitely a problem. It was time to see the flight surgeon.

The flight surgeon had been mobilized with the New Jersey Guard. Skip knew and trusted him. He studied Skip's X-rays for a few minutes and then sat down at his desk. Skip waited impatiently.

"Okay Skip, you have two herniated disks in your lower back at L2 and L3. I don't know if that happened during your recent ejection, or when you punched out the previous time. Those rockets seats do a great job saving lives, but they usually trash the spine."

"Does that mean I'm going to be grounded?" Skip asked anxiously. He was afraid he might lose his job with Pan Am.

"Not at all, it's just something you'll have to live with, although it may become a problem when you get older."

Skip relaxed visibly and let himself exhale. "Great, then I guess I can continue flying. I assume the numbness will eventually go away, right?"

The flight surgeon leaned over his desk and began to talk in an earnest, almost pleading voice. "Look, there is a greater issue here, something we are all wondering about...me...your friends in the Guard...and probably your family too. Why are you doing this? Why are you hanging your ass out like this every day? Surely, you realize that we are not going to win this war, and that it will go down in history as one of our nation's more notable failures. It doesn't take a pot-smoking, long-hair hippie to see that. I'm certainly not one, but I can see that clearly. Is all this worth dying for? Leaving your wife a widow, to raise your children alone, or with another man?"

Skip said nothing. He was at loss for words.

The doctor sighed and sat up straight. He had made a decision. "Okay, here's the deal. As a doctor, I can tell you with certainty that those long Misty missions are aggravating your condition. I'm not sure flying shorter missions will be any better, but I'm willing to take a chance. I'm going to release you for flying on the condition that you return to your squadron to fly regular strike missions. Fair enough?"

Skip started to protest and then changed his mind. The flight surgeon was doing him a favor and maybe even saving his life. "Fair enough, Doc," he said. "And...thanks for everything."

He returned to his squadron and flew for fifteen straight days, sometimes two missions a day. There were no problems. When it was over, Boris took him off the schedule. "Get out of here," he said. "I'll see you in three days."

Early the next morning, he stood in front of base operations, carrying a change of clothes in a small bag. The sun was already well above the horizon, and he could feel the heat from the moist, cloying air. It was going to be a scorcher today, for sure. There was usually a pilot or two to go along with him on such trips. But not today. He wondered where he would end up by day's end.

His thoughts were interrupted by the C-141 transport turning into the ramp in front of him, its four engines whining softly as the aircraft prepared to stop. This might work. He turned and walked into operations. "Where's that C-141 from?" he asked. "Okinawa," the sergeant said, barely looking up from the counter. "But you can't get on it. It's carrying hazardous cargo." Skip turned around disgustedly and walked back outside, his plans thwarted for the moment.

The aircraft commander from the C-141 was walking away from the aircraft, heading straight toward him. He was a young first lieutenant, "bright eyed and bushy tailed," as his father used to say.

"Good morning, Lieutenant," Skip said, as the young man approached.

"Good morning, Major, how's the war going?"

"We're still winning, as far as I know. They haven't killed me yet, anyway."

The lieutenant laughed. "That's always a good sign." He looked so young, twenty-four or twenty-five at best, half the age of airline captains flying the same size aircraft and making a third of their salary.

"Heading back to Okinawa?" Skip asked cautiously.

"Yep, soon as we refuel and take on some cargo. How about you? Where are you headed?"

"Okinawa...I'm going on...umm...official business. A classified mission actually."

"Great! Why don't you ride along with us? We'll be launching in about an hour."

Bingo! Skip thought. He sighed deeply. "I wish I could, but they say I can't because you're going to carry some kind of hazardous cargo."

"Who told you that?"

"The sergeant in operations."

The lieutenant snorted in disgust. "Come with me, I'll get this sorted out."

The two of them burst in the door, striding side by side, like two gunfighters ready for the shootout at OK Corral. The lieutenant's face was set with determination. He was about to show this fighter pilot that he wasn't the only one who knew something about combat.

The sergeant watched them warily, sensing trouble. The lieutenant approached him looking confident, almost casual. "Good morning, Sarge. The major here will be returning with us. We just got the word from the command post at Kadena. He has some business there, a classified mission of some kind, but they wouldn't tell me what it's all about."

Skip smiled to himself. *This was my kind of guy. Start out with a lie, prefera-bly one that is plausible and impossible to verify, and then launch the attack.* He waited to see what would happen next.

The sergeant shook his head vigorously. "Sorry sir, no can do. We're loading some Class A hazardous cargo on your aircraft. According to regulations we can't…"

The lieutenant leaned forward and affixed him with a steely-eyed gaze. Although he didn't raise his voice, his words took on a hard edge. "Listen Ser-geant, I don't give a shit if you're loading a baby hippopotamus for the San Diego Zoo, the major is going with us. Now, put him on the goddamn passenger mani-fest."

The sergeant sighed resignedly. He'd fought this battle many times and had always lost. He reached for the manifest. "May I see a copy of your orders, sir?"

Like the other pilots in the squadron, Skip always carried several types of orders in his pocket when he was about to escape for rest and relaxation. He had orders that covered every occasion—leave, TDY, R&R, even training. Most were outdated, bogus, or otherwise flawed, but they almost always worked. But this was a special situation. The lieutenant had mentioned a classified mission. He decided to pull out the big dog, his "Combat Fox" orders.

Operation Combat Fox was the mission that had sent Skip and the other Guard pilots to Vietnam in the first place. The orders were intentionally vague, stating simply that the bearer was authorized to travel wherever and whenever necessary to accomplish a classified mission. It was, as some people pointed out, a license to steal. Of course his orders had expired when he returned to Myrtle Beach to sign in. But there was no way the sergeant could know that.

The sergeant glanced at the orders, his eyes widening slightly at the vague and sweeping authority it seemed to grant, and then handed them back. "Have a good trip, sir."

"Thank you, Sergeant," the lieutenant said pleasantly. The two of them turned and walked out.

"Not bad," Skip said, as they walked toward the aircraft. "You have the mak-ings of a good fighter pilot."

"Don't I wish. But there's no way. Once a trash hauler, always a trash hauler I guess."

"There are lots of ways to be a fighter pilot," Skip observed. "It's a state of mind more than anything else."

"You ought to know. By the way, I assume you really are on a classified mis-sion."

Skip grinned. "And I assume that you really did get a call from the command post in Kadena about my mission."

The lieutenant laughed heartily. "Touché!" The two of them turned and climbed aboard the aircraft.

Skip settled in comfortably on the bench seat behind the crew. Now, he knew where he would end up tonight. The adventure was about to begin. Someday he would look back on this moment and wish he had never left Phu Cat.

KADENA AIR BASE

Okinawa, Japan
April 21, 1969

It was five o'clock at the officers' club, and people were trickling in for happy hour. Soon the room was filled with the buzz of people in lively conversation. The shades were drawn, and the lights turned down, setting the stage for the evening's activities. Skip was on his fourth double-vodka martini and feeling no pain, although he didn't feel drunk. The bartender eyed him warily, noting the camouflaged name tag and insignia on his flying suit. Visitors from Vietnam tended to get carried away, a practice that was looked down on but difficult to prevent. After all, they were fighting a war and were entitled to let their hair down sometimes. He decided Skip looked harmless enough and moved down the bar to serve another customer.

Skip ordered another drink and looked around the room moodily. It was crowded with people, mostly men, although here and there he saw a woman who looked like somebody's wife. He wondered what Christy was doing right now. Just getting up, he imagined, getting ready for school. She was always an early riser. He missed her so much. Damn her principal! They would have had so much fun in Hawaii. It didn't seem right.

He was jarred back to reality by a hand that grabbed his arm with a strong, friendly grip. "Skip! What the hell are you doing here?" He turned to face a large, stocky man, blond curly hair, sharp nose, and piercing blue eyes. He was wearing a tropical shirt with a wild pattern of flowers in red and green and a pair of tan slacks. His face looked familiar, but he couldn't place him.

"It's me, Gomo...Gomo Green, from Misawa."

Of course! He remembered him now, an easy-going, fun-loving guy who was always getting into trouble for one thing or another. The guys in the 531st used to call him the "married bachelor" because of his penchant for partying downtown and running with the single crowd, even though he had a wife living on base. He always liked Gomo.

"So, what's the deal, Skip? The last time I heard you were living in New York, flying with Pan Am. How did you end up here, sitting at the bar wearing that smelly flight suit?"

Skip laughed. "It's a long story. I got called up with the Jersey Guard during the Pueblo crisis. One thing led to another, and the next thing you know, I'm flying Huns in Vietnam, at Phu Cat, to be exact."

Gomo shook his head sympathetically. "Joining the Guard, that was your first mistake."

"I take it you're no longer on active duty."

"You got that right. I got out in '65, just after I finished a tour at Bien Hoa. Carol had been on my ass for a long time about the shitty lifestyle, long TDYs, and low pay, so I figure screw it, I'll try something else. I fly for Continental now, based in Denver. It's boring work, but everybody's happy, and that's what counts."

"So what are you doing here at the club, slumming with the likes of me?"

"I come here every time I'm in town. I bring the flight attendants, sit them down at a table, and watch all the guys go into a feeding frenzy. It's like chumming for sharks."

Skip smiled indulgently and shook his head. "Same old Gomo."

"Which reminds me, the girls sent me over to get you. Several of them want your body."

"This I seriously doubt."

"Oh but they will, trust me. Especially after I work my special magic."

Skip didn't want to go at first. He felt shy and awkward, not to mention slightly drunk. But Gomo's cheerfulness and irascible humor were infectious, and Skip allowed himself to be led away from the bar. This could be fun, he thought.

There were five women at the table, each attractive in a different way, two blondes, two brunettes, and a redhead. They ranged in age from mid-twenties to mid-thirties. Their hair was cut at different lengths and in different styles. Everyone was dressed casually in pastel-colored blouses and beige or khaki slacks. It was the finest looking group of women a man could expect to find under the circumstances. Skip could see what Gomo meant about starting a feeding frenzy.

He stood uneasily at the head of the table as Gomo gave him a long, flowery introduction. Gomo proclaimed him as a scholar, a gentleman, and the world's greatest fighter pilot, next to him, of course. The women listened to all this with looks of amusement. They had obviously heard this speech many times before. A space was cleared, and Skip was given a chair next to Gomo.

Everyone was friendly, and no one seemed to mind the intrusion. The women introduced themselves, going around the table one by one. At last, he turned to meet the one sitting to his right. When he looked into her frank, appraising eyes, he was speechless. She was beautiful. For a moment, he could think of nothing to say. He had the feeling something important was about to happen in his life, and whatever it was, he was absolutely powerless to stop it.

Her long, blond hair hung simply to her shoulders. Skip fought hard to resist the urge to reach out and touch its silky softness, to run his fingers through it. Her face was oval and exquisitely chiseled with classic Nordic features. She wore little makeup. None was needed. Only a small, lush circle of light rose lipstick framed her teeth, which were white and perfectly straight. She was dressed simply, in a pale blue, oxford-cloth shirt and khaki slacks. The two top buttons of her shirt were unbuttoned, hinting at the firm breasts concealed beneath. A thin gold chain around her neck and simple gold earrings completed the picture. She said her name was Lori Williamson.

Although her beauty was stunning, it was her striking green eyes that captivated him; eyes that seemed to look into the very depths of his mind and soul. At the same time, their corners crinkled slightly with amusement, as if she relished the thought of toying with this clumsy oaf sitting next to her, in a wrinkled, sweat-stained flying suit.

If Lori was aware of the profound impact she was having on Skip, she didn't show it. "So Skip, what's it like to be a legend in your own time?"

The teasing lilt of her voice disarmed him immediately, and he relaxed. "More like a legend in my own mind," he admitted. It was not an original quip, but they both laughed anyway.

She asked him more questions, wanting to know about the war, his family, and life in general. She listened carefully, moving smoothly from one subject to another, taking care not to lose him along the way. He answered everything, simply and without exaggeration. He found himself explaining in great detail how he had been shot down and nearly captured in Laos and painted a glowing picture of Christy and the kids. When it was over, she had gotten inside his mind effortlessly and, without him realizing it, now knew all she wanted to know about this man named Skip O'Neill.

When it was his turn, he asked about her life. She told Skip she was thirty-four and had been flying for the airlines for thirteen years. She was born and raised in San Francisco, the only daughter of a doctor and an interior decorator, who had dearly wanted her to go to college. She decided to see the world instead and quit school after the first year. But she was tired of flying now and wanted to return to college and study art, or perhaps creative writing. Skip asked her if she was married. She was not. She was away from home too much for that. She scarcely had time for a boyfriend, much less a husband.

She was staring intently at his face now, looking almost pensive. He shifted uncomfortably in his chair. "What are you looking at?"

"Your mustache. You'd be a very handsome man if you didn't have it, the kind of man who could easily sweep a girl off her feet."

He blushed; he didn't know what to say. Was she toying with him, making him feel foolish? Or was she serious? He didn't know.

"Of course, I hear fighter pilots in Vietnam like to wear those handlebar mustaches, like they were in the cavalry fighting Indians in the Wild West. Still…" She left the rest of the sentence hanging tantalizingly in front of him.

Skip started to reply but was interrupted by Gomo. "We're going to dinner in about thirty minutes. You're going to join us, aren't you?"

"I don't know. I…"

"Of course he is," Lori interrupted. "You are, aren't you, Skip?"

"I'll have to get out of this flying suit to go into the dining room."

"Well, I suggest you get your ass in gear, Major. Time's a wasting!"

Skip looked around and realized that other men had joined the table, and by now everyone was paired up. He hesitated. What if he left and…

Lori read his mind. "Don't worry about your chair. I'll take good care of it for you."

"It shows, huh?"

"Yes, but it's sweet, very sweet."

He rose stiffly and walked across the room, trying to look nonchalant and unhurried. As soon as he was outside, he dashed the two blocks to his quarters and bolted through the door, scrambling out of his clothes as he went. Thirty minutes. It was not much time. Five minutes later, he was showered and standing in front of the bathroom mirror, his face fully lathered, including the mustache. He paused for a minute, the razor dangling from his hand. It had taken him a long time to grow this mustache and train it just so, carefully waxing the tips of the handlebars each day. A man who could easily sweep a girl off her feet, that's what she had said. He raised his hand with determination and began to shave.

When it was over, he rushed into the bedroom and searched frantically through his small suitcase, cursing himself for packing so carelessly. He found a long white shirt with lightly embroidered panels on the front, a popular item for men in this part of the world. He put the shirt on, shrugged on a pair of khaki pants, and slipped into a pair of loafers. It was all he had. It would have to do. He turned and raced out the door.

He was back in his seat just twenty-five minutes after he had left. "Excellent timing," Gomo said heartily. "We were just about to eat. Hey! What happened to your moustache?"

"It was getting kind of itchy. It was time for it to go." His voice was strong and confident. He was slowly regaining control of himself.

He turned and looked at Lori. Her eyes softened. Slowly, she reached up and ran her index finger across his upper lip, testing its smoothness. "You certainly know how to respond to subtle hints, don't you?" she whispered.

He returned her gaze steadily and smiled.

"Subtle? You called that subtle?"

This time she was the one who blushed.

Skip scarcely noticed what he ate at dinner. He was too busy thinking about what was yet to come. He knew where this was going. It was only a matter of time.

"The crew bus is outside gang. It's time to go," Gomo said after they finished dessert. The others rose and started for the door, some pausing to pass phone numbers to men who had joined them. Lori rose also but made no effort to leave. The group filed through a wide, double door at the front of the dining room. The last woman to leave paused and glanced back. "Are you coming, Lori?" she asked.

"You go ahead. I'll take a taxi. The good major has offered to buy me an after-dinner drink." The woman nodded without surprise and left.

Lori turned and looked at Skip with her green eyes. "You were going to invite me, weren't you?"

"Yes I was, as a matter of fact."

"Well, that's very kind of you, but I'd rather take a walk. It's stuffy in here, and I ate too much for dinner." She took his arm, and the two of them left the club.

It was a beautiful night. A black-velvet sky full of stars peeked out from behind clouds that hung overhead, like fat, puffy sheep grazing in a peaceful meadow. A full moon had just broken free from the horizon, scattering light in its path, as it began its ascent. The ocean was not far away, and they were treated to soft balmy breezes that tasted vaguely of salt. They turned down a quiet street lined with houses. The lawns and shrubbery were carefully manicured, and the scent of tropical flowers provided an exquisite counterpoint to the salty air. They walked hand in hand, wandering aimlessly down the darkened streets, saying very little, each lost in their own thoughts. It was a journey Skip didn't want to end. But it did, and sooner than he expected. Rounding the corner at the end of one of the streets, he found himself approaching the building where he was staying. What to do now?

They stood in front of the building, their figures cast in pale yellow from the light over the door. She looked at him expectantly. Skip started to speak. "Lori, I…"

She reached up and laid her index finger over his lips, the same finger that had traced the smooth area where his moustache had once been. "Shush," she said. "Invite me in before I chicken out and run away." He put his arm gently around her waist, and together they walked through the main entrance and down the hall to his room.

The room was dark, save for a single lamp left on beside the bed. In the corner, shadows danced around an open suitcase. The hastily tossed clothes strewn around it told the story of his haste to return to her earlier in the evening. But neither of them noticed. They were facing each other now. He was surprised at how tall she was. Although the heels of her shoes were modest, her face was almost even with his. He reached for her and drew her close. "It's been awhile," he said simply.

"That's supposed to be my line," she replied wryly. "But for what it's worth, it's been awhile for me too."

Skip took his hands and burrowed them in her luxurious hair. Then he drew her near and kissed her. Her mouth exuded incredible warmth, with a sweet taste that was impossible to describe. There was no trace of the food and drink she had taken that evening, and he couldn't discern the presence of mouthwash or breath mints. How could that be? They continued to kiss, their bodies pressed tightly together. He could feel her warmth, and she could feel the urgency in his loins. Together, their feet performed an intricate waltz that drew them closer to the bed.

She did not protest as he laid her down. Carefully, he began to undress her, unbuttoning her shirt, and unzipping her slacks, interrupting his task now and then to cover her face with soft kisses. She lay anxious and compliant, raising her body at the appropriate moments so he could remove her clothes. To his relief, he managed to open her bra easily. Her breasts were perfect, just as he had pictured—not too large and not too small but just right. Her nipples were rock solid, standing proudly amidst a sea of excited bumps. He paused to take each one in his mouth. She moaned softly. He traced his fingers along the soft down of her belly and hooked them under the elastic of her panties.

"No," she said suddenly. "Not yet. It's my turn...stand up." He did as he was told. She sat on the side of the bed, unbuttoned his shirt, and took it off. Her hands moved softly across the tangle of cuts and bruises on his chest and looked up at him quizzically. He shrugged. She nodded, remembering his story about being shot down and began to kiss them one by one. His trousers came next, and she took her time unbuckling the belt and drawing the zipper down. They dropped to his ankles, and she held him steady as he stepped out of them. When they were off, she lay back on the bed. "Now," she said.

Skip was beside her in an instant, throbbing with excitement. She was a real blonde. He saw that immediately, as he took off her panties. He slipped a finger into her moist garden and discovered an incredible heat within. As he did, she uttered a throaty groan and pulled him toward her. He mounted her eagerly and then paused, looking down at those green eyes that were now glazed with excitement. For a moment, he felt like the ruler of the universe. Then he plunged into her, and the two of them melted into a single pulsating being.

The sun streamed through the window, forcing Skip to open his eyes. It was almost noon, not that it mattered. He wasn't going anywhere. He rolled over and regarded the tangled sheets beside him. Lori was gone. Nothing remained but a few strands of fine blond hair on the other pillow. He stretched and shuddered with pleasure. He was covered with her scent and could feel her essence on every part of his body. Reluctantly, he rose and walked slowly toward the bathroom, still thinking about last night. He felt surprisingly good, considering all the drinks he had consumed. It was if their lovemaking had purged all the poison from his body, making him whole and pure. He looked around the bathroom and saw no further sign of her, save for a few hairs in the sink. The shower and tub were dry. He decided that she had left shortly after he fell asleep and had taken a shower when she got home. It made sense, because she was scheduled to leave early this morning.

After he showered he stood in the middle of his room, still thinking about Lori. That's when he noticed the note on the bedside table. Curious, he picked it up, sat down on the side of the bed and began to read:

Dearest Skip,

You don't play fair my dear! Last night was not supposed to happen. In fact, I was determined that it would not happen. That's the way it is with me sometimes. Just when I think I am in control, I find out that I am not. One thing though, my moustache theory was right! You did sweep me off my feet, and I want you to know that. Well, that's it. I am leaving, and we will never see each other again. Sad isn't it? But it has to be. But I will never forget last night. Never!

Love and kisses,

Lori

Skip sat on the side of the bed for a long time, thinking about the note. She was right, they would never see each other again, and that was a good thing. But in his heart, he knew he wanted to see her again, wanted to see her so badly that his chest ached. Filled with anguish, his eyes moved restlessly around the room. As they did, he spotted another object on the bedside table that he hadn't noticed before. It was a simple white handkerchief, folded neatly, displaying the monogram "LW." He picked it up and inhaled her scent. Had she forgotten it, or had she left it as a gift, a lasting reminder of her presence? He was certain he knew the answer.

He folded her note carefully and placed it in his pocket along with the handkerchief.

Mandarin, Florida

April 25, 1969

It had been a long day, and everything that could have gone wrong had gone wrong. It began the first thing in the morning, before Christy even had a chance to drink her coffee. Maddie decided she didn't want to go to school and tried hard to convince her mother that she was sick. She was quite a little actress, but Christy wasn't fooled. To make matters worse, Cam announced that he couldn't find his school books, just as they were about to leave. This made an already late departure even later.

Things didn't get any better when she got to school. Her problem children, there were four of them in class, rose up as if on cue and began misbehaving. The war of wills, during which she struggled to maintain control of the class, lasted most of the day. Finally, there were the parent-teacher meetings in the evening. She hated them almost as much as she hated going to the dentist. It was always the same—parents of the good students lined up to find out what they already knew, that their kids were bright and well-behaved, while parents of problem children were conspicuously absent. Why couldn't it be the other way around? Well, the day was almost over, thank God. She had just picked up the kids at the baby-sitter's, and they were in the car, as anxious to get home as she was.

It had been eighteen months since Skip left for the airlines, and later, for Vietnam, and her life had been hard ever since. Sometimes it got to be too much, trying to be a mother, father, teacher, housekeeper, cook, family bookkeeper, and taxi driver, all at the same time. Somehow, she managed. But Skip would be coming home in less than six weeks. Life would be easier then. Her heart still ached when she thought about him. He had pulled a fast one with that Misty thing and almost made her a widow. Could she ever trust him again? She wasn't sure, but she would try. Meanwhile, he was definitely on probation. But that was all talk, and she knew it. The minute he walked through the door her heart, not to mention her body, would melt. She did love him after all. You're a real push-over, she thought, smiling to herself.

Mandarin was a small, sleepy town tucked along the east bank of the St. Johns River. The narrow county road on which she was driving, Mandarin Road, was unusually quiet that evening, as it wound its way through orange groves and passed under stands of cypress trees elegantly festooned with Spanish moss. The sun had morphed into a fiery, red ball and was about to disappear below the horizon, leaving long, dark shadows in its wake. There was a cool breeze blowing from the river, and she had rolled her window halfway down to taste it.

"Mommy, I'm hungry. When are we going to eat?"

"As soon as we get home, honey. I'll fix supper right away."

"Oh, you're always hungry," Cam said from the backseat. "Stop being a crybaby!"

Maddie whirled around in her seat angrily. "I am not a crybaby."

"Are too!"

"Am not!"

"Children, children, enough already. You're giving mommy a headache."

The approaching truck was going way too fast. Christy could see that right away. Also, it was weaving uncertainly, drifting back and forth between the centerline and the edge of the road. She wondered if one of his front tires was going flat, or perhaps his front end was out of alignment. It was a muddy, beat-up, old pickup truck, the kind many of the grove workers drove. She flicked on her lights and eased as far over as she could to let him pass.

Maddie and Cam began to squabble again, and the two of them were wrestling between the front and back seat. As they did, Maddie knocked over Christy's purse, dumping its contents on the floor. Christy took her eyes off the road, distracted by the melee going on beside her. "Madeline Nicole, you stop that right now. Get back in your seat! Cameron, you too!" When she looked up, the truck had changed lanes and was heading straight for her.

The next two seconds passed in dreamlike, slow-motion. She could see everything with dreadful clarity…the mud-spattered grill of the truck, the large crack in its windshield, even the faint outline of the cigar in the driver's mouth.

"Mommy!" Maddie screamed.

The two vehicles collided with a thunderous, metallic roar, and then everything fell silent.

The pain was bad, indescribably bad. The children! Were they all right? Christy tried to turn her head, but it wouldn't move. That's odd. Why won't it move? She decided to turn her whole body, so she could look for them. But that awful thing wouldn't let her. It held her firmly in place. Instinctively, she knew "that awful thing" was the steering column, and it was deep inside her. She could feel bubbles of blood expanding and contracting from her chest cavity. The children! Please God, don't let me die yet! I have to help them. Waves of blackness swept over her.

How long was she out? She had no idea. A Florida state trooper was struggling to open the door, but it was jammed tight. Now, he was reaching through the half-opened window, trying to pry the door lock open.

"Don't move, ma'am. Stay real still. An ambulance is on the way."

She thought she heard the distant wail of a siren, but she wasn't sure.

"It's going to be all right. Stay with me now…you hear? Stay with me!"

But it wasn't going to be all right, and she knew it. She had to tell him about the children. She managed to turn her head toward him and started to speak. But before she could, a foam of blood erupted from her mouth. Her eyes widened with shock and surprise, then became lifeless.

A Duval County deputy sheriff raced up to the car from the other side and froze at the sight of the hair, skull fragments, and brain tissue protruding from the windshield and scattered in streaks across the hood. "Oh sweet Jesus," he said, fighting back waves of nausea.

The truck was upside down, its roof flattened to the dashboard. The deputy and the state trooper approached it cautiously and bent down to look inside. As they did, they were startled by the sightless gaze of the driver, who had been crushed to death. The smell of booze inside the cab was overpowering. The deputy stood up quickly and tried to fight the rage that was welling inside him. "Dirty, rotten son of a bitch," he said, and kicked the side of the truck. "Dirty, rotten son of a bitch…Dirty rotten son of a bitch." Each time he repeated the mantra, he kicked the side of the truck.

"Did you know this guy?" the trooper asked.

"I knew him," the deputy replied grimly, "he worked over at one of the groves…when he wasn't drunk."

It was the ambulance driver who spotted the small boy lying in a crumpled heap in an orange grove, twenty yards away. Everything about him looked wrong, even from a distance. His hip was rotated ninety degrees from his body, and one leg was crumpled beneath him. He had been thrown clear of the car through an open window and died instantly when his head hit the pavement.

It was dark now, and the accident scene was a carnival of flashing red lights, flares, and floodlights. The air was filled with the sound of crackling radios. Firemen and paramedics wandered through the carnage searching in vain for lives to save.

Phu Cat Air Base

April 26, 1969

Skip was called to Colonel Rosie's office at two in the afternoon. When he arrived, the colonel took him inside, closed the door, and told him the awful truth: that his wife and children were dead, and he would never see them again. He did not believe it at first, but as reality began to sink in, he slumped in his chair shaking his head numbly back and forth in protest, fighting the urge to scream out in agony, waiting for someone to tell him it was all a mistake. But no one did, and soon the ritual of numb denial gave way to a flood of choked sobs. They sat quietly behind the closed door, Skip and Colonel Rosie, waiting for the horror of the thing to present itself fully, so it could be confronted in some rational way. Skip asked a few questions about the accident but scarcely heard the answers. His wife and children were dead. What more was there to say? By midnight he was gone, gathered up by a passing KC-135 tanker redeploying from Thailand to McCoy Air Force Base in Orlando.

The KC-135 pressed straight through to Florida, pausing only to refuel and change crews. For twenty-four hours, Skip sat huddled alone in the back of the aircraft, shivering in the cold cabin air, staring sightlessly out of a small observation window, the same question grinding over and over in his mind. Why had God done this to him? What universal purpose had been served by taking his wife and children away in such a cruel fashion? Outside the window, night turned to day and back to night, all in sync with the steady drone of the aircraft's engines. God chose not to reply.

Christy's brother Bob and his wife were waiting on the ramp when Skip stumbled out of the aircraft and into the bright Florida sunshine, red-eyed and unshaven, like a hermit leaving a cave. They took him away, and together they drove to Jacksonville.

Atlantic City, New Jersey

June 15, 1969

Skip always referred to the first year after his family's death as "the year that never happened." It wasn't that he tried to forget that year; he simply could not remember it. He tried many times, but it was like restoring a shredded photograph, with key pieces missing. There was a funeral in Nebraska; he remembered that well enough. And his family was buried in a small cemetery ten miles from Omaha. Christy's family was at the funeral, of course, and so were his mom and dad. There were others too, blurred images that hugged him, kissed him, murmured words of consolation, or shook his hand awkwardly.

The New Jersey Guard told him to take his time and report to his squadron at Atlantic City not later than June 15th. He arrived the morning of the fifteenth, two hours before a parade that would mark their release from active duty. He didn't want to be in it, but the group commander insisted, in fact gave him a direct order to do so. He was going to be awarded the Silver Star in a special ceremony during the parade. Boris and Slick were to be honored as well. When it was over, Skip walked away, without saying goodbye to anyone, and left the base, the medal still pinned to his uniform. He had a plan. He was going to kill himself.

His suicide could have been quick and easy, using pills or a gun. But he chose a weapon with which he was very familiar. He decided to drink himself to death. He had no idea how long this would take, so he started by renting a small, one-bedroom apartment in Somers Point, near Atlantic City. The name of the apartment complex, appropriately enough, was the Champagne Apartments. He gave the manager one month's rent in advance and signed the rental agreement without reading it. A month should be enough, he thought.

The more he thought about it, the more appealing his plan became. The haze of alcohol would surely ease his pain and suffering, and when death caught up with him, he'd probably not even notice it. After unpacking, he went to the liquor store and bought a case of vodka, along with several gallons of orange juice. He had five hundred dollars left after the purchases. It should be enough to see him through his last month on earth. He put the money in the drawer and got down to business.

It was tough going at first. He vomited a lot, as his body fought against the onslaught of poison. But things smoothed out after awhile, and he managed to stay in a steady state of inebriation, twenty-four hours a day. There was no phone, TV, or radio to distract him from his mission. Most of the time, he lay passed out on the bed. When he was awake, he stumbled from room to room in a drunken stupor, mumbling to himself and tripping over furniture. He was seldom hungry, but when he was, he staggered down the road to a nearby convenience store and bought junk food to sustain himself. The store clerks soon became accustomed to the sight of this wild-eyed, unwashed man who reeked of alcohol.

Skip dreamed about Christy every night. The dream was always the same. In it, she sat in a chair beside his bed, looking at him with sad and accusing eyes. The look on her face told him that she knew everything, about the lies he had told her, and about Lori. "How could you have done this to me?" she seemed to be saying. "How could you?" One night, the dream was so real that he leaped out of bed and threw himself at her feet, sobbing and begging her for forgiveness. But there was no chair beside the bed, and he just tumbled onto the floor, hitting his head on the radiator. This caused a deep gash over his eye, which bled profusely. Somehow, he managed to crawl back in bed, where he slept the rest of the night amidst a pool of blood.

After several weeks it became obvious that he was not going to die, no matter how much he drank. He was weary of the whole endeavor and no longer interested in the outcome. One morning, he rose unsteadily to his feet and went to the bathroom to confront himself. The man looking back at him from the mirror was a stranger, and a pitiful one at that. He had lost over thirty pounds, and his gaunt face was covered with a full beard. The large, ugly gash over his eye was just beginning to heal. He took a long hot shower and then shaved. Afterwards he drove to the local diner and ate a large breakfast of bacon, eggs, and toast. It was the first hot meal he'd had in over three weeks. It was a start.

The apartment was a pigsty after a month of binging, a tangled mess of discarded clothing, old newspapers, empty liquor bottles, and unwashed glasses. It took most of the morning to clean it. When he finished, he took all the vodka bottles, both empty and full, and tossed them in the dumpster. Exhausted from the effort, he sat down on the sofa and contemplated his new life among the living.

There was a pile of unopened mail in the corner. He gathered it up, laid the letters on the coffee table, and began opening them one by one with shaking hands. The mail conveyed a variety of messages, both important and routine—sympathy cards, utility bills, and a letter from his attorney concerning Christy's estate. His most recent bank statement reminded him that he would need to get a job soon, if he was to survive.

There were two letters that could hold the key to his future. One was from Pan Am and the other from the New Jersey Air National Guard. He opened the one from Pan Am first. They had obviously learned that he had been released from active duty and wanted to know when he would be returning to work. The letter also implied that if, for some reason, he wished to remain on military leave of absence that request would probably be approved. Skip decided not to return to Pan Am, not right away anyway. He needed more time to himself. He would ask for a leave of absence.

The letter from the Guard was routine. It had been forwarded from his old address in Florida. It simply stated that they had been unable to contact him and reminded him that he was obliged to provide a current address. It also contained a schedule of weekend training, or "drills" as they called them, for the next six months. He considered this carefully. Drills, annual training days, and flying training periods. He could make enough money from these activities to live on. Although he didn't want to see anyone or do anything, he had to eat.

It took another week to purge the last of the alcohol from his system. He slept most of the time, in a deep, dreamless sleep, waking up only to eat. When it was over, he put on clean clothes and went to the airport to pay a visit to the Guard.

The group commander seemed genuinely pleased to see him. Skip liked him and had the feeling he had been embarrassed about the picture the flower children sent to the guys in Vietnam, although he never said so.

"So, Skip," he said, "we've been worried about you. Where have you been?"

"Well, you know how it is. I've had a lot of stuff to take care of and a lot of thinking to do."

The commander nodded sympathetically, surveying Skip's haggard face and the ugly scar over his eye. "Lost a bit of weight, haven't you?"

He shrugged, trying not to look embarrassed. "Yeah…I was a little heavy anyway."

"Well, I wouldn't lose any more if I were you. What brings you here today?"

"Well, I dropped by to update my address and to let everyone know that I am ready to fly."

The commander considered this for a moment. One of the crew chiefs lived in Somers Point and had reported seeing him in a convenience store several times, drunk and disheveled. Not that he blamed Skip, of course, after all he had been through. But was he really ready to fly, both physically and mentally? He had to make sure. He decided to play it safe. "That's good, Skip. It's been over thirty days since your last flight, right? We'll have to get you re-current. Meanwhile, a lot of people have left the unit since we were released from active duty, and I'm up to my ass in paperwork. I need someone to lend a hand, and I have funds available to pay you. Are you interested?"

"Yeah, sure, I'd be happy to help."

"Good, you can start tomorrow. Welcome back." The commander wondered if he was doing the right thing.

*   *   *   *

Skip worked hard for the next few months and soon was back in the F-100. It felt good to fly again, and for a while, everything seemed back to normal. Then the moving cartons from Jacksonville arrived. There were only a few, as he had asked his brother-in-law to close down the house and sell what he could, but what remained was the very essence of Christy, Maddie and Cam. Slowly and carefully he took each item out of the box, unwrapped it, and laid it on the table and the surrounding floor. There were letters, post cards, photo albums, framed birth certificates, pictures drawn by the children, record albums, favorite books, and countless other things that chronicled their life. The last item he removed was the wax-encrusted Chianti bottle that had sat on his dining room table back in Omaha the evening Christy came to dinner and spent the night for the first time. The sight of the shattered remnants of his life arranged altar-like around him filled him with pain, a pain so enormous that it drove him back into the state he was in before he stopped drinking.

As if all this wasn't enough, the dream about Christy kept coming back, and by early winter he was drinking again; not to kill himself, but to blot out the feelings of guilt he was experiencing. He was still convinced that somehow his indiscretion with Lori had caused the death of his family. Although he was drunk every night, he took pains to report for work on time and in passable condition, no matter how bad he felt. He also tried his best to do his heavy drinking off base, away from the watchful eyes of his peers. He usually left work at four thirty and stopped for happy hour at a tavern nearby, just to warm up, so to speak. If there was a good crowd there, he would be feeling no pain by the time he left. Then, he drove to Atlantic City for the serious drinking.

The drive to and from Atlantic City was a perilous journey, especially when he was drunk. Once, a state trooper stopped him at 2 AM doing ninety miles an hour on the wrong side of the White Horse Turnpike. For reasons he never understood, the trooper let him go, ordering him to pull over to a deserted parking lot and sleep it off. Another time, a Somers Point police officer had him bent over the car ready to handcuff him, when his partner, who was in the Guard, recognized Skip from the Phu Cat days. He had been lucky both times. It was hard to believe that he didn't make the connection between his behavior and the fact that his family had been killed by a drunken driver. But he didn't.

Winters were hard and mean in Atlantic City. Icy winds howled down the deserted streets and along the boardwalk, cutting and slashing the faces and hands of those foolish enough to be outside. Most of the upscale bars and restaurants were shuttered for the season, and those that remained open catered to blue-collar workers, prostitutes, and petty criminals. But Skip's wants were simple—a warm place where he could get drunk every night, away from the prying eyes of his squadron, a place that was crowded and played music. He wanted to be with people but didn't want people to be with him.

His favorite hangout was a place called the Black Velvet Bar. It was one block west of Atlantic Avenue, on the fringe of a poor neighborhood. The bar was dimly lit, with sawdust on the floor, and the back area was occupied by two pool tables that never seemed to be empty. A combo performed every Friday and Saturday night, playing the best jazz he'd ever heard. Although most of the clientele was black, a few white people came by, mostly bikers and drug dealers, checking out the action with the black hookers who were always working the crowd.

Skip was viewed with suspicion the first few times he came to drink at the Black Velvet, because he was a white guy who obviously didn't belong there. After awhile, he was grudgingly accepted but mostly ignored by the customers, except for the hookers who took delight in cleaning out his pockets when he was drunk. But he was unfailingly courteous to everyone, especially the bartender, whom he tipped generously, and in time, the management let it be known that he was under their protection. The hookers left him alone and never stole money from him again.

When the summer of 1970 arrived, the city came to life like a tulip rising after a long winter's sleep. Tourists and vacationing college students from Philadelphia poured into town, filling up hotels and restaurants. The streets were alive once more, and the weather was warm and fair. The change in climate encouraged Skip to move to a different venue in search of people to be around, but not with. He began to visit the bars and discos between Pacific Avenue and the boardwalk. The vacation crowd liked to take naps after a long day at the beach and then start the evening of revelry around ten or even eleven. The bars seldom closed before three. Skip tried to follow this schedule whenever he could. The girls went to the discos to drink, dance, and check out the guys. Skip's boyish good looks seldom went unnoticed, even though he was thirty-five, but he wasn't ready to pick up girls, not yet anyway. But the girls were certainly ready to pick him up, and it was only a matter of time before one of them would succeed.

One morning in early August, he awoke to find a girl standing by his bed, holding a cup of coffee for him. She was young, scarcely over twenty, with dark straight hair parted down the middle and bright blue eyes. She was wearing a half slip pulled up to her armpits which barely concealed an enormous pair of breasts.

The girl handed him the coffee and watched with amusement as he checked out her breasts.

Skip sipped it slowly, trying to remember what happened last night. "Thanks. I really needed that...uh..."

"Joanne," she finished for him. "Joanne Vilano, remember?"

"Oh yeah, I remember," he lied.

She sat on the side of the bed, watching him with curiosity, while her fingers traced idle circles in the hairs on his chest. He felt a surge in his loins, a feeling he hadn't felt in a long time.

"Can I tell you something?" she asked hesitantly.

"What?"

"Well, it's kinda embarrassing, but, here goes. Last night was only my second time. The first time was with a boy in high school, and he...um...wasn't very good. But you? Oh my God! It was like awesome."

Skip smiled but said nothing. Her hand was down to his belly now. She was certainly learning fast

"And another thing," she continued, "it was so sweet of you to use that thing like I asked. I mean...my mom would kill me if she knew I carried them around. She's from the old school, you know? Stay a virgin until you get married."

Her hand was definitely in his shorts now. "So, how did you end up here last night?" he asked thickly.

"It was late, and my girlfriends had to go back to Philadelphia."

"And they dumped you, just like that?"

"Not at all. I told them to go ahead, that I was going home with you. Then I told you I was stuck in Atlantic City, which was technically true."

"Well, I guess I'll have to get you back to Philadelphia then."

"Nope, I called them this morning, and they are picking me up at three."

"Three? That's a long time from now. We'll have to find something to pass the time." He pulled her over to him, lowered her half slip, and started kissing her breasts.

"Ummmm," she said, and moved closer.

*   *   *   *

Rosie sat at his desk at the Pentagon, staring at the phone. He wasn't looking forward to the call he was about to make, especially after everything Skip had been through in the past two years, but it had to be done, for his own good. He was in luck. Skip was at the squadron that day. As he waited for someone to find him, he thought once again about what he was going to say. He decided he would play good guy for a minute or so, just to get Skip's defenses down, and then stick it to him.

Skip sounded normal when he answered the phone. It was obvious he was happy to hear from his old boss. "General Rosie, I heard about your promotion. Congratulations! It couldn't have happened to a nicer guy."

"Yes, well, even a blind hog finds an acorn once in awhile, as my granddaddy used to say. But enough about me. How are you doing these days?"

"Fine...fine, things couldn't be better."

"Really?"

"Absolutely!" Skip had no idea where this was going.

Rosie paused and took a breath. His voice turned icy cold and unpleasant. "That's not what I heard. I heard that you are a hopeless drunk and pretty much a joke around the squadron. In fact, they tell me the only reason they keep you around is because they feel sorry for you. It's all about pity, Skip. Nothing else."

The attack caught Skip by surprise. His face flushed with anger, and his hands began to shake. What's going on here? Why is he doing this to me? His voice turned cold. "In all due respect, General, I don't know where you are getting your information, but that's a crock of shit."

"I don't think so. I got it from a reliable, if somewhat biased source, a man who was on an inspection visit at your squadron a few weeks ago, a man who knows you very well. I asked him how you were doing, and he was more than happy to fill me in on the details. You may remember him, a fellow named Duke Christiansen?"

Skip nearly lost control when he heard Duke Christiansen's name. His voice was filled with rage, and he was almost shouting. Rosie wondered if he had pushed him too far. "Listen, General, in case you've forgotten, I'm no longer in the Air Force, I'm in the Guard. That means I don't have to take shit like that any more...not from you...not from anybody. What I do with my personal life is none of your fucking business...sir!"

Rosie remained unperturbed. "You're right, it is none of my business, and that's too bad, because if it were my business, I might be able to help you. God knows you need all the help you can get."

"Help me? That's a laugh. How? By calling me up and accusing me of being a drunk and a loser?"

"Well, that's part of it, but also by offering a way out of the mess you're in, a chance to start all over, and be the person you once were."

"I'm listening," Skip said. He was beginning to calm down.

"Okay, here's the deal. I have a friend, a colonel, who is the director of operations for the Air National Guard. He works here in the Pentagon, at the National Guard Bureau. He needs someone to manage all the fighter units in the Guard. It's a big job, and it will take someone very special to do it, someone who is in the Guard but understands how we do things in the regular Air Force. I told him I thought you would be perfect for the job, and he agreed to talk to you. By the way, he doesn't know anything about your personal life, about Christy and all that. Oh...I forgot to mention, it's an active-duty tour."

"Active duty? For how long?"

"For as long as you want, that's the feeling I get. The Guard Bureau is pretty short-handed these days. How many years of active duty do you have?"

"I don't know...fourteen maybe."

"There you go. You could probably get your twenty years for retirement. What more could you ask for?"

"Not very much, I guess. I'll have to think about it though."

"You do that. But don't wait too long."

"I won't and...uh...sorry for being so disrespectful a minute ago. I guess I got carried away."

"No problem. I was pushing you pretty hard, but I had to get your attention. We're both lucky, though. Had this been a face-to-face meeting, you would have probably punched me in the nose."

Skip laughed. "Probably."

Skip thought about it for a day or so and then called the colonel. What did he have to lose? A week later he was in the Pentagon.

$$* \qquad * \qquad * \qquad *$$

Someone told him when he arrived that working in the Pentagon could best be described by the word "long"—long hours, long meetings, and long walks to and from the parking lot. It was an amazing place, and Skip wondered how anything got done there. It was all so chaotic and stressful. Officers from every branch of the service were jammed together in windowless rooms and tiny cubicles, sometimes sharing a single telephone. There were nuclear submariners, paratroopers, fighter pilots, Green Berets, you name it, all working feverishly toward a single goal: to complete their tour and move on. As the saying went, the happiest day of their lives was the day they saw the Pentagon in the rearview mirror for the last time.

On the first day, Skip was greeted by a small desk overflowing with letters, memos, and telexes, all requiring his immediate attention. There were twenty-six fighter squadrons in the Guard, and his job was to look after them. There was no one to train him, and he received very little guidance. He was on his own. It was a formidable challenge, too much for his predecessor, who had left in frustration after six weeks, but Skip was determined to prove himself. It was tough going at first, and he worked long hours, typically leaving his darkened office late in the evening. But his hard work quickly paid off. Mindful of his communication skills and penchant for hard work, his boss extended his tour to four years. It was the beginning of a new career, and he approached each day with a joy and enthusiasm he hadn't felt in a long time. Maybe life was worth living after all!

After a time, the pain of losing Christy and the kids began to subside somewhat, diminishing to a dull ache that was constantly with him. Each year on Maddie and Cam's birthday he tried to imagine how much they had grown and what they might look like if they were still alive. And some nights, as he was drifting off to sleep after a hard day's work, he felt the bed sag and creak softly, and could sense the warmth of Christy's body as she slid in beside him. This never failed to bring tears to his eyes, although he comforted to think she might be with him, albeit on a spiritual level.

Skip's job left little or no time for a social life. This was good, for that meant no time for heavy drinking and brooding about the past. Still, he had needs that had to be fulfilled from time to time. His encounter with the twenty-year-old girl in Atlantic City had taught him that. The Washington, D.C., area was filled with single women, a ratio of four women for each single man, some said, and many came to the officers' clubs at Fort Myers and Bolling Air Force Base to meet men. He liked to make the rounds on Friday nights, when women of all sizes, shapes, and ages stood at the bar, three deep, and he seldom left without one of them on his arm. Usually he went to the woman's place, although occasionally he would invite one to his apartment, which was in Arlington, a few blocks from work. Either way was all right with him, as long as there was no emotional involvement.

After two years, Skip was promoted to lieutenant colonel and given a new assignment. There was no turning back now. He was on to bigger and better things.

LANGLEY AIR FORCE BASE

Hampton, Virginia
November 1978

Skip looked into the mirror, making a final adjustment to his tie. The image before him was different than the one that confronted him nine years ago, after his unsuccessful attempt to drink himself to death. This man looked young and confident, as if he was ready to meet any challenge thrown his way. He was attired in a neatly pressed, dress blue uniform, adorned with several rows of service ribbons, along with a pair of silver command pilot wings. The ribbons, there were fifteen in all, including two Silver Stars, fifteen Air Medals, and a Purple Heart, provided ample testimony that he held his own with the best of them during the war. A pair of silver eagles gleamed on his shoulders.

Since his latest promotion, he had received more than his fair share of ribbing about his youthful looks. He was used to being called "the boy colonel" both to his face and behind his back. Some said it scornfully, trying to mask jealously and resentment, others simply said it to tease him. But none of that bothered him. He had worked hard for nine long years to earn that promotion, slowly and patiently earning the respect of senior officers in the Air National Guard and the regular Air Force. Now he was a forty-year-old bird colonel, at the top of his game.

His assignment to Headquarters, Tactical Air Command at Langley Air Force Base, Virginia, had been unexpected. The Commander of TAC, a four-star general had specifically asked for Skip to be his adviser for Air National Guard affairs. None of that made sense to him until he learned that the commander was none other than General Winston Slade, the uninvited guest at his bachelor party in Omaha so many years ago, and the man who presided over his eventual demise after his accident in Misawa.

But General Slade was not the only familiar face he saw when he arrived at Langley. Rosie was there too, now a two-star general and director of operations. Best of all, his old friend Bob Lewis, a colonel like himself, was on the TAC staff. He had not seen Bob for more than fourteen years, and it took them hours of talking and drinking to catch up on old times, much to the dismay of Bob's new wife, who was much younger than Bob and not used to the fighter pilot way.

Skip looked at his watch anxiously. He was supposed to meet Bob at the bar at five thirty, and it was already quarter of six. Bob said there was a woman coming by later for a drink, a woman he wanted him to meet. He had been through this kind of thing many times before and usually tried to avoid blind dates, setups, or whatever you wanted to call them. But Bob was his friend, and Skip didn't want to hurt his feelings. He washed his hands quickly, left the washroom, and headed for the bar.

Bob was there waiting when he arrived, perched atop a bar stool, the usual saturnine grin on his face. "It's about time you got here. I would say being late is an automatic round on your tab, wouldn't you?"

Skip slid onto the stool beside him, wearing an easy grin. "You know what? I am going to buy the first round, even though clearly, if we rolled for it, you would lose, as you always do. Do you know why?"

"Why?"

"Because I am in an extraordinarily good mood tonight, and there's nothing you can do to piss me off."

"I'll drink to that."

"So will I…if the bartender ever takes our order."

The bartender set the drinks in front of them, two ice-cold, double-vodka martinis. The two men gazed at the drinks solemnly and then raised them for a toast. "To Corky," Bob said, "Our fallen comrade and fellow Blunderbird."

"To Corky," Skip replied.

They finished the first drink in short order and ordered another round. "You must have gotten laid last night," Bob said suddenly.

"Why do you say that?"

"Because you said you were in an extraordinarily good mood, remember?"

"I did say that, but that's not the reason. Actually, there is no specific reason. It's just that life is good right now, and I realize how lucky I am."

"We're both lucky, my friend. We've been through a lot of shit in the past twenty-odd years, especially you losing Christy and the kids." Bob paused for a moment, uncertain what to say next. "But somehow we landed on our feet."

Skip quickly changed the subject. "Speaking of getting laid, where is this princess who is supposed to come in and attack my body?"

Bob looked at Skip with alarm. "Look Skip, there is something you have to understand. This woman is a real lady. If you think you're going to get laid tonight, forget about it. She's a very special person, someone I thought you would enjoy meeting."

Skip started to make a sarcastic reply but thought better of it. It was obvious that Bob was dead serious. "Okay, okay," he said finally, "Don't get your bowels in an uproar. I'll behave like a perfect gentleman. It won't be easy, but I'll give it my best shot."

An hour passed. They ordered another round and drank it. It was obvious that she wasn't going to show up. Bob glanced at his watch nervously. "Listen," he said finally, "I hate to do this to you, but I promised my wife that I would be home by seven. We're taking the kids to a movie tonight."

"Not to worry. I understand. You go on. We'll do this another time."

Bob rose from the stool quickly and prepared to leave. "By the way, it's highly unlikely, but if by chance you get to meet her don't forget…"

"I know. She's a real lady, and I'm not going to get in her pants."

*   *   *   *

Skip eased back on the bar stool and surveyed his surroundings. Happy hour was in full swing now. People were lined up at the bar waiting for drinks, everyone talking at once, and the air was thick with cigarette smoke. How often had he been part of this scene in the past twenty-five years? Too many times, he decided. It was getting old. He was getting old. The evening had started on a positive note. Now, he felt unsatisfied, and vaguely unfulfilled. He looked around the room idly, trying to decide whether to have dinner in the club or at a quiet restaurant off base. That's when he saw the woman standing in the doorway.

She was a vision of elegance, a beauty by any standard. She was dressed simply, a tweed skirt hemmed just above the knees, soft, brown, calf-high leather boots, and a beige cashmere sweater. An elegant scarf in rich colors of rust and burgundy was draped over her shoulders and fastened at the neck with a gold pin. Her dark brown hair was done up in a simple bun, a style that would look old on most women but looked just right on her. A wide leather belt that matched her boots accentuated her slender waist. She was a tall woman, at least five feet eight inches, maybe more. Skip guessed she was in her early forties. Her face looked vaguely familiar, but he couldn't place it. Her eyes darted around the room anxiously, as if looking for someone. Once or twice, she started to walk into the room, then changed her mind and retreated to the doorway. She was obviously distressed. The woman he was supposed to meet tonight, he thought. That has to be her!

The woman took one last look around the room, then turned and headed across the lobby toward the main entrance. Skip jumped off the bar stool and started after her, threading his way hurriedly through the crowd gathered between the doorway and the bar. By the time he reached the lobby, she was reaching for the door. "Excuse me!" he called out. "Ma'am?" She hesitated for a second, her hand resting on the door handle, and turned around. His jaw dropped in shock and surprise. It was Penney Denison, the wife of his flight commander at Presque Isle.

"Skip? Skip O'Neill?" Her face broke out in a beaming smile, and she rushed over to hug him. "Oh my God...is it really you?"

They stood in the hallway for a minute hugging and talking excitedly, much to the amusement of the passing crowd entering and leaving the club. Realizing that they were creating a scene, Skip took her gently by the arm and led her to a small sofa along the wall. "Listen," he said with mock seriousness, "I have to move fast, because I know how this always goes. I never get more than five minutes alone with you, before your husband comes and screws things up. So tell me, how are you, how is Tom?"

A look of pain crossed her eyes, and she looked down, avoiding his gaze. "I...uhh...lost Tom...about nine years ago...not too long after Christy and the kids were killed."

"Oh my God, Penney, I had no idea. I am so sorry. What happened?"

"Nobody knows for sure. He was an adviser to the South Vietnamese Air Force, flying a mission down in the Mekong Delta somewhere, and the aircraft blew up...just like that. Can you believe it? After all those years...and he was gone in a split second."

Skip nodded sympathetically, holding both of her hands in his. "That must have been very hard for you."

Penney put on a brave smile. "Look who's talking. I can't even imagine what it would be like to lose my spouse and my children, all at the same time. I doubt if I could have gone on after that."

"It wasn't easy, that's for sure. But listen, enough of this gloomy talk. What brings you to the club tonight?"

Penney smiled ruefully. "It's a long story. A woman I work with has been after me for weeks to meet a single friend of her husband. I hate that kind of thing and have been putting her off. But she can be very persistent, so I agreed to stop by for happy hour tonight, just to have a quick drink with her husband and his friend. I was running a little late, and by the time I got here, they were gone. It was just as well, though. I didn't want to do it anyway. How about you? What are you up to tonight?"

Skip grinned mischievously. "Almost the same thing happened to me. Only, my 'date' wasn't a little late, she showed up an hour and a half late. Can you believe it? By the time she got here, my friend had already left. And get this, when she does show up, she waltzes up to the doorway to the bar, glances around the room, and then splits. What an airhead! If she wasn't so good looking, I would have just said sayonara baby, and let her go. But I did the right thing and chased after her. As it was, she was almost out the front door when I caught her."

By the time he finished the story, Penney was doubled over with laughter and could hardly speak. "You?" she managed to say. "You?"

Skip spread his arms expansively from his sides. "Ta-da. Your dream date has arrived."

They were creating another stir among the people passing through the lobby, but this time they didn't care. They were having too much fun. "So, what's the verdict?" Skip asked suddenly.

"The verdict?"

"Yeah, the verdict. I know how these 'meet-for-a-drink' deals work. If the girl likes the guy, she stays for dinner. If she doesn't, she has a drink and leaves."

"But we haven't even had a drink yet," she said teasingly.

"I know, but I'm starving. Can't you at least give me a clue?"

She paused and chose her words carefully. "I think I like the guy very much."

"Good, then it's all settled. Let's head for the dining room, while I'm still strong enough to walk. And by the way, dinner's on me."

She laughed. "Damn right it is. You just stepped over the line, Colonel. We're now officially on a date." She slipped her arm through his, and together they walked to the dining room.

$$* \qquad * \qquad * \qquad *$$

The courtship between Skip and Penney lasted over two years. It was not that they were uncertain about their feelings for each other, for without doubt, they were very much in love. But the memories of Christy and Tom were always there, unseen ghosts that would never go away and never let them lead a guilt-free life together. Many of their friends pointed out that they might as well be married.

Penney lived alone in a charming old Victorian house in downtown Hampton that she and Tom had renovated before he left for Vietnam, and Skip spent almost every night there. He was careful not to do that when one of her grown children was at home, but otherwise, they were living as man and wife.

Skip and Penney might never have gotten married had it not been for her youngest daughter, who was still in college. Tracey Denison could not understand what was taking her mom so long to make up her mind. Skip was a good-looking guy, and Tracey liked him very much. So did her two brothers, for that matter. What was she waiting for? Was it her dad? She vaguely remembered "Uncle Skip" coming to their house for dinner when they were living in Presque Isle. Her dad had seemed to like him well enough. So what's the big deal?

She finally confronted her mother one crisp, fall evening when she was home from school. She had a date that night and decided to spend a few minutes with her mom and Skip before she left. Her mom was in the kitchen preparing dinner. Skip was upstairs in the den, slouched in an easy chair, eating popcorn and watching a football game. She took in the scene and suddenly became annoyed. It was so…so…Norman Rockwell…so phony! Who did they think they were kidding? It was all a crock!

She walked into the kitchen and leaned against the counter, tossing her long, dark hair carelessly over her shoulder.

"Got a date tonight, honey?" Penney said, scarcely looking up from her cooking.

"Yes, with Craig."

"Craig? Hmmm. Been seeing a lot of him lately, haven't you?"

"Not as much as you've been seeing Skip," Tracey said sarcastically.

Penney looked at her daughter sharply. "What is that supposed to mean?"

"Well, you know, when someone asks a question like that, it usually means are things getting serious. And that's what a lot of people have been wondering about you and Skip…especially after two years."

Penney was getting angry. "It's not the same thing at all. Skip and I are not a couple of kids dating. We're just friends."

"Just friends? That's a laugh. You two are living together for God's sakes. You think I don't know that…that my brothers don't know that? Give me a break!"

Penney's face flushed with anger, and for a minute it looked like she was going to throw her cookbook at her daughter, but she got herself under control.

"That is none of your business," she said. "How dare you talk to me like that?"

Tracey realized she had pushed her mother too far. She walked across the kitchen and put her arm gently around her mother's shoulders. "Look, Mom, I didn't mean to be disrespectful, honest. It's just that I get so frustrated some-times. I mean, Skip is a fine man, and I like him a lot. No, I take that back, I love him. And I believe that if you burrowed deep enough into my brothers' hearts, you'd find that they love him too, not that they'd admit it, of course. It would spoil their macho image. And I know that you two love each other. I can feel it. So what's the problem?"

Penney shook her head miserably. "I don't know, honey. It's just…"

"It's my dad isn't it? You feel that marrying again would be disloyal, right?"

"Yes, something like that."

Tracey looked at her sternly. "Do you know what my dad would say if he were in the room right now? He'd say Penney, what the hell are you doing? I've known Skip O'Neill since he was a runny-nosed second lieutenant in Presque Isle. He's a good guy, and a lot of fun to be around. He'll make you laugh, and that's a good thing. If you love him, go for it. Otherwise, stop wasting his time."

Penney started to say something, but the doorbell rang. Tracey's date had arrived. She picked up her sweater, kissed her mother on the cheek, and started out the door. "Take care. See you later," Tracey said.

Skip came downstairs, and walked into the kitchen. "What were you and Tracey talking about?"

"She thinks I should either marry you or stop wasting your time."

Skip thought for a moment. "She has a point, you know," he said finally. "So…what do you want to do—marry me or stop wasting my time?"

She put her arms around him. "I think I should marry you."

"Good, so it's all settled."

"Not so fast. Aren't you forgetting something?"

"What?"

"The proposal…I expect a formal proposal."

He looked at her uncertainly and then kneeled on the kitchen floor before her. As he did, he thought about that moment on the sidewalk in Nebraska when he proposed to Christy. Was she watching him now? If so, what was she thinking? Somehow, he thought that she would approve. "Penney Denison, I love you very much and want to spend the rest of my life with you. Will you marry me?"

"Skip O'Neill, I love you very much and want to spend the rest of my life with you. Yes, I will marry you."

They were married in early spring in the chapel at Langley Air Force Base, to the delight of friends, family, and well-wishers. Bob Lewis was the best man, and Penney's father gave her away. Penney's daughter was the matron of honor, and her sons proudly participated as ushers. After the wedding, they went to St.

Maartens for a honeymoon. When they returned, Skip rented out his small condo and moved into her Victorian home. The couple settled down for a long and happy life together.

One afternoon in late fall, Penney told Skip that her latest mammogram had revealed a small lump which the doctor wanted to examine further. It was nothing serious, she assured him, but it was better to be safe than sorry. She died six months later.

*   *   *   *

Penney was buried with Tom in a small family cemetery in Illinois. Most of her family was there when they laid her to rest. They were mostly strangers to Skip, people he had never met. He felt awkward and out of place, being among them at such a private moment. In many ways, it was a painful re-enactment of what he went through when Christy died. But this time, there was no numbing loss of reality and no ranting and raving against an evil and demented God. Why should he? She was with Tom now, and that was as it should be. Sadly, he returned to his small condo, resigned to live the rest of his life alone.

New York University Medical Center

December 31, 1999

Skip opened his eyes, and look around cautiously. The room was not spinning for a change. Thank God! In fact, everything looked normal, except for the slight blurring of objects along the wall. He licked his parched lips and tried to turn his head toward the bedside table. He needed a drink of water. The room tilted precariously to the left and quickly righted itself, causing another bilious wave of nausea to crest at the back of his throat. He gagged and swallowed hard, driving it back. Not so fast, he thought. I'm still in charge here, and I don't feel like puking right now. What the hell were they putting in the IV, anyway? Whatever it was, they were bringing in the big guns now. Were they trying to hustle him out of his room? They better not, because he had a deal. January 1st, 2000…the millennium…that was his checkout date, and he wasn't leaving a minute earlier.

After a few minutes, his stomach settled down, and he began to doze, cursing the omnipotent god who controlled the contents of his IV. When he awoke the second time, Nancy was leaning over him adjusting the tubes attached to his arm. "I'm a little thirsty," he said. "Is it happy hour yet?"

"It's always happy hour for you, Colonel, didn't you know that?" She reached over and placed a container of cool water under his chin. He took the straw into his mouth and sucked greedily. "Ahhh," he said, when he was finished.

She took the empty container. "I'll refill this with lots of ice and place it on the bedside table, so you can grab it any time you want. You can reach it, can't you?"

He shook his head gloomily. "I can reach it okay, but every time I try, the room moves and snatches it away."

She nodded sympathetically.

The room was quiet, save for the usual sounds outside his door. She fussed with his sheets but made no move to leave. He listened to the steady ticking of the clock, which made him feel better. It sounded like his grandmother's clock, the one with the walnut case and two silver Great Danes, lying one on each side. There was no clock in the room, but he heard the ticking, all the same.

"I'm getting out of here," Skip said suddenly.

She looked at him with surprise. "Really? When?"

"New Year's Day…that's the day I check out. Kinda symbolic isn't it? Out with the old millennium and in with the new."

"You must be terribly excited," she said doubtfully.

"I am. There are a lot of people waiting for me. Are you working tonight?"

"No. It's New Year's Eve, remember? I'll be in tomorrow, though."

"Even better. We can say goodbye then."

"That would be nice," she said. "I'm going to miss you."

"I'm going to miss you too, Nancy. I really am."

She turned and started for the door, hoping no one would notice the mist of tears in her eyes.

"See you tomorrow!" he called after her.

"Yes, see you then," she replied.

After she left, Skip fell back on the pillow and gazed thoughtfully at the ceiling. A bright shaft of winter sunlight splashed across his bed, taking away the chill he was feeling. New Year's Eve! Twelve more hours until checkout, more or less. Did the hospital have a late checkout policy? He smiled at his own joke. He wondered what he looked like these days. He wanted to look his best when he left. There was a mirror across the room, but it was too far away. The last time he looked, he had been confronted by a bald little man, looking for all the world like Yoda in the "Return of the Jedi." Handsome, I'm not, he had thought at the time.

The IV tugged at him gently, trying to pull him away. It was a clever and cunning adversary, a relentless tide that pulled him farther and farther out to sea, waiting patiently each time for him to struggle back to shore, before it took him away again. But it didn't matter. Just a few more hours, and it could do whatever it wanted with his wasted body. He closed his eyes and let it take over, drifting him back to sleep.

He was awakened an hour later by the sound of Dr. Webster talking to a nurse nearby. "How are you feeling today, Colonel?" he said. He hated himself for asking that question. It sounded so hollow, so phony. It was obvious that his patient was dying, that he had only days, if not hours, to live. There were times when he hated his job, and this was one of them.

Skip's voice was strong but slightly slurred. "Doing good, Doc. Happy New Year to you...almost anyway." He was having trouble focusing his eyes.

"Thanks. The same to you."

"Doing anything special tonight?"

"Not really."

"Me neither."

The doctor busied himself reading his chart and then warmed the stethoscope inside his lab coat before putting it on Skip's chest. There was nothing more he could do for his patient, and they both knew it.

"I've got this dying thing all figured out," Skip said

"Pardon me?"

"I said...I've got this dying thing all figured out."

"Well, I'm glad somebody has, because I sure don't."

"It's no big deal. I'll tell you the secret."

The doctor looked at him speculatively. His patient looked exhausted and barely able to speak, much less tell a story. But he was ahead of schedule, and his rounds were almost over. What the hell, he thought, and drew up close to listen.

"Remember when Chuck Yeager was the first man to break the speed of sound in the Bell X-1 back in 1947?"

The doctor nodded. "That was before I was born, but I read about it in school."

"Right. The sound barrier was a big mystery in those days, and some engineers speculated that his aircraft might break apart if he tried to go through it. But no one knew for sure..." He paused significantly.

The doctor waited for him to continue.

"No one doubted that the X-1 could go supersonic, but the question was, who would fly her? There were plenty of guys around, but they chose Yeager. Why? Because he had guts and was the best in the business. When the big moment arrived, and the B-29 mother ship dropped Yeager and his X-1 out of the bomb bay, he fired up the rocket engine, and the next thing you know, he was through the barrier, and on to the other side, just like that. And you know the most interesting part?"

"What?"

"There was no ceremony when he landed, no party to celebrate the return of the fastest man in the world. The military wanted to keep it all hush-hush. So what does he do? He goes home to his wife. He was tired and beat to hell anyway...especially since he had two broken ribs, courtesy of a fall he took from a horse two weeks before...an injury he 'forgot' to mention to the Air Force, because they would probably have delayed the test. But about 4:30, his friends and colleagues showed up, he mixed a pitcher of cold martinis, and the party was on. Nothing fancy...just a gathering of friends and family."

He stopped talking, and for a minute, it looked like the story was finished.

The doctor looked puzzled. "That's an interesting story," he said, "but what does it have to do with death and dying?"

"It has everything to do with it. Don't you see? People have been speculating about death since the beginning of mankind. Valhalla, the Sun Chariot, heaven and hell...you name it, someone has a theory about it. But nobody knows for sure what happens after you die, right? No one has come back and said, 'Look, I've been there, and this is what it's all about.'"

Skip was exhausted, and spent. The doctor was not sure if he could continue. But somehow he managed. His voice was barely above a whisper, and he spoke with great effort. "Here's my plan. When my turn comes, I'm going to step back, take a deep breath, and run straight at it. I'm going to run like hell, like I'm not afraid of anything or anybody...and just hit it head-on. Just like going through the sound barrier. And with any luck, I'll pop right through to the other side, with a big grin on my face...just like Chuck Yeager...ready for the party to begin...a gathering of family and friends."

He closed his eyes, starting to drift away again. The doctor sat quietly in his chair, stunned by the intensity of emotions that swept over him—pity, sadness, compassion, and even a sense of his own mortality. They all hit him at once. At first he didn't know what to say. Slowly he rose to his feet and looked down on the dying man. "You know what, Colonel? It makes a lot sense...more sense than anything else I've heard on the subject."

"I'm checking out tomorrow. Will you be coming by?" Skip mumbled.

The doctor knew what he meant and didn't question him. "Yes, I'll be making the rounds tomorrow."

"Good, we'll say goodbye then."

*   *   *   *

He almost missed the whole thing. In fact, he would have missed it, had it not been for a thoughtful orderly who turned his television on at precisely five minutes to midnight. It was the sounds that woke him up, the music and laughter and cheering. He tried to focus his eyes on the screen, but it was only a blur of bright colors. It was bitter cold outside. He sensed that, even though his window was closed. The countdown started, and the people began to shout...Ten...nine...eight...seven...six...five...four...three...two...one...and the band started playing "Auld Lang Sine." Cars were honking outside on the FDR Drive, and he could hear noisemakers, firecrackers, and people cheering. The millennium...he had made it! He was overwhelmed, caught up in the sheer joy of the moment. But the IV started tugging again, this time with the force of a riptide. He struggled against it, savoring the sounds of happiness and joy around him one last time. Then, he relaxed, and let it sweep him away.

*   *   *   *

He was finally there, but it was not what he had expected. There was no celestial music, no fluttering of wings, no final release. Instead, he stood in darkness, save for a pinpoint of light that shined far away on the horizon. Instinctively, he turned and walked toward it. He walked at a steady pace, on the strong, sturdy legs of a young man who feared nothing the world had to offer. He knew that the light was where he was supposed to go, and he was not afraid.

The light was much closer than he expected, and as he approached, it began to morph, first into a shining, elongated ellipse, and finally into a doorway. It was the barrier, the thing he had vowed to dash through fearlessly, unmindful of what might be on the other side. But there was no need to run, and no need for bravado, for he realized that it was not a barrier at all, but rather, an entrance to a place he was destined to be. The way lay open; all he needed to do was walk through.

He met no resistance when he stepped through the doorway. But there was no one to meet him, no gathering of friends and family to celebrate his arrival. In fact, there was nothing at all on the other side, save for a vast expanse of white concrete, baking under a blazing sun. The scene seemed vaguely familiar. It reminded him of a fighter base in the Southwestern United States, in Arizona or Nevada perhaps, except there were no aircraft...no hangars...no buildings...and no people. Just a vast expanse of shimmering heat and unearthly silence. He squinted against the blinding sun, wondering what to do next. Then he saw her...like a mirage in the desert heat. To say she was an aircraft, or even an F-100 Super Saber, would trivialize the essence of her being. She was absolutely beautiful...and she was waiting for him, canopy open, ladder on the side of the cockpit. She was gleaming silver...not painted in drab camouflage like the birds in Vietnam...and there was no markings of any kind to mar her sleek body.

He walked up to the aircraft, noting that his parachute and helmet had been carefully placed at the bottom of the ladder. Fascinated, he began to walk around the aircraft, all the while, running his hand lovingly over her hot shiny skin. She was in pristine condition, new tires and brakes, not a drop of fuel, oil, or hydraulic fluid to be seen. As he rounded the tail, he saw the crew chief standing by the ladder. He was simply attired in a pair of fatigues, unadorned with insignia or name tag. His hair was silver, and his face looked ageless. His eyes were warm and respectful, yet possessed a strange inner glow.

"Is this bird ready to go, Chief?" Skip asked.

"Yes sir."

Skip nodded, picked up his chute and helmet, and started up the ladder. As he settled into the cockpit, the crew chief scrambled noiselessly up the ladder behind him, and together, they began the ritual…lap belt, shoulder harness, parachute lanyard, ejection seat pins…everything smooth and precise. Neither of them spoke. For a second, Skip looked down to adjust the rudder pedals. When he looked up, the crew chief was gone, and so was the cockpit ladder. He surveyed the cockpit and tried to remember when he had flown an F-100 last. Thirty years ago? Thirty-five? It didn't matter. He was ready. He flipped on the battery switch and watched the cockpit come to life, with flashing lights and the soft whirr of gyro motors. At the same time, he heard the sound of a compressed-air cart starting up. He sat quietly for a minute or two, enjoying the sounds, sights, and smell of the cockpit. He felt at home. Then, he pointed his index toward the sky and made a twirling motion, the standard signal for engine start. When he pressed the starter button, the air cart roared to life, and things began to happen. First, rpm, then oil pressure, ignition, engine temperature, hydraulic pressure…each event in sequence, each depending on the one preceding. It was like a complex symphony played by precise and accomplished musicians, and he was the conductor.

There were systems to check before he could taxi, but he didn't bother. Nor did he turn on the radio and navigation equipment. It would be a very short flight, and he wouldn't need them. The crew chief reappeared and held the wheel chocks in his hand, waiting expectantly. Skip eased the power forward, and the aircraft moved smoothly out of the parking spot. As he did, the crew chief snapped to attention and gave him a smart salute. Skip returned the salute, gave him the traditional thumbs up signal, and turned onto the taxiway. When he looked back, the crew chief was gone, and so were the wheel chocks and the air cart. In fact, there was nothing left on the shimmering white concrete to show that he had ever been there.

Taxiing out to the runway was cool and pleasant. The bird was so light that it took little or no power to keep it rolling. With the canopy open, and oxygen mask hanging loose, he could feel the warm, dry desert breeze blowing across his face. He felt good; better than he had in a long time. Suddenly he remembered that he hadn't called for taxi clearance. He smiled to himself and thought, "No control tower, remember? No buildings, no aircraft, and no people. Relax and enjoy the ride." As he approached the runway, he began to feel thrill and excitement surging through his body, and his heart began to race. This always happened just before takeoff. He closed the canopy, fastened the oxygen mask around his face, and taxied into the takeoff position.

It seemed to him that the runway went on forever. For all he knew, it did go on forever. He set the brakes and advanced the throttle. At full power, all instruments were in the green and rock steady. She was ready to go. He released the brakes and snapped the throttle into afterburner. It kicked in with a solid, reassuring thump. The bird shot down the runway and left the ground so quickly that he scarcely had time to raise the landing gear before it started climbing at an astonishing rate. At fifteen thousand feet, he spotted a fat puffy cloud sitting all alone, anchored to the bright blue sky. Impulsively, he buried the nose below the cloud and did a slow lazy barrel roll around it, pausing at the top to admire the view of the desert through the top of the canopy. It felt so good that he did another one in the opposite direction. The cloud flashed by him and was gone.

At forty thousand feet the aircraft showed no signs of slowing down. It continued to streak skyward with its nose pointed straight at the sun. Soon he was soaring to heights he had never visited, and he was elevated to a state of indescribable happiness. It was as if all the moments of his life had fused into this single point in time and space. And he began to laugh joyously and make tight dizzying rolls around the sun.

At sixty thousand feet he was still climbing...and laughing...and rolling around the sun...and laughing...and rolling...as the sky slowly faded into darkness.

978-0-595-67328-5
0-595-67328-7